The Ranger's
Dog Tags

P. J. MacLayne

The Ranger's Dog Tags
Copyright © 2021
by P.J. MacLayne

The Ranger's Dog Tags is a work of fiction. All names, characters, events and places found in this book are either from the author's imagination or used fictitiously. Any similarity to persons live or dead, actual events, locations, or organizations is entirely coincidental and not intended by the author.

ISBN-13: 978-1-7349587-1-3

Published in the United States of America.

Acknowledgments

As always, thanks go to K.M. Guth, for her cover design and other graphic assistance, as well as a last-minute suggestion on the book's description.

To Cornelia Amiri, for her invaluable assistance in editing this story as well as her constant encouragement.

And to Angela Pryce of Angela Pryce Editing, for her sharp eyes and showing me the way of colons.

Chapter 1

The squad car screamed down the street, its red and blue lights tearing through the darkness. I feathered the gas pedal and waited for a second set of headlights to pass. Dolores, my salsa-red F-type Jaguar, growled in anticipation.

Thank goodness no one else was out on the streets of the small town of Oak Grove at three in the morning. When I let Dolores loose, I'd break traffic laws left and right on my way to the Aldridge house. Eli's house. No matter how fast I drove, the fire trucks would get there first.

I pulled back onto the street as Lando's voice came through my phone again. Anxiety bled through the speaker. "Scotty hasn't heard from Eli either, Harmony."

Lando was the first person Eli hired when he started his business, and Scotty joined them next. They—Eli, Lando, and Scotty—sometimes reminded me of the three Musketeers.

The knot in my stomach tightened. I blew through a stop sign and mashed on the gas pedal. Ten blocks to go. "Have you been able to get into the camera feed?"

"No. The signal cut off after a blinding flash. It came from behind the cameras, not from outside."

Five more blocks. Ahead, no red glow colored the night sky. I pretended to stop at the intersection of Elm and Fifth. Two blocks. "How about the tracking app?" I asked. Several years ago, Eli had created a GPS tracker but never released it to the public. Only Eli, Lando, and I had it installed on our phones.

My question was met with a long silence. "I'm blocked," Lando admitted. "We were messing around and made a dare a few days ago. Eli blocked me. If I can hack into it in less than five days, I get a bonus. He's going to win this time."

Or lose, depending upon how I looked at it.

One block. Red, blue, amber and white lights flashed, piercing the canopy of the oak trees lining the street. I choked down the bile in my throat and wrangled Dolores into an empty spot between two police vehicles half a block from the house.

"Let me try." I switched to the app and chose Eli's contact. As hard as I stared at the screen, the dot beside his name remained a solid red instead of changing to green. Either his phone was off, or he'd blocked me, too. I refused to believe the other option, that something awful had happened to Eli and it had also destroyed his phone.

I killed Dolores' engine and, after waiting for another police vehicle to zip past, climbed out.

They'd called for reinforcements. This had to be worse than terrible.

Smoke obscured my first view of the house. Smoke, but no flames. At least, none that revealed themselves through the multitude of flashing lights. I elbowed my way through the small crowd of neighbors gathered to watch the show until I reached the police barrier. With one hand, I shaded my eyes to seek a familiar face among the police and fire-fighters swarming the scene.

Officer Bo Holt, the town's rookie, found me first. "Harmony. Thank God you're not in the house. We were worried." He raised a hand to forestall an anticipated flood of questions. "Let me call this in."

I ignored the police mumbo-jumbo that poured from his lips and strained to make sense of what was happening. Three fire trucks lined the circular drive. One poured a steady stream of water on the roof, even though there were no flames. Another hose ran through the front door, but appeared to be unused.

I still had Lando on speaker, and his voice broke through my stupor. "Harmony. Harmony. What's happening?"

"The house is on fire. But it isn't. I don't understand. I'll call you back when I figure it out. I have to talk to other people right now." I pressed the screen, ending the call without giving him a chance to protest.

I wasn't lying. Chief Hinds, Oak Grove's fire chief, and Chief Sorenson, the police chief, headed my direction. The two of them together at the scene of a minor house fire rang its own alarm bells. Worst case scenarios played out in my head.

Someone shoved a foam cup into my hands as I sat at the wobbly card table that served as a command center. I sipped, not tasting anything but warmth, focused on my text messages. Lando was on his way to check Eli's house near Orlando. Scotty was heading to the office there. From here, north of Pittsburgh, I couldn't do anything. I needed to get back to Dolores and start the long trip to Florida to join in the search.

A fireman appeared with two more folding chairs and opened them up for Hinds and Sorenson. I wondered which one was playing the good cop and which the bad? Claire—Chief Hinds—opened the questioning. "What can you tell us about the fire?"

Nothing, but I didn't say that. "First, you tell me. Did anyone die?"

"What makes you ask?" Claire exchanged a glance with Chief Sorenson. Her gray hair shimmered like a halo in the glow of the headlights. She insisted on being called Claire, unlike Chief Sorenson. Some days I forgot he had a first name.

"The two of you together at the scene of a simple house fire? It makes me assume the worst."

"Nothing is ever simple when it comes to you, is it, Miss Duprie?" Chief Sorenson asked.

This was the beginning of an argument I couldn't win. I was too tired and worried to play games. I didn't even straighten my back or pat my bun into place, my normal reaction to his commanding presence. "Do I need to call my lawyer?"

Sorenson shook his head. Somehow, I found the fact that he wore a short-sleeve shirt and khakis, instead of his uniform, comforting. "Not unless you want to convince me you set fire to the house you renovated. If that were the truth, I'd be asking for a mental health evaluation, not arresting you. Perhaps we should ask a different question. How did you know about the fire from your apartment across town?"

"Easy." I held up my phone. "Eli's security app entered panic mode. I didn't even know it existed until it woke me."

Claire leaned across the table. "Interesting. Can you recreate it?"

"If I dug around, I might find it, but you'll hate me for the headache you get."

A corner of her mouth twitched. "I'll take your word for it."

"That's not why you pulled me aside."

"No. We're concerned for your safety."

So, she was the good cop. When would Sorenson jump in with his part?

I took my time reading a message from Lando with no real update before answering. "Let me ask again. How can a simple house fire be a threat?" I repeated my other burning question: "What else requires the presence of top law enforcement and fire officials? Meaning you two. So, who died?" I studied their faces, but their stoic expressions revealed nothing.

"We'll do a secondary sweep of the house after the hot spots cool," Claire said. "The initial assessment indicates no one was inside."

Good to know. "But…" I prompted.

She fidgeted with the ring on her right hand. "Based on eyeball reports from my senior officers, the fire may have been started by an incendiary device. This was no accident. If it hadn't been for the sprinkler system, there's a good chance the house would have been destroyed."

It was too much to take in. I stared at the ground. Then the sky. Then the house. When my phone vibrated, I stared at it before checking the two messages that came in. One from Lando. One from Scotty. Nothing from Eli.

Scotty's was short and complete on the preview screen. "*No one here.*"

I switched to Lando's. I didn't have time to read it because someone jiggled the table. When I looked up, both Claire and Chief Sorenson were staring at me.

Sorenson's left eyebrow arched. "Something interesting to share?"

Like a kid caught reading a comic book, I put my hand over my phone's screen. I debated my answer. Sorenson had enough of his own problems, and there wasn't anything he could do about mine. But he'd pressure me until I caved. Still, I could hold off for a bit. Long enough to read Lando's message.

"*Eli isn't home. Checked the house. It looks fine. No sign of a disturbance. His car isn't in the garage.*"

He was talking about Eli's house in Florida, a thousand miles away, not the one in front of me.

"Miss Duprie?" Sorenson repeated, his voice harder.

I placed the phone on the table, then set my hands on my lap to hide them. I clenched and unclenched my fists. Clenched them again. My fingernails dug into my palms. I forced the words from my constricted throat.

"Eli is missing."

More words spilled out, and I was unable to stop them. "He should have responded to the alarm. There's been nothing. He's not at home or at the office. When I call him, it goes straight to voice mail like his phone is turned off. He never turns his phone off." Unless he was in bed. With me.

"Besides, it's Monday. Technically, Tuesday now. It's his night to kick back and review changes to coding languages. I talked to him before I went to bed and everything was fine."

Tears ran down my cheeks. I didn't hide them. "And there's nothing I can do. He's in Florida and I'm here."

Out of nowhere, an old-fashioned cotton handkerchief appeared in Sorenson's grasp. He thrust it towards me.

I accepted it, took off my glasses, and swiped at my eyes. "Throw in the suspicion that the fire was deliberate and everything is worse," I sniffed. It was ten times worse. Or more.

Chief Sorenson allowed his professional demeanor to slip. Wrinkles formed on his forehead, and he frowned. "Maybe his battery died, or he's out of range of a tower and doesn't realize it. Perhaps he's just getting snacks."

For over an hour? Besides, Eli had been on his third beer when we talked. He didn't drink and drive. But it was nice of Sorenson to try to comfort me. I wiped my eyes, blew my nose, took a shuddering breath, and attempted to hide my fears.

"I'll assign an officer to patrol here tonight," Sorenson told Claire, "while your crew finishes the cleanup." He turned to me. "I'll assign another to keep an eye on your place as a precaution. I don't expect anything else will happen, but I want to eliminate the possibility of you being a secondary target. By morning, you'll have heard from Hennessey. We'll find out this was all a coincidence."

Except, I don't believe in coincidence.

Chapter 2

I hung around until the last hose was rolled up and stowed. Claire assigned a truck and crew to remain on site to monitor the situation in case any hot spots remained.

The brightening sky held the promise of sunrise when I headed home to my empty apartment and my empty bed. No matter how many times I called Eli's number, he didn't answer. Lando and Scotty had no luck either, despite their search grid, which included every convenience store in Eli's Orlando neighborhood and beyond.

I stared at my closet and debated my next move. My suitcases were stored in the basement and I couldn't get to them without bothering Luke and Joe, my elderly landlords. Was I even allowed to leave town before the authorities determined the cause of the fire? There would also be the insurance company to deal with.

A sob stuck in my chest, driving out my breath. I sank onto my bed and forced myself to cough. Coughing turned into sobbing and wild tears. I covered my face with my pillow, not wanting Joe and Luke on the floor beneath me to overhear. Somehow, I must have drifted off.

The pounding on my front door woke me. I ignored it, not ready to face the world. I couldn't resist checking my phone, however, and nearly threw it against the wall because no message or missed call from Eli showed on the display.

My self-imposed isolation didn't last long enough. Joe and Luke had keys to my place and weren't afraid to use them in case of an emergency. Which this was, from their point of view.

"Harmony," Joe called from the front room, his voice tight with anxiety. "Harmony?"

Reluctantly, I rolled over. I owed them too much to ignore them. "Give me a minute," I called. At least I was dressed, although in the same clothes I'd worn all day yesterday. I didn't care if they smelled like smoke. I took a few minutes in the bathroom, tucking my brown hair into its habitual bun, but there was nothing I could do about my red, swollen eyes.

I walked to the front room and into Joe's outstretched arms. Luke, from behind, turned it into a three-way hug. It took me a few minutes to realize that Chief Sorenson, in full uniform, stood by the front door. That explained how Luke and Joe knew what was going on.

"Any word?" Sorenson asked. The dark circles under his eyes made me wonder if he'd been up since leaving the scene of the fire.

Even with the added strength provided by Luke and Joe, I could do no more than shake my head.

Sorenson acknowledged my response with a tired nod. "I've reached out to my counterpart in Orlando. He's not aware of anyone fitting Hennessey's description having contact with law enforcement last night. He'll keep an ear out. Although, like me, he believes Hennessey will turn up when he's ready." Hennessey being Eli.

No news was good news, my mother used to say. But like a mosquito bite, I couldn't leave it alone. "Has anyone contacted the hospitals?"

"That's the next step, but you need to slow down," Sorenson frowned. "It's been less than twelve hours. Granted, this behavior is out of character for him."

Not really. He had a bad habit of disappearing. But not like this. And if Chief Sorenson wasn't worried, he wouldn't have called Orlando.

Luke pulled himself out of our huddle. "Let me get a pot of coffee going. We need to think logically."

That was my line, but I needed the reminder. Besides, I didn't want normal. I wanted Eli. I checked my phone for the ten thousandth time. Nothing had changed. I needed to call Eli's office and see if anyone there had heard from him. Darla, his administrative assistant, would keep things running for a day or two. But without his presence, the business would unravel.

Joe shoved a coffee cup into my hands, startling me out of my contemplation. I didn't remember sitting in my easy chair, but there I was. Out of habit,

I blew across the top of the cup before taking a sip. "Okay," I said. "Logic. If Eli's phone died, he would have recharged it and called by now. If it broke, he'd go to the office and call from there."

I took a deep swallow of my coffee. The hot liquid soothed my aching throat. "Even if he was in a meeting, either Lando or Scotty would message me. Anyone see a flaw in my thinking?"

"Not yet." Sorenson sat down on the loveseat, and Joe put a cup of coffee in front of him—on a coaster, earning my approval. Sorenson nodded his thanks before adding, "Unless Lando and Scotty slept in and no one at the office knows what is going on."

It amused me that he called Lando and Scotty by their first names. He usually didn't call anyone by anything but their last name or title. I guess he'd never been introduced to them in the couple of times they'd visited Oak Grove.

But Sorenson's theory made sense and was easy enough to check. I shot off a text to Lando. *"Any word? You at work?"* And waited. For less than a minute, although it felt much longer.

"No update. At the office. Pretending to work like everyone else."

I looked up and shook my head. "Nothing. What's the next step?"

Sorenson rubbed his chin. "In these days of patient privacy, hospitals won't release any information to you. Especially because you aren't the next of kin."

Which gave me an idea. I texted Lando again. *"Did you check his parents' house?"*

"Not there."

Another theory shot down the drain. "Lando says he isn't visiting his parents. Where else do we need to check?"

"You won't like it." Sorenson grimaced. "It wouldn't be the first time a man disappeared to spend time with a secret lover."

Logically, it made sense. My heart screamed that it wasn't true. My voice quavered despite my efforts to hold it steady. "Is there a way to check without access to Eli's financial information?"

"Phone records. And we'd need a warrant for those. Which we won't get, since he is in Florida and I have no jurisdiction. If we want to go down that path, he might have had a burner phone."

I took another sip of my coffee. It tasted as bitter as the concept of Eli having a mistress. Or was I the hidden girlfriend? "We're getting nowhere." The itch returned. The desire to hop into Dolores and speed all the way to Florida. I couldn't scratch that itch yet.

My phone chirped. Not with Eli's personalized ringtone, but the call came from a Florida area code. Torn between hope and dread, I swiped my screen to answer. "Hello?"

"Harmony?"

It took a moment to match the voice to a name. "Darla? Have you heard from him? Tell me you have news."

"No." Her voice broke. "And I hate to call you, but this is pay week and Eli signs the paperwork first thing on Wednesdays and today is Tuesday. It has to get processed tomorrow."

Money was the least of my worries, but not everyone was as lucky.

"How can I help?"

"I talked to Kris." Kris O'Keefe was the company's lawyer. "She said you can sign it as representing Eli. I'll send it to you, you sign it; and send it back."

I was a simple researcher with Eli's company, not a vice-president or anything fancy. "What?" I sputtered. "Me? Where did Kris get that idea?"

"The paperwork you signed the last time you were here? Kris says Eli set you up as his backup. I don't fully understand the legalities."

I didn't either. But now I understood the sour look on Kris's face and Eli grinning like a banshee as I scrawled my signature in each highlighted spot. I trusted Eli, so I hadn't asked many questions.

"Let me get Kris. I'll put you on hold."

I'd never paid attention to the hold music before. The instrumental version of an old song—'Build Me Up Buttercup'—played in my ear. Buttercup was Eli's nickname for me. The crack in my heart widened.

I stood. "No offense, but this is a business call. And no, there's no word on Eli."

With the bedroom door closed, I changed my shirt while waiting for Kris, and brushed my hair before putting it back into a bun. Little changes to instill self-confidence. Kris scared me.

"I told him it was a bad idea. He didn't listen to me." Kris grumbled. "You know how he gets. So, you have total authority over the company in his absence."

"That doesn't seem right. When he mentioned it, I thought he was joking."

"The clause doesn't kick in for twenty-four hours. I insisted on adding it as a safety valve."

To protect Eli from me. As if I'd ever hurt him. But it made sense from her point of view. "I can't get there in a few hours. And the equipment up here is destroyed. How do I take care of payroll? I don't want anyone to not get paid."

She didn't answer right away. I imagined her running her fingers through her bob-cut blond hair, her habit when she was thinking. "Let me confer with the accountant and some other folks," she said. "I'll get back to you."

By the time I emerged from my bedroom, Chief Sorenson had left. He had a whole city to protect and serve, not just me. Luke and Joe had stayed and stilled their quiet conversation when I walked down the short hallway.

"Well?" Joe asked.

A harsh laugh reflected my nervousness. "As of five o'clock this afternoon, I'll be the head honcho of a whole damn corporation. Shifter Technologies. If Eli doesn't show up, that is."

Luke's eyes widened. "How does that work?"

"Eli set it up the last time I was in Florida. He didn't explain all the ramifications of the paperwork he had me sign because he knew I'd protest. Always thinking ahead." But how could he have imagined this situation?

"Are you going to handle it from here?" Joe asked.

"Before the fire, I would have. Now, it's too hard to make it work. If I get the go-ahead from whichever detective is handling the investigation into the fire, I'll leave for Florida in the morning. I can count on you guys taking care of things here, right? Like my mother's African Violet?"

"Of course," Joe answered, "But what do you know about running a technology company?"

Nothing, I realized. I shrugged. "I'm about to get a crash course."

I spent the afternoon packing, answering calls, cleaning my refrigerator. A quick trip to the clothing store was in order because all but one of my business suits were stored at Eli's damaged house.

Between calls to me, Darla spent the afternoon finding people with contacts to local hospitals. As Chief Sorenson had predicted, none had information to share. Not even to friends.

The call from Claire was more informative. A state investigator was coming to town to aid in the probe of the fire and finding out who set it. With the electricity still off at the house and the equipment ruined, I assured her she didn't have to worry about the security system. We'd identified the one flaw in the setup: no electricity and no back-up generator rendered the system useless.

Precisely at five, Darla sent me the email with the payroll paperwork. I printed it, signed it, and ran the little hand-held scanner I used for research jobs over it. Thank heavens the scanner still worked. I hadn't used it in forever. By five thirty, the paperwork was on its way back to Darla to forward to the payroll firm. Under other circumstances, I would have gotten a thrill out of the setup. But all it did was confirm Eli's status as still missing.

Everything was coming together too easily. Like a lamb headed to slaughter, I followed my shepherds. I didn't like it but didn't see any other way.

Chapter 3

I felt like the Bandit in Cannonball Run, except I headed South instead of West. I made the drive to Florida in eleven hours when it should have taken fourteen spread over two days. This was partly because I started while it was still dark and missed rush hour traffic through Pittsburgh, partly because I stuck as much as possible to the interstates and didn't do any sightseeing along country roads going through West Virginia, and partly because I didn't run afoul of any officers of the law.

Dolores helped, sensing my urgency. Each time I pressed the gas pedal, she responded with a growl of joy. I swear she used less fuel than normal, because I didn't make as many stops as expected to refill her tank.

Even though I had the key to Eli's place, I couldn't force myself to stay there. Oh, I drove by it, but no light leaked out from the windows, solidifying my decision to get a room at a hotel. I couldn't handle the emptiness of his absence.

What I didn't have was a key to the office. I'd never needed one. So, in the morning, I delayed until I was sure Darla and others would get there first. While I waited, I made a side trip to Eli's and went into the house to look for clues. Or him. My heart cracked more when I didn't find either.

The house was a single-story pale-yellow stucco 1980s design with a two car garage in a typical Florida subdivision. The only thing that made it stand out from its neighbors was the double-sized lot. Eli had planted an assortment of trees and shrubs along the edge of the property to maintain a degree of privacy. Juniper bushes created a barrier under the front windows.

Inside, it was only slightly less bland with cookie-cutter furnishings. The first time I'd visited Eli, I'd teased him about forcing him to go to second-hand shops to look for furniture with personality. The interior looked liked he'd walked into a warehouse-type store and picked out entire 'rooms'. The only parts of the house that felt like him were the Florida room—which featured a pool with one of those 'never-ending' current generators for exercise—and his bedroom. I saved the bedroom for last as I wandered through the house, looking for anything that didn't belong.

The bedroom was the one room in the entire house where I was comfortable. The dark wood of Eli's dresser and desk and his personal mementos made it feel warm and welcoming. But it couldn't comfort me today.

The earthy scent of his aftershave hit me like a

baseball bat. I clung to his desk chair, steadying myself as I studied the room. The bed was made but wrinkled, and pillows were stacked against the wrought-iron headboard where he'd been sitting the last time we talked. His laptop lay open on the bed, the screen dark. There was no sign of his phone or wallet, either on the nightstand or the tray on top of his dresser.

It was the wrong thing to do, but I snagged his dog tags from the tray and slipped them around my neck. My heart shattered more as the tags nestled between my breasts.

With hope dredged from my diminished reserves, I scanned the office's parking lot as I pulled in. Eli insisted on no reserved spots, but the space near the front door, the one with shade in the afternoon, was always left empty for him. Today, the spot remained vacant.

In fact, a lot of spaces were unoccupied. I guided Dolores into one farthest from the doors. If I stayed in Florida, I'd need to buy her a cover to preserve her paint job from the damage caused by the harsh sun. The thought of having to stay sent a shiver down my spine.

I sat in Dolores with the air conditioner running and imagined calming scenery. Tall hills covered in snow-coated pine trees, scarlet-colored sunsets, a stroll along the beach with my favorite man. The crack in my heart deepened.

Each second stretched into several as I put off the inevitable. I worried everyone would resent me for walking in and taking over Eli's job.

A rap on the window startled me out of my ruminations. Lando, one hand shading his eyes, stared through the glass. I lost the bet I'd made with myself. Although he'd cut his hair, it was still blue.

I rolled down the window. "Hey."

"Are you going to sit out here all day or are you coming in?"

He must have seen me on the security cameras. "I just got here."

"It's been fifteen minutes."

It didn't seem that long. "I keep hoping he'll show up." No need to explain who 'he' was.

"We all hope for that." Lando straightened, and at full height he loomed over Dolores. "It's getting hot. Come inside."

I couldn't put it off any longer.

I gestured to the half-empty parking lot. "Where is everyone?"

"They're out searching for Eli. We gave them each a picture of his car and we're tracking their routes on a map in the office." Lando kicked at a fallen palm frond. "Don't worry, they volunteered and are using vacation time."

That was the last thing on my mind. "Here's my first executive decision. This afternoon we'll send a second batch if we need to and everyone will receive their normal pay."

Lando hooked his arm around my waist and urged me forward. "I knew there was a reason I liked you. By the way, how did you get here so soon? We didn't expect you until tomorrow."

"The roads were clear, and the wind was at my back."

Lando grinned. "And you stayed within the speed limit the whole way, right?"

I ignored him, refusing to incriminate myself.

When we got to the front door, he opened it with an exaggerated bow. "After you, m'lady."

The only proper response was to sweep by him, nose in the air.

"Harmony!" Fiona Varela, the receptionist at the front desk, chirped. She pushed a button on her phone and made the announcement, "Harmony's here!"

The speakers throughout the building repeated her words. "Harmony's here!"

Voices called out in greeting. It felt like going to a bar where everyone knows your name.

Like a conquering hero returning home, I pushed my way through the door to the workroom. Darla, looking years older than she had a few months ago, walked down the center aisle. She opened her arms. "Don't just stand there," she said. "Come here."

We hugged, tearless, strength to strength, leaning on each other as we would need to lean on each other in the coming days. I felt tall compared to her.

She stepped away, patting her short, gray hair into place. "I've been pulling together paperwork for you. Let's get to work."

I grinned, knowing who the boss really was.

The trip to the executive hallway took forever as I stopped to say hello and chat on the way. I noted how many employees shook hands or patted me on the shoulder. I figured it was a way for them to link to Eli. Or because I was playing boss and they wanted to get on my good side.

Lando had tagged along with Darla and me. He had a habit of playing bodyguard. Normally I found it amusing at best and irritating at worst. This time I found it touching. And convenient. I had plans for him, and he'd set himself up so he couldn't object.

Eli's darkened office sat in the middle of the short row of rooms, with a conference room on either side. The first time I'd visited him, he'd explained he'd picked it so that no one assumed they were higher on the totem pole of executives and managers because their office sat next to his. I stopped in the doorway to give myself time to adjust to the emptiness, then turned to Darla.

"Not here. I'll set up in the small conference room if it isn't booked." That would put her office across the hall from me, conveniently close.

She nodded. "I'll clear the schedule. Kris wants to talk with you right away. Do you want coffee?"

It figured. Kris had been missing from the greeting committee.

"I'm not used to the Florida climate," I said. "How about something cold?" What I wanted was

23

my homemade iced tea, but that wasn't happening.

She winked. "Gotcha. Lando, come help me."

It was nice to be alone for a minute, contemplating the setup. I rested my hand on the chair Eli habitually sat in during meetings. I didn't want to sit there, replacing him, but I didn't want anyone else to use it, either. Besides, the end of the table wouldn't give me the room to spread out paperwork the way I liked. I switched the chairs around, so Eli's occupied the middle spot on one side. I pushed the extra chair into a corner.

The swap earned Darla's nod of approval when she returned, a stack of papers in one hand, balancing a tray with a pitcher of ice water and a glass on the other. Lando trailed behind her, loaded down with a collection of office supplies, a laptop, and a can of diet soda.

"I told Kris and Marty they'd have to wait a few minutes," Darla said. Marty Hvidston, an older man who was so skinny that if he turned sideways, he disappeared, was the company's accountant. While he didn't dislike me, he mostly ignored me.

I nodded. "I want you and Lando here, too. We're going to have to work as a team. Are there any supervisors we should include?"

Darla answered. "Kris wants to bring you up to speed on top-level information. I've set up a separate meeting with the supervisors and a third one with the staff." She jerked her head towards Lando, who was busy making sure the laptop projected to the oversized TV screen on the wall. "She won't be happy to include either of us."

Lando raised his hands to shoulder-height. "You know me. I want nothing to do with management stuff."

"But I want you here as moral support. And as Eli's friend. And mine," I insisted.

Darla's mouth tightened. "Remember, you signed Kris's paycheck."

I'd gasped when I saw the number on that check. If Eli figured she was worth the money, I wouldn't fight to change it. But I wouldn't let her walk all over me, either.

"Then it's settled. Lando, are you done?"

"Yep, ready to go. Darla, on your to do list, add getting the techs to give Harmony access to Eli's files and email. We can get Kris to approve it, if necessary."

Darla nodded. "I see most of his email. However, some are private and for his eyes only. Harmony will need to see those. We'll ask Kris for approval for Harmony to have access to them."

I needed that access yesterday. Maybe those emails held a clue to what had happened to Eli. "Let's do this," I said as I logged onto the laptop.

❊ ❊ ❊

The meeting ran for hours. Well, an hour and a half, but it felt longer. I found myself staring out the window at the cluster of palm trees at the end of the parking lot. It was fine when Marty showed slides detailing the overall financial health of the company—and it was in excellent health—but when he got into specifics; it felt like pulling the numbers together for the Oak Grove Library's Board of Directors; tedious and boring. As much as I loved numbers and spreadsheets, I didn't care how many rolls of paper towels were used in a month. But the details would be important if I ended up staying around long-term, so I tried to remain alert.

I spotted Lando covering his mouth to hide a yawn, Darla twiddling her pen like a majorette's baton, and declared myself in need of a break. I'd make a trip to the restroom and then check in on the hunt for Eli.

Kris followed me to the ladies' room. I didn't think too much about it, but as we washed our hands, she stared at me in the mirror. "We need to talk," she said, looking away.

"I thought we just did."

She shook her head and stuck her hands under the air dryer. "Personal stuff."

She was right. And it wouldn't help to delay. So much for my plans. "Your office or mine?"

Kris closed her eyes and loudly inhaled. Her lips moved, and I had the impression she was counting to ten. "Mine. It's more private."

If I wanted to establish my position as top dog, I'd make her come to my temporary digs. But I needed her as an ally, not an enemy.

"Give me a few minutes to find out if there's been an update on Eli and I'll meet you there."

Chapter 4

I purposely made Kris wait for a few more minutes than was polite, to show her who was boss. To make up for it, I brought along a fresh cup of coffee, made the way Darla said she liked it. I took a Coke for me, needing the caffeine boost.

I swept into her office without knocking. I wanted her out of her comfort zone, hoping it would force her to be honest. Besides, it always upset me that it looked like Eli had spent more money on setting up her office than his own.

While she took a drink from her cup, I set my can on her four-person table not on a coaster, put my hands behind my back and stared out the window. I stayed there long enough to make the silence uncomfortable.

"What did you want to say that couldn't be said in front of everyone?" I asked, turning and fingering the dog tags around my neck.

"You're a lot more like Eli than I realized," Kris said. "But it will take me time to trust you."

I dipped my head in acknowledgment. "You didn't hide your feelings when Eli had me signing all that paperwork a few months back. I didn't understand how far-reaching it was. I thought it was a convenience for him, if he was at a meeting somewhere and out of communication."

"That may be how he explained it to you, but he knew better. I made it very clear to him what he'd set up."

A new scenario thrust its ugly way into my brain. "You don't think he planned his disappearance, do you?"

"I considered the idea. But it's so out of character, I can't force myself to accept it."

"Just like the suggestion he has a mistress. We both understand this business is his first love."

Kris stiffened. "Who suggested he has a mistress?"

"Chief Sorenson. Standard police response. He didn't believe it either. But without access to Eli's private email and electronic devices, we can't disprove it."

"How can you just stand there and sound so detached?" she asked, her voice cracking.

"I've learned to hide my personality and pretend I'm someone else," I explained. "Right now, I'm pretending to be a combination of a cool, calm, collected CEO and a private investigator." I looked out the window again, rolling the chain that held the dog tags between my fingers. "If I allow myself to think about Eli any other way, I'll be in a puddle on the floor and no use to anyone."

She came and stood beside me. There was

nothing to see but a small strip of grass with a picnic table, and a fence blocking the view of the alley. "What does the PI side of you say?" she asked, all business again.

I used one hand to brace myself against the wall. "That this isn't a game and I have to stop pretending it is. Eli is in trouble. Big trouble. And I don't know how to fix it."

Lunchtime pizza for the employees was on me. On my dime, not the company's. I wasn't comfortable spending the company's money, even if Eli would do it.

Plate in hand, I wandered between groups, making small talk and listening to the stories being told. I hoped for a tidbit that would spark an idea of where to look next, or to find a shred of truth among all the speculation. But, like the employees who had been scouring the streets, I came up empty.

My ramblings had me intersecting with Lando and Scotty more than once, and I figured they were doing the same thing as me. Scotty surprised me. The quieter of the two, he'd normally grab a couple pieces of pizza and head back to his cubicle. He mingled instead. Where Lando was tall and his blue hair stuck out like a beacon, Scotty was of average height like me and his brown hair made it harder to follow him as he moved around the room. I made a mental note about using him for undercover work.

All too soon, another group of employees headed out on their search and rescue mission while I got pulled into another meeting. I hoped it would keep my mind off Eli. It did. Mostly. I don't think anyone noticed when my thoughts drifted away, and I fantasized following a back road somewhere and finding a dazed but otherwise healthy Eli.

For the rest of the afternoon I sequestered myself in my makeshift office, getting up to speed on the details needed to keep the business running. I hung around until the last employee headed home, although I had to force Darla to leave. I suspected she'd put in a lot of unclaimed overtime in the last few days. I had plans, even if they were no more than fast food, my hotel room, my cell phone's police scanner, and my personal laptop.

But Lando and Scotty had something else in mind. They ambushed me as I locked the front door and stepped into the muggy evening air.

"We're taking you out for supper," Scotty said. "There's a new Thai place we want to try."

I hated to turn them down—I'd never tried Thai food—but my priority was Eli. "Sounds good. I'll take you up on the offer another time."

He and Lando exchanged a glance. I tried to read its meaning and came up blank.

"We've got an ulterior motive," Scotty confessed. "We figure it's time we clue Eli's folks into what's happening."

And I was the best person for the job. Eli's mother Tillie, and I talked occasionally. She always invited me over for supper when I came to Florida, with or without Eli. Rob, Eli's father, I wasn't so sure about. Whatever appetite I had disappeared.

Lando's van was in the shop, or so I'd heard. "There isn't room for all three of us in Dolores," I said, stating the obvious. "And I don't want to leave her here."

"We'll take my car. It's got a back seat." Scotty's car was a nondescript tan-colored four-door sedan. The kind I would drive if I didn't want to be seen. He'd bought it off an old man who only drove it to church on Sundays, or so the story went. The few times I'd ridden in it convinced me the motor wasn't stock. "How about we meet you at Eli's in fifteen minutes?"

I shook my head. "I'm not staying there." I ignored the look they exchanged. "I'm staying at the hotel on Twentieth. I have to change, so give me half an hour."

Lando nodded. "Got it." The fact that he didn't push me on the hotel decision made me suspect that he approved.

❀ ❀ ❀

I'd debated with myself about spending the money but broke down and got a suite instead of the cheapest room. Since I was spending the money anyway, I got an upgraded suite.

The microwave, mini-fridge and coffee maker were standard. The extra space and sitting area were expected. The jacuzzi tub was a bonus. I didn't expect the balcony, which overlooked more than a parking lot. I imagined myself sitting there, sipping sweet tea, watching the ducks on the nearby lake. I hoped the ninth floor was high enough to eliminate mosquitoes and no-see-ums. What I didn't think I'd ever use was the working fireplace… not unless I had Eli to cuddle with as we watched the embers flicker. We'd made plans to take time off and go to a mountain lodge for a week in December. I swallowed back the lump that formed in my throat.

A stop at a convenience store gave me the opportunity to pick up a few essentials. Soda, munchies, and an aspirin substitute for my developing headache. I had to reach around a little old lady to get a small container of creamer. Later, I'd track down a grocery store for fresh fruit.

Back at the hotel but before I emptied my bags, I turned on the television for background noise. It was set to a local news channel, and I didn't bother changing it. I never watched TV, except for the weather.

As I fixed my hair and washed my face, I half listened to the newscaster drone on about local items: the new Disney prices, the rush hour traffic, the crashed car mired in the underbrush near the Saint Johns River that had been spotted by a fisherman. There was also a new shelter for the homeless.

It took too long for my stressed brain to process what I'd heard. I rushed back to stare at the screen. They'd moved on to the stock market report. But if it was on the news, it was on the web.

I paced by the desk while waiting for my laptop to load. I should have taken Eli's advice and bought a faster one. As I logged in through several layers of security, I choked back a sob.

I had to dig for the hotel paperwork with the WiFi password. Then click through the hotel policies. And the welcoming website. Then wait while the search engine hunted for the news channel's home page.

When there was a knock on the door, I didn't look out the peephole to see who was there, expecting Lando and Scotty. I thought they were the only ones who knew where I was. Rookie mistake.

I didn't anticipate being greeted by a brick wall of a man with deep brown skin when I opened the door. If I wasn't mistaken, that was a gun in a holster under his left arm. And a police badge attached to his belt.

"Miss Harmony Duprie?" he asked with a voice as mellow as a ray of springtime sunshine.

"Do you sing?" I blurted. It was the first thing that came to mind.

A slow smile spread across his face. "Not in public, ma'am. You are Harmony Duprie, right?"

"Yes. And you are, Detective…?" I let my voice trail off.

The smile got bigger. "Horace. Detective Timothy Horace. Orlando Police Department."

I stepped aside to give him room to get by. He needed a lot of room. "You're out of your jurisdiction, aren't you, Detective?"

"We have a mutual aid agreement with the locals." I didn't think his smile could get any bigger, but it did. "Although it's pretty one-sided."

I could imagine. "I'd offer you something to drink, but I'm not set up for guests."

"No worries, Miss Duprie, I won't be staying long."

"Are you the official welcoming committee? Or the bearer of bad news? What do you know about Eli? Was he in that car they found this afternoon? Is he all right?" The words poured out of me, along with my fears.

He held up a hand. "Whoa. Slow down. I was asked to introduce myself because I'll be your liaison while you're here. I don't fully understand why, but your Chief Sorenson contacted my chief and convinced him you needed one. I don't have all the details, but what's this about a car?"

Liaison, right. More like my handler, I expected. "How did you find me? I didn't tell anyone where I was going to stay." I sat at the desk and refreshed the news channel's website.

He peered over my shoulder. "Pure luck. I was on my way to the police station here in North Crystal and spotted your car. That's part of the limited information I received. I took a chance. And the gentleman at the front desk gave me your room number."

"Scared him, did you?" I asked as I scrolled through the latest news reports.

"Maybe. But not you."

I had bigger things to worry about. "What do you know about the car found on the bank of the Saint Johns this afternoon?"

"Nothing. Not my jurisdiction. Why?"

"You were told why I'm here, right? He's missing. Eli Hennessey. My boss. Lover. Boyfriend. Partner. Whatever words you want to toss around. It's been three days since someone tried to blow up his house in Oak Grove. Three days since anyone has heard from him. And I don't believe in coincidence, Detective."

Chapter 5

The hotel room felt smaller with Detective Horace hovering over me as I waited for the news channel's website. I found the article, with a video attached. Unfortunately, the film was taken from a distance. Even using full screen, the shots of the car were too blurry to identify any features.

"Is that his?" Detective Horace asked.

"I can't tell. The color is right—black—but there are lots of black vehicles on the road." The driver's side was crumpled, and the rear window shattered. My stomach churned. What if Eli had been in that car?

There was a knock on the door. Horace instinctively moved his right hand toward the interior of his suit coat where he kept his gun. "Are you expecting someone?"

I'd forgotten about Lando and Scotty. "Yes. Two of Eli's friends and coworkers. We plan to talk to his parents tonight."

He relaxed. "Make sure it's them first."

Like I didn't know that.

I made a show of looking through the peephole before opening the door. "About time you got here," I said before I let Lando and Scotty in. "Be on your best behavior. We have a visitor."

"Eli?" Lando asked, hope evident in his voice. He walked inside and halted. Scotty almost ran into him.

"Guys," I said, "Meet Detective Timothy Horace of the Orlando Police. He's been assigned to work with me—us—to find Eli." Or keep me in line. "Detective, Lando and Scotty. Lando's the taller one."

"Officially?" Scotty asked. "That'll be a first. You do your best work on the sly."

I wanted to swat Scotty but didn't.

"Excuse me?" Horace raised an eyebrow and studied me.

Heat rose in my cheeks. "Long story. Let's get back to business. Guys, would you be able to identify Eli's car in a bad video?"

Lando rolled his shoulders and popped his knuckles. "His Acura Integra? Sure. There aren't many of that model left on the road."

At the thought of one less, a shudder spiraled down my spine.

"Let's see the video," Scotty said.

In silence, we watched the replay. Lando reached past me and hit the button to play it one more time. The reporter's voice grated on my nerves as he stretched out the little information he had to match the length of the video.

Lando straightened and shook his head. I fiddled with the dog tags.

"I don't know." Lando pursed his lips. "Maybe, but I'm not sure. Scotty?"

Scotty frowned. "I'd be guessing. Can it be traced by license plate and VIN?"

Horace nodded. "Yes. But that won't prove the identity of the occupant. Let me make a call." With a chin jerk, he stepped out into the hall, closing the door behind him.

This wasn't the way I'd expected my evening to go. The news report hadn't mentioned which hospital they'd taken the victim to, so I couldn't reach out for more information.

"What's with the mountain?" Lando asked, dropping onto one end of the couch.

"That was fast work," Scotty said, "getting the cops involved." He took a seat at the other end.

I sat between them. "I didn't call them. Chief Sorenson pulled some strings. Horace claims he spotted Dolores by chance, but I don't believe him. I need to check for a tracker."

Lando whistled. "Sorenson did that?"

I shrugged. "Who else? I only told a few people I was leaving. And I'm not of any interest to an Orlando cop."

There was a hard rap on the door, and Lando jumped up to answer it, but checked the peephole first.

"Dude," he said, as Horace walked in. "You need to step away after you knock. All I could see was your chest."

Horace grinned. "It was a great tool when I was a street cop."

"I bet. What did you find out?" Lando stuck his hands in his pockets.

No hesitation. Straight to the point. From the frown that disappeared as quickly as it had appeared, I got the feeling Horace wasn't used to that approach.

But it didn't seem to faze him. "Between privacy laws and the fact that the victim is still being treated in the ER, all I got was male, early thirties, brown hair. Not much to go on. They didn't find a wallet. And there were no plates on the car."

The description fit Eli, but it fit lots of other men, too. "The lack of plates and wallet indicates a stolen vehicle," I mused, "which eliminates Eli." I waited for my gut to guide me, but it wasn't helping.

"How about the VIN?" Lando asked.

"The car hasn't made it to the police lot yet for processing. We're pushing to get it moved up on the list of priorities."

"What's the procedure for getting me into the hospital and seeing if I can identify the patient?" If nothing else, Horace might slip and tell me the name of the hospital.

He shook his head. "It doesn't work that way. You aren't the next of kin."

"You've got power of attorney, Harmony," Scotty pointed out.

Horace's eyes narrowed, like he was recalculating.

"For the company. I don't believe it works for personal legal issues. I'll ask Kris tomorrow." I cocked my head. "And I'd rather not upset Eli's folks if it turns out to be some random dude in a random black car."

"If you've got a picture of your friend, we can get it to the hospital staff to see if it's a match." Horace frowned. "Identifying marks will help, too."

I started with the photo. Eli was camera-shy but I had a few of him, mostly taken when he wasn't expecting it. I scrolled through the gallery on my camera to find one that showed his entire face. "Will this do?"

He blinked and stared at the picture, then took the phone from my hand and studied it. "He looks familiar. But the name doesn't ring a bell. Where have I seen him before?"

As far as I knew, Eli had never been involved with the cops except for business. Not even a speeding ticket. "The grocery store?" I suggested. "A basketball game?" Although Horace looked more like a football player.

"The wife does the shopping. I don't follow basketball. I golf."

I would never have guessed.

"Are you based out of the central office, Detective?" Lando asked.

"Yes." Horace gave me back my phone. "Why?"

"Eli drops by every six months or so to check in with the chief. Make sure he's still happy with our software. Maybe that's where you've seen him."

"You lost me."

"Orlando PD was one of Eli's first customers. He worked with the chief to work out the bugs. The Department still gets a big discount as a way of saying thank you."

Eli had never mentioned that. There were a lot of things about him I didn't know.

"This Hennessey is the software geek?" Horace asked, his voice tense. He held out his hand. "May I see that picture again?"

I passed it back to him although his reaction set off a tingle at the back of my head. I rubbed the chain around my neck and waited.

He shook his head. "I'm not sure. But that explains why the chief gave me this assignment. People disappear all the time. Start a new life or whatever. He doesn't take an interest in them. Most cases are handled by the neighborhood patrol officers. Heck, I thought he was upset with me and I couldn't figure out why.

"Instead, he underplayed it." Horace's lips formed a tight line. "I have to approach this from a different angle."

"You've got a lead," I said. "Use your connections and go to the hospital and compare the photo to the victim. It's that easy." Or I'd sneak in. Buy some scrubs from a second-hand store or fake being sick and go to the Emergency Room. First, I needed to find out what hospital the patient was in. There were only about a dozen to choose from.

"I'll need a warrant."

And that would take forever. I didn't have forever.

"Can you send me that picture?" Horace asked, as he reached into his pocket. "Here's my business card with my email address."

"It'll come from my business email." I'd never set email up on my phone, and had no plans to, much to

Eli's amusement. The thought made me catch my breath.

"Okay." He didn't move. What was he waiting for? Didn't he have places to go, people to see, judges to talk to?

"How else can we help, Detective?" I poured on the charm. "My phone number so you can call me with updates? I'm afraid I don't carry business cards."

The corners of his mouth turned upwards. "This isn't the way this is supposed to go. I'm supposed to be in charge."

"Harmony has that effect on people." Lando chuckled. "She looks harmless, but somehow throws you off balance. I haven't figured out her tricks yet."

And that's the way I liked it.

From one pocket, Horace pulled out a little notebook like all cops carry. He pulled a pen from a different one. I wondered how many pockets he had. Where did he keep his keys? His wallet? His handcuffs?

But he was waiting, and I rattled off my number, while trying to determine where he stashed his spare ammo.

He flipped a page. "Any identifying marks?"

I visualized Eli's naked body. Another mistake, but I powered through the memory, ticking them off on my fingers. "Scar, left shoulder blade. Another scar, right forearm. Small birthmark, lower right arm." And my favorite. "Ranger tattoo, left hip."

His eyebrows shot up. "As in hockey?"

"No. As in Army Ranger. He doesn't like to advertise his service, so keep it a secret if you can."

Horace nodded, snapped the notebook shut, and slid it and the pen, back into his pockets. "I realize you have your hopes pinned on this guy, but you might want to pray he isn't Hennessey. Word is, he's in rough condition and might not make it."

I practically shoved Detective Horace out the door. I had work to do, and he was in the way. If the man in the hospital was Eli, I needed to get to him. Pronto. And I didn't want to wait for all the delays of the official process.

Lando and Scotty were typing away on their phones, searching out other news websites. If one carried the report, others did. And one of them might mention the hospital's name.

"Send that picture, Harmony," Lando said. "We'll figure out where the guy from the accident ended up. As slow as the elevator is, we'll know before the detective turns his car key."

Lando's optimism was just what I needed. "Tell me that Eli's okay. That he wandered off in one of his programming comas and he's squirreled away in a hotel, ignoring the rest of the world. That the guy in the hospital isn't him."

Lando and Scotty wrapped their arms around me in a group hug. "We want to believe that Harmony,"

Scotty said. "But we have to deal with reality. Stay strong. We're here to help. Not just me and Lando, but everyone who works for Eli. We had our own meeting while you were with the managers and agreed to help you however we can."

Scotty pulled away to study my reaction. "They appointed me as a spokesperson. Anything they're afraid to tell you in person, they'll share with me so I can pass it on to you."

He grinned and shook his head. "I swore I'd never get involved in management. But here I am, because of you. And Eli."

I pulled him in and rested my head on his shoulder. I'd give myself this moment to be weak. I suspected I'd need every bit of strength I could muster soon. Too soon.

Chapter 6

The hospital security guard didn't look convinced, and he didn't look like he'd be easily manipulated. I tried the simple approach. "I want to see if it's my friend. It's probably against protocol," I said. "But figured it was worth a try."

Lando, Scotty and I had started with security instead of medical personnel because the doctors were slammed. Three ambulances had pulled in during the short walk between Scotty's car and the entrance to the emergency room.

I fluttered my eyes and tried to appear pitiful. Looking at the guard's boots, not at him, I held up my phone, displaying a picture of me and Eli. "Can you check and see if it's him? I don't want to upset his parents if it's a false alarm."

"I can't allow it." He shook his head. "There are procedures and regulations."

The tears that leaked from my eyes were real. "I understand the rules, but surely they don't apply in this case? If it's my friend, I know his allergies and his doctor's name and other information the doctors and nurses need. Wouldn't it be better to check?"

His eyes narrowed. "Can I take your phone? I'll see if I can't find a nurse with time to check it out."

For the second time in the night, I handed my phone to someone I didn't fully trust. My insecurities screamed, but I'd do anything for Eli.

The security guard disappeared through the locked double doors leading to the treatment area. I took a chair in the waiting room, as far away from anyone else as possible. It was an old habit. I didn't want to catch any stray germs. Lando and Scotty sat on either side. I expected them to pull out their phones as a distraction. Instead, they each reached out and held my hands. It made the silent wait more bearable.

I'm not sure how long we sat there. Half an hour? Forty-five minutes? But eventually the security guard returned. In another rookie mistake, I hadn't checked his nametag. I made up for it. Jason. I didn't know if it would do me any good, but it was better than calling him 'guard' in my thoughts. Angry thoughts mostly, as I cursed him for taking so long.

But the slight smile on his face flipped my attitude. He held out my phone. "Our chief nurse has agreed to let you take a peek at the patient."

Lando, Scotty, and I stood.

Jason shook his head. "Just the lady."

Scotty squeezed my hand. "Bring us back good news, Harmony."

I couldn't foresee any way there could be good news. Either it wasn't Eli, or he was badly hurt. I followed Jason through a maze of doors and hallways until we reached a closed-off room.

"Wait here for the nurse," he said, before heading back the way we'd come.

Arms crossed and eyes on a dark spot on the opposite wall, I did my best to ignore the steady stream of staff flowing by. Their scrubs seemed to follow a color code, but I couldn't puzzle out what it meant. The nurses wore blue, but who were the people in brown and purple?

After too long, a nurse stopped in front of me. Her gaze raked me from top to bottom. She put her hand on the door and said, "No photos."

My phone was tucked into my purse and the thought hadn't crossed my mind, but I nodded. "Of course not."

She slid open the door and went into the room. Tentatively, I followed, unsure of what I would see.

I walked into a half-remembered nightmare. A bed in the middle of the room. Chairs pushed against the walls. Machines beeping, tubes and wires everywhere. Stark white sheets covered by thin paper spotted with fresh blood.

Then there was the man, motionless, his neck in a brace, his midsection covered by a white blanket. I cataloged every bruise, scrape, and cut on his arms and legs before allowing my eyes to travel to his face.

My heart stopped.

Not the face of the man I loved, but it was Eli. The swelling and bruising made an effective disguise, but it wasn't good enough to fool me. I grabbed the door frame to help me stay upright.

The nurse read my face. "What's his name?" she asked in a dispassionate tone.

"Last name Hennessey. Two ns, two ss. First name Matthew. Middle name Elijah. He goes by Eli." If I adopted her attitude, I would get through this. Detach myself from the man and get through the facts.

She typed the info into the computer mounted on the wall. "Date of birth? Blood type? Allergies? Past surgeries?"

I rattled off his birth date and what I knew of his medical history. His dog tags supplied his blood type, A-positive. "As far as I'm aware, he isn't allergic to anything. He claims he's allergic to peas, but that's just because he doesn't like them."

She chuckled. "Sounds like my husband. Are you two married?"

"No, we're in a long-term relationship. His parents live here in town. My friends out in the lobby can tell them what's happening."

The rhythmic beeping of one of the machines sped up, and an alarm wailed. The nurse punched a button on the wall. Within seconds, staff stormed into the room. I shrank into a corner to stay out of their way, hoping they wouldn't throw me out.

Whatever they did worked, and the beeping slowed and returned to normal. Everyone, including the original nurse, left the room. I was alone with Eli.

I sent a quick text to Lando and Scotty to tell them to get Eli's parents—and hurry. Then I pulled the rolling stool beside the bed. I wanted to hug him, but there wasn't a way to get my arms past all the wires. Gauze and tape and bandages covered everything within easy reach. I settled for placing one hand on his forearm, a spot that appeared uninjured.

"What have you gotten yourself into, Eli?" I half-whispered. I leaned forward and touched my lips to his cheek. I hoped it would be the reverse of the fairytale, where the prince kissed the princess to wake her. It didn't work. His eyes didn't flutter. His slow, labored breathing didn't change. Not even his little finger moved.

"Stay with me, Sweetie." I stroked his shoulder. "We'll get through this together."

I'd heard once that even someone in a coma could hear the people around them. I wouldn't sing to him and annoy the patients in the neighboring rooms, but I could talk.

"Did I tell you about Sarah and Freddie? He talked her into moving in with him. I take credit for it, because if it wasn't for me, they might never have met."

He didn't respond, but I didn't expect him to.

"The City Council wants to put together a fall festival. Kind of like the Bird Watching Festival in the spring. It's too late for this year, but they're looking for volunteers for a committee to organize it next year."

A different nurse came into the room to check Eli's vitals. She glanced my way but said nothing. After updating the information in the computer, she left.

I tried to figure out what else to talk about. It had to be pleasant news, nothing negative. The task was harder than I'd figured.

"You should see Joe and Luke's flower garden." That was a safe topic. "All the summer flowers are in bloom. The black-eyed Susans are gorgeous this year. They were one of my dad's favorite flowers. Joe and Luke are having a heck of a time keeping the birds out of the sunflowers. At this rate, they won't get any seeds for themselves."

My throat dried out, but I didn't want to leave the room in search of something to drink. I might get lost and not find my way back, or someone might decide I wasn't allowed there.

A muscle in Eli's arm twitched. I took it as a positive sign. I watched his face, but everything remained still. The beeping of the machine stayed steady.

I rolled my shoulders to ease the growing stress. "Oh, Eli," I whispered. Unwished for tears rolled down my cheeks, and I wiped them away. He was a strong man. He'd be okay. I had to believe it.

Voices in the hallway shook me from my moment of despair. Eli's parents had arrived.

"You'll have to leave," the nurse said, before I had a chance to hug Tillie and Rob, Eli's parents.

"We can't have too many people in here."

Tillie opened her arms. "Harmony."

Taking my hand off Eli's arm hurt. It was like I was abandoning him. But I didn't have a choice. I dredged up what I had left of my internal strength to support her as she glimpsed Eli. Between Rob and I, we got her seated before her knees buckled.

"What happened?" Rob asked.

The nurse answered. I never had checked her name tag, and for once in my life, I didn't care. "It was an accident. That's all the troopers told us. They're investigating."

I didn't add what I knew, which was next to nothing.

"He's lucky they found him today," she continued as she checked the levels in the various bags of fluid dripping into his body. "The weather is predicted to turn bad this weekend and the fishermen will be off the river during the thunderstorms."

Tillie grasped my hand and squeezed. "What's wrong with him?"

"The doctor will explain when she comes in. I'll let her know you're here." The nurse nodded at me. "You can wait in the lobby."

"No." Tillie tugged on my hand. "I want her to stay."

The nurse shrugged. "If the alarms go off, leave the room." She glared at me. "Understood?"

The message was clear. I was the interloper. I had to leave, even if Tillie and Rob stayed. My reluctant nod satisfied her and, after one more glance at the readings on the machines, she strode out the door.

When she was gone, no one spoke. It was better that way. If Tillie or Rob didn't ask questions, I wouldn't have to lie.

"We've got him stabilized, but he's not out of the woods," the doctor, a blond-haired woman who looked younger than me, explained. "His body started to shut down due to dehydration, but he's responding well to treatment. We'll run additional tests as soon as he's up to it. Based on experience, he may have broken ribs, but I don't believe any other bones are fractured. Until I'm more comfortable with his overall progress, I won't order a full set of X-rays."

"Is there anything else you'll be watching for?" Rob asked, too calm for my comfort. Maybe it came from his military background. In some ways, he and Eli were alike, while in others, they clashed.

"Concussion and internal bleeding. We won't be able to rule either of those out without further observation and tests." The doctor stuck her hands into the pockets of her lab coat. "I don't want to sugarcoat the severity of your son's injuries, but I also don't want to alarm you for no reason. There's a lot of wait and see involved. As soon as I feel it's safe, we'll arrange for him to be moved to the ICU."

"How long until he regains consciousness?"

She shook her head. "It varies from case to case. He's under light sedation now to aid in the healing process, but it could be anytime now, or it could take days."

I heard the unspoken 'or never.'

Tillie gasped. "But he's always been so healthy and takes care of himself. I can't remember the last time he was sick."

I had a feeling she didn't know about the injuries that had left his scars.

"And his health may have saved his life," the doctor said. A machine beeped out of rhythm and she checked the display. "I suggest you folks go home. Get some rest. Staff will contact you if anything changes."

A nurse peeked her head in the door. "Doctor, we need you in 32C."

"On my way." She nodded in our direction. "We'll take care of him," she said as she whisked out the door.

Tillie shook her head. "I can't leave him like this."

I'd stay forever if they let me.

Rob held out his hand. "Come on, honey, all we can do is sit here, worry, and be in the way. That won't do Eli any good."

How was he staying so calm? Sure, I was ice-cold stoic on the surface, but inside I was putting together all the shattered pieces that fell apart again each time I looked at Eli.

The way Tillie's lips turned down told me she wasn't convinced, but she stood. "It doesn't feel right to leave."

"These chairs aren't comfortable enough to sit in for long," I said. "Once they get him moved to ICU, you can spend more time with him."

The combined pressure was too much for Tillie. Her shoulders dropped. "We'll come back early tomorrow. Maybe he'll be awake by then."

My heart wished the same. My head told me not to hope too hard.

Chapter 7

Lando, Scotty, and I watched the taillights of Rob's car disappear around the corner as he and Tillie headed home. They were barely out of sight when Lando grabbed my arm. "Give us the lowdown, Harmony. How bad is it?"

I leaned against him. "Not going to lie. It's bad." As the three of us walked back to Scotty's car, I filled them in on what the doctor had said. And what she hadn't said, but I'd inferred.

"She's not positive Eli will make it." To hide my tears, I turned and watched the edge of sunshine brighten along the horizon. Besides, I didn't want to see their reactions. It might be more than I could handle.

Lando kicked the front tire of Scotty's car, hard enough to rock the vehicle. "Damnit," he swore, followed by a string of harsher language. "Why aren't we in there with him?"

"Because we can't do anything about it." Scotty slapped his palm against the hood. The sound echoed in the still early morning air.

"He'll know we're there," Lando protested.

I shook my head. "No. He won't. I can't explain it, but when I talked to him, nothing moved. He didn't even blink. It was like talking to a shell without a man inside."

The memory proved too much. I stuck my hands in my jean pockets to hide the way they trembled and leaned against Scotty's car. I needed a rock to support me, but my rock lay almost lifeless in a hospital bed.

Lando opened the passenger side door and sat in the front seat, his feet planted firmly on the ground, his elbows on his knees, his head lowered. "I don't want to leave."

"Me neither." Scotty jumped up on the hood and crossed his legs.

I wouldn't argue. "Good. You can keep me company. If anything changes, I want to be only a few steps away."

The back seat of Scotty's car wasn't comfortable, but I curled up on it, pretending to sleep. Lando even found a shawl in a box of cosplay accessories in the trunk to use as a cover. Scotty tuned the radio to a local classical music station to chase away the silence. None of us wanted to talk.

I clenched my phone, praying for good news and dreading bad. To ease the burning of my tear-reddened eyes, I closed them. Just for a minute.

It wasn't the wake-up call I expected.

"I brought you some food. I hope you're okay with breakfast burritos," Detective Horace said.

If I stayed quiet and didn't move, would he see me?

"Good morning, Miss Duprie."

Yeah, he knew. I searched for my glasses and put them on as I sat up. I didn't even pretend to be cheerful. "How long have you been here, Detective?" I asked, hunting for my phone, wanting to check for missed calls. I found it under the shawl, but there were no messages waiting for me.

"Long enough to get the answers to my warrant and figure out what you were doing out here. But what I don't understand is how you wormed your way in to see him. There's a lot you haven't told me."

"My priorities have changed in the last few days."

His posture softened. "You'll need to cooperate with me to help us determine what happened."

"I can't promise how much help I'll be. I have other things that need my attention." My gaze wandered over his shoulder to the Emergency Room entrance.

"Whatever information you can share to assist us in identifying a suspect will be appreciated."

That got my full focus. "This was deliberate."

In the front seat, their mouths full of food, Lando and Scotty started babbling. I raised a hand to stop them. "Detective?"

His lips formed a tight line. "A quick look at the car was all I needed. The red paint transfer in the scrapes on the side made it obvious."

I grabbed onto the information like a lifeline. All the energy I was spending on worry could be turned towards figuring out who had run Eli off the road. "I assume you'll be contacting all the local repair shops? Although chances are, the car used was stolen."

It was Horace's turn to raise his hand. "I know how to do my job."

Of course he did, or he wouldn't be a detective. I had to be nice to him. I didn't have access to the computer systems he used. Or did I? Did Eli have a back door to them? Most likely. If I found his secret username and password, I could hack their system.

Lando asked the question I'd bitten back. "Did they locate his phone when they searched the car? Or his wallet?"

Horace scrunched his eyebrows. "Those items weren't listed in the report."

"How about his Glock?" I hadn't checked Eli's house for his gun, but he always kept it with him.

"He carries?" Horace asked.

"He's licensed for concealed carry. It's a Glock 19 from his military days, although he's always talking about buying a newer model."

I let the information sink in, then added, "I also have a gun, although mine is a Beretta. She's locked up in my hotel room because I haven't checked if my permit is honored in Florida."

His jaw dropped. Before he answered, my phone buzzed. "Hold that thought, please." I checked my messages and looked up with a slight smile. "Tillie says they're moving Eli to ICU."

Horace's jaw dropped further. "How do you know? Did you bribe a nurse?"

"His mother. Tillie is his mother." My confidence in the detective dropped a notch.

"The report lists her as Natalie. And his father as Benjamin."

"Right. She goes by Tillie. And he goes by Rob."

"Tillie I can see. Where does Rob come from?"

My grin was genuine. "Family secret. Do you know, Lando?" It was a lie of omission, but I'd been sworn to secrecy by Tillie.

"Nope. Eli never mentioned it," Lando answered.

The perfect opening. Or closing. "Speaking of Eli, I'd like to check on him. Do you mind, Detective?" Where he was standing blocked me from getting out.

He nodded and stepped aside. "I'll verify the inventory of the car and be in touch. Say in an hour? Where can we meet?"

I had too many conflicting demands on my time. What I wanted more than anything was to be beside Eli, holding his hand. What I needed to do was go run his company and do my best to hold it together. I couldn't do both at the same time. And where was I going to find time to hunt for whoever had done this to Eli?

I switched into executive mode. "I should have some free time around noon. We can meet at the office. Lunch on me, if that's allowed."

He blinked, processing my change in personality. "Business as usual, Miss Duprie?"

I counted to ten. Twice. Then I straightened my spine, squared my shoulders, and channeled Chief

Sorenson's command presence. "If you think anything about this is normal, Detective, it's time for you to rethink your priorities."

He crossed his arms and stared down at me, his height giving him an advantage in the battle for top alpha. But I'd learned the tricks and could stare back forever. He blinked first, chasing the Florida sun out of his eyes.

"What does it take to intimidate you, Miss Duprie?" Horace asked.

I didn't answer the question. "Noon then? Chinese?"

I didn't stay with Eli very long. They were getting ready to run tests. But the few moments were enough to tell me nothing had changed. He was still lost, a silent shell. I dropped a kiss on his forehead before the nurse hustled me out of the room.

As Scotty drove me back to the hotel, I filled him and Lando in. "I'll ask Tillie to put you two on the approved visitors list. That way you can check on Eli yourselves."

"Should we ask for Darla to be on the list, too?"

"We can ask. I don't know if the hospital limits the number of people allowed in. Or if she can handle seeing him the way he is."

Scotty pulled up to the hotel's front door and I got out. I wanted a shower and a change of clothes before heading into the office. "Why don't you guys plan on coming in after lunch? I'll approve the late arrival."

I expected a snarky response but didn't get one, proving just how tired they were. I should have given them the entire day off but didn't want to be accused of playing favorites.

Fiona was on the phone, so I waved to her as I used my employee badge to unlock the door to the back room. Which was easier for me. I wasn't in the mood to deal with Fiona's overly bright, almost artificial personality. It always bothered me until I became immune to it. That, and her obvious crush on Eli.

The change in mood hovered over the room like fog. I got a few hands raised in greeting, but no one said as much as hello. I guessed Lando or Scotty had called in and shared the news.

I wasn't inundated by a flood of questions about Eli or his condition. Everyone appeared to be burying their worries in their work. Which is exactly what I planned to do.

Overnight, someone had transformed the conference room into something that resembled an office. The table had been replaced by an actual desk. A large bouquet hid the open cupboards that had been cleared of their contents.

Darla followed me in with a glass of ice water in one hand and a stack of paperwork in the other. "I've got them sorted in order of importance," she said as she put everything on top of the desk. "The way Eli liked them. On top are venders trying to get our business. Garbage, mostly, but Eli liked to look through them. Then comes the invoices needing to be paid. Nothing unusual today. Next comes the part he hated. Letters to customers that are behind on their bills. Usually it's because city officials are slow with budgeting or whatever, but there are a few we have to remind regularly. I've got a standard letter put together for each that you just need to sign."

"And the one in the bright red folder?"

She smiled. "That's reserved for out-of-the-ordinary requests. This one is from a high school teacher wanting to bring a group of her students for a tour of the facility. Eli had a way of explaining we're a small operation and not very interesting."

I disagreed with his assessment and would look at the request. "Do you do this for Eli?"

"On the days he doesn't get to the mail first."

That sounded like Eli. "Thanks. I appreciate you keeping me on the right path. It'll take me some time to get the hang of things." I hoped Eli would get better before I figured out his methods. "But as much as I appreciate the water, I have the feeling this is a coffee kind of morning."

"Sugar and creamer?" Darla asked.

"I'll get my own. I don't want you to interrupt your duties to take care of me."

She closed the office door and put her hands on her hips. "And I want everyone to accept that you are in charge. If I have to play the role of the dutiful secretary to make that happen, so be it. Whatever it takes to keep the business running until Eli is healthy again. He will get better, won't he?"

Did she want the truth or lies to make her feel better? I went for a combination. "He's in rough shape. I don't know all the details. But he made it through the night and that has to count for something. Since I'm not next-of-kin, I only know what Tillie shares with me and what I see for myself."

Darla squeezed her eyes closed and nodded. "Thanks for being honest. We'll just keep this between ourselves, right? I wouldn't want the word getting out to Eli's competitors. They might use it as an opportunity to try and undercut the company."

I wanted to ask her about the competition, but now wasn't the time.

Chapter 8

Chinese for lunch solved two problems. First, it gave my coworkers a treat to help boost their spirits. Second, when Detective Horace showed up, it wouldn't seem like I was doing him a favor.

He arrived at five until noon. Actually, he pulled into the parking lot fifteen minutes early but waited to come inside. I knew, because I'd asked the techs to give me access to the security cameras.

I didn't meet him at the door, but had Fiona call Darla to escorted him in. Another method to establish myself as being in charge and keep him off balance. It was better that way until I trusted him and figured out his intentions. Or his boss's motives. I didn't want to be on his bad side, either. A fine line to tread.

The small plate of food he carried into my office didn't look like enough to satisfy me, let alone him. That wouldn't stop me from enjoying the assortment Darla put in front of me.

"How can I help you, Detective?" I asked, lifting a forkful of fried rice to my mouth.

"You puzzle me, Miss Duprie, and that makes me uneasy. How did you and your friends get to the hospital before me?"

I swallowed. "Easy. More than one news station carried information about the accident. We dug around until we found one that mentioned the hospital by name. Getting in to see Eli was harder. I convinced them I could supply his medical history so they could provide proper treatment. It helps that I'm a civilian and don't have to wait for a judge and a warrant."

One side of his mouth rose. "You make it sound logical."

"Logic is what I'm best at." Sometimes I applied it in unique ways, but he didn't need to know that. "Now it's my turn to ask a question. Any word on the car that hit Eli?"

"Nothing from FHP yet." He read my puzzled look. "Florida Highway Patrol. They are in charge of investigating the crash."

I scribbled myself a note to research Florida's law enforcement agencies and how they operated.

"Back to my questions," Horace said. "It's the pattern of your knowledge that's troubling. How you knew about the fire in your hometown before it was reported by neighbors. How you got to Florida so fast. It was like you were ready to come. How you walked in and took over this company with no resistance. How you figured out Hennessey was missing before anyone."

I wondered who was feeding him information. It had to be an employee. I'd have to track that person down and figure out the proper response. As a security-oriented organization, there shouldn't be any leaks.

"All of that can be explained. Logically explained. First; Eli had designed a security system for the house, and the system alerted four people, including me, to the fire." Well, it would have alerted four people if Eli's phone had been working.

"And how did you pinpoint the time that Hennessey went missing?"

Was he trying to catch me in a lie? "I'm afraid you've been misled. I can't tell you when Eli had his accident. I can narrow it down to between nine on Monday evening when Eli and I talked, and three Tuesday morning when the fire started. Logic, Detective. And my turn again."

I twirled some egg noodles onto my fork but didn't take a bite. "Have you checked Eli's car for fingerprints? If his wallet, phone, and gun were stolen, the culprit may have left traces of his identity behind."

"Or worn gloves. And yes, the team is looking for clues in the vehicle. Standard procedure. Now, back to you. How did you get here so fast?"

I arched my eyebrows. "Really? You've seen my car. And I travel light. What isn't logical is how you tracked me down so easily." I scrawled another note to remind me to ask Lando and Scotty to help me check Dolores for a tracking device.

He ignored my challenge. "Your car may be quick, but the legal system isn't. How did you bypass it to get access to run this company?"

It was my turn to ask a question, but I'd let it slide. Once. I leaned back and tented my fingers. "Now, that part isn't logical at all. When Eli set this up several months ago, he told me it was to cover him when he attended conferences and similar events. I didn't realize the power he'd given me until Kris, the company lawyer, explained it when I got here."

While he processed my answer, I took a bite of my sesame chicken. I had one more question for him, but the timing wasn't right.

"It all seems logical," Horace said after a lengthy pause. "It's the long chain that bothers me."

I could see that from his point of view. "If you discount me, what other theories have you developed? It wasn't road rage, because in a case like that, the other driver wouldn't have robbed Eli. Have you requested his phone records to check if he got a call that would explain why he was on the highway?"

"All the standard investigations are in progress, Miss Duprie. You realize that I won't share details with you while you are still technically a suspect?"

"And you understand that I may not trust you, either, Detective?"

Horace nodded. "That's fair. Since you understand police work, I'd like to hear your theory."

"I don't have one. I've gone over my last conversation with Eli and can't pinpoint anything out of the ordinary. There's no logical reason for him to have left the house. Until you can get your hands on his call logs, I'm as puzzled as everyone else."

My cell phone buzzed and I grabbed it, hoping for a call from Tillie. Instead, the screen identified the caller as Claire, the Oak Grove Fire Chief.

"Excuse me, I have to take this." I swiveled so my back was to the detective, giving me the illusion of privacy. Still, I kept my answers short.

"Hey, Claire…"

"Yeah, it's hot and muggy here…"

"I'm holding up," I lied.

"No kidding…"

"I thought they handled cases at the federal level…?"

"Sure. I give permission. With one caveat. Get a tech guy to take the hard drives out of the computers and hold on to them for me. I don't want anyone to access Eli's code…"

"I'll stay in touch…"

"Thanks. Bye."

I ended the call, stared at the wall for a moment, then turned back to face Horace. "What do you know. That was Chief Hinds of the Oak Grove Fire Department. The ATF wants to take over the fire investigation as a training exercise. She doesn't believe it. Neither do I. At least they asked permission."

"Like you would tell them no."

I grinned. "It wouldn't be the first time."

"You've told the ATF no?" Horace's eyes widened.

"Not the ATF. I've never dealt with them. The FBI is a different story, and I'm not free to share it."

He rubbed his ear. "Okay, let's go back to the original point. Why would the ATF investigate a house fire?"

I stirred my fried rice with my fork as I thought. "If I have to hazard a guess, it's tied to Eli. He's got some crazy high security clearance and I can see the feds wanting to make sure it wasn't compromised. But wouldn't that be the job of the FBI or Secret Service?"

"I believe that's handled by another government agency. I'm not sure because I've never dealt with it. I'll ask around."

Or I could research it and find out for myself. I added it to my list. "Will you be getting warrants to monitor Eli's bank accounts? I know which bank he uses, but don't have access to his records. He kept everything electronically."

"We can do that. If anyone uses his cards, we might retrieve a video."

I neatly printed the name of Eli's bank on my notepad, tore off the sheet and handed it to him.

Horace stood, pushing his barely touched plate toward the center of the desk. "I need to check in with the chief. It looks as if things are going to get complicated."

"Welcome to my life, Detective," I said, as I rose to escort him to the front door.

A cursory reading of the list of Shifter Technologies' customers didn't give me any insight into why a federal agency would get involved. The list was police department after police department, including a Native American Tribal Police Department. The only exception was the Oak Grove Fire Department.

That was a work in progress, so it didn't surprise me to see a zero in the contract amount column.

But Eli would occasionally do jobs not under the company name. It was a way to keep his skills sharp, he'd told me. Darla didn't have that list. I wasn't psychologically ready to dig through Eli's desk to look for it. Not when other people were around to see me crying. I'd save the task for the weekend.

A knock at the door interrupted my thoughts. "Any update from the hospital about Eli?" Kris asked.

"No, but they wouldn't call me. I haven't heard from his parents, either. Which I'm taking to mean that nothing has changed."

"That's not right." She sat and leaned forward with her elbows on my desk. "He made you medical power of attorney, didn't he?"

"What's that?"

"Oh, shit. He didn't tell you." She rubbed her hands together. "It's possible to designate a person to make decisions for you in case of a medical emergency when you can't decide for yourself, even if you aren't related. It's strictly for medical and has nothing to do with legal or financial obligations. It was widely used by same-sex partners before the marriage laws were updated. I've dealt with a few cases where partners hadn't set up POA, and they weren't pretty."

"What does that have to do with me and Eli?" I pushed my laptop aside so I could see her face better.

"He wanted to make you his medical POA. I wouldn't do it, because I like to separate my work here from personal matters. If anything ever came down to a court battle, it creates a cleaner division of legal decisions."

"In other words, it shows you didn't talk him into it," I said. But I wondered if she had tried to talk him out of it.

"Exactly. Anyway, I thought it sounded like a good idea, with as much time as he spends with you up north. So, I referred him to a friend to get it done. Eli never mentioned it again and I don't know if he followed through with it."

How would I find out without rooting through Eli's paperwork? "It doesn't seem that important. It's not like Eli's parents will keep me from seeing him or deny him proper care."

The conversation replayed in my head as I waited for the ICU nurse to verify that I was on the approved visitors list, which made me wonder who else was on it or needed to be. Tillie would add Lando and Scotty if I asked, but Rob had never approved of Lando.

Only one guest at a time was allowed in Eli's room, so I had to wait for Tillie to leave. We shared a hug in the hallway.

"Any change?" I asked.

She sniffed back a small sob. "Nothing. The only time he moved was when the staff turned him to prevent bedsores."

I tightened my hold on her. "He's breathing on his own, right? That's got to be a good sign." The oxygen tube in his nose was standard procedure.

"And they aren't seeing any signs of internal bleeding," she told me.

"That's great news."

She let go of me. "They brought in a portable X-ray machine. They made me leave the room while they used it. The results aren't back yet, as far as I've been told."

I wanted to find a nurse and demand answers, but it would take time for a specialist to read the X-rays. "I'm sure they'll tell you as soon as they can. Now, why don't you go home? Rest. I'll stay with Eli. You've been here all day."

She pulled out a tissue and wiped her eyes. "Rob came and sat with him for a while. Gave me a break. But I could use some sleep. You'll call if anything changes?"

"Yes. Tell Rob I said hi."

If I used my imagination, I could pretend Eli took each breath without a struggle. Except for the new wrappings around his chest, nothing had changed. The stark white room seemed dark despite the sunlight peeking in through the window.

I sat in the uncomfortable visitor's chair and rested one hand on Eli's arm while using the bed to support the book I pulled out of my purse. I'd stopped by his house and grabbed the one he'd been reading the last time we talked. Even if I didn't understand it, I could read it to him. It would suit him better than one of my typical romances or biographies.

I stayed until almost midnight, when shift change happened and the new nurse sent me home. By then my voice was hoarse and my throat sore. As I drove back to the hotel, I had that prickly feeling of being followed, but was too tired to deal with it. With no clear culprit in my rearview mirror, I blamed it on my weariness and worry.

Chapter 9

I ignored my alarm when it went off. It was Saturday, and I could sleep in a few minutes. But I had an agenda and didn't want to delay too long.

First thing I did when I rolled out of bed was start a pot of coffee. My throat hurt. I hadn't talked that much since presenting my thesis for my master's degree.

I took advantage of a morning breeze to drink my first cup while sitting on the balcony and watching seagulls wing their way over the lake. The hot coffee eased my throat.

I wasn't the only one enjoying the morning. Several people stood at the edge of the lake, throwing bread into the water, feeding the fish. Two men stood a little way away from the water, talking. I'd have to take time to walk along the lake's edge and relax.

But I had things to do and places to go. At least I wouldn't have to deal with any law enforcement types. I hoped.

Tops on my list was figuring out who to trust. I

needed to start from a position of trusting no one. A very lonely place to begin.

The probability that someone at Eli's company was betraying him, and me, cut deep. But that was the only way to explain Detective Horace's insider knowledge.

Being in charge meant I had access to everything, including employee applications and hiring paperwork. Sure, everyone had gone through a security check when they were hired, but I wanted to drill deeper into their past.

Even though the company had less than fifty people, the level of research I planned would take forever. I needed to narrow my search.

With a third cup of coffee in my hand, I pondered the options and watched a man stroll along the lake's shore. The family that had been there earlier were gone, likely spending their day at one of the area's attractions. Nothing out of the ordinary, but instinct yelled at me.

I studied the man. And identified a pattern. Every few steps he'd scan the hotel. His attention focused on the lower floors, and he didn't seem like an immediate threat. Was he waiting for someone? Or casing the building, preparing to rob it? I picked up my laptop and moved inside, the hopeful beginning of the day dampened.

I retrieved Betsy, my Beretta, from her locked case and put her in the top drawer of the nightstand. Only as a precaution.

❃ ❃ ❃

No one seemed to follow me on my way to the hospital, but I checked the rearview mirror more often than needed. The prickly feeling wouldn't go away. I tried all the tricks. Switched lanes. Made turns at the last minute. Pulled into a parking lot and studied the traffic. Nothing worked. If I had a tail, they were good. Professional grade. And that made me nervous. Perhaps my lack of sleep and too much caffeine had kicked my imagination into overdrive.

I reached the hospital's parking lot and let go of the breath I didn't know I'd been holding. No one had attempted to run me off the road. There'd been no high-speed chase. But I was glad the parking space was in view of the valet stand. Dolores would be safer with a constant stream of people nearby. For added security, I made a side trip to talk to the valets and slip them each a twenty, when they promised they'd keep an eye on her.

In what had become my new routine, I shared a hug with Tillie in the family waiting room outside the ICU. "Any change?" I asked.

"No." Moisture gathered in the corners of her eyes. "I thought for sure he'd wake up today."

"There's a lot of the day left. What do the doctors say?"

Tillie smiled. "There's some good news. No broken ribs, although his chest is badly bruised."

I'd have to ask Horace if Eli's car had an airbag and if it had deployed. "That's wonderful. Is Rob coming in today?"

"When I left home, he was in his workshop. He claimed to be working on a shelf I asked for a long time ago, but mostly it looked like he was destroying scrap wood with the saw. It's his way of burning off stress."

I understood. "Don't worry about hurrying back. In fact, you can stay here and take a nap." The dark circles under her eyes revealed how little sleep she'd gotten.

She glanced longingly at the empty recliner. "Yeah, I could do that." She kissed me on the cheek. "I'm glad you're here."

Tillie was right. Nothing had changed. It was as if I'd only been out of Eli's room for a minute. If I strained my eyes, I could imagine that his chest rose and fell with each shallow breath.

I rearranged the chair and pulled his book out of my purse. I'd start where we'd left off. Chapter Three.

"Are you learning anything?" the nurse asked when she came in a few minutes later to check on Eli.

"Me? No. I don't understand most of what I'm reading. But he does, and that's all that matters."

"Your voice is what matters. I can't prove it by the vitals, but he rests easier when you're here. His mother doesn't have the same effect on him. And his father's voice makes his blood pressure go up. We like it when you are here."

Her words encouraged me to keep going. "Is his mother still here?"

The nurse nodded. "Fast asleep. Unless we get some noisy visitors, I think she'll keep sleeping."

That gave me more time with Eli. I opened the book again and continued reading.

That sensation returned when I left the hospital. The one telling me to stay on my toes, that someone was watching me. I stepped off the sidewalk and pretended to check my messages. Everyone else kept on walking. No one seemed out of place.

I blamed it on my lack of sleep. Deep down, I didn't believe my own excuse.

I wanted to head back to the hotel and grab a nap myself, but I was in this for the long haul and needed more clothes. Actual food would be good, too. Food came first. Besides, the drive to the grocery store would take me off the major streets and let me identify the tagalong, if I had one. That was the plan, anyway.

The trip was uneventful. No obvious cars in my wake. No tingle at the back of my neck. So, I took my time in the store loading up on fruit, including varieties that the stores in Oak Grove never carried. I'd always wanted to try star fruit.

I also picked up some of my favorite snacks and a six-pack of a local beer, a small mirror and a selfie stick, and duct tape. I resisted the urge to buy seasonings. Meals hadn't been an issue yet, but I wasn't eating much. The prospect of supper every night in the hospital's cafeteria didn't thrill me.

As if on cue, the tingle returned as I stashed the groceries in the trunk. Instinctively, I reached for Betsy, but she was at the hotel. I had no choice but to play the game. Not knowing the back streets and alleyways like I did in Oak Grove put me at a disadvantage.

Or I could play it straight, as if unaware of any danger. Lull the tail into complacency. Then look for the opportunity to make a move at the last minute.

Part of the problem was the amount of traffic, even on the backstreets. I didn't want to risk getting anyone else involved. But if I couldn't go fast, I could do the opposite. Drive five miles under the speed limit. Anyone who didn't pass me when they had a chance became a suspect.

It took four miles, but the ploy worked. The tan-colored sedan never made a move to pass and let other cars go by, filling the gap between us. With the car's image securely stored in my brain, I went for a drive.

Even though it wasn't rush hour, traffic on the interstate was heavy. I guided Dolores through openings, switched lanes whenever I wanted. I wished for an open road and a heavy foot on the gas pedal, but that wouldn't happen. Not now, not here in the middle of Orlando.

Not wanting to go too far, I exited before the attractions. Then turned under the interstate and took the onramp heading the opposite direction. I was thrilled to see I'd lost my tail somewhere, without even trying. Score one for me.

My joy was short-lived.

The hotel parking lot was nearly empty, and I got a premium spot near the side entrance. That way I didn't have to carry my bags through the lobby. It also put me closer to the elevator. The stairs to my apartment in Oak Grove didn't bother me but climbing up eight stories wore me out.

I found spots for all my groceries, then tackled my next project: putting together a makeshift tool for checking Dolores' underside for a tracker. I'd seen enough 'bugs' in the last few years that I figured I'd recognize one in a place it didn't belong.

I should have parked in a sunnier space. I had to rely on the small flashlight on my phone to brighten any suspicious spots. As I knelt on the ground, I wished for a friendly neighborhood mechanic who would put Dolores up on a lift.

Luck was with me. The little black box was too obvious, attached to the car's frame near the middle of the rear bumper. It took only a few seconds to pull it off. I juggled it, debating my next move. The car two spots away with a Texas license seemed like a good option. But guilt struck. I didn't want an innocent bystander to get hurt. Instead, I walked across the parking lot and stuck the tracker on the garbage dumpster.

I didn't know whether to be mad at Chief Sorenson or thankful for his concern, but either way seemed out-of-character for him. Was I placing blame on the wrong person?

When I considered it, the bug seemed too easy to find. Instinct pulled me back to Dolores. I picked up my makeshift tool and continued my tour. I felt foolish when a family spilled out the door and tried to figure out what I was doing, but I ignored their stares.

Sure enough, a second little black box clung to Dolores' frame near the passenger's door. A quick tug and it came off in my hand. It didn't match the first one. My theory about Chief Sorenson placing it shattered. The second tracker joined the first.

I trudged up the eight flights of stairs to get some sorely needed exercise. Six sets up, I paused to catch my breath and stare out the window overlooking the lake. A man stood there. I checked off the list in my memory. Same build, same clothes, same habit of scanning the hotel every few minutes. Either he was casing the place or waiting for someone. It had been a long wait.

One other option came to mind. He was watching for me.

Without the luxury of guessing if he was a bad or good guy, he became a threat.

Chapter 10

I didn't know the rules of the game I'd been sucked into, so it was time to create my own. I'd start with a trip to the mall. If I needed to run Eli's company for very long, I had to have more than three outfits. I didn't know any local clothing shops, so the mall would have to do.

I'd learned not to sacrifice quality for quantity. The first store I chose not for its selection, but for the mirrors reflecting anyone entering. I wanted to see if I was being followed. The reflection revealed no sign of a stalker.

My second planned stop was at the other end, a store with a reputation for well-made clothing. I didn't even window-shop, power-walking all the way. Still, I waited for the prickly feeling to come back. It never did.

I took my time picking out several basic suits and additional matching blouses. If I mixed-and-matched, I'd be set for weeks. It wasn't until I finished checking out that the sensation of being watched returned. With the crowd around the checkout area, I couldn't pick out anyone who didn't fit.

How had they found me? The only tracker on my phone was the one Eli had coded. And only Lando had access to it.

Unless…

Unless whoever had stolen Eli's phone had turned it on and gotten through his security. If his phone was active, I'd be able to turn the tables and track them.

I stopped at the store's entrance pretending to read my messages. In reality, I was checking Eli's app. The spot that should show the location of his phone remained unwaveringly red. My theory had been proven wrong. I'd have to do this the old-fashioned way.

I flitted from store to kiosk. Always looking, never buying. Watching the flow of traffic and looking for a point where people had to change their path to veer around an unmoving obstacle. That's how I found him.

He stood outside a store directly opposite from the one I was in. I couldn't risk taking his picture and letting him know I was on to him, so I memorized his face while browsing through birthday cards. Short brown hair, almost a buzz cut. A large nose and ears that lay flat against his head. Eyes a little too close together. His lips drooped on one side, like a stroke victim's.

He didn't look as if he was interested in what the store was selling—fabric. And he didn't have the air of a man waiting for his wife. No checking his watch or his phone, looking everywhere but where I was. It was time to disappear.

I wandered through a few more stores, knowing he moved with me. The shoe store provided me the opportunity I'd been looking for. In plain view, I tried on a pair, returned them to the shelf, then did the same with a second pair. But as I ducked behind some shelves that blocked his view, I found the other entrance, which led directly to the parking lot.

Luck stayed with me. A delivery truck was parked in front of the store, giving me additional coverage as I made my escape. As I headed back to Dolores, I wondered how long it would take the man to realize I'd left. How much time did I have to spare before he'd come looking for me? How had he found me in the first place?

It didn't seem possible a third tracker had been placed on Dolores. Besides, that wouldn't explain how he'd traced me in the mall. Had I been bugged?

With my purchases stashed in Dolores' trunk, I dumped the contents of my purse on the passenger's seat. I dug through all the normal items. A package of tissues. A paperback book, Moon Baby. My contacts case. A little metal box of breath mints. A pair of nail clippers and a mirror.

I didn't remember buying that brand of mints. Ever. How long had they been in there?

Curious what they looked and smelled like, I opened the tin. Or tried to. Only the lid was stuck, and I didn't want to break a fingernail. The nail file on the clippers should do the trick.

I tried to stick the file in the opening, but nothing budged. Now I was determined to figure out this puzzle. I flipped the box upside down to see what I'd missed and found my answer. Two tiny screws, one at each end.

It was a clever setup, with screws so small the nail file was too wide to fit in the slot. Not even the tip.

Frustrated, I considered my next step. I wanted to break open the case and see what it held. With that no longer an option, I needed a unique way to get rid of it. Dropping it in a trash can seemed boring. I considered placing it under the tires of a nearby oversized pickup so it would get crushed. Or setting it on the roof of a nearby car with California plates. How long would it stay there?

I ended up throwing it under an SUV passing by and waiting until they were gone to retrieve it. Although it was damaged, it hadn't popped open like I'd hoped. I tossed the debris in the garbage and called it good.

As I drove to the hospital, I considered the bigger question. How did the tracker get in my purse in the first place? The list of possibilities was short. The old lady who bumped into me at the convenience store while I reached for creamer the other night. Thursday, when I'd been greeted by everyone at the office. A hospital staff member when I'd been focused on Eli in the last few days. The easiest person to blame was the old lady. I feared the worst-case scenario, a co-worker.

I brushed my worries aside and headed to the ICU, texting Tillie as I waited for the elevator.

We met in the hallway. A smile softened her weary face. "He moved!"

"His mother said he moved?" I asked the nurse as I settled in by Eli's bedside.

She sighed. "It was an involuntary action when I checked his reflexes. Which are functioning. But she needs to cling to as much hope as possible, so I didn't want to discourage her."

She seemed more talkative than the other nurses I'd dealt with. I read her name tag. Amy. "What else can you tell me based on your experience?"

She fiddled with the blood pressure cuff wrapped around his upper arm. "You know it's against the rules for me to share patient info, right? Good try, though."

"I apologize. I shouldn't have asked you to do that."

"What I can tell you," she said, "Is that doctors still can't predict when a patient will come out of a coma."

Goosebumps rose on my arms. That was the first time I'd heard the word used to describe Eli's condition. I'd heard stories of people being in a coma for months or even years. Everything suddenly seemed ten times worse.

"Are there any signs to watch for?"

One side of her lips rose. "It's not like in the movies, where a patient sits up and starts talking. Typically, they will wake up for a minute or so, then gradually stay awake longer over many days."

So, I was in it for the long haul. I'd have to rethink renting the room at the hotel. But I wasn't comfortable staying at Eli's, either. I needed to look for one of those short-term vacation rentals. Or get Darla to do it for me. I'd get Joe and Luke to clean out the fridge and send a couple boxes of my stuff. No, that was going overboard.

"Thanks," I said as Amy made notes in Eli's chart. She locked the computer when she left. No way for me to snoop in his records. Instead, I adjusted the chair and opened his book. We'd stopped at Chapter Ten.

It surprised me when Rob showed up an hour later to take a turn sitting with Eli, but I was glad he did. For both Eli and Tillie. She needed an actual break. Still, it was awkward when we met in the waiting room. He wasn't the hugging kind, and a handshake seemed too impersonal. I ended up placing my hand on his upper arm to establish a connection. He didn't brush it off.

He also didn't ask all the questions Tillie would have. It made it easier on me, because I didn't have to give answers that weren't quite true. Instead, he read my face, nodded, and headed to Eli's room.

Despite heavy traffic, I enjoyed the drive back to the hotel. Sure, I checked for cars going the same direction as me, but the tingle of danger never appeared.

I'd needed the nap, although I felt guilty about not using the time to dig through the personnel records. In fact, the rest made me feel good enough to go to Eli's and get a new book. I remembered seeing the biography of Ada Lovelace, an early pioneer of programming, on his bookshelf.

I took a different route to get there, just to explore the neighborhood. There wasn't much to see. Each home looked like a duplicate of the one next door, a typical Florida subdivision. The streets had been laid out with T intersections, instead of crossing each other. Slowed traffic down.

It also meant there were no alleys, one of my favorite escape routes. And that I had to keep a constant eye for children playing in the streets.

I parked in Eli's driveway and gathered my courage. It would never get easier, entering the house and knowing he wouldn't be there. Once inside, I hurried from room to room, giving each a perfunctory glance, making sure nothing had been disturbed. I needed to purchase several of those devices that turn lights on and off to make it look like someone was at home, even if all that accomplished was keeping the neighborhood kids from trying to break in to go swimming.

His room was the last on my tour. The scent of his aftershave had faded, making it feel even emptier. I grabbed the biography from his shelf and hurried back to Dolores, tugging on the door to the house to make sure I'd locked it.

Rob had left when I got back to the hospital. It saved me from another awkward greeting in the hallway. I rearranged the chair, opened the book, laid one hand on Eli's arm, and started reading.

Hospital staff kicked me out shortly before midnight. At a stop sign on the way back to the hotel, I watched two boys climb over a fence and into someone's backyard. It triggered a fear that I'd forgotten to lock the door from the house to the patio at Eli's. I'd never get any sleep if I didn't go check.

The detour took me to the back entrance of the subdivision, which I'd discovered while exploring. The street ended up not quite opposite Eli's house, at one of those T intersections. Still, my headlights lit up part of the yard and movement at the edge caught my attention, too big to be a cat or a dog.

I made a wide turn to get more coverage from my headlights. A shadow moved behind one of the azalea bushes. I wished for Betsy as I drove down the street and turned at the corner. I pulled to the side, turned off my lights, and contemplated my next move.

First, I needed to park closer to the house. Lights off, I drove down the street until I found a place with enough room to make a U-turn. Going so slow I was almost going backwards, I crept to the end of the block, around the corner, and stopped a few doors down from Eli's. This spot provided a view of the yard while still being unobtrusive.

And yes, someone skulked from bush to bush, shadow to shadow. The body's outline made me guess it was a man. Out of habit, I reached for Betsy. She still wasn't there. I didn't have any other weapon except for my wits, which were running low.

With the engine and the overhead light turned off, I opened the car door and slid out, praying I wouldn't be noticed. Like in a cartoon, I hid behind the trunk of a tree. Not a grand old oak, but a palm tree. It would have to do.

I couldn't figure out what he was up to. He didn't act like a homeless person looking for a hidden place to sleep. But he didn't seem to be hurting anything, either. I tucked Eli's dog tags into my shirt so no stray beam of light would hit them and reveal my presence. Then I slid to the next tree.

A door banged open. "Muggles!" a woman yelled. Just Joanna Garcia, getting her cat in for the night. Happened like clockwork at twelve-thirty. Muggles was good at coming when called, and soon the door banged shut. I stuck my head around the tree to figure out where the man in Eli's yard had gotten to in the meantime.

A flare of light—small, but bright—revealed his location. It glinted against an object in his hand. A glass bottle, maybe. A neighborhood kid out drinking, hoping not to be caught? The light rose until it met the top of the bottle. The flame flared and fire replaced darkness.

The shadow man raised his arm and drew it back into a throwing position.

I didn't have time to dash across the street and tackle him. But I remembered one weapon I had—my voice.

Chapter 11

Once upon a time and far away, we practiced yelling in our self-defense course. I drew on that memory now, filled my lungs. And screamed.

My shout echoed in the night. His throw faltered. The light arched through the darkness, bounced against the wall and landed in the juniper bushes that lined the front of the house. He bolted towards the neighbor's yard and beyond.

I had two choices. Chase after the arsonist or put out the fire. The bushes were expendable. Eli's home wasn't. I dialed 911 and grabbed the garden hose.

The sidewalk across the street was hard on my bottom, but it was dry. I sat and waited for the solo fire truck crew to complete their work. Two units had shown up, but I'd kept the fire from spreading and the second one left after a few minutes. There were smoke stains on the stucco, but they'd wash away with a pressure washer.

A fireman, still in his big yellow coat, came and sat beside me. "You did good, not assuming you would be able to control the fire by yourself."

The crew rolled up their hoses. "I didn't want to guess what accelerant was used or its properties. It was too risky to assume water alone would do the job."

Like a snake shedding its skin, he slipped off his coat and bundled it up on the sidewalk. "You've done this before."

I shook my head. "I've had the misfortune of being involved in a situation that gave me the opportunity to pick up on the lingo and learn the basics. But I'm no expert, Lieutenant." I hoped I guessed his rank correctly.

"It's rare I run across someone who admits they don't know it all," he chuckled.

"Did you find the bottle?"

"Parts of it. When it hit the stucco, it shattered. I assume the suspect meant to break the window and set fire to the front room. If you hadn't stopped him, the plan would have worked."

"Will the fire department handle the investigation, or turn it over to the police?"

"The higher-ups will make that decision. We don't have anyone trained in arson investigations. Our expert retired a few months back, and the budget isn't there to hire a new one. Small town. Why?"

"I'll expect their call. I assume the 911 operator saved my contact information. Oh, and I should warn you that the ATF may get involved."

"The ATF doesn't handle brush fires, ma'am. Or attempted arson on a private residence." His polite words held a rebuke.

"Right. And yet, for reasons known only to them, they took over an investigation up north. On a house owned by the same man who lives here."

My statement was met with a long pause while the lieutenant processed the information.

"Is that where the owner of the home is now? Up north? And that's why you're watching the house?"

I wished for a jacket to warm me in the sudden chill. "He's my boyfriend, for lack of a better word. He's in the hospital. United Care East."

❋ ❋ ❋

If it weren't for the man at the lake, I'd be able to relax. I'd slept in and wanted to enjoy my coffee in peace. But he was there, again, and had brought along a camp chair. He stared at the water and not the hotel.

No one expected me to be at the hospital until after lunch. That gave me an hour to research everyone's backgrounds. Not near enough time, but it would be a start.

I eliminated the people who had worked with Eli the longest. They were his most loyal employees, and I couldn't see any of them trying to hurt him. Scotty became my unofficial cut-off point. Everyone after him remained on my list. That only eliminated ten people.

Darla remained on the list, although I didn't

believe her to be guilty for a second. Still, with Eli's life at stake, I wouldn't skip anyone just because I liked them. I'd do the research and ease my mind.

I wished for access to the police resources I normally used, but I wasn't in Oak Grove anymore. I'd learned which sites online to trust and which ones were worth the money they charged.

In one way, it felt good to get back to what I excelled at: Research. It felt terrible that my research might reveal things about my coworkers I didn't want to know, but I couldn't count on the cops doing anything more than a quick look. I had more to lose.

Thankfully, everything about Darla came back clean. She'd been stopped for speeding once and had a couple of parking tickets, but that just made her a real person. I checked the clock and saw I'd used up forty-five of my minutes. Many times I'd spent several hours looking up one topic, but I didn't have that luxury with this project. I needed to streamline my research.

Then I remembered that list on my desk. Each item would only take a few minutes. The most important was the status of my concealed carry permit. Did Florida recognize it?

As I headed downstairs to make my trip to the hospital, the weight of Betsy in my purse comforted me. I hoped I wouldn't have to use her, but I wasn't defenseless.

But her presence didn't stop the prickles that started when I pulled out of the hotel's parking lot. I didn't understand it. No one else left at the same time. The street had little traffic, and no one stayed behind me for more than a block or two. I kept one eye on the rearview mirror, but never spotted a threat. I was imagining things.

The lady at the ICU front desk waved me through. That meant Eli was alone. Rob and Tillie often drove to Tampa on Sundays to visit Eli's older brother, Simon, and his family. It was a good diversion for them.

"Has anyone been in to see him today?" I asked the nurse checking his various bags of fluid. Not Amy, but it was the weekend, and I didn't recognize most of the faces.

"Nope." She tugged on the sheet to smooth out a wrinkle. "Rumor has it a cop came by, wanting to ask questions, but the charge nurse cut him off at the pass. No warrant, no access. Not that your friend is in any shape to answer questions."

Which Detective Horace knew. And he had a warrant. A different cop asking about last night's fire might not have access to that information. As I settled in to read, I made a mental note to find out who was in charge of the investigation.

I closed the book and laid my hand on Eli's. We'd reached the end, but I didn't want to leave. Even if all I did was sit in silence, I hoped at some level he'd know I was there. Avoiding the various cuts, I used my other hand to stroke his head. They'd shaved off most of his hair to clean out the glass and dirt and stitch up the cuts that needed it. His new scars would be hidden under his hair when it grew back. I wondered if his head had hit the windshield. I never had found out if his airbag went off.

Funny, but I felt safe sitting there. All the hospital security, I guessed. No one who didn't belong would get in. But the quiet was a little too quiet.

No one ever claimed I could sing, and I wouldn't torture Eli by trying, but humming didn't require me to be good. I stroked his cheek around the tubes and wires and did just that. Hum, that is. His favorite song, 'Build Me Up, Buttercup.'

Then, it happened. I swear it did. The smallest amount of pressure under my hand, as if he tried to lift his. Then it vanished. I studied his face and started humming again. Nothing. The moment was over. It gave me hope there would be more.

I didn't leave until the staff chased me out when they came to do Eli's scheduled care. With no solid plans, I had time to plot my next steps.

The minute I walked out into the sunshine, that sense of security disappeared. I recognized my mistake. The hospital had more than one door. I should have used a different one each day. Not that it would make much of a difference. These people knew what they were doing and had the time and patience to do the job. Besides, I couldn't hide Dolores.

I didn't understand their motivation. They knew where I was staying and where I went regularly, so why follow me around? Trying to shake them would accomplish nothing. So, I did the unexpected by doing the expected. I headed straight back to the hotel. No stops, no switching lanes, no side streets. Let them figure that out.

Thankfully, the hotel's WiFi signal reached into the laundry room. I wouldn't leave my clothes unguarded by going back to my room as they washed. I got a Shifter, Inc. employee searched and cleared while my clothes swished around in the washer and another while they tumbled in the dryer. But I needed to cut the list down even farther.

A vague memory nagged me. Something about not getting bids. I sat mesmerized, watching the last load of clothes go around and around, trying to bring the idea to the front of my brain. Another hotel guest loaded up her washer and muttered about how much it cost, and how the last hotel she stayed at was cheaper. And I remembered.

About a year ago, Eli had problems with his contract bids being undercut. He'd wondered how his numbers were getting leaked. If last year's and the current problem tied together, I could eliminate any of the newer employees. I was disappointed that only three people had been hired in the past year and could be taken off the list.

As I folded my clothes to carry upstairs, I realized I had another problem. What to read to Eli next? The internet was full of informative articles, but all the equipment in his room might interfere with the WiFi signal. I settled for downloading several white papers he'd be interested in. He'd be behind when he came to. I shoved back the rest of that thought. If he came to.

Chapter 12

"How does this much mail and paperwork pile up over the weekend?" I asked Darla as I settled in at my desk Monday morning.

She shook her head. "Mondays are always like this. I swear the post office deliberately saves up mail to give us a headache."

"Is there someone I can bribe to change that?" I stirred half my usual amount of creamer into my coffee. I needed it strong after staying with Eli until midnight again.

"You really are like Eli, aren't you? He asked me that same question more than once. How is he doing?"

I wouldn't lie to her, but I wouldn't tell her the whole truth. After all, I had no proof that he'd blinked several times when no one was there but me. "He's not getting any worse. According to the nurses, that's a good thing." The evident weight loss wasn't, but I'd keep that to myself and not allow it to get me down. I tapped the paperwork. "Okay, what do I need to tackle first?"

❀ ❀ ❀

Mid-morning, Darla knocked on my open door. "Miss Duprie? Do you have a minute? There's someone here to see you."

Darla knew better than to call me 'Miss Duprie,' so, this wasn't going to be good. At the same time, it had to be important. I turned off my computer display and sat back in my chair and made a wild guess. "What agency is he from?"

Her eyebrows shot up. "You expect more than one? He's with the FHP. Florida Highway Patrol."

"It was an interesting weekend. Offer him coffee and bring him in."

Her glare told me I wouldn't get off that easy. She'd be after me for answers I didn't want to share.

The man hovering in the hallway had the look of being ready to get down to business. That suited me fine. I stood to greet him.

"Miss Harmony Duprie?" He reached for my extended hand. His shake was firm but not overdone. It gave me hope that we'd get along.

"Yes. Have a seat, Trooper."

"Sergeant, actually. Sergeant Alex Richon."

Not the normal chain of command, then. I'd done my homework. I nodded. "How can I help you, Sergeant? I assume you're here regarding Eli's accident?"

His brows knotted. "My information has the victim's name as Matthew. Matthew Hennessey."

"Yes. His middle name is Elijah. He goes by Eli."

He pulled out one of those ever-present little notebooks and wrote in it. "What can you tell me about the night of the accident?"

"I've given that information to the Orlando PD. Haven't they shared it with your department?"

"Yes, ma'am, but I'd like to hear it from you."

Each time I recited the story it got harder, not easier. In my head, I could see Eli lying in his hospital bed, unresponsive. "We talked Monday night. A week ago. Everything seemed normal. We discussed our days and plans for Tuesday."

"I understand he'd been drinking."

"A couple of beers. But his style of drinking goes like this. The first beer goes down smooth and fast, the second beer he sips on until it gets warm and he tosses it. The third beer? If he drinks more than a few swallows, it's unusual." I couldn't remember if there had been a can on his nightstand.

"You have the keys to his house?"

"Yes, just like he has the key to mine." A wave of panic splashed over me. "Did they recover his keys? I need to get his locks changed. And contact my landlords to change the lock to my apartment."

"Let me check." Richon pulled out his phone and poked at the screen. I waited impatiently while he tapped and scrolled. Why hadn't I thought of the keys before?

His eyes narrowed, and I wondered if he needed glasses. He finally looked up.

"A set of keys is listed on the inventory, but there isn't a picture. I can get you one, if you like."

"Yes, please. For my peace of mind."

"Will do. Can you tell me the last time Mr. Hennessey's car was serviced? And where?"

"He mentioned it several months ago. I don't remember the name of the garage offhand, but it should be in his records. He keeps an actual paper file on his car because it's one of his hobbies." I caught my breath and reached for a tissue. He'd never drive that car again. I didn't think it was salvageable, based on the photos. And how long until he could drive at all?

Richon gave me a moment to compose myself, which allowed me to ask my own question. "Why are you handling this, Sergeant, instead of a trooper?"

One corner of his mouth rose. "You caught that?"

It wasn't my first go-round with police command structure. I sat back in my chair and stared at him, waiting for an answer.

"All I can tell you," he said, "is that there's pressure from higher up. I don't know why or who."

A knock on the door interrupted us. Darla stuck her head in. A deep worry line creased her forehead. "Sorry, but you have more visitors."

"We're almost done here," I said. "Can they wait?"

She placed two business cards in front of me. I picked them up, read them, and shuffled them. "Is the big conference room available, Darla? We won't have enough room in here."

Richon pushed his chair back. "I can come back later."

I handed him the cards. "I'd like you to stick around. This could get interesting."

The conference room was too big for the four of us, but it was better than being cramped. I'd asked Darla to put Kris on standby in case anything came up that affected the company and to contact Detective Horace. He took up enough room for two people.

Darla put a pitcher of ice water and a variety of soda as well as a carafe of coffee on the counter. I fixed myself a cup and took the seat at the head of the table. Eli's chair. It was a strategic move, and fun watching them eye each other, trying to figure out the correct spot to sit. Sergeant Richon ended up to my left and the two newcomers to my right. I waited until everyone got settled.

"You all know who I am. I've been delegated to act on Mr. Hennessey's behalf while he is incapacitated." All eyes focused on me and I counted to ten to find my equilibrium. "While we're waiting for Detective Horace of Orlando P.D. to join us, we might as well get started. Do you want to introduce yourselves? Sergeant Richon, why don't you go first?"

He nodded. "Sergeant Alex Richon, Florida Highway Patrol. I'm assigned to the case involving Mr. Hennessey's accident."

I swiveled to face the man on my right. I guessed him to be in his mid-forties, but he had the look of someone with many more years of experience. "Captain Leonard Williams. North Crystal Fire Department. I'm handling the investigation into the fire at Mr. Hennessey's house last night."

"What?" Richon blurted out.

"Sorry," I said. "We didn't get that far in our conversation. But wait, it gets better."

"Better?" he asked.

I turned my attention to the woman with short, blonde hair seated next to Williams. Slight in stature, she moved like a gymnast, all bundled-up energy that could explode when needed. "I'm not sure about Miss Duprie's definition of better," she said, "But I'm Special Agent Vanessa Salters with the ATF. I'll be collaborating with Captain Williams."

"The last time I hosted an inter-agency meeting," I said, swirling my coffee in its cup, "was in my apartment and I used a sheet for a projector screen."

Salters held her hand over her mouth, making me suspect she was hiding a grin. Williams frowned. Richon didn't take the statement so well. He stiffened. "How big was the fire? I didn't catch it on the news this morning. And what's this about a meeting?"

"Thanks to quick action by Miss Duprie, the fire was contained quickly and the only real damage is to several bushes," Williams said. "We've verified the information she provided. The house across the street has one of those doorbell cameras and it caught the action."

Oh, shit. "Any legal procedure to make sure that footage doesn't find its way to the internet?" I asked.

Salters nodded. "Already taken care of. I pulled a few strings, stretched the truth, and the only copy of the video is in ATF files."

"That's a relief. Thank you."

Richon cocked his head. "Allergic to the media?"

"Something like that. In this case, I want the person responsible for what's happening to have as little information as possible."

"You've done this before," Salters said, as if accusing me of a crime. "What is the story behind a meeting in your apartment?"

I shrugged. "Nothing much. Just the Oak Grove police chief, a sheriff's deputy, and a couple of FBI agents."

Williams sputtered into his coffee. Richon's stare could have burned a hole in my shirt. Salters laughed. "I'm going to have to get my hands on that report."

"It doesn't exist. Not with my name in it. It was unofficial, anyway, like this one."

"So, let's get down to business. How are these two events tied together?"

"Here's the thing. It's not just these two." I got up and walked over to the whiteboard. Remnants of other meetings remained, and I was reluctant to erase them. I only felt a little remorse wiping away a drawing of a pixilated dragon.

"A timeline might be helpful." I wrote 'Eli disappears' followed by 'house fire' and notated it as Monday.

"The fire was Saturday night," Williams objected.

"That was the second fire. Eli also owns a house in Oak Grove, and someone firebombed it the night of the accident. He fell off the network before the fire, although the fire was the reason we found out. Is that logical?"

Salters clasped her hands behind her head and leaned back. "That's the incident that brought the ATF into the picture. But I wasn't told why. Any ideas?"

"No. It came as a surprise to the Oak Grove Fire Chief. Do you have a theory?"

"All I know is that we got pressure from up the line."

"Same story here," Richon said.

"I'll add more events. Maybe it'll clear things up." I didn't think so, but they were the experts. "I arrived here Wednesday night. Detective Horace contacted me on Thursday night. Eli was found on Thursday." I erased both entries and switched their positions. "Technically, Eli was found first, although he wasn't identified. Any objections?"

No one said anything.

"It was late Thursday or early Friday that I identified Eli. I wasn't paying attention to the time. On Friday, I figured out I was being followed. I assumed it was someone with the Orlando PD, but I have no proof and Detective Horace isn't here to defend the department." I knew I sounded overly matter of fact, but I was hiding behind logic to conceal the desperation that encompassed me.

"How do you know you were being followed?" Salters asked, her voice tight.

I glossed over the question. "I recognized the signs. And on Saturday I located two trackers on my car." I added them to my list. "That's the same day I found a 'bug' in my purse. Anyone want to claim responsibility?"

Richon whistled. "That's not FHP's style."

"While it is something the ATF might do," Salters said, "it wasn't us. Not that I've been told."

"Then we'll blame it on the Orlando police for now." I studied the list. "Where were we? The fire Saturday night or Sunday morning, however you want to count it." I squeezed the notation into the last available space. "Am I missing anything?"

Salters used a finger to tap the table, but no one said a word. The almost-silence was broken by a knock on the door. I opened it, expecting to see Darla and Detective Horace. I didn't anticipate a third person being with them.

Darla frowned and shrugged. I guessed she hadn't been introduced to the newcomer.

I'd handle it. "Detective, I'm glad you could make it. But who is your guest?"

The man was tall, but he didn't match the detective in height. And he clearly thought he was in charge. He didn't wait for Horace to answer and pushed by him. "I'm Special Agent Rodney Putnam with the DCSA."

Chapter 13

Special Agent Putnam didn't offer a handshake. I disliked him immediately. Behind me, someone blew out a breath of air that sounded like a hiss.

"Interesting group of people you've gathered, Miss Duprie."

"I'm not familiar with your agency, Agent. Oh, I'm sorry, *Special* Agent. May I see an ID?" It was an art form, insulting him while being as sugary as sweet tea. Like a Southern belle saying, "Bless your heart."

While I waited for him to pull out his wallet, I studied him. Buzz cut black hair, shoes shined to the point of reflection, creased pants and a white shirt under a dark blue suit coat. Military or ex-military was my determination. Neither made me happy.

He flashed a badge and handed me a business card. It looked real, but I had no way to check at the moment.

I didn't have the time or inclination to stick with social niceties. "Where do you fit into this puzzle, Special Agent?"

"Are you familiar with Mr. Hennessey's security clearance?"

Straight to the point. Maybe there was hope for him yet. "All I know is that he's got some super-duper secret squirrel level of security. I never asked him about it. I always assumed it had something to do with his years in the military."

"Close enough. His clearance is renewed every five years. This is the fifth year, but he shouldn't have come up on my list for three more months."

There it was. I waved towards an empty chair. "Join the crowd. I've got a sergeant instead of a trooper, a captain, the ATF, and now…" I looked at his card… "the freaking Defense Counterintelligence and Security Agency, all getting pressure from up the chain, and no one knows why. And I can't forget the detective assigned to be my watchdog or liaison, depending upon your point of view. Which is weird either way, because I'm a civilian. Oh, did I mention the man haunting the lake by my hotel?" I added a sideways note in the margin on the whiteboard, the only place I had left to write.

"And Eli is in the hospital and what I want to do is crawl into the bed beside him and hug him and make him feel better." I drew in a shallow breath, all my constricted lungs could hold. "Instead, I'm dealing with all of you and running his company." I tossed the marker I held onto the ledge at the bottom of the whiteboard. It bounced out and fell to the floor. No one moved to retrieve it.

I was done. Over it. I didn't want to play detective

anymore. I slumped into my chair and buried my head in my arms.

"Which agency will take the lead in this? What is the protocol?" Richon asked. I recognized the voice but didn't look up.

Salters chuckled. "I don't believe there is a protocol. To the best of my knowledge, a group like this has never worked together."

A murmur of agreement rippled through the room.

"I was warned about this," Horace said.

"Warned?" asked Salters.

I lifted my head.

"According to Police Chief Sorenson of Oak Grove, Miss Duprie's hometown, it's not that she breaks the rules, it's more like they dissolve when she's around. His words, not mine."

That was one way to put it.

"This may be unorthodox," Salters said, "like everything else in this case, but I suggest you remain as Miss Duprie's primary contact, Detective. The rest of us can do the cloak and dagger stuff, while you become the public face for law enforcement. Your bulk won't hurt either, since she needs a bodyguard."

I straightened my spine and shook my head. "Not going to work."

"Why not?" Horace asked.

"If my theory is correct, this is an inside job. Someone here holds a grudge against Eli."

Five sets of eyes fastened on me. Salters leaned forward. "You've captured our attention. Go on."

"Over a year ago, Eli mentioned that his bids for jobs were getting undercut by his competitors. His prices are already on the lower side of the market and it seemed suspicious. He hasn't mentioned it recently and I'm not aware of the current status of the situation, but I'm not seeing many new customers lately.

"A few months ago, he was worried that one of his competitors was involved in a series of incidents aimed at me. I won't go into detail, but it turned out to have nothing to do with him."

"Chief Sorenson sent me that report," Horace said. "there was no mention of Hennessey in it."

There should have been. Eli helped me capture the culprit. "It came up in a private conversation, based on my own research."

"That still doesn't explain why you suspect it's an inside job," Richon objected.

It seemed clear to me, but I kept going. "An additional point. There was no reason for Eli to be on the road last Monday night. But when it comes to his employees, he is loyal to a fault. If one of them called him asking for help, he'd kick into hero mode and go rescue them."

"That gives us the means and the opportunity. What's the motivation?" Salters asked.

I felt like a rubber ball, my attention bouncing around the room. "One of the oldest on the books. Revenge."

I let the word sink in before explaining. "Eli also told me that when he started the business, several other companies went under because he offered a better product and better prices. My theory is that someone tied to one of those companies got a job here. I'm digging through personnel records and past employment histories, but I don't have time to do it right."

"You'll need to go deeper than their applications," Putnam said. "It's easy enough to leave a gap in your history and say you were going to school or something."

I nodded. "Exactly. Which is why I'm dissecting their social media. Running searches on the names, finding out their hobbies, who they are married to, looking for anything that's out of place. You do background checks, Special Agent, so you know the drill."

"Yes. And I have access to databases you don't."

I had more access than he would expect, but that was my secret. "Are you suggesting what I think you're suggesting? Is that legal?"

A shadow of a smile crossed his face. "Aren't you the one that makes rules disappear? I can truthfully say my job is to make sure Mr. Hennessey's clearance isn't compromised during his illness."

Everyone went through a security check when they were hired, including me, so I wasn't worried about the DCSA finding any illegal activities in the reports. "I'll get you the list."

Salters rubbed her hands together. "I'll handle the undercover aspects and work with the agent up north to tie the two fires together. Sergeant, has the FHP developed any leads into the accident?"

"We're checking traffic cameras, but the area

where the incident occurred isn't in range of any of our static units."

"There's a flaw in your theory, Miss Duprie." Horace pushed himself away from the wall he'd been leaning against. "The first fire and the accident occurred the same night, a thousand miles apart. If everything is tied together, that means more than one person is involved."

Salters shrugged. "It's easy to hire someone to commit arson. Hell, you don't even have to pay, sometimes. A few arsonists do it for the glory, the joy of watching a building burn and not getting caught. As much as I like Miss Duprie's theory, we need to keep our minds open to other possibilities."

Nothing wrong with that, but no one jumped in with their own ideas.

"Another issue," Horace said. "I can't stay with Miss Duprie twenty-four seven. And I doubt the department has the manpower to assign a rotating shift of officers."

"I don't do bodyguards, anyway," I said firmly. "They're annoying."

Horace walked over to the whiteboard and picked up a red marker. "You are being followed. And bugged." He underlined the pertinent notations. "And someone is potentially casing the hotel you are staying at. You still think you don't need a bodyguard?"

"I'm not convinced that an agency represented in this room isn't responsible. No one has tried to approach or hurt me."

"Because they're setting you up," Salter snapped.

"Getting you comfortable, so you ignore them. Then they'll follow you on a trip to the coast, find a spot to run you off the road, and bam! You end up dead or in a coma like your friend."

I'd always been able to protect myself. Mostly. Hell, Eli could always protect himself. Mostly. What had changed? If this unidentified enemy took on Eli on his home turf and won, what chance did I have? I closed my eyes so no one would read the fear in them.

"Miss Duprie?" Salters urged.

"Hold on. I'm considering my options." Not that I had many. "I don't suppose any of you approve of the idea of me as bait to draw out…" I didn't get to the end of my sentence before a chorus of objections rose.

"Absolutely not!" "Hell, no." "Are you crazy?"

I held up my hands. "Okay, okay, I get it. I'll hire a bodyguard. But not the detective. Give me recommendations for companies with women on their staff."

❁ ❁ ❁

I ended up with the numbers of two agencies, one from Horace and one from Salters. Because I still had my doubts about Horace, I already had a preference, but I would interview both.

So they didn't need to parade through the employee area, I escorted Horace, Williams and Richon out the rarely-used back door. Putnam and Salters hung back. She handed me a second copy of her card.

"When you have some spare time," she said, "I'd like to take you out for a drink. I'd even settle for lunch. You've got stories to tell, and I'd like to hear them. They might be relevant to the case."

I couldn't imagine how. "I don't know when I'll be able to get away, but that sounds good. Stay in touch."

She nodded and gave me a side-hug. "Remember, I've got your back," she whispered before leaving.

What did that mean? I didn't have time to figure it out because Putnam was waiting for me. "Can we talk in private?" he asked.

What deep, dark secret was he going to reveal? "Sure, my office is just down the hall."

A muscle in his right cheek twitched. "You aren't using Mr. Hennessey's office?"

I waited until I closed my door to answer, first swallowing hard to get the lump out of my throat. "I can't work up the courage to even go in there to retrieve paperwork. Darla brings me everything. One of these days, I'm going to have to check his drawers and file cabinet for anything private that needs to be handled."

Putnam nodded. "Which leads to the concern at hand. It's possible that Mr. Hennessey is in legal possession of secret government paperwork. I need to retrieve the documents."

I chewed my bottom lip but didn't ask questions. He wouldn't give me the answers, anyway. "If Eli has these papers, Special Agent, I have no idea where he keeps them. And unless they are in a folder marked 'Top Secret' I wouldn't know them if I saw them. How do you propose I look for them without knowing what they deal with?"

"We can search together."

That made sense. "Not now, I've already spent too much time not dealing with business issues."

"Perhaps this evening after everyone else has left for the day?"

It had to be done, even if it cut into my time with Eli. "Six thirty tonight? Call when you get here, and I'll let you in."

I escorted him out the back door and shut it behind him. I rubbed my forehead. The headache would last the rest of the day, but it might ease up if I got some food into my stomach. It was too late to order for the entire staff, so everyone would be on their own.

I eased into my office, hoping Darla wouldn't notice and descend on me, demanding answers to questions I didn't want to think about. A few minutes alone would help me regain my mental equilibrium.

But someone was sitting in my chair. It wasn't Goldilocks. And Betsy was in my purse, locked in the bottom drawer of the file cabinet. The thud of my heart vibrated in my ears. The blond hair peeking over the top of the chair stirred a recent memory. "Special Agent Salters? What are you doing here?"

She swiveled to face me. "I spoke to my boss, and he agreed to my plan. You don't need a bodyguard. You have me. Let's go to lunch and talk about it."

Chapter 14

"You railroaded me," I complained as we settled into a booth at a little diner a few blocks away. Eli usually ate lunch at his desk or in the employee break room, so I'd never been to this diner. But Vanessa promised I wouldn't be disappointed. Yes, she'd insisted I call her by her first name. "I was tired and overwhelmed and didn't have time to think."

She grinned. "That was the idea. I didn't want to give you a chance to say no until you listen to my proposal. And treating you to a decent meal couldn't hurt."

A waitress in a pink uniform came by to get our drink orders. The menus were in a holder on the table and I browsed their selection.

"The meatloaf is fantastic," Vanessa suggested. "If they have any left. Better than Mom used to make. It goes fast. Ask for brown gravy."

Comfort food was just what I needed, but I checked the rest of the menu out of curiosity. If the food held up to her promise, I could see myself coming back. By the time the waitress—Bea, according to her name tag—returned with our sodas, I'd talked myself into trying the meatloaf.

Vanessa ordered first. "Meatloaf, mashed potatoes, brown gravy on both, and corn."

"I'll have the same, but green beans instead of corn," I said.

"You gals are lucky," Bea said. "We've got two pieces left. Let me go reserve them for you."

While we waited for her to disappear through the swinging doors that led to the kitchen, I checked out the other customers. An assortment of business-people, a few college kids with their books and electronic devices piled on their tables, and one family. I felt like I blended in, but Vanessa was an anomaly. Too wary. Her eyes never stopped roaming the dining room.

"Here's the issue," she said, startling me, "If you're dealing with the DCSA, it's some high-level shit. You won't find a bodyguard that can handle it. Even I don't have that level of security clearance, but I've got enough to make Putnam and his cronies happy. Plus, I've been stuck behind a desk for a few months, recovering from an injury, and I'm bored. You're the perfect solution to get me back into the field."

"You're using me?"

"Absolutely. At least I'm honest about it. There's something about Horace I don't trust. I can't figure out why."

She got a point for that. "How do you see this working? You can't hang out in my office and I won't share my hotel room."

"I noticed an empty desk in the front room. I'll snag that, bring my laptop, and do my job. As for living arrangements…"

She waited while Bea brought our food. The slice of meatloaf was so thick I wondered if I'd be able to eat even half of it. The rich aroma of the gravy alone made me realize how hungry I was. I'd have to bring Eli here someday. I put down my fork, my appetite suddenly gone.

Vanessa noticed but didn't comment. "Now, about your living arrangements. You said you're in a hotel? You aren't staying at Mr. Hennessey's place?"

I shrugged. "I'm not comfortable with him not being there."

"Got it." She chewed on a forkful of corn. I took a tiny bite of the meatloaf. It was better than what I make, so I took a second, bigger bite.

"I've got a proposal," she said. "Don't say no right away. My roommate got married a couple of months ago, so I have an empty bedroom. I rent the first floor of an old house. It's nothing fancy and needs work but has character." She scrunched her eyebrows. "I don't know anything about architecture, but I think someone said it was Victorian? I may be way off base."

She had me at Victorian. I suspected what would come next. "What are you hinting at?"

"Move in with me. It'll be short term, but long enough to get the current situation settled. You'll have a private furnished room and a small, shared bathroom. The kitchen and living room are also shared."

It could work until Eli came home. "I insist on paying rent and my share of utilities."

"I won't fight that."

"Does it have a garage? I don't want to park Dolores on the street." That might be a deal-breaker.

"Dolores?"

"My car. She's a salsa-red, F-type Jaguar convertible."

Vanessa whistled. "Cool. I didn't spot it at the office. Where are you keeping it?"

I'd stopped by an auto-parts store on my way to work and bought a generic cover. It didn't fit perfectly but was good enough to protect the paint job.

"She was there. Camouflaged."

"The house has a garage, but it's full of junk." Vanessa drummed her fingers on the table. "I bet if we shuffle stuff around and take a run to the dump, we can make enough room for your car." She grinned. "We including the two guys who rent the second floor. They work undercover security at Disney but won't talk about it. One of them has a pickup we can borrow."

There had to be a catch. "I suppose you think the three of you can tuck me in a back room and never let me see the light of day with the excuse of keeping me safe. Thanks, but no thanks."

She chuckled. "You're sharp. I considered it, but it won't work. You have to be out and about for us to get the bad guy to show himself."

A compromise of sorts. I could live with that.

"You have internet, right? Maybe not-speed-of-light, but a good connection?"

"Yep. It's a requirement for the job. I have a separate account for guests you can use."

I was running out of objections.

"One more thing I should warn you about," Vanessa said. "Every six months or so, the owner decides to sell the place, puts it on the market and sets an unreasonably high price. We have to play along with the occasional sucker who wants to look around."

That was almost a deal-breaker. I valued my privacy and hated the idea of looky-loos wandering through my bedroom. On the other hand, I wouldn't be spending much time there.

"I'd like to see it before I make a commitment," I said. "How about tomorrow at lunch?"

"Sure. Tonight, I'll hang out with you until you lock yourself into your hotel room. Then I'll meet you in the morning and escort you to work."

I pushed at the remnants of the meatloaf, amazed I'd eaten most of it. "You'll be in for a long night. I'll stay with Eli until midnight or until the staff kicks me out. The cafeteria will be closed and there isn't any place for you to stay."

Her eyebrows lifted. "Midnight?"

"Every night." The lack of sleep would catch up with me sooner or later.

"I'll see what I can work out with hospital security. Tonight, I'll tough it out. It's all part of the job, Miss Duprie."

If we were going to be roommates, that wouldn't work. "Call me Harmony."

❋ ❋ ❋

My afternoon appointment was with Elena, the sales manager, to review the contracts that were close to being finalized, and to see if any of them needed my personal attention. As much as Eli liked to grumble about the differences in their philosophies, he and Elena balanced each other out when it came to contracts. And Eli knew it. That's why she still worked for him.

"That's not what Eli promised," I said, leafing through the agreement for the joint venture involving three Maine police chiefs. The price was higher than the number Eli had quoted in the initial conversations.

"Do you know how much time went into making the software work for this?" she asked.

"He did a lot of the work when he was in Oak Grove with me," I reminded her.

"You can't go in there!" Darla's loud voice in the hallway leaked into my office. Elena and I exchanged a glance, and I stood. "Let me check this out."

Darla sounded more angry than fearful, so I left Betsy in my purse, strode to the door, and yanked it open. "What's going on?"

With her arms crossed and her feet planted firmly, Darla blocked the doorway to Eli's office. Lando, down the hall a short distance, bounced on the balls of his feet, ready to spring into action. Vanessa, looking more curious than worried, stood behind him. On the other side, Kris and Marty had come out of their offices to see what was going on. The two men Darla had accosted stood with their backs to me.

They turned when I spoke. One, I recognized. Rob, Eli's father. The other man's face looked like a bad cartoonist had drawn a picture of Eli. I made the presumption that it was his brother, Simon.

"Can I help you, Rob?" I asked, keeping my tone casual, hoping to defuse the situation.

"We need to get into Eli's office, and she won't let us." Rob jerked his head in Darla's direction.

"Then she's doing her job. No one is allowed in there besides me and her. What do you need?"

"To get things set up for the business consultant I'm hiring to run the company until Eli is better."

From the corner of my eye, I watched Kris slip back into her office. Lando started down the hall, but I held up my hand to stop him. "What makes you think that's necessary?"

"As Eli's father, I'm his representative. It's my responsibility."

I wondered if Simon had put the idea into Rob's head. "That would be true, if Eli hadn't made other arrangements. Several months ago, he signed off on legal documents setting up what would happen if he was unable to work. The paperwork was notarized and properly filed. Whether he shared that information with you or not, it doesn't change the outcome. I'm in charge for now."

A vein in his right temple pulsed. "What the hell do you know about running a business?"

"Besides my years of experience in running a public institution? And the business courses I took as part of my master's degree? And the time Eli and I spent collaborating on many of his projects? Do you need more?"

"A library isn't a business."

"Have you ever run one? In fact, do you even know what a library does these days? It offers more than books on shelves."

"You don't know how to manage money and you'll run the business into the ground. Eli will have to start all over. After all, how deep in debt are you, spending money on fancy cars and expensive clothes on a librarian's salary? Or did you talk Eli into buying them for you?"

Lando covered his mouth with a fist and coughed. I shook my head. "Eli and I never played 'You show me yours, I'll show you mine' with our bank accounts. I suspect we're fairly even, not that it's any of your business. That's between me and Eli."

Rob drew a deep breath, a big, bad wolf getting ready to blow the house down. "I'll get a lawyer and we'll see who's in charge."

Kris marched out of her office with a thick file folder. She thrust it towards Rob. "Give that to your lawyer. It's copies of all the paperwork giving Harmony total control of Shifter Technology Incorporated in case of Eli's absence or being unfit to do the job. It also includes forms giving her POA for medical, financial, and personal legal matters."

"Kris?" I asked, not taking my eyes off Rob.

"You said you didn't want to pursue it, but I asked the lawyer that Eli consulted about the medical form. He told me about the rest of it and sent over copies of the paperwork. I figured they might come in handy."

"I didn't sign anything like that."

"You didn't need to. It was all handled by Eli and his personal attorney."

Over Rob's shoulder, I could see that Darla looked as if she was afraid to breathe. The tension was a fog bank swirling in the hallway. I had to end the confrontation without further damaging my relationship with Eli's family.

"I appreciate your concerns for the company, Rob, but we have it covered. There's no one here who isn't willing to do what it takes to make sure that when Eli returns, his business will be in as good shape as it was the last day he was here." I wished that was true. I feared there might be an exception.

"What it takes is a consultant to run it for him." Rob's face reddened.

"That's your opinion. Eli's was clearly different. I'm honoring Eli's wishes for the company."

Until that moment, I don't think Rob had ever seen me as anything more than Eli's occasional girlfriend. He seemed taken aback that I would stand up to him. That for every argument he presented, I had an answer. He was running out of steam, and that made him even angrier.

During the entire face-off, Simon stood silently behind his father. I stuck out my hand.

"Simon? I'm sorry we had to meet like this. Eli has talked about you." Mentioned was more like it. On rare occasions. There was a ten-year age gap between the brothers, and Simon had mostly ignored Eli when they were kids, according to Eli. Even as adults, their relationship was superficial.

Simon hesitated, then grasped my hand to be polite. But I wasn't some newbie. I squeezed back and pulled, a gentle tug. Just enough to force him into my space where I was in charge.

His eyes widened, and he let go. I caught him rubbing his hand. He opened and closed his mouth, then opened it again. "We'll take it to your lawyer, Dad. Let him figure it out."

"You can do that," Kris said. "It'll be a waste of your money. He'll take one glance at those documents and tell you to go home."

"You sound awfully sure of yourself," Rob said.

"I am. If I wasn't good, Eli wouldn't have hired me."

I wanted to give her a high-five, but that would have to wait for later. I had to get Rob and Simon out of the office first. "Rob," I said, fiddling with the dog tags hanging around my neck, "I understand how hard this is for you, and appreciate that you want to do right by Eli. But don't you think those of us who work with him every day understand what he wants for the company better than a consultant ever could?"

Rob clasped the file folder with both hands. "I thought this was the one way I could help Eli. There's nothing I can do to make him get better any faster, and when Simon suggested this, it seemed like the perfect solution. I'd get to be a hero for my son again."

"And I took that away from you."

His eyes scanned my face. "Yes," he said bluntly.

I felt bad for him. Honestly I did. But not bad enough to let him ruin the progress I'd made in a short amount of time. I moistened my dry lips. "All of my research," I said slowly, formulating my answer, "indicates that Eli will have a long recovery. Physical therapy, speech therapy, occupational therapy, and more. He'll need plenty of help along the way. You can be a major part of it."

Rob frowned. "You know all the right words. Why don't I trust you?"

"I can't answer that question. Only you can."

His stare was a challenge. I didn't blink. His lips formed a thin line, and he tapped the file. "Don't think I won't have my lawyer look at these."

"Please do, if it will make you feel better."

Rob dropped his eyes, then pushed past Simon and the small crowd gathered in the hallway. Simon frowned, pointed his finger at me and shook it. "Expect an injunction," he threatened, then followed his father. Coward.

"Show's over!" Lando yelled. "Back to work. Let's make Eli proud."

I closed the gap between me and Darla. She was shaking and moisture pooled in her eyes. I wrapped my arms around her. "Breathe," I whispered in her ear. "You did great."

Chapter 13

"In all the years I've worked for Eli," Darla said, "I've never seen his father here. So, what got into him?"

Darla, Kris, Lando, and I were squeezed into my office. Vanessa had opted to join the party, but she stood in the corner rather than dragging in yet another chair.

"If I had to make a guess, Simon pushed him into it. Why, I can't tell you. Simon and Eli have never been close, and I don't think it was out of the goodness of his heart." That was my theory, anyway.

"Hire a business consultant, fire him, and Simon takes over?" Vanessa suggested.

"It seems farfetched, but the idea entered my mind. But why? He's got a job and a family in Tampa," I answered.

"Unless that information has changed recently." She grinned. "I have connections that can check it out. I'll justify it by saying I'm eliminating him as a suspect."

Lando smirked. "Suspect. Right. But the way you handled Simon was amazing, Harmony. Showed him who was boss. Then you roped in Eli's dad by being all kinds of sweet and caring." He held up his thumb and forefinger, not quite touching. "Had me this close to tears."

I wished for something soft to throw at him, but had nothing, so I ignored the last part. "Kris, what are the chances they could get an injunction like Simon suggested? I can see him nagging Rob until he's too tired to fight back and goes along with the idea."

Her lips tightened. "It could happen. A shady lawyer who knows a shady judge requests an emergency hearing and I wouldn't get notified. Even then they'd have to lie. But I've got friends in the court system who'll keep an eye out for such shenanigans."

"Anything else we need to watch out for?" I asked.

"Public relations," Darla said. "I've already handled a call asking about long-range plans for the company. If word gets around that Eli isn't in charge, customers may want reassurance about its stability."

"I'm not the person for the job. I avoid media with a passion. Is there anyone we can assign the PR responsibility to?" I asked.

"Fiona," Lando said promptly. "She's bugged Eli about doing PR spots for her classes. Plus, I've heard her dealing with difficult people on the phone. She's a wiz."

"Done. She'll need a new title, a desk, and a raise. Darla, can you make that happen? We'll have to get someone to cover reception duties."

"Can we have her run everything by me? I used to do occasional announcements for Eli, and I know what he'd want," Darla said. "Put Paul from the support desk in her spot. He wants to move to daytime instead of evenings, and he already knows how to work with customers. And Annie mentioned wanting to switch to evenings. It'll make the support workload heavier for a few hours during the day, but that will be a short-term problem."

I needed to spend more time with the other employees, listening to their wants and dreams. "After things settle down, I want to review staffing. Find out who else feels stuck in their current spot and where they'd like to be. I won't make any promises, but I can be aware."

"It sounds like something Eli should take care of," Darla said, "when he returns." She sucked in a breath. "Oh."

I couldn't reach her from across the desk to hug her. Lando put his hand on her shoulder. "Eli will be back. You can count on it."

The pain of Eli's absence hit each of us at different times. Me, it kept hitting again and again. It was a punch in the gut when I unlocked his office for Special Agent Putnam. I pretended to have a hard time getting the key out of the lock to give myself time to recover.

"What are we looking for, exactly?" I asked, placing my hand on Eli's desk and waiting for the room to stop shaking.

"Several documents likely stored in a locked drawer or file cabinet. The top sheet will be stamped with a security level, unless he's mixed up the order of the pages."

The first step was to locate the right drawer. The desk was too easy. I knew where Eli stashed the key: in the locked top drawer, stuck inside an old pack of gum. The bottom left hand-side was where Eli stored files for current projects. I unlocked it and pulled it open.

"You can look, but I don't think you'll find what you're searching for."

Putnam knelt on the floor and sifted through the files, occasionally pulling one out and fanning the pages inside. He reached the last folder and shook his head. "Nothing."

I'd wandered over to the four-drawer file cabinet while he worked. It was already unlocked, which was good, because I'd never seen that key. It was also bad, because that meant the documents Putnam needed weren't stored there.

Where else would Eli store something private? His office didn't have a closet. He used a coat rack on the rare chilly days he wore a jacket.

I returned my attention to the file cabinet, stuffed with records going back to the start of the business. It would take forever to examine each one. "What do you think?" I asked as I surveyed the disorder. "Most of these are labeled by date, with no indication of a name anywhere."

Putnam scratched his jaw. "You could stick a file in here, date it with anything, and no one but you would guess what it contained. Security by obfuscation."

That sounded like Eli. "Is there a date in the paperwork that might have a special meaning?"

"I've not seen the documents, but chances are they have a variety of dates. Check for his birthday. Your birthday. His mother's birthday."

That would take hours. Hours I didn't have. "That doesn't sound like Eli. Leaving a file cabinet containing secret government papers unlocked. There's got to be another place where he kept them."

"Did he ever take work home?"

"All the time."

"That's where we'll check next."

But not tonight. I itched to get to Eli's side. "How urgent is finding the paperwork?"

"It'll wait until tomorrow. I'll arrange for a patrol to guard the house until then."

An idea sparked in my tired brain. "What are the chances that the fire Saturday night was a cover for trying to break in, steal the documents, and hide their tracks?"

Putnam's eyes widened. "It's a possibility I hadn't considered. I assumed we'd find the paperwork here."

"So did I. But unless Eli has a hiding spot we don't see, we were wrong."

"I need to make a phone call. While I do, would you look at any file in here that might be of interest?" He tapped the cabinet and didn't wait for an answer before leaving.

Where would Eli hide something? The top drawer seemed too obvious. In every movie ever, the search always starts at the top and the file gets found in the second drawer. I sat on the floor and started at the bottom.

The random files I pulled contained snippets of hand-written code and notes. It was like a diary of his journey in developing his early programs. I didn't understand much of it. Heck; I didn't understand most of it. But it was important to him, so I returned each folder to its original location.

As interesting as the glimpses into Eli's mind were, they held no clues to the secret documents. There was still the unspoken question—why did Eli have them in the first place?

As I pulled out yet another file to examine, Putnam came back. "That's taken care of," he said. "There'll be two sets of eyes on the house at all times. Are you finding anything?"

"Nothing that you need. Without breaching security, can you tell me why Eli has these documents? It might be the key to where to look."

He slid open the top drawer halfway, to make sure the cabinet remained stable. "It's a project for a different agency. I can't provide details because I don't know them."

I closed the bottom drawer. "If it's one of his side projects, chances are they are at the house. Where, I can't say. He made a point of not working on those when I was around."

He put away the file he was scanning and shut the cabinet. "In that case, we should continue the search there. Tomorrow."

If I took off early, I'd preserve more time to spend with Eli. Make up for what I lost tonight. I'd have to check with the boss and verify it was okay. Except I was the boss.

"I'll meet you there at four, if that works for you."

He nodded. "I'll make myself available. Will you be bringing along Special Agent Salters? She's been hanging out in the hallway. Is there something I should know?"

"You must not have been copied on the memo. She maneuvered me into accepting her as my bodyguard, for now."

He chuckled. "It's about time one of us got the upper hand. I've been studying your file, and it's interesting."

"The government has a file on me?" I squeaked.

"How many times have you dealt with a federal agency? Your interactions with the FBI alone created a sizable record."

There wasn't any way to change that.

Putnam was full of surprises. "I've recommended that you be given a low-level security clearance until Mr. Hennessey returns to work. I'm aware you aren't a programmer, but if questions arise regarding business transactions, you'll be authorized as a point-of-contact."

It was necessary, I supposed, but that didn't mean

I was happy about it. I'd always feel like a government spy was looking over my shoulder. I'd put up with it for Eli.

No one looked over my shoulder as I sat beside Eli's bed, reading. I had a copy of the medical POA in my purse, half-afraid Rob would try to block me from seeing Eli, but my fears were unfounded. Vanessa prowled the hospital, staying out of my way; but probably getting in the way of security. She wasn't allowed to enter the ICU, so I had a moment of peace.

The night's reading material was one of the security blogs Eli followed. Dry reading, and I stopped frequently to make sure of the pronunciation of words and names. It seemed wrong, but I was tired of talking. All I did anymore was talk, at work and here at the hospital. For someone who was used to saying only a few words all day, it was a strain.

I resorted to humming again. Any song that popped into my head. Folk songs. John Denver. Three Dog Night. Snatches of the popular music from my college days. I rested my hand on his, humming 'You Are My Sunshine,' when it happened.

His hand moved. It wasn't my imagination. I looked up and his eyes were open. "Welcome back, Sweetie. Are you going to stick around for a while?"

He opened his mouth, but no sound came out. I pushed the button to call the nurse, then wet my finger in my bottle of water and touched it to his lips.

He blinked and his normally pale blue eyes, now a muddy gray, focused. Then he closed them again.

"Eli, open your eyes. Can you hear me? Please wake up."

Amy, the nurse, rushed in. "What's going on?"

"He woke up! Just for a minute, but his eyes opened!" I could feel my cheeks stretch as I smiled for the first time in a week.

She checked all the displays. "It's a start. May be hours, may be tomorrow, or it could be in five minutes when it happens again. My best guess is tomorrow. So why don't you head home and get some sleep?"

Home was a long way away. But at least I might rest easier in my hotel bed, knowing Eli had made a turn for the better. "Let me text his mother and then I'll leave." It would give me a few more minutes to hope and watch for another miracle.

Chapter 16

"If he didn't move now and then, I'd think he was a statue," I told Vanessa. She'd shown up as promised at my hotel in the morning and was drinking a cup of coffee while I finished getting ready. She'd spotted the man by the lake while enjoying the view from my balcony.

"Could be a local working on his tan," she said. "but not this early. My gut says we need to check it out. Not we as in you and me, but we as in the ATF."

"I could do it in the right disguise. Gray wig, an old lady dress, false teeth, makeup. I just don't have the time to put all the pieces together."

Vanessa sputtered into her coffee. "What?"

"Throw in some heavy orthopedic shoes and a cane and I'm gold." I grinned. "Maybe the guys who live upstairs from you can teach me a few tricks."

"You've done this before?" she asked, glaring. "Don't think for a second I'll let you try anything like that. Not while I'm watching you."

It would be a fun challenge. Slipping away from Vanessa, that was. But as long as all the legal agencies did their jobs, I shouldn't need to resort to going undercover. I had other things to worry about. I poured what remained of my coffee down the drain. "Are you ready to go?"

It was weird knowing I was being followed and not having to worry about it. Vanessa's little white car had no trouble keeping up with Dolores while blending in with traffic. I wonder what modifications had been done to its suspension. But the silver pickup behind her bothered me. It didn't follow us into the parking lot, so maybe it was coincidental. Right.

As Vanessa helped me put the cover over Dolores, I asked, "Was that silver truck a friend of yours?"

"You noticed it, too?" She tugged on the corner of the cover to get it in place. "No one I know. I'll ask around to see if one of the other agencies involved sent out someone to watch your back. They weren't trying to hide."

"I had the same impression. It doesn't make sense."

"Are we still on to check out my place during lunch?" she asked as we walked into the office.

I nodded. "Unless Darla has scheduled an emergency meeting, I'm good."

"Another day in paradise, eh?" Vanessa joked.

It might be paradise for some, but it wasn't something I ever wanted. I was living in my personal hell.

❋ ❋ ❋

The neighborhood needed work. Lots of it. Before we even got to Vanessa's I was ready to back out of the deal. Lawns were barren of grass. Houses needed new siding or paint. Junker cars were propped up on concrete blocks. More than one house looked like it should be razed. Not your quintessential Florida postcard development. It didn't seem like an area an ATF agent would choose to live, but Vanessa seemed immune to her surroundings.

We turned a corner, and the character of the street changed. The houses, although old, needed only minor repairs. At least they were clean. Most had grass and flowers. The cars in the driveways had tires. If this was Vanessa's neighborhood, I could make it work.

She pulled to the curb in front of a house with faded blue paint, patchy grass in the yard, and two forlorn-looking pots of red geraniums on the porch. They needed to be watered and pruned, and given new potting soil. Or tossed and replaced with new ones. I had a vision of pots of brightly colored flowers hanging from the edge of the porch's roof.

I'd have to replace the decorative trim first. Half of it was missing, and I wasn't sure what remained was original. The house was a Victorian, but not one of the grand old houses scattered around Oak Grove, like Eli's. I wondered what shape the interior was in.

I didn't have to wait long to find out. Vanessa hopped out with a cheerful, "We're here!"

139

The inside was better than expected. Sure, the front room needed new carpet and the kitchen cabinets needed replaced, but everything was clean. I'd want to give the rooms more life by changing the color of the walls, but I supposed white was standard for a rental.

The two bedrooms were small but adequate. I suspected they'd been the original parlor, split in half. The shared bathroom was a recent addition to the house, but it faced the backyard and didn't ruin the lines of the architecture.

I wondered what the upstairs was like. A locked door blocked the stairway, so I couldn't peek. How much would it cost to return the house to its original glory?

"What do you think, Harmony?" Vanessa asked, and I picked up on a note of anxiety in her voice.

"It'll work." On a short-term basis, anyway. If I stayed too long, I'd start making improvements without the landlord's permission. Fix a crack in the wall here, change the light fixture there... "Is the backyard shared? Who owns the empty lot next door?"

"The backyard is a joke. There's no shade, so it gets too hot to spend any time out there. And I don't know who owns the property next door."

I knew nothing about Florida landscaping. What trees would grow here?

"Oh, one more thing," Vanessa continued. "We don't have central air. Each room has a window unit, and they do a good job unless the temperature breaks a hundred."

Another reason I disliked Florida. But I'd only be here for a short time. I hoped.

❀ ❀ ❀

Eli's house seemed unchanged, frozen in time. Special Agent Putnam hadn't arrived yet, so I sat in Dolores with the air conditioner running, reclined the seat, turned up the radio, and tried to relax.

But the feeling of being observed made relaxing difficult. I'd spotted the watcher hidden in the bushes at the edge of the yard. He hadn't left his post to demand my identification, and I assumed he'd been given my description.

I closed my eyes to ease their burning. It had been a long day of shuffling paperwork, and reminded me how much I hated the business side of management. But I had to get it done to move Fiona and the others into their new positions.

A rap on my window woke me. I reached for Betsy, and blinked to focus. Then I popped open the door.

Putnam stood there, a touch of a smile on his face. "My apologies," he said. "A meeting ran late."

I didn't bother asking what the meeting was about. He wouldn't tell me. "That's okay. I hope we have more luck here than we did at the office."

A welcome rush of air conditioning met me when I opened the front door. It carried no trace of Eli's aftershave. The emptiness forced open another crack in my heart.

I surveyed the spotless living room to give myself a moment to recover. "I'm not sure where to start."

"Where's his desk?"

"The bedroom. But he was as likely to work in the kitchen or sitting by the pool."

"We'll start with his desk. I don't imagine he stored the paperwork with his cereal or in the freezer."

In spite of myself, I smiled, liking this side of Putnam.

While he examined the desk, I checked Eli's nightstand. And under his bed. And his pillow. Nothing.

"Having any luck over there?" I asked.

"None. The document isn't here. Does he have a safe?"

"There's a gun safe in the spare bedroom. I've never seen him put anything in it besides his rifles and ammo, but it won't hurt to look." I snagged the key from the tray on top of the dresser, then automatically checked to make sure the dog tags still hung from my neck. They'd become a part of me already, and most of the time I didn't even feel their slight weight.

Eli only owned a few guns. He wasn't a hunter but liked to go to a gun range once in a while. I tried shooting his rifle once but missed the target and ended up with a bruise on my shoulder.

I stepped aside to allow Putnam to examine the contents of the safe. It looked like I expected: Everything in its place, no random papers on the bottom. Putnam took a rifle out and examined it, military-style, then put it back without a word. I guessed he was satisfied with what he saw. He closed the safe door with a metallic bang.

"What now?" I asked, as I locked it.

"The easy way didn't work," he said. "So, we tackle it the hard way. Search every room, every drawer, every potential hiding spot, including the cereal boxes and the freezer."

I was glad he retained his sense of humor. It might make up for the fact that I'd lost mine.

He started in the spare bedroom, so I got out of his way and tore apart the front room. I looked under the sofa, flipped over each cushion, stuck my hand into the cracks. I tilted his recliner to look under it and lifted the back cover to peer inside. Each book and magazine on the coffee table got flipped through and dangled to see if anything would fall out. I even checked behind the pictures hung on the walls. Nothing. I didn't expect to find anything. It wasn't Eli's style.

Putnam and I finished at the same time. He tackled the kitchen, and I took the sunroom. Not that it had any hiding spots. The patio chairs had slotted seats and backs, and the heavy plastic container where he stored the pool chemicals only took a minute to dig through.

For the sake of saying I'd done it, I checked the bathrooms. Even behind and inside the toilet tank. I came up empty.

While Putnam rattled around in the kitchen, I returned to the bedroom. After checking the laptop bag, I closed Eli's laptop and put it away. One by one, I removed every book and leafed through them. I ran my hand under the shelves and across the back.

When I peeled back the covers on the bed, a wave of his scent reached me. Once again, his absence struck me. I choked back my emotions and continued the hunt. Putnam joined me in the bedroom, and we wrangled the mattress off the box springs and peered between. I was positive he could have done it by himself but was trying to make me feel better.

He tackled Eli's dresser while I checked out the closet. The cardboard boxes that held his mementos and souvenirs remained taped shut, just like the first time I'd seen them. The thin layer of dust on the tops told me they hadn't been disturbed. I wasn't tall enough to see on top of the built-in shelf and saved the task for Putnam. Instead, I buried myself among Eli's clothes, checking pockets and sliding my hands up the sleeves of his jackets. I wondered if I should take one to wear, like a high-school girlfriend. Except it would never be chilly enough to wear it.

"Find anything?" Putnam asked with no enthusiasm. I guessed he'd come up empty-handed.

"No, but you're taller than me. Will you check the shelf?"

I busied myself straightening the sheets and blankets on the bed. Eli would be upset to come home to a messy room. Not that he kept it perfect all the time, but he didn't keep pizza boxes and fast-food containers sitting around, either.

As I expected, Putnam was empty-handed when he finished checking the shelf. "I don't get it. I was sure the documents would be here. Have you seen an inventory of the contents of his car?"

I'd been more concerned with what wasn't in the car than what was. "No."

"It's a good thing I know where to get it then. I'll reach out to Richon tomorrow." He looked around the room. "That's all we can do for now. I'll request the friendly shadows outside maintain surveillance for a few more days."

"What's bothering you, Special Agent?" I read it in his eyes. He was worried about something.

He grimaced. "I have to check, but I don't believe the papers were in the car. If Hennessey had them, they would have been taken by whoever ran him off the road."

And stole everything else, I speculated. I concentrated on breathing. In and out. In and out. This spy versus spy stuff was way above my pay grade. But I spotted a flaw in Putnam's theory.

"If someone got their hands on the documents, they wouldn't be following me around. Or setting fires to Eli's houses. That feels like payback."

"Your logic is sound, unless there are two forces at play; and we're both right. Which reminds me, where is Special Agent Salters?"

"She figured I'd be safe here with you, so she's running an errand." Or taking a nap. "She said to call her when we got done."

"We're finished, unless I'm hit with a sudden burst of inspiration or spot something we've missed. I'll stay with you until she arrives."

I leaned over to pull out a wrinkle in the

bedspread and the dog tags fell out of my shirt. As I tucked them back inside, an almost-memory from several years ago struck me. Something about a necklace and a closet. And an unfinished wall. But that was in a Victorian home, and Eli's was too new. But he might have modified this closet to create a hiding spot.

"Hang on a sec." I took the two swift steps to the closet. Once inside, I turned around to examine the inner wall next to the door. In both my apartment and in a certain bedroom in Eli's house in Oak Grove, that space still showed the wall studs. The perfect hiding spots. But, as I expected, the area had been covered with wallboard. "Never mind," I said. "Good idea, but it didn't work out." Disappointed, I sent a message to Vanessa. I was ready to go spend time with Eli.

Chapter 17

"Any changes?" I asked the nurse at the ICU desk. She had a pink carnation pin on her collar, a spot of cheerfulness in an antiseptic white world.

She moved her mouse, but I couldn't see the computer screen, so I had to wait for her to read the notes. "His mother reports he woke up for a few seconds, but the monitors didn't catch it. I told her the next time to ring for a nurse right away. Same goes for you."

Sure, if I wasn't too busy savoring the precious moments. I hadn't told him how much I love him the last time. I wouldn't make that mistake again.

One hand holding a book, the other on his, I assumed my normal position at his bedside. I'd picked up the first in a fantasy series he'd probably read in college from his house. Two pages in, I remembered reading it a long, long time ago. It felt like bumping into an old friend I hadn't seen for years.

Amy's arrival to check on Eli fit perfectly with my need for a break. I got a drink of water, stretched, walked up and down the hall, thought, and worried. How long could I keep this up? No progress had been made on the hunt for Eli's attacker. At least, not that anyone had shared with me.

I returned to his room and stared out the window at the fading light. It would be dark soon, but the bright city lights would hide the stars. I wished I could drive up to the Point—Oak Grove's hang-out spot—put down Dolores' top, wrap myself in a blanket, and track falling stars in the night sky. How long until I'd have the chance to do it again? I feared winter would move in first.

Damnit, I was too old to be homesick.

With one chapter completed, I closed the book and stroked Eli's hand. It was nearly midnight and the nurses would kick me out soon. There'd been no repeat performance of him waking up like I'd hoped.

"I'm not giving up on you, Eli Hennessey. One of these days you'll wake up for real and I'll be here to see it." Or only a few minutes away, as long as it wasn't rush hour. "Until then, remember I love you."

He groaned. And licked his parched lips. I grabbed the tube of balm on his bedside table and rubbed some on them.

"Is that better, Sweetie?" I asked.

His eyes opened. He blinked. And blinked again. I pushed the nurse call button but didn't want to miss my chance. "I love you, Eli. Don't forget that. No matter what happens, I love you."

His eyes focused, and he turned his head to stare at me. His mouth opened. No sound came out.

Amy rushed in. "He's awake. Good deal. Mr. Hennessey, I'm one of your nurses, Amy. Would you like a sip of water?"

I moved so she could take care of him. Amy lifted a glass of water with a straw in it to his mouth. His Adam's apple bobbed as he swallowed. He licked his lips. A sound came from his mouth. More of a groan than a word, but I heard the meaning behind it. "Stay." Then his eyes closed.

I wanted to shake him and wake him up again. In my dreams, that was all it would take. But I knew better. With my hand on his shoulder, I waited for a sign that he'd reopen his eyes.

"Show's over," Amy said. "But it was a good one. We should see more events like it, and they should last longer."

I thought the words she didn't say: Eli was back. He was going to be okay.

After a short internal debate—text or call Tillie— I decided a text would be better. That way I wouldn't wake her up, and she'd be greeted by the good news in the morning. Then I floated down the steps to meet Vanessa. She'd asked me to meet up in the cafeteria. If she had something up her sleeve, I was in the mood to play along.

Before joining her at the table tucked away in an

alcove, I got a cup of hot mint tea to soothe my throat. She already had a cup of something in front of her, so I didn't feel bad about not buying her anything. I didn't know her well enough to guess what she liked.

"So," she said once I sat down, "I had an interesting conversation with a security guard."

"Interesting as in how?" I asked, after waiting for the warmth of the tea to trickle down my throat.

"He approached me because I don't fit the normal friend or family member of a patient profile. I don't belong. He picked up on it last night but let it slide. When I showed up again tonight, it set off the alarms in his head. I flashed my badge to calm him down."

"Is that normal?" I knew nothing about hospital security. Did Oak Grove's tiny facility even have any?

"Nope. Seems like they are on high alert for some unknown reason. His guess was that a big-name celebrity had been admitted, but no one mentioned who."

"You think it's tied to Eli."

Vanessa nodded. "Yep. Pressure from above. Sounds familiar."

"If we find out who is responsible for the push, would that help solve the case?"

"Truthfully, I don't think so. I can't imagine they were involved in the crash. My guess is that Mr. Hennessey has a friend in high places who wants to make sure every rock is turned over to find his attacker. And the people watching you are part of the favor. They want to keep you safe because of your relationship with Hennessey."

There was one flaw in her theory. "Eli has never talked about knowing anyone with the power to do any of this."

"Because he didn't want to name drop?" she hazarded.

"Where does that leave us?"

"It changes nothing. You've got enough to worry about. In the meantime, I've already touched base with the others. We're going to get pictures and license plates and see if we can identify the guys watching you. We don't want to jump to any conclusions."

I swirled my tea in the cup, processing the information. "What can I do to help?"

"Nothing. This is entirely on us. With the guard's help, I got a picture of tonight's watcher and sent it to Putnam. He'll run it through DCSA's database."

"You're enjoying this." I was torn between being happy for her and sad that it was at Eli's expense. And mine.

The left side of her lips quirked. "I haven't had a challenge like this in months. There I was, stuck doing research on fire patterns in the 70s compared to the past few years, and now I'm part of a group effort with three other agencies. Four, if you count hospital security. Enjoying it? Heck, yeah."

How could anyone get tired of research? I wanted to probe for more information, but when I opened my mouth, a huge yawn came out.

Vanessa grinned. "Time to get you to bed."

It was past time. The surge of adrenaline I'd experienced when Eli awoke had faded. By the time I got back to the hotel, I'd be ready to crawl under the sheet.

The typical Florida afternoon thunderstorm made its appearance early. When I went to drink my morning cup of coffee on the balcony, it was pouring, and the wind blasted water into every corner. My watcher wasn't by the lake, and I hoped he'd found someplace safe and dry.

It would be a good day to stay holed up in the hotel room, start a fire in the fireplace, and read. But I wouldn't do any of that. Eli's company couldn't run without me. I snorted and laughed at myself. It was running just fine. All I was useful for was signing paperwork. But I headed to the office, anyway.

Around eleven, Darla poked her head in my door. "You've got a visitor, Harmony."

I spotted the mountain in the doorway as soon as I looked up. It was impossible to miss him. I set aside the report I was reading and rose. Vanessa hovered in the hall behind him. It didn't look like good news.

"Detective," I said, "come in and have a seat. Do you want coffee?"

"No thanks. I won't be staying long." He planted himself in front of my desk. Was he trying to intimidate me by making me look up at him? He didn't know me very well.

"I was asked to update you on the investigation," he said.

By whom, I wondered, but didn't ask.

"The car we believe ran Mr. Hennessey off the road has been located," he continued.

"Let me guess." I leaned back in my chair, so it was easier to watch his face. "It was reported stolen before that night. The agency that found it hasn't been able to pull prints or other identifying information from it."

"Correct on both. We did locate numerous hairs in the carpet. They matched the owner."

They'd tried. "No sign of Eli's phone or anything?"

"No, but the warrant came through and we are examining the records."

He had my full attention. "And the last person he spoke to?"

"Was you, Miss Duprie. In fact, the last two calls he received were from your number."

Had I talked to Eli earlier in the day? "It's possible. We often talk shop during work hours. What time were the calls?"

"The last one was at eleven PM. May I see your phone, Miss Duprie?"

This was my cue to tell them to wait until my lawyer was present or they'd gotten a warrant, but I knew they wouldn't find what they were looking for. So, I dug my phone out of my purse and unlocked it before giving it to him.

Horace took a few moments to examine the records, then passed the phone to Vanessa. She glanced at the screen and nodded before handing it back to me.

"Spoofed," she said. "There's no record on your phone to match the one on Mr. Hennessey's. It explains why he answered the call."

"He would have known it wasn't me as soon as the person who called started talking," I argued.

"Unless they convinced him you were in danger, that they had both your phone and you," Horace said.

It sounded like the plot of a movie. One I didn't want to appear in.

"Eli and I never kept our relationship a secret." Well, we had tried and failed miserably. "And there are several ways to locate a phone number, even for a cell phone. But if you are correct, Detective, the caller would have needed personal information about me to convince Eli I was in danger. Which leads me right back to the conclusion that it's someone who works here."

Vanessa nodded. "We agree. Putnam is pushing to have the records checks expedited. In the meantime, we'd like you to move in with me today instead of waiting for the weekend."

"Your Chief Sorenson asked me to pass on a message," Horace said. "Stephen Sallis is out of prison, on compassionate release. He has an untreatable cancer. Sorenson said to be careful."

I caught my breath.

"Who's that?" Vanessa asked, her hand instinctively reaching for her weapon.

"He's a minor crime figure with delusions of grandeur. I had a supporting role in his capture." Sallis been responsible for the disaster that played out after Jake, my ex-boyfriend, gave me a replica of a stolen necklace. "You think he's going to show up looking for revenge?" I unlocked the drawer holding Betsy and my purse, took her out, opened the chamber to verify it contained a round. Then I laid her on the desk near my right hand.

"This isn't a game, Miss Duprie," Horace growled.

"And I'm not playing, Detective. You may not approve, but it won't be the first time I've shot someone if that's what it comes down to. I'll even aim for center mass."

"Can you shoot someone you work with?" Vanessa asked.

Could I? Shoot Fiona or Annie or anyone on the floor? I didn't have an answer.

Vanessa read my thoughts. "That's why you need to let us do our jobs," she said.

Chapter 18

I couldn't argue with Detective Horace and Vanessa. Well, I could, but they were right. So, after lunch was delivered, Vanessa and I took her car to the hotel. It had more room for my belongings. The front desk clerk gave us a couple of cardboard boxes because I didn't have room for everything in my suitcases.

There wasn't enough time to settle in at Vanessa's. I hung up most of my wardrobe while Vanessa put the food away in the kitchen. Then, it was back to work.

I needed more coffee to get through the spreadsheets and printed-out PDFs from Marty. There wasn't a logical reason he'd given me paper copies, instead of attaching the files to an email or telling me where he stored them, so I could look at the up-to-date versions whenever I wanted. I had to force myself to pay attention while he droned on about the increasing electricity and water costs and how to cut their usage to save money.

"If everyone turned off their computers and monitors when they go home, it'd be a start," he said. "And we should cut back on the air conditioning. Set it to turn on in the afternoon."

I nodded and took notes to make it appear I took him seriously. "What else?"

"Don't water the grass as often."

I had a vague memory of Eli talking about using recycled water for that but added it to the list. "Good ideas. Why don't you send out a memo and ask if anyone else has suggestions? Is that a project you'd be willing to tackle?"

"I'm a numbers guy," he said. "I'm not good with social interaction."

I'd noticed. He came off as standoffish. He wouldn't mingle with the other employees even on the days I provided lunch. That's why I'd made the suggestion, wanting to change that. "You can do it by email. Or put a box in the breakroom. You don't have to talk to everyone."

He scratched behind his ear, and his oversized glasses jiggled. "Sure, I guess so."

"Thank you. I'll add a note in your file so Eli's aware of your help when he does your yearly review." I hoped Eli had a process for annual evaluations.

To my surprise, Marty looked uncomfortable with my response. He rubbed an eyebrow, as if resisting the urge to pick at it. "Yeah, okay."

I poured on the charm, determined to win him

over. "Thanks for preparing this report for me. I'll give it the attention it deserves. If you think of anything else, my office door is open." I flashed a broad smile.

He stood and gathered his papers. "I reported to Eli once a month."

"Got it." Did all women make him this uncomfortable, or had I lost my touch?

He left, and I stared at the empty spot. The meeting hadn't gone as I'd hoped, and I couldn't figure out what I'd done wrong. Normally, I could get people to loosen up and work with me. I'd have to ask Darla for his personnel file to check for clues.

❊ ❊ ❊

The messages from Tillie brought a mix of emotions. *'He woke up twice today. I was there the second time.'* Good news, but the following message broke my heart. *'He doesn't know who I am.'*

I'd read about the potential for temporary memory loss. Or in some cases, long-term. I didn't expect it to happen to Eli. But none of this should have happened.

I sent a response, telling her not to lose hope. He'd get better.

It had become a habit that at the end of my workday, Darla, Lando, Scotty, Kris and I met for a few minutes. The 'public' reason was to debrief me on how the day had gone and give me a heads-up on the morning's priorities. The real reason was to update them on Eli's progress. Then we'd decide on what to share with the rest of the staff. Darla would compose an email first thing in the morning to send to the employees.

It seemed a good way to communicate, but it bothered me that it fed information to a potential suspect. I was the only one who knew that.

On the way to my new, temporary home, I stopped to buy hangers and a bathroom shower caddy, avoiding the hospital until Tillie left so I wouldn't have to comfort her in the hallway again. Tired down to my toes, I didn't have the energy to spare for her.

Vanessa insisted we take her car instead of driving separately, and I didn't fight with her about it. It made sense, but I resented the loss of freedom. Not having to pay attention to traffic also gave me more time to worry.

I flipped through my phone, wondering how my number had been spoofed. While I was at it, I deleted the records of spam calls. Companies wanting to sell me insurance for car repairs or give me a better interest rate on my credit cards. I never answered numbers I didn't recognize.

But something caught my eye. "Ah, shit," I whispered.

Vanessa slammed on the brakes and pulled into the parking lot of a small strip mall. "What?"

"There's a missed call from Eli the night of the accident. I never heard my phone ring. If I had answered, could I have saved him?"

She held out her hand. "Let me see."

With a too-familiar action, I handed her my phone. She studied the screen and muttered, "I wonder," before taking her phone out of the cupholder. She punched the screen and held it to her ear.

"Detective," she said after a few seconds. "Salters here. In that log from Hennessey's phone, does it show a call placed at one AM? No? Thanks. Duprie got a spoofed call of her own then. We didn't see it because we weren't looking for it."

Horace's response was muffled and the words indistinct.

"Right," Vanessa said. "Tomorrow."

"What?" I asked.

She put her phone away and handed me mine. "We continue as planned. Nothing has changed. I keep an eye on you and everyone keeps doing their jobs. In the long run, this is an interesting tidbit that supports the prevailing theories.

"Look at it this way. Hennessey got his call at eleven, yours came in at one. Chances are he'd already been run off the road. If you'd answered, no telling what story the suspect would have spun. You might have ended up in Hennessey's house up north when it was firebombed."

Goosebumps rose on my arms. I stayed silent for the rest of the short trip, considering my options. Truth was, I didn't have any. I'd been forced onto a narrow path, and the only way to go was forward. Until they arrested the guilty party, Eli wouldn't be safe, and he was my top priority. I was just collateral damage.

At the hospital, we stopped at the bottom of the staircase that went up to the ICU. "See you around midnight," I said.

Vanessa shook her head. "I'll go up with you. Call it instinct."

I wasn't feeling the prickly sense that warned me of danger. "Maybe it's the security guard trailing us. Is that your acquaintance from last night?" I jerked my head towards the uniformed man down the hall.

"That's him. Cute, but married."

I didn't say a word as we started the trip upstairs, but I wondered which guy at work I could fix her up with. Lando wouldn't do; their personalities would clash. Scotty, on the other hand, in his quiet way, would be an interesting match. I wouldn't even consider anyone else until I identified Eli's enemy.

By the time we reached the fourth-floor landing, Vanessa was puffing. "Only nineteen more steps," I said in encouragement.

"You've counted the stairs?"

"Yes. There are ten on the first half of each floor, and nine on the second. That makes a total of seventy-six steps."

She grinned. "I'll take your word for it."

I expected her to leave when we reached the fifth floor, to wander wherever she wandered off to. Instead, she took a chair in the ICU's family waiting room.

"I'll stick around for a few minutes," she said. "Until the prickles go away."

My danger meter was off, or I was so tired it didn't register. I'd have to trust her gut. Not a position I liked being in, but Eli waited for me. He just didn't know it.

I stopped at the desk to check in and get an update and had to tell the new nurse who I was. She verified I was on the list of allowed visitors. "How's Eli doing?" I asked after she'd approved me to enter.

"He had a rough day." She frowned. I peeked, but her sweater covered her nametag. I'd given up on trying to remember everyone's names. "It started when we removed the bandages from his chest, but between not recognizing his mother and not understanding where he is, he got agitated. The doctor worried we were going to have to sedate him, but luckily, he fell asleep before it became necessary. No guarantees on how he'll do tonight. Call if you need us."

If she was trying to scare me, she was doing a good job. I nodded but sent out a silent prayer for things to get better.

He laid unmoving when I entered the room, his chest barely rising with each breath. That wasn't anything new, so I planted a soft kiss on top of his still-healing head. Then I put the chair next to his bed, placed my hand on his, opened the book and escaped into the land of imagination.

Somewhere in the second chapter, his breathing shifted. I looked up, and his eyes were focused on the ceiling. "Well, hello there, Sweetie," I said. "How are you feeling?" That was a stupid question. He probably felt like crap. "I love you," I rushed to add, desperate to make sure he heard it.

He blinked and turned his head towards me. I

stood so it would be easier for him to see me. "Hi," I said again, my knack for conversation gone.

His tongue darted out to moisten his lips. A single word fell from his mouth. "You."

I was supposed to call the nurse but craved this moment of just him and me. "Yeah, it's me."

He licked his lips again, and I grabbed the balm. As I smoothed some on, his eyes stayed glued to my face.

"You," he croaked when I finished, "I remember you."

I should have hit the nurse call button, but there was something I needed to do first. I leaned down and touched my lips to his. No pressure, because I didn't want to hurt him. And his feeding tube was in the way. "I love you, Eli Hennessey."

His hand pushed on the back of my neck. That's what greeted Amy when she walked in—Eli and I getting reacquainted.

Chapter 19

Amy chuckled, alerting us to her presence. "You two need to take a breath. We don't want Mr. Hennessey to pass out from the lack of air."

I took my time breaking the kiss. "I was about to alert you." The tube that fed Eli oxygen was out of place and I straightened it.

Then I attempted to stay out of the way as Amy did the things she needed to do, but Eli wouldn't let go of my hand. She didn't seem to mind and worked around me, except when she changed his gown. I moved and tried not to pay attention to the green, black and purple bruises covering Eli's chest.

When she left, Eli blinked his eyes rapidly, as if struggling to stay awake. They'd close, then pop open, and he would search the room until he found me. I made it easier on him by propping myself on the edge of the bed.

"It's okay if you go back to sleep," I told him. "I'll stay." At least until they sent me home.

He licked his lips. He did that every time he got

ready to talk. "Butter," he said, then tried again. "Buttercup."

His eyes closed, and I figured he was out for the night. Still, I stayed where I was, waiting for his breathing to settle into an even pattern.

With a deep inhale, his eyes fluttered open. "Safe," he whispered.

"Yes, you're safe, Eli."

He shook his head. "No. You."

So, that's what was bothering him. "Yes, Eli, I'm safe."

He closed his eyes again, but I wasn't ready to leave. I held his hand and hummed until I got a cramp in one leg and had to stand and stretch it out. He didn't stir, so I brushed my lips against his forehead and tiptoed from the room.

Vanessa was asleep in the family waiting area when I got there. I hated to wake her, but we needed to get to the house and to our beds. Everyone but me was getting time to sleep.

Which explained why I slept through my alarm in the morning.

"You should have woken me," I complained to Vanessa as we pulled out of the driveway of her—our—place.

She chuckled. "I tried. Nothing but dumping ice water on you would have worked. And I don't have another set of bedding to loan you. Besides, you needed the sleep. And you're the boss, so who's going to yell at you?"

No one. But Darla would look at me with disapproving eyes. Lando and Scotty would worry about me, even though I'd sent all three a text to say I'd be late.

On the way to work, I noticed Vanessa checking the rearview mirror more than necessary for the amount of traffic. I twisted, trying to get a glimpse of whatever was bothering her. "Our normal tail back there?" I asked.

"Silver pickup, check. It's the car behind him that has me worried. Black sedan, heavy window tint, no tag on the front." She stepped on the brake, then hit the gas to give herself maneuvering room.

"Sounds like one of the three-letter agencies. Pains in the neck, all of them. Present company not excepted."

She glanced at me and laughed. "The extra rest did you good. You've been too tired to put up a fight."

I couldn't argue the point. Especially when Vanessa chose that moment to make an unneeded right-hand turn. I grasped the dashboard to steady myself.

"Hold on," she said, from between clenched lips. "I want to see how good these guys are."

I braced myself as she made a hard left. Her car responded well. Not like Dolores, but not bad. "Upgraded struts?" I asked.

"Yeah, and a few other extras."

It might be fun to match her car against Dolores when this was all over. "How is it going?"

"Lost the truck. The black car is still with us, although he's pretending not to be."

"Which agency is being left out of our fun?"

"FBI. DoD. Hell, as complicated as this case is, I'll throw in the bloody DHS. Take your pick." She made a couple of swift lane changes. "He's got to know we're aware of him. What would you do?"

"At home, I'd head down an alley that would be hard for him to negotiate. There was one time when I stuck to the back streets and led my tail right to the steps of the cop shop, where a friend on the force waited."

"Sweet. I can work with that."

She pushed the phone button on her car's radio. "Call," she said. "Horace. Cell."

He answered immediately. "Good morning, Special Agent Salters. How may I help you?"

"So formal," Vanessa muttered. Then, "Detective, I know you don't work traffic, but I have an opportunity you won't want to miss."

While the two of them worked out the details of an officer running a stop on the black car, I sent a text to Darla telling her I'd be late. Well, later. I blamed it on traffic. Always a convenient excuse.

"How about that?" Vanessa said after she'd hung up. "There happens to be a unit in the neighborhood. All we have to do is sit back and enjoy the show."

It didn't take long for a police cruiser to become part of the parade. It surprised me when the lights and siren didn't come on right away. I understood a few minutes later when another car joined us with the unmistakable hulk of Horace at the wheel.

He pulled in between us and the black car just as the first car lit up. Vanessa slowed and parked on the curb. Horace came in behind us. As if reluctant to comply, the black car flashed its lights. The first cruiser sounded its siren again. The black car turned on its emergency blinkers and drove a short distance down the street, ending up in a convenience store's parking lot. As they passed by, I saw two men—one driving, the other in the back seat.

I reached for the door handle to get out of the car, anxious to see who our followers were, but Vanessa laid her hand on my shoulder. "Let the police deal with it."

The officer approached the car, and the driver stuck his hand out of the window. The papers he held rustled in the breeze. They were more than a driver's license and insurance card. Horace took a defensive position by the car's rear bumper.

After looking at the paperwork, the officer walked back to Horace. Even with the window rolled down, I couldn't hear their conversation. Horace took his turn examining the documents and shook his head.

"What's going on?" I asked.

Vanessa frowned. "You've got me. I've never seen anything like it."

Horace strode up to the open window and handed the driver the paperwork. His mouth moved occasionally, but mostly it looked as if he was listening. Finally, he stood, rubbed his hand over the top of his head, and watched the car pull out and slowly drive down the street.

I didn't understand. My frustration grew while

Horace talked to the police officer. "What's going on?" I asked again.

Vanessa drummed on the steering wheel. "Maybe they couldn't make the traffic stop stick?"

That wasn't right. Cops could always come up with something to authorize a stop, even if they let you go later.

Horace headed our direction and Vanessa rolled down her window. "That was interesting," he said, leaning against the car so he could see us.

I twisted as far as possible to face him. "What was that all about?"

"He claimed diplomatic immunity and the paperwork backed him up."

I still didn't understand, but I didn't have any experience with the topic. Oak Grove didn't attract many foreign visitors. Or anyone important.

"Diplomatic immunity?" Vanessa repeated. "That makes no sense. Which country?"

"Some little island in the Pacific Ocean. Never heard of it, but dispatch verified it's legit. The driver, a minor secretary to a secretary, claimed he just happened to be going the same way as you. There isn't a way to disprove it, and diplomatic immunity means we can't touch him."

"I wonder if it has anything to do with the documents Special Agent Putnam is looking for?" I said.

"I considered the same thing." Horace rolled his neck. "Although what a little island in the middle of nowhere would have in the way of secrets is beyond me."

"I'll contact Putnam," Vanessa offered. "Will you send me a copy of the incident? My clearance is higher than yours, Detective, so he might be more willing to discuss how we can ensure Harmony's safety with me."

"How many diplomats does this country have?" I asked. "This one got caught so easily, he'd be foolish to try again."

With a shrug, Horace straightened. "Putnam will get us the answer. Until we hear from him, go about your business as usual, Miss Duprie. You're in good hands with Special Agent Salters."

He tapped the roof and stepped back. Vanessa shifted into drive and pulled back into traffic. "Heck of a way to start your day," she said.

"Did this kind of thing happen to Eli and he never told me?" I wondered out loud.

"You'll be able to ask him yourself soon."

"If he remembers."

She didn't deny the possibility that he wouldn't. "We're discussing how to handle it when he can be questioned about that night. All four of us are going to want answers, but only one of us will ask the questions. I'm out of the equation, but Richon and Putnam are duking it out. It's fun to watch from the sidelines."

"How is your investigation coming?"

"Slowly. We know what was used as an accelerant but tracking down the culprit will be tough. My guess is that the fire here was set by a first timer who got his instructions off the internet. My counterpart up north is seeing the same thing."

We pulled into the parking lot at the office. "In fact, they've released the location. The house is available if you want to get repairs started."

I wouldn't be there to make sure it got done right. That hurt.

I hoped that was the end of the excitement for the day and longed for a moment of quiet to review the paperwork stacked on my desk. Nothing urgent, according to Darla, but I felt guilty ignoring it.

A notation about petty cash on Marty's spreadsheet made me curious. Where was it kept? I hadn't spotted any cash in Eli's office. Darla would know. I stood in her doorway and waited until she got off the phone. "Who's in charge of petty cash?"

"Me, pretty much." She opened her desk drawer to show me a banker's bag. "I use it for things like the occasional book of stamps, tips for deliveries, birthday cakes. I keep some here and the rest is in the safe."

"Where is it?"

She grinned. "In the corner. Over there. Disguised as a plant stand. No one ever gives it a second look."

She was right. With the long fern fronds dangling down its sides, I would have never guessed. "Do you have the key?"

"No key. It's a combination. That side is up against the wall. Eli usually hands me money from his wallet when I run low."

That didn't help me at all.

"What else does he keep in it?"

"His copyrights, trademarks, paperwork from when he started the company. Kris has copies, and he keeps copies in his safe-deposit box, but he likes keeping the originals here."

And maybe the top-secret documents Putnam was searching for. "Tell me if you need more cash. When Eli gets back, we can sort it out."

"I'm glad you're here, Harmony. I don't know what we would do without you."

It was sweet of her to say, but the truth was that I felt like a fraud. There wasn't a damn thing I could do to bring in new customers. What would happen if Eli's memory loss extended to his coding skills?

My mother would have told me I was borrowing trouble. My father would have congratulated me on preparing for the future. I'd never be as good as Eli, but it wouldn't hurt to have a basic idea of what he did. I had an office full of experts to ask for help in getting started.

Chapter 20

I was studying Marty's printouts when Kris knocked on the door. "It's go time."

She'd changed into a black suit with a pale blue shirt, not the multi-colored flowered one she'd worn to work.

"Go time? Go where?" I asked.

"The courthouse. Eli's father filed for an emergency injunction and his lawyer skipped the 'notifying the other party' portion of the process. A friend in the clerk's office clued me in. We have time to get there before the hearing starts."

"What should I bring?"

"Yourself. That's it. I have the documents we need." She raised the briefcase she held.

I pulled my purse out of the drawer and followed her. A part of me hoped it was a bad joke, that Rob wouldn't do this. In my heart, I knew better.

As we strode through the main room, Vanessa grabbed her jacket from her chair. That jacket. The blue one with the bright yellow letters 'ATF' on the back. Her holster and weapon were in her other hand as she charged out the door. "Where are we going?"

"Courthouse," Kris said, her face a thundercloud.

"Count me in. Whose car are we taking?"

We took Kris's, with me in the front with Kris, and Vanessa in the back. Kris used the quick trip to explain how the hearing would work. It was different than the criminal trials I'd taken part in. Nobody had to wait outside to be called as a witness. All I had to do was follow her lead.

The courthouse wasn't what I expected. It looked more like an old brick office building than anything judicial. Functional but boring. No marble pillars, no grand, sweeping staircase entrance, no gold dome on top. I'd have to research its history when I had the time.

Kris had her choice of empty parking spots. I guessed it was a slow day. Vanessa and I stashed our guns in the car's trunk before heading inside. The deputy in charge of security passed us through without changing his expression. It disappointed me he didn't react to Vanessa's jacket.

We sat in the last row of chairs in the courtroom. Further up, I recognized the back of Rob's head. Two men sat by him, one on either side. I figured one was Simon and the other the lawyer.

Five other men clustered around the judge's bench, the only furniture in the room with personality. The fine old wood was darkened by age, and the scrollwork appeared to have been carved, not glued on. The judge looked as old as the bench, with white hair and deep wrinkles in his dark amber-colored face. They were talking numbers. Numbers in the hundreds of thousands of dollars.

"Contract dispute," Kris whispered.

I nodded and was glad I had her to protect me. Well, protect the company, but for the moment, we were the same thing.

The conversation at the bench went nowhere for the longest time. The judge seemed as bored as I was. He broke into the discussion, requesting additional documentation. The men gathered up their papers, shook hands, and left.

That didn't seem normal to me, but if it worked for the participants, who was I to complain? Kris' phone pinged, and she checked the screen before shaking her head. "They sent the paperwork to the office for the hearing. They want to pretend to meet the court's requirements without actually fulfilling them. Wait here."

She went and held a quiet discussion with the deputy at the back of the courtroom. His only reaction was a slight nod, but Kris looked satisfied when she returned to her seat. In fact, I suspected she was eager for our case to get started.

The judge shuffled papers. The bailiff stood by the bench, hands loosely clasped. He had the art of waiting down to perfection.

The back door opened, and a lone man entered. He whispered to the deputy and took a chair next to Vanessa. He and Kris acknowledged each other. I wondered who he was and what he was doing there.

The judge passed a piece of paper to the bailiff who read it out loud. "In the case of Hennessey versus Shifter Technologies, Incorporated and Harmony Duprie," he said, "Will the parties approach the bench?"

I started to rise, but Kris laid her hand on my shoulder. I got the hint and waited while Rob, Simon and the lawyer took their places on the right-hand side of the courtroom. Then Kris stood, and I, Vanessa, and the other man followed her example. Vanessa slipped into the first row of seats behind the little railing that separated spectators from the front of the courtroom. Kris, the man I didn't know, and I took chairs at the table on the left side of the room.

Kris leaned in to whisper in my ear. "That's Clinton Essex, Eli's personal lawyer. He's the one who wrote up the other powers of attorney."

Rob talked to his lawyer, and he didn't sound happy. I stared straight ahead and ignored him. Finally, I could read the name on the judge's nameplate: Schemmer.

"Appearances for the record," the judge droned.

Rob's lawyer stood. "Pierre Kinder for the Plaintiff."

Then it was Kris's turn. "Kris O'Keefe, representing Shifter Technologies, Incorporated and Miss Harmony Duprie."

Clinton Essex also entered his appearance as representing Elijah Hennessey, owner of Shifter Technologies, Inc.

"No!" Rob shouted before Kinder glared at him.

Judge Schemmer raised an eyebrow but didn't comment. "Mr. Kinder, I've read your filing. Mr.

Hennessey, my sympathies on your son's condition. However, Mr. Kinder, I am confused by your lack of mention of the attorneys for the defendant."

I peeked at Kinder, but he didn't seem upset.

"Your Honor," he said, "Initial discussions with Miss O'Keefe and Miss Duprie didn't go well. I thought it best if we moved forward in a formal setting."

"I see," Schemmer said, in an even tone. "Miss O'Keefe?"

"I request that the motion for injunctive relief be dismissed, Your Honor. I've brought copies of the legal documents granting Miss Duprie full authority for Shifter Technologies if Mr. Elijah Hennessey cannot perform those duties. Mr. Hennessey, the father, was provided with copies on Monday of this week."

There was a shuffling noise behind us, but I didn't turn to look. I was trying to read the judge's face and getting nowhere. He tented his hands and leaned back in his chair.

Kris held up a stack of paperwork she'd retrieved from her briefcase. "I've brought copies for the court, Your Honor. Because of the late notification I received of this hearing, I was unable to file them in a timely fashion."

"Bailiff," the judge said in a monotone.

The deputy approached our table, and Kris handed him the legal documents. Then he gave them to the judge, who flipped through the sheets.

"What about you, Mr. Essex?" the judge asked.

"Several months ago, Mr. Elijah Hennessey requested documents be drawn up to give Miss

Duprie power of attorney in regard to medical decisions. After further discussion, he added legal and financial POA's, with similar conditions as to his health and state of mind. I've brought copies for the court."

The bailiff seemed amused by the process as he once again played mailman.

Schemmer glanced at the papers before leaning forward. "We've been joined by some distinguished visitors. Do either of you have an interest in this case?"

I turned to look. Putnam sat beside Vanessa.

She spoke first. "Special Agent Vanessa Salters, ATF."

Putnam came next. "Special Agent Rodney Putnam, DCSA."

The bailiff's mouth formed an 'O' but the judge remained unfazed. "Would either of you like to speak to this case as a friend of the court?" he asked.

Putnam stood. "Your Honor, Mr. Hennessey does business with several government agencies. I'm not at liberty to disclose the details. We are vetting Miss Duprie to be our contact until he can resume his duties. In addition, she is helping the agency with a matter of some urgency."

The judge nodded. "I assume you can't say more than that, but the fact that you are seated on the defendant's side of the courtroom is an indicator of the agency's current position?"

Putnam smiled. "Correct, Your Honor."

Rob ran his fingers over his head and whispered to his attorney.

"Moving along," Schemmer said. "Special Agent Salters, what does the ATF have to do with this matter?"

"Miss Duprie is a material witness in a case under ATF investigation involving property owned by Mr. Hennessey. We were made aware of a potential threat to her safety. Until it is resolved, I've been assigned to provide protection."

Schemmer's eyebrows lifted. "I have questions, but this is not the appropriate forum. Are we missing anyone?"

"The FHP is responsible for the investigation into Mr. Hennessey's incident. Miss Duprie has been of assistance to Sergeant Alex Richon, who is handling the case. He was unable to be present, but is available by phone, Your Honor," Vanessa said. "And Detective Timothy Horace of the Orlando PD is acting as a liaison of sorts. He wasn't able to clear his schedule to be here at such short notice."

"I see." Schemmer stared at me, and I looked back, making sure to blink. I didn't want to challenge his authority.

He turned his attention to the other side of the room. "Mr. Kinder, in light of the provided evidence, what justification do you or your client have to continue with this motion?"

Kinder and Rob held a whispered conference. Simon, his back turned to us, listened in. I tried but couldn't catch enough words to string a coherent sentence together.

"Your Honor," Kinder said. "My client's original concern stands. Miss Duprie is unqualified for the position and he wants nothing more than to ensure that when his son recovers, he'll have a job to go back to."

A job? Didn't Rob realize that Eli was the heart and soul of Shifter Technologies? No fancy MBA would understand that. Under the table, Kris put her hand on my knee to calm me down.

"Miss Duprie," Schemmer said, "we haven't heard from you yet. Not that you don't have plenty of people speaking for you. What are your qualifications, other than Mr. Hennessey's trust?"

Kris nodded, and I swallowed hard as I rose. "Your Honor, I hold a master's degree in Library Science with a minor in Library Administration. I have four years of experience as a research librarian and have worked as an independent researcher. This past year, I spent three months in a temporary position as Chief Librarian for the City of Oak Grove, while the lady holding the position was on family leave. I've been working with Eli—Mr. Hennessey—in the position of Director of Research for Shifter Technologies. In addition, I'm a consultant for the Oak Grove Chief of Police as a crimes statistician."

I thought I saw a small smile, but it disappeared. I swallowed again and kept going. "I've been assisting Eli—Mr. Hennessey—in developing new markets and expanding existing ones. My relationship with the other employees of Shifter Technologies allowed me to step in and make an almost seamless transition to support the company in Eli's temporary absence. I hope the court will allow me to continue on as I've started.

"Your Honor, I understand the concerns of Eli's father and family." That was as close as I would come to acknowledging Simon. "We all want the best for Eli. We just disagree on how to accomplish that. I urge the court to support Eli's—Mr. Hennessey's—clear wishes in this matter."

Schemmer did smile. "You didn't mention having a law degree, Miss Duprie."

I cocked my head. "Because I don't."

"You should reconsider your choice of professions. After Mr. Hennessey returns, of course. You'd make a good attorney." He banged his gavel on his desk. "In the matter of Hennessey versus Shifter Technologies, Incorporated and Miss Harmony Duprie, the petition is denied. Miss Duprie, good luck."

And one of the weights around my shoulders fell off.

I wanted to cheer. Maybe throw confetti. I did neither. "Thank you, Your Honor," I said in unison with Kris. We let Rob, Simon, and Kinder leave first. Simon shot me a dirty look on the way out. I responded with my iciest stare. I wouldn't be intimidated.

Chapter 21

Putnam walked with us to Kris's car. "I'm glad it worked out. I didn't want to pull out the big guns."

What was he talking about?

"I received information on Simon Hennessey. The company he works for is bankrupt. It'll close unless someone buys it and keeps it afloat."

I didn't even know what Simon did for a living.

"So," Vanessa said, "you think Simon cooked up the scheme to get some MBA to buy a failing business and keep his job on Hennessey's dime?"

My thoughts took it further. "You don't suppose he had something to do with running Eli off the road?"

"Gut reaction?" Putnam shook his head. "No. I was observing him in the courtroom. He doesn't have the balls to do it himself, or the money to hire someone competent enough."

"Have you made any headway in checking out the other employees?"

"We've eliminated a quarter of them. Progress is slow, and we're not finding anything out of the ordinary. Frankly, Miss Duprie, you're the biggest anomaly."

I wondered how deep he'd dug. I had a few things I'd rather not share. It seemed safer to switch topics. "By the way, I found out there's a safe in the office, used as a plant stand. I don't have the combination for it, and neither does Darla. Kris, did Eli tell you?"

"Nope. He's good at keeping secrets."

I rolled my eyes. "That's an understatement. Would a locksmith be able to open it?"

"Depends upon the manufacturer and model." Vanessa grinned. "I used to hang out with one. That was his standard answer."

"Are you still in touch with him?" Putnam asked.

Her grin got wider. "Nope. Ended up busting him. He used his skills in a side business of an illegal nature."

Would Jake be able to open the safe? The thought struck me out of the blue. I quickly locked it in a corner of my brain. The last thing he needed was to be drawn into this mess. He'd settled into the job in Cleveland, from everything he told me. The supposed expert jewel thief had become a bartender and was considering buying and renovating a house in the neighborhood near the bar. He'd jump right in to help Eli—they were cousins, after all—but I didn't want to destroy the life he was building.

I should call him and tell him about Eli anyway. Shoot, Eli and Jake were more like brothers than Eli and Simon.

"I might know someone," Kris said. "But what are you looking for?"

"Official paperwork," Putnam said. "That's all I can say. Miss Duprie has given us access to potential storage locations, but we haven't located it."

"I'll talk to my boss and see if we have any local contacts." Vanessa nudged Putnam with her elbow and jerked her head towards the courthouse. I turned to look… and wished I hadn't.

Rob and Simon were leaving the building with Kinder leading the way. In a move so smooth it seemed practiced, Vanessa and Putnam stood in front of me, pushing aside their jackets, so their weapons were accessible.

But Rob wasn't a threat. I'd expected to savor the rush of victory again, but a wave of sadness washed over me instead. His eyes on the ground and his shoulders slumped, he didn't glance in our direction. I wanted to give him a hug and tell him it would be okay.

I pushed through the barrier created by Vanessa and Putnam. "Thanks. They don't scare me."

Vanessa chuckled. "Didn't think so. We want to make sure they know who they are messing with. Not Hennessey's father, but the brother. We don't trust him."

Rob and company got the message. Kinder pivoted and led them away from us. Simon couldn't resist and shot us a double middle-finger salute before hustling to catch up with his father.

"Real mature." I let go of the breath I'd been holding while steeling myself for an argument I didn't want.

"We'll keep an eye on him," Putnam straightened

his jacket. "Make sure no one bribes him to get access to Hennessey."

"Are you trying to scare me or reassure me? Is that even possible?"

Putnam lifted an eyebrow. "In my line of work, Miss Duprie, anything is possible."

The stairs to the ICU seemed longer than normal as I stopped at each landing to peer upward, checking that no one waited to intercept Vanessa and me. I was beginning to understand why she and Putnam were so protective. If someone got to me, I could be used as a tool to get to Eli.

Who could be behind all of this?

I left Vanessa behind in the waiting room to check in with the nurse. She was the same one as last night. Short black hair, tiny earrings. Since her sweater covered her nametag again, I named her 'Sweater' in my head.

"He stayed awake for half an hour while his mother visited," she said "While he still didn't recognize her, at least he talked to her. He started on a liquid diet today, which he complained about, but finished the soup and applesauce. The doctor is considering moving him out of ICU."

That was the best news I'd had in weeks. Except I'd have to worry about how to protect Eli when the move happened. Before settling into the visitor's chair, I shot off a text to Vanessa. She could work with her friend in security to develop a plan.

I resumed reading where I'd left off the previous night. Two pages in, the back of my neck tingled, a sure sign I was being watched. When I looked up, Eli's eyes were open.

"Hey, Sweetie." I stood and leaned over to plant a soft kiss on his mouth.

He blinked and smiled. The feeding tube was gone, but red marks lingered on his face from the tape that had held it in place. Why hadn't the nurse mentioned the change?

He licked his lips, preparing to talk. "Do it again."

"Do what?"

He tried to smile. "Kiss me."

"No problem." I leaned over and we touched lips. His were chapped and rough, but it didn't matter. His hand pushed against the back of my head and deepened the contact.

No nurse interrupted us, but I didn't want to spend the entire time kissing him. Well, I did, but I wanted to talk to him, too.

Richon had requested that I not ask Eli about the accident, so I wouldn't influence Eli's memories. I didn't want to worry him by discussing work. That left the weather. And sports. And the news, which I censored.

But he had questions of his own. "How long have I been here?"

"It's been a week." A small white lie. No mention of the days he'd been lost.

He winced. "I don't remember what happened."

I crafted my answer with care. "You have a brain injury. It'll take time for it to heal."

"That's what the nurses say, but I don't trust them." His eyes closed, but he wasn't asleep. I waited.

"There's lots I'm missing," he said. "The lady who says she's my mother. She looks familiar, but I can't get the full picture. It makes me feel bad." He frowned. "And my dad tells me I should pretend to make her happy."

"Do you remember your father?"

He shook his head and winced again, as if the movement hurt. I massaged his shoulder with light strokes to ease the pain. "No," he answered. "But it's easier to say I do than fight with him."

I made a mental note to discuss the situation with the nurse. I didn't want Rob to interfere with the healing process.

"But I recognize you." Eli squeezed my hand. "You're my safe spot. Why aren't you here all the time?"

How did I explain to him I was running his company? "What do you do for a living?"

He scrunched his eyebrows and furrows formed on his forehead. "I get flashes of computers. And numbers. But I don't think I'm an accountant."

"You code software." Or did. Would it come back to him?

"Huh. So, I'm smart?"

"You're a freakin' genius."

"You're just saying that because you love me." His eyes closed. "Sleepy. But I don't want to sleep. I want to stay awake and talk to you."

"Sleep is how you'll heal."

"That's what the nurse said. Will you stay with me? I don't want to be alone." His voice trembled.

Was he scared? Another fissure formed in my heart. "I'll stay as long as they let me. And come back tomorrow. Deal?"

"Deal. Can I get a goodnight kiss?" His eyes popped open, and he grinned.

Eli was back. Or at least a part of him I knew well. The parts he'd hidden from me had me worried.

On the way out, Sweater stopped me. "I forgot to mention it to his mother," she said. "when they move your friend out of ICU, he'll be more comfortable if he has shorts or sweatpants. When he starts physical therapy, he won't have to worry about covering up."

"What happened to the clothes he was wearing when he was brought in? I should take them with me and wash them." What was left of them. I assumed they'd had to cut his shirt off to work on him in the ER.

"His mother took them, according to the notes."

They were in good hands. "Thanks," I said, then headed to the waiting room to meet up with Vanessa.

Vanessa laughed as I poured a glass of water on the geraniums by the front door. "I count on the rain to keep them alive. I don't have a green thumb."

"Tomorrow, I want to go shopping. We can pick

out some hanging baskets." I poked at the edge of the porch's roof. The wood was solid. There was even a hole to use for the hanger.

"Settling in?"

Is that what I was doing? I didn't plan to stay for long. Once we figured out who'd attacked Eli, there'd be no reason for me to remain. "Consider it a hostess gift."

"You're funny. A hostess gift. You're paying rent, remember? Do you need help taking the cover off your car?"

Because she had a meeting, we were driving both cars. I didn't want to be without a vehicle. Cleaning the garage to make room for Dolores was on tomorrow's agenda. One more thing to stop worrying about.

And while I understood Vanessa's concern, I was tired of being watched. If things worked out, I'd sneak out of the office and take some time for myself. I deserved it.

The stack of morning paperwork Darla placed on my desk seemed unusually slim. "Are we missing something?" I asked.

"Nope." She grinned. "It's just an easy day. Eli used them to visit with the staff. Especially the support folks. That way he got to hear first-hand about the customers' issues."

I only knew the basics of the software. How could I help the pros?

Darla read the panic on my face. "You don't have to do everything the way Eli does. You need to find your own style."

Wise words. She was right. I'd been trying so hard to fill in for Eli, I'd forgotten my experience. What would I do if I had free time at the library? Shelve books. One of the most unappreciated jobs, but one of the most important. But with no books to put away, I had to come up with something different.

Or I could dream of Eli making a miraculous recovery and returning to work on Monday. But that only happened in bad books.

At lunchtime, I snuck out the back door. By the time I walked around the building and to Dolores, Lando was waiting for me. Darla must have ratted me out.

He smirked. "Going somewhere?"

There was no sense in lying. "A department store. Eli needs a few things. And then to check out his house."

"I drop by the house every day. Even the guys keeping surveillance on it don't bother me anymore. But we can go if it makes you feel better."

"It will."

He waved at a cop going by as we took the cover off Dolores. "We never used to see the police," he said. "Quiet neighborhood, small business, no one causing any trouble. Now, it's three, four times a day."

"Is that a problem?"

"Nope. Just a curiosity." He put a hand on Dolores' hood. "Can I drive? Please?"

No one but me drove Dolores. Except Eli. I considered making an exception as a thank you. One time. But the prickle at the back of my neck started and decided for me. "After this is over, maybe. Before I go home, ask me again."

"That's cool. But can I tell you a secret? We enjoy having you here and hope you stay."

"Everybody?" I teased as I pulled into the street, watching for the familiar silver pickup. There was a serious intent behind the question.

"Hell," he said. "Office gossip says even Kris likes you after yesterday. And she doesn't like anyone. Except Eli. And Darla." He ran his hand across the top of his head. "I've always thought she had a crush on Eli, and who doesn't like Darla?"

Someone who didn't like me. Or Eli.

Chapter 22

I eyed the racks of athletic clothing and realized I didn't know what size Eli needed. He'd lost enough weight that his old clothes wouldn't fit.

But sweatpants had adjustable waistbands. I picked out several pair, along with some shorts. And socks. And boxer briefs. I thought they might be more comfortable than what he usually wore.

I was overdoing it. Eli had an excellent wardrobe, and I'd never needed to buy him clothes. But I liked it.

Lando pretended to browse the dress shirts, but his attention was on me. That didn't bother me, but the man on the other side of the men's department, near the nightwear, did.

He fit in perfectly with the other customers. Middle-aged, slightly bald, with a bit of a beer belly. What sent the red flags flying was that every time I glanced in his direction, he was staring at me.

It wasn't my imagination, either. I switched to a spot that put Lando between me and him. In a few minutes, he'd moved too, so I was in full view again. Coincidence? Not in my book.

I'd finished my shopping, anyway, and headed for the checkout. Lando trailed behind me.

"You have an admirer," he said.

"You mean my tail?" I jerked my chin in his direction. "He's not very good at hiding."

"Not him." Lando cocked his head. "Don't peek. Over in shoes. Had me doubting myself. But he's keeping an eye on you."

I fought the urge to turn and stare. Were they double-teaming me now? I forced a smile to my face as the saleslady rang up my items and took too long to bag them.

"It's time to check Dolores for bugs again. I don't have a scorecard to identify the good guys from the bad," I told Lando as we headed for the exit. "It's irritating. I'd like to figure out who they're with."

"What makes you assume they're together? What if two different organizations are in competition? Is there a way to make them confront each other?" He rubbed his hands. "We could have fun watching the sparks fly."

"I like it. Now, how to make it happen? Did they both follow us?" I asked as Lando held the door open.

"Yep. And they figured out they're both following you. Shoe guy sent clothes guy the stink-eye."

We reached the sidewalk, and I handed Lando my bags. "I'm going to fake looking for something in my purse. Tell me what happens."

"Clothes guy stopped inside. Shoe guy has

disappeared. Guess he didn't like having a rival. Fun game, eh?"

Except it wasn't a game. "I'm tired of it, Lando. I haven't been given the rules and I don't know how to win."

"I've been doing my own research," Lando said as we walked towards Dolores. "making sure all these agents are who they say they are. They checked out, but they aren't playing by the rules, either."

"And they admit it. Someone is pulling the strings and they won't say who." I bent over as if looking at something on the ground. "You recognize the man three cars down from Dolores? By the yellow Jeep?"

"Shoe guy. He must have left by another door."

Shoe guy was average height, average build, average everything. The kind of man who dissolved into the background unless you were looking for him. A professional.

But not professional enough, because Lando had spotted him. It reminded me of the time I'd been tailed in D.C. The FBI had claimed the men following me had been hired by Sallis, but I'd never bought their story.

Which one bothered me more? The pro was more dangerous but understood his boundaries. The amateur was more likely to make a mistake. Someone in between spelled trouble.

I opened Dolores' trunk and Lando put the bags inside. My options were limited. I chose the least logical.

"Let's go have a conversation with Mr. Shoe Guy." With a soft thunk, I closed the trunk. I adjusted my purse on my shoulder and made sure Betsy was on top of everything else. "Are you with me?"

Lando's smile lit his face. "Can I tackle him if he pulls anything funny?"

I should have told him no. I was the one with the gun and didn't want him to get hurt. "Use your best judgment." Something I was guilty of ignoring. But I brought up an image of Eli as I'd first seen him in the emergency room to light my fire.

Mr. Shoe Guy saw us coming and ducked behind a green pickup with a 'for sale' sign in the back window. By the time we reached his hiding spot, he'd vanished. Like a wind-blown baby spider, he'd floated away, leaving no trace.

Lando and I looked. And searched. And hunted. Around cars, under cars, between cars. "Now what?" he asked when we met back at Dolores.

I blinked in the overly bright noonday sun. "We go to Eli's as planned. And keep an eye on the mirrors the whole way. With any luck, the fact that we got a look at him will scare him off." Good words, but I didn't believe them, not for a second. But I had to protect Lando. He didn't have a military background like Eli. His experience was all fun and games on the computer.

"I don't like it," Vanessa said when I filled her in on the excitement. "Mixing amateurs and professionals is a recipe for trouble. Present company not excepted." Worry darkened her eyes.

"I've been playing by the rules. Not that it's helping." I stroked the necklace holding Eli's dog tags. "It's been over a week, and not one of you has a lead."

It might be time to go rogue. But I didn't have a place to start. Orlando was too big, and I didn't know a tourist trap bar from an outlaw underground haven from a front for drug sales.

"That's not true." Vanessa scooted backwards in her chair and pushed my office door shut. "Putnam messaged that they got their hands on footage that appears to show Hennessey's car. The video is being analyzed to identify the other cars caught on camera at the same time. They're hoping to find potential witnesses."

It was a start. "Are they checking with gas stations and fast-food restaurants for security tapes from the night of the incident?"

"Yes, but it's a long process. We're talking upwards of a hundred establishments."

I wasn't in Oak Grove anymore, where a quick count gave me a total of seven shops at the main exit to the interstate.

"Can I help?" In what spare time, I couldn't say.

"FHP has it covered. They've put a small task force on the project."

"Pressure from above?" I asked.

"Apparently." Vanessa huffed. "We haven't been able to connect the dots and figure out who's responsible. We're all good at what we do, so can you imagine how frustrating that is?"

"Yes. I've been there a few times myself. Now

consider being in a spot like that without an organization backing you up."

"You've got three agencies helping."

Not really. They were working for themselves. If they suspected I had anything to do with Eli's accident, they'd bust me in a heartbeat. Vanessa was there as much to monitor me as to protect me, and I wouldn't forget it.

"By the way," she continued. "We've lined up a locksmith to look at the safe. He'll come on Monday if that works for you."

"Monday's our busiest day," I told her, "but I'll make it happen."

I wasn't sure what to expect when I arrived at the hospital. Tillie had sent a message telling me how long Eli had been awake and how he'd remembered her. And that they were moving him to a different room if everything went well overnight. I passed on the word about buying him clothes. We could stay in friendly communication, even if Rob disapproved of me.

Vanessa stuck close until I reached the ICU. Her friend the security guard trailed behind. Overkill, because no one glanced my way. I ignored how uncomfortable the attention made me because nothing would deter me from my goal.

I waved to the nurse at the desk and headed toward Eli's room. The lights were dimmed, and he was asleep. Same story, different day. I had hoped but didn't expect anything had changed.

But it was different. He was sleeping this time, not in a coma. If I read to him, I'd disturb his rest. And I felt guilty reading to myself and not sharing it with him. Instead, I pulled out my phone. There were people I hadn't been in touch with for too long. They'd have to settle for texts, but that was better than nothing.

The silly cat videos Sarah sent started a case of the giggles. I tried to keep quiet, but when a kitten totally messed up a jump, it became a lost cause.

"Nobody laughs around here," Eli said. "I miss hearing it."

"Hey, Sweetie, I didn't mean to wake you. How did your day go?" Lame, but it was a way to get him talking.

"At least I didn't sleep the whole time. But you know what would make it better?" He reached up to stroke my cheek.

I had an inkling. "What?"

"A hug and a kiss from my favorite person."

"If you're referring to me, I can make that happen."

I leaned down, and his arm wrapped around me, drawing me closer. He felt stronger, although nowhere near his previous strength. Then I stopped thinking and concentrated on doing.

"So, what were you laughing about?" he asked when we eventually finished saying hi.

"Kittens. Sarah sent a link to a cute video."

"Have I met Sarah?"

"Yes. She's one of my best friends. She sells real estate." I waited for a flicker of recognition in his eyes, but none came. "Short brown hair, about my height, she's dating Freddie. Does any of that sound familiar?"

He didn't answer for a long time. "There's so much that's out of reach. Nurses keep asking me who I am, where I am, and who they are."

"And you tell them what?"

His eyes glittered from the sudden moisture that formed in them. "I'm in the hospital, but I don't know why. I can't remember getting hurt. And the people who come to see me..." He paused. "I'm beginning to recognize the nurses, but the lady who says she's my mother... I don't know her, and I should. It makes me feel guilty, so I call her Mom to make her happy. You're the only one I remember."

"What's my name?" I was treading in dangerous territory.

"You're Buttercup. Something about yellow flowers, but I haven't found all the pieces yet."

"What's my name?" I asked again.

He squeezed his eyes closed. "Give me a minute. It's on the tip of my tongue. I almost found it earlier today. Can I get a hint?"

What was the right way to handle it? Make him figure it out?

"Kiss me again," Eli demanded. "That will help me grab the memories."

I didn't believe my lips were magic, but I'd play along. I touched my mouth to his and waited. Nothing.

"Again. More."

I obeyed. His eyes fluttered open and he grinned. "Harmony. Harmony. Harmony Duprie. Internet researcher extraordinaire."

Had he known it all along and played me for a kiss? It's not like I'd turn him down if he asked. But he hadn't mentioned that I worked for him. That bothered me.

"Do you remember your name?"

His grin turned to a frown. "Eli fits. But there's more. Why does the name Matt keep popping into my brain?"

"Your given name is Matthew Elijah. You told me you went by Matt until you got to high school, when you decided you liked Eli better."

He picked up the controller and adjusted the height of the backrest to a sitting position. "Which do you like?"

"You've always been Eli to me." Not quite true, but close enough to count. Before I fell in love with him, I'd called him Elijah.

"If you like it, I'll keep it."

It needed to be his decision, not mine. But how to tell him that? I chickened out and switched the subject. "Is there anyone else you remember?"

The wrinkles in his forehead deepened. "Tall guy. On the scrawny side. But his hair is a different color every time I picture him. Sometimes it's brown, sometimes blue, and then it's bright red. In a Mohawk. Who is that?"

"That would be Lando. He switches his hair color all the time. Or used to, anyway. Lately he's been staying with blue. Good guy."

"Then why hasn't he come to see me? No one has come to visit. Don't I have any friends?"

The pain in his voice stung, and I rushed to soothe it. "The doctors limited the number of visitors. Your parents and I are it. Once you move out of intensive care, the restrictions will loosen." I hoped. And if I needed to throw my weight around to make it happen, I would. "Lando asks about you every day."

"Am I that hurt?"

It was the question I'd been dreading. I reached up and rearranged his pillow to hide the pain in my eyes. "What have the doctors and nurses told you?"

"They keep talking about what good progress I'm making and avoid answering. Will you tell me? I trust you."

I shoved back the panic that rose. Would he be able to handle the truth? "Put the pieces together. You're in the hospital in intensive care. Your memory is iffy. There are machines monitoring you every minute and you have how many IVs? How bad do you think you were?"

"Did I die?"

The air rushed from my lungs and it was my turn to fight unbidden tears. "No. You were close but got rescued in time."

"What do you know about the accident? I remember worrying about you. But why? Tell me what happened."

"I can't. I wasn't there. You need to talk to the FHP first. I don't want to give you a false memory."

"You don't understand. If I don't get it out right now, I'm afraid it'll slip away from me. And the next time I'm asked about it, the information will be gone." He ran his hand across his head. "Why is my hair so short?"

"They shaved you to clean the cuts. Now, about what happened. Hold that thought. I'll be right back."

I dashed to the nurses' station. "Can you call security and ask them to bring Special Agent Salters to Eli's room? He wants to talk about his accident, and I'd like a witness."

She didn't seem fazed by my request and reached for the phone. "I'll handle it."

Chapter 23

Eli's eyes were shut when I returned to his room, I wondered if I'd missed our opportunity. "Eli?" I whispered tentatively.

"Where did you go?"

"I'll explain later." I turned on the voice recorder app on my phone and placed it near his head. I tried to recollect the words the cops had used when they questioned me a few years ago on drug trafficking charges, but I'd been too nervous to pay close attention. I'd have to wing it.

"For the record, this is Harmony Duprie and Eli Hennessey. Eli, what do you remember about the night of the accident?"

He scowled. "Is this a game?"

"I'm an unreliable witness. This way no one can say I put words in your mouth."

"You wouldn't do that, Buttercup."

"Not on purpose. This is to protect both of us." The old Eli would have understood. This Eli seemed unsure but willing to let me take charge. I wondered if the personality change was permanent.

He licked his lips, a sure sign he was thinking. "I talked to you. But you weren't here. You were home. But not my home. I can't talk you into moving here. With me. But you're here now. I like having you here."

I decided not to interrupt his rambling. If he wandered back to the topic of the accident, it would be more believable.

"I got another call after we talked." He squeezed my hand. "It's all mixed up. The number was yours, but a man called. You didn't let someone else use your phone, did you?"

A whispered cough alerted me to a new arrival. With the barest nod of my head, I acknowledged Vanessa's presence. Eli didn't seem to notice.

"Then what happened?" I asked.

"I was driving. I shouldn't have been. But I had to rescue you. But you didn't need rescuing. It doesn't make sense." Eli's voice rose a few notches, and I stroked his cheek to calm the panic.

He fell silent, and I checked the app to make sure it was still recording.

"I was driving. Headed East. To the Cape, maybe? I don't understand why I needed to go there in the middle of the night. I stopped to get gas." He spoke haltingly, like he was pulling the words from under a boulder.

"Did you talk to anyone?"

"At the gas station? No. Yes. A guy getting gas at another pump. He came over to check out my car.

Said he owned one back in the day. Only his was green. Or red. I'm not sure."

"What color was his car? The one at the other pump?"

"Blue? Green? No, red. Because later he was chasing me. I should have been able to out-maneuver him. But the steering felt funny. The car wasn't handling right. Like a tire went bad."

Vanessa coughed again and I ignored her. Unless he'd run over something in the road, there wasn't a reason for a tire to go bad. Had it been vandalized?

"Do you remember what the man at the gas station looked like?"

Eli frowned. "No. He's a blurred face. No beard, no mustache. Nothing special. No glasses. Just a face," he repeated.

I chose not to push him. I'd leave that to the professionals. "Then what happened?"

He licked his lips and closed his eyes. "I have flashes. Scraping against bushes. Water in front of me. Trying to get my seatbelt off. Can't find my phone. Where is everyone? Shouldn't the police be here? It's sunny, but I can't open my eyes.

"It hurts. Everything hurts. Help me. Please. Somebody help me."

Pain radiated from his cry. He'd gotten lost in the agony of his nightmare.

I couldn't take it. "Eli. I'm here. You're safe. Everything's going to be okay. Come back to me, Eli."

His eyes popped open, and he sat upright. "Shit, what happened?"

"You went too deep into your memories and weren't ready for them." It was the best explanation I could come up with.

His eyes darted around the room. "Who's that?" he asked, focusing on Vanessa.

We hadn't planned for this. I didn't know how to respond. But Vanessa came to the rescue, striding forward with her right hand extended.

"I'm Vanessa Salters, part of the team investigating the incident. Pleased to finally meet you, Mr. Hennessey. Harmony and I bumped into each other earlier, so she knew I was here and had the presence of mind to reach out when you wanted to talk."

She was slick and earned a couple of notches in my assessment. No mention of her title or agency. No lies, just not the whole truth so as not to alarm Eli.

"As long as she was around, I thought it would be a good idea to have an official witness to my recording," I explained as they shook hands. Eli seemed to do it because he couldn't avoid it.

"You'll send me a copy?" Vanessa asked, as if I hadn't already planned to.

"Of course."

Eli eased back on his bed, wincing as he moved unused muscles. Weariness flooded his face. "Did I tell you everything you need?"

Vanessa avoided the whole truth again. "You confirmed a few leads we were already following. And gave us a few more. Thank you for your assistance. Now, I'm going to borrow Harmony for a minute or two. She'll be right back."

Eli nodded and closed his eyes. I followed Vanessa into the hallway. She put her hands on her hips and faced me, making sure I stood where Eli could see me if he tried.

"Good work in there," she said. "I'll pass along the recording to Richon as soon as you get it to me."

Was that a hint? "Nag, nag," I muttered as I scrolled through my contacts for her number. I attached the recording to a text and hit send.

"When Hennessey slipped into that last memory, I thought you would lose it and I was planning my intervention. But you held it together. That's impressive."

I didn't know whether to take her at face value and was too drained to expend any energy on figuring it out. "It was pure instinct."

"Got it. Now, get back in there and take care of your friend. I'll see you later."

Eli's breathing was steady, almost a snore, when I returned to his room. The trauma of his memories must have been too much, and I figured he'd sleep for the rest of the night. Still, I settled by his bed and placed my hand on his.

To my surprise, his eyes fluttered open. "You came back."

"Of course I did. I'll always come back to you." Or he would come to me, but that was a discussion for another place and another time.

The smile that came to his face was faint, but there. "I like that. And as much as I love having you here, I think I'm going to take a nap. I'm worn out."

"Go ahead. Tomorrow is Saturday, so I'll be able to come earlier."

He yawned. "Can I have a goodnight kiss?"

There was only one acceptable answer.

"Do you ever sleep in?" Vanessa grumbled as she emerged from her bedroom around eight.

"The coffee is fresh." I rotated the cup in my hands and stared at the backyard, plotting its future. Sarah was on the job, finding the owner of the house and the lot next door. Although I had no plans to stay here, the house cried for a lot of tender loving care and I knew the person to make it happen: Me. In what spare time, I hadn't figured out.

"What are your plans for the day?" Vanessa sat across from me, avoiding the papers I'd piled there.

I stacked them neatly to give her some room. "I'm waiting to hear from Tillie if they move Eli today. Something about a special unit where he can receive intensive therapy. In the meantime, I'll hit up a grocery store for fresh fruit. Find a laundromat. And are we going to work on the garage today? Parking Dolores in the driveway, even covered, makes me nervous."

"It's in the plans for this afternoon. And didn't I tell you? There's a washer and dryer in the garage. The guys use it on Sundays, we get Saturdays. The rest of the week is first come, first served."

One less thing I had to worry about. I could multi-task as I did laundry. "Do you want to go first?"

"Naw, it'll take me a bit to wake up. It's all yours. My shelf is the lower one above the washer if you need soap."

I made a mental note to buy a clothes basket and detergent. And another note to figure out how to get my clothes from Eli's house in Oak Grove and get them cleaned. I hated to ask Joe and Luke to do more than they already were, overseeing the insurance adjusters and contracts for the repairs.

"I won't be following a routine, so you won't need to shadow me all day."

Vanessa chuckled into her cup. "That's not the way this works. You can't ditch me that easily."

Good thing she didn't know about the short walk I'd taken around the neighborhood earlier.

❋ ❋ ❋

"I don't like it," Vanessa said. She stood in the hallway at the hospital, one hand on her hip and her head cocked as she studied our surroundings. "There's no way to secure the area. Anyone can wander through here."

We stood far enough away from Eli's new room that he couldn't overhear us. All of his attention was on Tillie anyway, as she fussed with his covers and the window shades.

"He's listed as private, so no one knows he's here," I said.

"Yes, but unless the door is kept closed all the

time, anyone walking down the hall can look in and see him. What if a nosy reporter strolls by and recognizes him?"

Eli's face, while gaunt, looked more and more like what it should every day. I could understand her concern. "What do you want to do about it? We don't want to interfere with his treatment."

She rubbed the back of her neck. "I'll talk to hospital security. They must have handled cases like this before."

"I'll leave it up to you to figure out. Right now, I need to get Eli's mother to relax before she drives him up a wall. The stress she's creating won't do him any good."

Easier said than done. All her pent-up mothering instincts were hunting for an outlet. He needed a nap, but she wasn't giving him a chance to rest.

After she fluffed his pillow for the umpteenth time, I intervened. "It's good, Tillie. Why don't you head down to the cafeteria and get something to snack on? You deserve a break."

"But Eli…"

"I'll take care of him until you get back. Go." I shooed her away.

The nurse—this one named Maria—chuckled as she came into the room. "Thanks. I was about ready to make her leave myself. I'll make sure the doctor orders no visitors when Mr. Hennessey's therapists are with him."

"What kind of therapy are you talking about?"

"Physical therapy to start. Both major muscles and fine movement. Then there will be a train of experts to evaluate what else he needs. That will help us suggest a proper facility for long-term rehabilitation."

"I can hear you," Eli growled.

Maria grinned. "At least his speech wasn't affected."

I plastered a smile on my face while my heart sank. I'd figured Eli would be back to his old self in two or three weeks. It looked like I wouldn't be going home for a long time.

"Then there's occupational therapy," Maria continued. "What's your job, Mr. Hennessey? Or do you want to be called Eli? We'll be seeing a lot of each other."

Was she flirting with him? Then she winked at me and I got the message. It was part of her bedside manner.

"Eli is fine," he answered.

I wouldn't have to worry about him reverting to Matt. I waited to see if he'd volunteer information about his company without prompting. The question hung in the air, like a balloon losing its helium and slowly falling.

Maria typed her notes into the computer. "We can discuss it later. But you have a big decision to make. Do you want beef or chicken broth for lunch?"

Chapter 24

Eli was in good hands. I slipped into the hall, propped myself against the wall, and studied the carpet and my options. My remaining hope that he'd make a quick recovery, and I'd be able to return to Oak Grove floated away. Like a bee in a spider's web, I was stuck.

A pair of athletic shoes stopped in front of me, and I looked up into Vanessa's face.

"Security is handling it," she said. "It appears the floor you are standing on needs sudden, urgent repairs. Construction is slated around Hennessey's room. Assigned staff will be allowed through the barriers, but visitors will have to go the long way around."

I studied the little Hispanic woman strolling by. Was she an international assassin? And the tall, gray-haired man who trailed behind her—was he a retired CIA agent providing extra security? Barriers wouldn't stop either of them, but if Vanessa was satisfied, I'd accept her professional judgment.

"They'll add extra walk-throughs on this floor," Vanessa continued, "to keep an eye on things."

Was she trying to convince me or herself?

Maria came out of the room. "The move wore him out and he's asleep. Why don't you take a break?"

I hated to leave him, but I had a list of things to do. And Tillie would be back to keep him company.

❁ ❁ ❁

"Vanessa," I said.

"Got it." She leaned forward to get a view through the side mirror. "Black sedan, three cars back."

We were on our way to the hospital. We'd made a start on cleaning the garage, and my laundry was finished. I'd bought enough groceries for the week. Tomorrow would be for cooking and filling the freezer.

"Do you want me to ditch it?" I feathered the gas pedal, testing Dolores' reaction. Perfect, as always.

"The safe option is to ignore it. They know where we are going."

Or was this a new player? I turned the radio to a rock station. Some old-fashioned head-banging hair band. The music matched my mood. "Let's see how serious they are."

I braked hard to make a sudden right-hand turn. The silver pickup behind us squealed its tires but stayed with us. The sedan had enough time to react and followed in our tracks.

They were serious. "Want to play?" I asked Vanessa. "It's a good way to relieve stress."

Vanessa grinned. "I'd like to see what you and this car can do."

That was the encouragement I needed. "Place your bet. Which one do we lose first?"

"The truck. They aren't that good."

I plotted my move. The interstate called my name. The closest on-ramp was a mile away. With all the traffic on the street, I played nice. No lane changes, no sudden turns. If nothing else, I'd lure them into complacency.

My target was past the next set of traffic lights. If I timed things right, I'd be able to use that in my escape. What I hoped for was the tail end of a yellow signal. What I got was pure green. No help at all.

I waited until the last possible second, crossed every solid white line imaginable, and zoomed up the ramp. The silver truck wasn't nimble enough to follow. The black sedan should have had time to react but didn't.

Solo, I merged into a gap in the traffic. Adrenalin pumped through my veins. I had no outlet. "Did I misread the situation?" I asked, stepping on the gas pedal to make a smooth transition into the next lane.

Vanessa let go of the dash. "I read it the same way. It's not paranoia if someone is out to get you."

"Then why didn't they follow?"

"Bad driver? The car wouldn't handle it? They got called off?" She shrugged. "We don't know who they were, so we'll never get the answer."

"There are lots of things we don't know, and I don't like it. It's been a week and your agency hasn't made any progress on the fires. And you're supposed to be the best. Putnam has disappeared without an update on the background checks. And what's up with Richon? At least the mountain showed up when we needed him."

She studied her fingernails. "You realize I can't tell you everything."

I found an open spot in the fast lane and encouraged Dolores to pick up speed. "I get that. But you aren't telling me anything. That whole story about diplomatic immunity is bogus. Whoever it was realized they'd been spotted and were ordered to back off."

It was a shot in the dark, but the thin line formed by Vanessa's lips told me I'd hit pay dirt. Her silence spoke volumes.

"Message received." We flashed by the exit to the office and I kept going. "But at some point, you'll have to trust me. It works both ways. I've done everything I can to cooperate and I'm still being treated as a suspect."

"Where are we going?" Vanessa's voice rose a note or two as we flashed by another exit.

I leaned forward and looked for the sun. "East, apparently. Daytona. Northeast, technically, Dolores needs a workout."

As my foot fluttered on the gas pedal, I wondered how far Vanessa's law enforcement powers went. Could she arrest me for a traffic violation? Today wasn't the day to test her tolerance, so I'd stay a mile or two above the speed limit. Most of the time.

The miles flew by, and I switched the station to one that played soundtracks from movies. Not my normal choice, but it filled the void in the conversation. I could out-silence Vanessa any day of the week. She should be glad I didn't torture her by singing along.

As we approached the Deltona exit, about twenty-five miles before Daytona, I decided the fun was over. If we turned around now, I'd still have plenty of time to spend with Eli. The drive had done me good, and I'd almost been able to forget my worries.

I slowed, took the exit, turned under the interstate, and headed up the onramp on the other side. Vanessa didn't question what I was doing, still giving me the silent treatment. It would get uncomfortable if we didn't break the stalemate before we got home.

I'd reached cruising speed when I spotted them. Vanessa saw them, too. On the opposite side of the road. Two black sedans.

"Shit," she said.

"Who are they?"

She bit her bottom lip.

"So, who am I going to piss off when I remove their tracker?" I asked.

"You won't find a bug." Her mouth quirked. "No matter how hard you look."

The mile markers showed our progress, but my mind was going nowhere. The GPS wasn't attached to Dolores, or on me. I'd been extra careful with my purse and checking my clothes each morning. Unless Vanessa sneaked into my room when I wasn't paying attention?

Or…

"It's you, isn't it? You're wired. You've been

pretending to protect me when what you're doing is trying to find evidence against me." A sudden rage engulfed me. "I'll move out tonight. Unless you plan to arrest me on some bogus charge first. You can keep the rent."

I adjusted the rearview mirror to get a better long-range view of the cars behind us. She'd betrayed me when I thought we'd had a chance of being real friends. And she'd done it when I needed a friend the most. "Who are you answering to, Special Agent Salters?"

With a push on the gas pedal, I let Dolores fly. The sooner I retrieved my clothes from her house, the better. There were plenty of hotels to stay at until I found a new place to live.

Vanessa sucked in a breath as we blew past a string of cars in the right lane. "Slow down. I'm not wired. There's a tracker app on my phone. That's all."

I didn't ease off the pedal. "Who has access to it?"

"My boss."

"And?"

"Richon."

"And?" I glanced at her. Under her Florida tan, her face had paled. I pushed Dolores to go faster. "And?"

"Putnam and his agency. Will you slow the fuck down?"

I did better. It was a gift from the heavens. A spot with no traffic. And a paved strip between the two sides of the interstate for law enforcement use only.

I slammed on the brakes—

Feathered the clutch—
Shifted down—
Cranked the steering wheel—

I ended up facing the opposite direction. The perfect bootlegger's 180. My favorite maneuver.

I didn't have time to check Vanessa's reaction. She didn't scream. I gave her points for that. But the soft string of curse words that emanated from her side of the car was the satisfaction I craved. I fed Dolores enough gas to get to the pull-through and watched in my mirror as the black sedans screamed by.

It took thirty seconds until I spotted a break in the traffic and joined the flow at a more leisurely pace. I needed to find a back road for the return to Orlando. The Highway Patrol would be on alert, and I doubted Vanessa could pry me out of the fix I'd gotten myself into. The adrenalin rush was over, and I needed to get back to her house.

"Is this the game you want to play?" I asked her. "Because I have more tricks up my sleeve. Or maybe you and your cohorts can give me some respect." I didn't hide the edge in my voice.

"You could have killed us," she hissed. "Along with people who have nothing to do with this."

"I know my car and her capabilities. And my skill level." I'd turned into a brick of ice. No feelings. "I studied the variables and made an educated assessment."

"You're crazy."

"I can be."

We'd reached the Deltona exit again, and I took it, but then followed the road towards town. If I remembered correctly, a winding route started at Deltona and ended up north of Orlando. It destroyed my plans for extra time with Eli but kept us off the interstate.

I ignored Vanessa as she punched at the screen of her phone. "If you make a left in about a mile, it'll put us headed south to Sanford," she said. "We can rejoin the interstate there. I've called off the troops."

"All of them?" I slowed and watched for the intersection.

"Every last one. Cross my heart. The route will give us time to talk."

I didn't believe her, but I'd give her a chance to redeem herself. I'd already said everything I wanted to say. I made the turn. "So, talk."

"There's a lot I can't explain. Security and all that."

Or she wasn't willing to tell me about it.

"Your history provides difficulties," she said after a long pause.

If she was waiting for a reaction from me, I'd missed my cue.

"Putnam got his hands on records the rest of us aren't able to access," she continued. "He hasn't shared everything, but enough for us to agree to the current setup."

"What did he tell you?" I kept my eyes on the winding road.

Vanessa chuckled. "I'm actually envious of your history of busting criminals. Some big-time players, too. All while maintaining your persona of a small-town librarian. If I didn't know better, I'd think you were running a crime syndicate and using legal means to destroy the competition."

"That sounds like the plot of bad fan fiction."

"If you say so. I haven't read any. Fan fiction, that is." From the looks of the apartment, she didn't read much at all. Her loss.

"Turn right in two miles," she said. "My point is, you're too perfect. The poor little rich girl who does everything wrong, then gets everything right. Busts the bad guys and gives the cops all the credit. Wins the heart and business of the hero. Saves the townsfolk from the villains without getting hurt. You can't be real."

At least she didn't bring Jake into the conversation. Maybe they weren't as good as they thought they were.

I jinxed it.

"We're still trying to figure out where another Hennessey fits in," Vanessa said. "Eli's cousin. His name is Jake, right? He's disappeared."

"Jake got a job in Cleveland months ago." I braked for a slow car in front of us. "He doesn't stay in touch."

"Oh, we know. Problem is, if he's getting paid under the table, there's no proof he's working. We can't locate him."

The cops always tried to make Jake the bad guy. Sure, he'd done a few illegal things in the past, but he'd changed. "There's nothing criminal about that as long as he pays his taxes."

"Have you talked to him lately?"

What was she fishing for? "I haven't heard from

him since I texted him about Eli. And I'm not trying to track him down. I have other things to worry about."

"The turn is just ahead," Vanessa said, staring at her screen.

I signaled, slowed, and merged onto the onramp. At the top, a sheriff's car sat in the median. "You said you called off the cops. Were you lying to me again?" I asked, my voice as sharp as a knife.

"I did. It's a coincidence. Stick with the traffic flow and you'll be fine."

It wasn't like Dolores didn't stand out, no matter how I drove. I kept my eyes forward and my hands on the wheel and stayed in the center of the lane, next to a semi. It lowered the opportunity for me to become a random target.

I clung to the spot, keeping my eyes on my mirror, trying to identify a light bar on any of the cars behind us. Five miles down the road, I relaxed. A little.

"And that's my point," Vanessa said. "It's too perfect. Breaks in traffic when you need them and a truck at the right moment. How can one person have so much luck?"

"You're jaded. All you do is fight criminals and pretty soon everyone is a criminal to you. Instead of looking for the good in people, you see the bad. Even if it's only in your imagination." I shot her a disapproving glare.

"If things were perfect in my life, Eli wouldn't be in the hospital. I'd never have been arrested. Or drugged, kidnapped and held at gunpoint. And I'd be in my apartment in Oak Grove, reading. I haven't had time to read since I've been here."

Yes, I was feeling sorry for myself. And homesick. I needed a friend and Vanessa's betrayal burned deep. I'd never tell her how badly she'd hurt me.

She stared out the side window and didn't respond. As road signs marked our passage, I started a new list. Find a hotel. Figure out the most important things to pack. Text Sarah and tell her to quit gathering information about the house. I wouldn't be buying it.

She interrupted my rumination. "I want to trust you, Harmony, but there are too many coincidences. And you're at the center of all of them."

"I don't believe in coincidence."

"Then explain what's going on."

I slammed my hand against the steering wheel. "What do you think I've been trying to do? And you are supposed to be helping. Instead, you've made me your prime suspect. Typical lazy police work. Name a suspect and find evidence to prove it instead of searching out the evidence and then find the perpetrator."

"That's a low blow."

"Is it? Because right now it feels like the truth." I added finding a PI to my list. And a bodyguard. For both me and Eli. I still had the names of the agencies that had been recommended forever ago on my desk.

Chapter 23

I signaled my turn to take the interstate exit closest to the house.

"Aren't we going to the hospital?" Vanessa asked.

"I need to pack first. I'll make arrangements to get the rest of my things once I find a place."

"I can't let you do that."

"And you'll stop me how? Arrest me? On what charges? Hold me as a material witness? My lawyer will play the get out of jail free card so fast your collective heads will spin. He may be retired, but he's still as sharp as they come."

"He won't do you any good from that rinky-dink town where you live."

I hit the button on the dash. "Call. Dan. Mobile."

Vanessa reached over and ended the call before the connection was made. "You won't need him."

"Too bad. He loves a challenge. The minor cases he handles help him relive his glory days when he won a case before the Supreme Court."

"Wait. Wait a minute. You use a lawyer who

argued in front of the Supreme Court and you have his personal number?"

"And won," I reminded her. "He and my dad were close friends. I amuse him, so he keeps me around. My parents were killed in a mountain climbing accident, you know. So much for my perfect life."

The house loomed ahead. Two black cars were parked in front of it, not trying to hide their presence. I pulled to the curb a block away.

"Who are they?" I asked, with one foot on the brake and the other hovering over the gas pedal.

"I don't know."

We sat in silence. I considered my options. Chances were, they'd already spotted us. Dolores wasn't easy to hide, and I didn't have the right connections to go underground.

"Which agency are they with?" I asked.

"My guess is Putnam's. He's not responding to my message."

"So, now we have agencies not cooperating and fighting between themselves. And you wonder why civilians don't trust law enforcement." A thought struck me. "Or maybe they aren't cops at all?'

I unfastened my seatbelt and reached for my purse. I wanted Betsy close by.

"We should consider the possibility." Vanessa pulled her service revolver from its holster and checked that a round was loaded.

I wondered if it was all for show. I didn't trust anything anymore. Not even my own eyes. And I really didn't believe the bright yellow car pulling in behind us. Two cars back, but in the first free spot. And unmistakable.

I flung open my door, half-expecting gunshots to follow. Or men in black running in my direction. Nothing.

So, I turned off the engine and pulled out the keys. "Stay here," I said, as if I were in charge. Before Vanessa could stop me, I hopped out of Dolores, half-bent to decrease my profile, and dashed towards the yellow car. The driver's side door catapulted open, and the driver got out, his arms spread wide open.

I didn't launch myself into Jake's welcoming hug. But I didn't stop him from wrapping his arms around me, either. The familiar scent of his custom after-shave surrounded me, and his unshaven whiskers tickled the top of my head.

"What trouble have you gotten yourself into this time, Angel?" He tugged me closer. "And why is there a gun pointed at us?"

Jake hadn't pulled us to the ground, and I twirled to see Vanessa lowering her weapon. She holstered it and walked in our direction.

"She's on my side. Kind of. It's hard to explain. I don't know the whole truth," I told Jake in an under-tone. "She's a cop. So, watch yourself."

He stiffened. Jake's reputation with law enforcement was less than stellar. "How deep in are you? Do I need to rescue you?"

But Vanessa was a few feet away. I'd fill him in

later. "Not yet. You'll know if and when the time comes."

"Sorry," she said. "I misread the situation." She appraised Jake with a bold sweep of her eyes.

Bullshit. I didn't believe her excuse for a second. She'd tried to intimidate us. But I understood her instant attraction to Jake. His sparkling dark eyes and brilliant smile had pulled me in too, when we first met. Hadn't Putnam's information included his picture?'

She held out her hand. "Hi. I'm Vanessa."

I jumped in before Jake could get in trouble. "Special Agent Vanessa Salters with the ATF. Vanessa, this is Eli's cousin, Jake."

She took an instinctive step back. "Jake Hennessey? Where did you come from?"

I needed to diffuse the tension. "You mentioned his name three times and summoned him."

One side of Jake's mouth rose. He took a step forward and held out his hand. "Special Agent."

Her face looked like she'd been eating lemons, but Vanessa shook the offered hand. "What are you doing here?"

With an unwavering smile, he answered. "Harmony texted me about Eli's condition. I came to help. Tillie gave me this address, and here I am. Is there a problem with that?"

"Can you prove it?"

The plastered-on smile stayed in place. "Will the gas receipts and fast-food wrappers satisfy you? I'm afraid I don't have a hotel bill. I took a nap at a rest stop in North Carolina."

"Where are you staying?"

"I thought I'd bunk with Harmony until I could find a place." He winked at me. "It wouldn't be the first time."

"Except I'm moving out. Now. I haven't figured out where I'm going, but there are plenty of hotels. And no, Jake, you can't stay with me."

He put his hand to his heart. "Curses, foiled again." He jerked his chin up the street. "We'll talk about it later. After we deal with the goons heading this way. Unless they're your friends, Special Agent?"

Funny how Jake could be so polite and still make the title sound like an insult. Vanessa turned, and with a move made smooth by practice, drew her gun. "Get Harmony out of here."

"In the car, Angel. Now!" Jake shoved me into the driver's seat. "You too, Salters."

I crawled into the back seat to make room for them. Vanessa ran around to the passenger's side of the car and Jake slid into the driver's seat.

"Salters!" Jake barked, leaning over to crack open the door for her.

"No, wait. I recognize one of them." But she positioned herself so the door acted as a shield.

I didn't move. Until we got an all-clear, I was staying right where I was.

"Identify yourselves," Vanessa shouted. The two men stopped and held their hands away from their bodies. More than a few people in their yards turned to see what was going on. I prayed there'd be no gunfire and no stray bullets.

"Salters. I'm Rono Tirada. We did the updated laws session together a year ago. Remember?"

"Shit.' Every muscle in her back relaxed. "What are you doing here?"

The men resumed walking and Vanessa closed the car door and went to meet them.

"ATF, eh? What have you gotten into, Angel?"

"Not me. Eli. I'm collateral damage."

He started his souped-up Charger, and the familiar sweet rumble of the pipes was welcome music. "Crawl up here," he said, patting the passenger's seat. "Let's go for a ride and you can tell me all about it."

The temptation was strong. Even a short ride with no cops around would be a breath of fresh air. And it would give me time to explain the situation without worrying about anyone overhearing.

But if we left, it might result in another car chase. While I had law enforcement on my side—sort of—Jake didn't have that luxury.

"I want to see what they're up to," I said. "See if they have any leads into the fires."

"Fires?" Jake's hands tightened on the steering wheel. "How many fires are you talking about?"

"Only two. The first one was at Eli's house in Oak Grove. The second one happened at his house here."

Jake turned on his blinker. "You can tell me the story over drinks. It'll give me a chance to contact some friends, too."

I'd met a few of his friends in Oak Grove, and none of them were pillars of the community. But their connections might be exactly what we needed to fill in the gaps the official investigators couldn't.

"We'll do that, Jake, I promise. But not now. I've raised enough hell for one day."

"What did you do?"

I grinned. "A bootlegger's 180. In the middle of the interstate. At full speed. I might need to buy new tires after that stunt."

For the first time in my memory, I left Jake speechless with his mouth hanging open.

"But I didn't know if I was being followed by the good or the bad guys when I did it. Not that it would have mattered. Both sides are pissing me off."

His jaw dropped lower, he shifted into first, then revved the engine. "What the frig have you gotten yourself into, Angel?"

❊ ❊ ❊

I shouted out the window, telling Vanessa I'd be right back, and locked Dolores as we rolled by. Jake did the speed limit and not a fraction faster. By the time they got to their cars, we'd be out of sight. By the time they found us, we'd be sitting in the neighborhood bar a few blocks away, working on our first beers. Or not.

The little bar wasn't much more than one long, narrow room with beat-up wooden tables. Not a bar stool in sight. The jukebox was unplugged, and the TV muted on the weather channel. A few old men kept the bartender company. Except for the over-whelming stench of stale beer, it was the perfect place to talk.

Jake was on his third beer and I was finishing my

first when I got halfway through the story. I'd been doing all the talking, and he hadn't interrupted me. I noticed how tightly he gripped his beer bottle when I recited the events in the courtroom, when Rob tried to take over the company. And when I told him about Sallis being back on the streets, his face became expressionless. A bad sign.

But Jake knew his limits. His fourth beer sat in front of him, getting warm, when I finished my story. My second beer was in the same state. I finished talking just in time, because Jake jerked his head towards the front door, which he'd been keeping an eye on.

"We have company." He stood, his face lit with his salesman's smile, and waved. Then, with the ease gained from hours of experience, Jake cleared the debris on the table next to us. He jiggled it to sit next to ours before Vanessa made it to the back of the room.

"Agent," he said, holding out a chair for her. "I wondered how long it would take you to show up. We parked out front to make it easy to find us. Beer? It's on me."

It always amazed me how he worked an audience. I wasn't impervious to his charm, but it didn't hold the same power over me as it did most people. Before Vanessa even got settled, the bartender placed a bottle on the table for her. More of Jake's magic.

"It's an Orlando company's unique brew. There's an interesting lime note. Have you tried it, Special Agent?"

Vanessa picked up her bottle but didn't take a

drink. "This won't work if we don't use first names. I'm Vanessa and the guys at the house are Rono and Luis out of the Huntsville office. They're here for a conference that starts Monday and came by to say hi. And no, Harmony, they weren't the ones following us."

Shit.

Jake leaned back in his chair and, with one finger, traced the trail left by a drop of condensation running down the side of his beer. "Angel filled me in on what's been happening while we waited for you."

"It's a complicated case," Vanessa agreed. "It breaks all the rules. Playing it by ear hasn't worked out either."

"That's because it's Harmony we're talking about. You need to draw outside the lines and on the next page. Maybe in a different book."

"And I suppose you have a grand plan?" Vanessa snapped.

Jake's smile spread ear-to-ear. "Oh, I have plans. But Harmony won't put up with any of them. Rightfully so. Instead, we'll start by going to visit Eli. I'll find a place to stay. And she will go back to your house. Because even though she doesn't trust you, it's the safest place for her right now.

"That will give me a few days to do my own digging and come up with something better. Agreed?"

Vanessa's eyes met his. "Agreed."

Even if she was willing to go along with it, it didn't mean I had to.

Jake reached over the table and put his hand on top of mine. "Agreed, Angel?"

I wanted to say no. Jake waited, batting his puppy-dog eyes until I caved.

"There is one stipulation," he said, directing his gaze at Vanessa. "You and your cronies have to drop the pretense that Harmony is involved in any of the crimes. You're doing it to cover your butts and appease your superiors because of your lack of progress in identifying the actual suspects. Otherwise, I'll hide Harmony so deep you'll need the FBI, the CIA, and the Secret Service to find her. Understood?"

I caught my breath. Had Jake gone too far?

"You can't do that," Vanessa challenged.

"Between her money and my connections? Try me." Jake's smile never flattened, but his stare was ice cold.

It was the first time he'd ever publicly acknowledged he knew about my hidden wealth. We'd always played the game that it didn't exist, and both of us were happier that way.

The two of them were locked in a war of wills as Vanessa returned his stare. I sipped my beer, content to wait for the outcome.

Jake won. Vanessa blinked first. Just as I'd anticipated. I was the only person who had ever beat Jake in a stare-down, and I wasn't sure he hadn't let me win.

Vanessa rolled her shoulders, relieving their stiffness. "I can handle my boss, but I can't speak for the other agencies."

She'd had no problem promising to call them off during the chase earlier. What was the truth?

Jake extended his hand. "Allies, then, Special Agent Salters?"

It was a treat watching him manipulate her. She reached across the table to grasp his hand "Allies."

Their handshake lasted a moment too long, and I didn't interrupt the battle. To my unpracticed eye, Vanessa appeared to let go first. Another win for Jake.

He picked up his beer, put it to his lips and tipped his head back. His Adam's apple pulsed with each swallow. When he'd emptied the bottle, he sat it on the table without as much as a whisper of a thunk. He stood, rock solid.

"I believe Harmony has been patient with us long enough. She wants to go see Eli. Are you ready, Angel?"

Past ready. But I was impressed that Vanessa hadn't questioned Jake's nickname for me. I suspected I'd hear about it later. "I'll see you later, Vanessa. Don't wait up."

"Hell, no. I'll follow you there. I still have a job to do."

Jake and I shared a glance, and I nodded. Well, it was more like the barest movement of my head, enough to tell Jake we'd play along this time.

"Key, Jake," I said when we got outside. I squinted in the brightness of the Florida sun after the darkness of the bar.

"I'm good. I only had four beers."

Which he could handle, but it would still put his

blood alcohol level over the legal limit. "Key," I repeated.

"You're no fun." He winked as he pulled his keys out of his pocket and tossed them my direction.

They made a high arc, and I snatched them cleanly out of the air on their downward path, then unlocked the Charger. "Where can we meet?" I asked Vanessa, who hovered a few feet away.

"The family waiting room. Call me when you're ready to leave."

She was pretending to cooperate. I'd see how long that lasted.

Chapter 26

The Charger was a delight to operate, as always. It was the car Jake had used to teach me how to *really* drive. But there were no fancy tricks this time. I stuck to the script and the easiest road to get to the hospital, keeping one eye on the mirror the whole way.

I never spotted anyone who didn't belong. Vanessa stayed behind us the entire trip. Either she'd kept her word about calling off the harassment or switching cars had done the trick.

We'd stopped by the house first. It wasn't on the way, but I didn't want to leave Dolores parked on the street. I'd moved her to the driveway and covered her.

After parking at the hospital, I headed for the door closest to the ICU and had to correct myself. As Jake and I waited for the right elevator, I realized I didn't know how many stairs it took to get to the fourth floor.

The security guard hanging around at the nurses' desk gave us a hard looking over, checked his phone, then nodded. I guessed that since Jake was with me, the guard assumed he was good, too. I asked the lady at the desk to add Jake to the approved visitors list. I needed to add Lando and Scotty, too, but she seemed stressed, and I didn't want to add to her work.

Eli's room faced west. He was watching birds flocking outside the window when we entered after making our way through the obstacle course of cones and security tape.

"Hey Sweetie." With the back of his bed nearly upright, I didn't need to lean very far to kiss him. I'd planned for a quick touch of our lips, but he turned it into more. Much more. It became one of his claiming his territory kisses, and I remembered that Jake hovered near the door.

I ended the kiss sooner than Eli wanted, but planted a peck on his cheek as a consolation prize. "See who came to visit," I said cheerily, but wondered if Eli would recognize Jake.

The lost look in his eyes was the answer I didn't want. Eli frowned and deep lines formed in his forehead. I'd warned Jake about the possibility, and he handled it like a pro.

With his familiar grin lighting his face, he strode forward, offering his hand. "I'm Jake, your cousin. I heard you had a bit of an accident and came to help."

"Jake? But Jake's just a kid. One I have to get out of trouble all the time."

"I've grown up. I'm here to get you out of trouble this time." He kept his hand out until Eli shook it. And held on to it.

"How do you know Buttercup?'

Shit. Could Eli handle the truth?

Jake laughed. "I met her first. I'm responsible for you two getting together. Although I'm jealous that you won her heart, I admit you're made for each other."

The perfect response, walking the tight line between lying and volunteering too much information. It seemed to satisfy Eli because he let go of Jake's hand and reached for mine. "So, I got the girl? You were always the one chasing the ladies."

"I stole a girl or two from you back then. But you took the prize."

They were talking in a code I didn't understand. Had they moved up in history? Was Eli remembering more?

My brain battled between the joy of Eli regaining his memory and the worry that he'd be unable to handle the confusing relationship between Jake and I.

"What are you doing these days?" Eli asked. The moment had passed. I was both saddened and relieved.

"I'm a bartender. In line for management as soon as business picks up. Profits have been increasing since I fingered the guy giving away free drinks to his moocher pals. They stopped showing up and real customers are coming back."

Eli grinned. "Still causing trouble."

I smiled, too. Jake, the eternal bad boy, becoming the protector of good. Or was it a story he'd made up to distract Eli?

An aide came in with a food tray. I hadn't realized it was suppertime, but between coming down from the adrenalin rush and the beer, I wasn't hungry. After doing the checks to verify Eli was Eli and the food was his, she set the tray within his reach and left. Eli stared at the covered dishes but didn't swing the tray across the bed.

"Here, let me help you," Jake said, reaching for the bedside table.

Eli shook his head. "I'm not hungry."

Jake lifted the covers from the various dishes. "Jello. Naturally. Some sort of broth. How original. No wonder you don't want to eat. I need to sneak in some real food. A steak or a big juicy cheeseburger. Applesauce? What was I expecting? It's sprinkled with cinnamon. That's a good place to start."

Eli shook his head and looked away. "I'll pass. Save it until you leave. I don't want to eat in front of you."

Clear as day, he was lying. I crossed my arms and glared. "You love applesauce. Tell me the truth. Why don't you want to eat?"

He rolled so his back was to us. "I can't do it. Last time I tried, I ended up with food all over me. The nurse had to clean me up and change my gown, then feed me like a baby."

"Hurt your pride, did it?" Jake asked. "Was she cute, the nurse?"

"If you go for the grandmotherly type."

Jake snorted. "Okay, here's the deal. Roll over. I'm going to help you. You hold the spoon, and I'll guide it where it needs to go. Ready?"

Then I watched the most amazing thing ever. Jake propped himself on the bed, opened the silverware packet, removed the spoon, and placed it in Eli's shaking hand. Together, they dipped out a spoonful of applesauce and, ever so carefully, Jake helped Eli put it in his mouth.

Not a drop spilled. In fact, Eli may have licked the spoon.

"Alright!" Jake said, a little too cheerfully. "Let's try again."

The second attempt was as successful as the first. And so were the third and the fourth. The fifth seemed sloppy, and I realized Jake had let go of Eli's hand halfway through the motion. But Eli found his mouth, anyway. A small, but important, success.

Where had Jake learned to do that?

They finished the applesauce, and Jake picked up the jello. Orange. Eli didn't like jello, and fake orange ranked at the bottom of the list. He shook his head. "No, I'm done." He raised his quivering hand and laid it on his chest. "I'm worn out."

"I'll let you off easy this time," Jake said as he picked up the broth, "but drink this."

To my wonderment, Eli did. I felt a twinge of jealousy. I should be the one taking care of Eli. Was this how Tillie felt? But Jake had been so good, so careful with Eli. There had been times he'd treated me like that. Back before he'd gotten me arrested.

Jake and I didn't talk on the return trip to the house. Vanessa—and only Vanessa—trailed behind us. I decided Jake was planning his next steps, and I was trying to figure out mine.

I longed to spend the entire day on Sunday with Eli, but that wouldn't give me time to research long-term rehab facilities for him. Or to restart digging into the personnel records since Putnam hadn't reported any success. Or reported anything, if I was honest with myself.

It hit me as we pulled up to the house. "I've been a bad friend, Jake. I haven't even asked how you are. We haven't talked in forever. So, how are you doing?"

He stared out the windshield and watched Vanessa unlock the door and disappear inside. "You know, that hurt. Even after you told me the whole story. But when we walked into Eli's room, it hit me, how rotten of a shape he is in. You say he's doing better? Better than what?"

"From what I can find on the internet, in another day, maybe a few hours, if he hadn't been found, he'd be dead." I choked out the words. No matter how hard I tried, I couldn't separate myself from my emotions and think logically. Not when it came to Eli.

"And that's why I'll forgive you for not thinking about me. I don't know how you're handling every-thing that's been thrown at you."

"Did you quit your job? You were settling in so well."

"I haven't had a proper day off since the boss fired the fool who was ripping him off. So, when I mentioned wanting to come here, he gave me two weeks off.

With pay, even. He owed me big." He chuckled. "I'll tell you how I caught the guy another time. We're making Salters nervous sitting here."

He was right. She stood in the doorway, pretending to check the mail. "Where are you going to stay? I'd offer you the couch, but Vanessa and I are fighting, and the two of you would be on each other's nerves the whole night."

"As much as I'd love to irritate her, it'll wait until things get settled. I'll grab a room somewhere. Don't expect to see me for a few days. I've got to locate some old friends to help us out."

"Be safe, Jake."

"I will, Angel." He pulled me over and planted a kiss on my forehead. "I'll be in touch."

He waited until I was in the house to pull away. From one guard dog to another. Vanessa sat in the front room, flipping through TV channels, trying to find something to watch.

She didn't mince words. "Do you trust him?"

"He took a bullet for me once. The question is, should you trust him?"

I wasn't above irritating her and left the question hanging in the air.

"And?" she finally asked.

I considered my response. Then I answered with a different question. "How much do you think I trust you right now?"

Her face reddened.

"Let's try this again," I went on. "Is there any reason Jake should trust you at this point?"

241

"I'm a federal law enforcement officer. Of course, he should trust me!"

"Or is that a reason not to trust you? Stalemate."

❈ ❈ ❈

I didn't wait for Vanessa to wake up before going for my morning stroll. But she was waiting for me on the front porch when I returned.

"You can't be doing that," she said.

"What? Taking a walk around the block? You told me this is a safe neighborhood, and I have Betsy." I tapped the pocket of my lightweight jacket.

"A walk is fine. Going without me and not leaving a note isn't. You freaked me out, disappearing that way. My reputation and my job are at stake."

Manipulation much? That was my territory. "Your job and reputation are on the line every assignment. I'm not special." I sat beside her on the front porch steps.

"Not like this. I've got no clue who's calling the shots, but your boyfriend isn't your average computer geek. What's he hiding?"

"I've been asking myself the same thing ever since all of you started poking around. The bad part is, I can't ask him. He doesn't remember."

"Richon wants to interview him. See if he can add anything to what you got out of him."

"His doctors need to clear him first. And it might be good to have one of them in the room. Because I won't be allowed to be there, and I'm worried about how Eli might react to his memories or nightmares."

"Noted. I'll pass along the word."

"How did you get roped into being the go-between instead of Horace?"

Vanessa grimaced. "You noticed. They haven't officially pulled him from the case, but he's done a disappearing act. I don't know if he's gone undercover or if his chief decided it was out of their jurisdiction."

"Can you imagine Horace going undercover? How do you disguise a mountain?" I worked hard to maintain a straight face, but a little giggle may have leaked out.

She blinked. A couple of times. Then she chuckled. "Mountain, huh? I can see that. What nickname do you have for me?"

Would she consider it an insult that I didn't have one? "You don't expect me to answer, do you?"

She bought it. "I'll get it out of you somehow. I am trained in all the best questioning techniques."

"Interrogation, you mean? Been there, done that. You'll have to come up with something new."

We sat in the sunshine, not talking. Finally, Vanessa stood and stretched. "Coffee?"

I nodded.

"Don't do it again, Harmony," she said before heading inside.

I didn't answer. She didn't want to hear the truth.

I missed sitting on my steps to read the morning newspaper while patting Piper, Joe and Luke's dog. I missed listening to the birds instead of the constant drone of cars. If I added a sunroom to the back, it would give me a place to sit and the house would help block the noise.

The garage was almost clean, and I was worn out. How many years and how many renters' worth of stuff had contributed to the accumulation? We'd found a still usable bookshelf to add to my room, but most things were broken beyond repair.

I'd called the hospital to check on Eli before we started. Rob and Tillie had stopped by but had left. Sunday was their day to hang out with the grandkids. Eli's morning was filled with anticipated visits from various therapists. Oh, and Jake had come by, early bird early, to help Eli eat breakfast. The nurse giggled as she told me that Jake had smuggled in some bacon. Jake had probably flirted with her in his usual way, allowing him to push the boundaries. As long as it benefited Eli, I didn't care.

My bun had fallen out, and I played with a straggling lock of hair while sipping on a soda and watching the last of the trash getting loaded into a pickup. I was settling in and didn't like it. But Eli remained my priority. I needed to take a shower and go visit him. It was almost lunchtime. If Jake could get him to eat, so could I. I tried to figure out what to sneak in for him but came up blank.

❀ ❀ ❀

He was snoring, so I didn't have to check if he was still breathing. Running background checks from my phone wasn't easy, but it filled the time while Eli slept, recovering from a rough morning. It got to the point where I had too many pages open and too many apps running, so I closed everything and started fresh. In the process, I got into Eli's tracker program.

That's when I spotted a green light flashing for his location.

Chapter 27

I had the honor of sitting up front with Horace while Vanessa sat in the back. My initial plan was to hop into Dolores and chase down the location on my own, but I didn't know that area of town. So, I called Vanessa for help. She'd never been there either and convinced me to contact Horace.

He knew the neighborhood, and not in a good way. Although he wasn't thrilled that we'd interrupted his Sunday afternoon golf game, he was happy we hadn't gone to the location on our own. The street was known for drug deals and addicts.

The house we pulled up to didn't appear to be a dealer's house, and it was out of place compared to the houses on either side. Although it was an older home needing repairs, the weeds in the yard were cut back and no junk cluttered the front porch.

Horace squared his shoulders and placed his hand near his gun as he strode up the sidewalk. He'd instructed me to stay in the car, but Vanessa got out and stood by the driver's side door, ready to spring into action if needed.

The cracked front window of the house rattled when Horace pounded on the door. I'd seen a face peeking out that same window a few seconds earlier, so someone was at home.

The door opened, and Horace announced himself. He and the house's occupant had a brief conversation I wasn't able to hear. He turned and gestured for me to join him.

He'd moved inside by the time I climbed the two rickety wooden steps. Vanessa stayed behind, playing guard dog. A tiny old woman met me at the door. Next to Horace, she looked like a toy. A matching old man sat on the worn-out couch across the room.

"Come in, honey," the woman said, "Before you let out the cold air."

The temperature inside felt as hot as outside, but I did as she asked. The hint of coolness from a wheezing air conditioner in the window reached me, then disappeared.

"You want something to drink?" she asked. "I'm Nellie, and this is Archie. We're so glad you dropped by. We don't get much company. Please, have a seat. You, too, Detective."

I was afraid that Horace would break any of the furniture, all of which had seen better days. "Water would be good, thank you," I said, as I gingerly sat in an afghan-covered rocking chair. Horace remained standing.

"Show them the phone," Nellie said as she bustled into the kitchen.

Archie grinned. "Never mind her. She's been bossy for years. What do you want to know about the phone I found? And how did you know I had it?"

"Where did you get the phone, sir?" Horace asked.

"Tell them the story," Nellie called from the kitchen.

Archie shook his head but smiled. "I am, Honey," he called back. "So," he said, turning to Horace, "I went fishing last week. I go now and then when she is with her church friends." He jerked his head towards the kitchen.

Nellie came out with two glasses of water, one for me and one for Horace. "He'd go every day if I let him."

"Anyway," Archie continued, "I wanted to try a new spot. Headed East on Colonial. There are a couple of places to fish off bridges. That way my old knees don't have to deal with fighting uneven or swampy ground."

I sipped my lukewarm water, wanting to scream at Archie to hurry and get to the point. But he'd get there in his own way, and I had to be patient.

"I got a few bites but didn't catch anything. Then my line got caught by the wind and snagged in some brush. I didn't want to break the line because I was using one of my favorite lures and hated to lose it.

"I walked to the riverbank where the bushes were pushed down and broken, so it wasn't too hard most of the way. The last few feet took some work, but the lure was right there if I could just reach it. Do either of you fish?"

"Get on with it," Nellie said, sitting beside Archie on the couch.

He patted her hand. "I thought they might understand about having a favorite rod and lure," he grumbled. "Anyway, when I cut the line, the lure dropped. I leaned over to pick it up, and that's when I found it."

I dredged up my last bit of patience.

"What did you find?" Horace asked.

"The phone. I asked the other guy who was there if he lost his, but he'd left it in his car. The one I found was beat up and looked like it had been there awhile. It wouldn't turn on and the screen was cracked, but I brought it home, anyway. Even if I ended up throwing it away, I didn't want to leave it there."

Nellie interrupted. "I reminded him that maybe the phone needed charged. Our cord didn't fit. But I took it with me to choir practice yesterday and asked around. A girl in the youth group had the right one, and we plugged it in during rehearsal. We turned it on later, but between the cracks in the screen and being locked, we couldn't figure out the owner. It's in my purse if you want to see it."

It took all my strength to remain calm and let Horace handle it. "Yes, please," he said.

Nellie hustled down the short hallway. I sipped on my water and tried to look relaxed while my stomach churned.

She returned with a skinny black rectangle held gingerly between her fingers. It could be any phone. Or Eli's. It was impossible to tell. She handed it to Horace. He passed it to me. With shaky hands, I hit the button to bring it to life.

Through the spiderweb of cracks and chips, I

studied the screen. I didn't have to look long. The face that stared at me was the same one I looked at in the mirror every morning.

"Well?" Horace asked.

"This is Eli's. But it's locked, and he uses the fingerprint reader to lock it."

"He didn't share his pass code?"

I shrugged. "It never came up in conversation."

"So, it's the right phone?" Nellie asked.

Horace nodded. "Yes. And we appreciate your cooperation, especially for allowing us to interrupt your Sunday. It may help us solve a crime."

"I always wanted to be a detective," Nellie chirped.

"Glad we could help," Archie added.

"May I offer you a reward?" I asked. I didn't expect them to say yes but wanted to try.

Nellie smiled. "Oh, no, honey. Just knowing we helped is our reward."

"Can I give you a hug?"

She opened her arms. "I'll never turn down a hug."

I used the opportunity to slip a twenty into the pocket of her sweater. I wanted to give her more, but it was the right amount for her not to question where it came from. Hopefully, she'd think she'd put it there months ago and just forgot.

"What are the chances of Putnam finding what he's looking for?" Vanessa asked, leaning forward from the back seat of the cruiser.

"Eli is good at keeping secrets," I pointed out. "I can't imagine him taking pictures of the documents

Putnam wants, but I've seen stranger things. I won't rule it out completely."

"Should we call him?"

"We've already ruined Detective Horace's day off. By the time Putnam gets here from Tampa, it'll be late. Let's set something up for tomorrow. That way Lando can help. Eli may have stored company secrets which we need to protect. And Lando set up the phone originally, so he's familiar with it."

I wished there was a way for me to get into the phone first, to make sure there was nothing too personal on it. But that opportunity wouldn't present itself.

"You won't need me for anything, right?" Horace asked.

"Your chief giving you grief?" Vanessa tapped me on the shoulder. I turned, and she winked.

Horace took too long to answer. "The department is always stretched during tourist season."

It was always tourist season in Orlando. He was up to something he couldn't share. But what?

I didn't mention the phone when I visited Eli that evening. All it would do was worry him. When I got to his room, he was asleep, and I settled into the most comfortable chair and pulled out my own phone. I'd put the time to good use working on delving into employees' backgrounds.

He rolled over before I'd gotten very far, and I looked up to see him staring at me. He licked his lips and, with shaky hands, reached for the water bottle by his bed. I wanted to rush over to help, but he needed to relearn to do things for himself. With the help of the straw, he got a drink without spilling a drop. Progress.

"Sometimes," he said, returning the container to the bedside table, "When I wake up and you're not here, I worry that you've left me. That you're never coming back. Where do you go?"

I didn't think he was ready to hear about his company yet. I found a spot to sit on his bed to be close to him. "Let's see. Yesterday I did laundry and bought groceries. Today I went for a drive to clear the cobwebs out of Dolores' motor."

His eyebrows scrunched together. "Dolores?"

"My car. Her name is Dolores."

"I remember. You name everything."

I'd avoided one trap. "Well, not everything. I haven't named my shoes. Or my purse."

I made him laugh. And wished I hadn't. He winced and put a hand to his side.

"That hurt. What did I do?"

"Your ribs got banged up in the accident. Do you want me to call the nurse and ask for some pain meds?"

"No, I'll rest for a few minutes and it'll ease up. I was hurt worse than this in the Rangers. We were in some God-forsaken African country when I was shot. The company medic wrapped up my shoulder while we waited for the whirlybird. Have I told you about it?"

"You've mentioned your service, but don't talk about it."

"Didn't want to worry you, I suppose." He stroked my cheek, then pulled his hand away. "Wait. I was a Ranger?"

"Yes. Before you started programming." I untucked his dog tags from under my shirt and pulled them over my head to hand to him. "These are yours."

With the look of a little boy at Christmas, he plucked them from my hand and studied them. "I gave them to you?"

"No. I 'borrowed' them from your bedroom when you were missing. I hoped they'd provide a connection to lead me to you. It didn't work out that way, but it makes me feel better to have a piece of you close. We can ask the nurse if you're allowed to wear them."

"Lean over."

Huh? "Why?"

"I want to put them back on you. Your wearing them makes me happy."

I was glad to oblige. I tipped my head and waited while he fumbled to get the chain over my bun. Once the chain settled around my neck, he tugged it to bring me closer. I expected a kiss, but he put his lips to the dog tags themselves before tucking them between my breasts.

"Now you have my kiss next to you all the time," he whispered.

My heart fluttered. I closed the distance between his mouth and mine and showed him how much his gesture meant to me.

"So, I was a Ranger," Eli said after some time. "Did we know each other then?"

"We didn't meet until several years later. And you didn't tell me about your military experience right away. You're not ashamed of it, but parts are still classified."

"Explains the nightmares I've been having."

"Do you want to talk about them?" My head rested against his shoulder and he hugged me closer.

"I'd rather talk about something else. Something that won't give me bad dreams. Tell me about what sports I like."

Safe subject. "Let's start with basketball."

❄ ❄ ❄

With a cup of coffee in one hand, and swatting mosquitoes with the other, I sat on the front steps, wondering how Vanessa would take the news. I planned to change the rules and she wouldn't like it.

Behind me, the squeak of the door hinges alerted me to her presence.

"Ready to go?" she asked.

I patted the stairs after knocking off a palmetto bug. "Have a seat, Vanessa. We need to talk."

"You'll be late for work if we don't leave now."

I was the boss. No one could yell at me. Not the Board of Directors or the City Council. Besides, I'd already texted Darla.

"That's not your problem. Your problem is where you are going to be while I'm working. Your invitation to use a desk at Shifter Technologies has been revoked. If you and the others want to pretend I'm a suspect, I'll treat you accordingly. Your access to the company's internet has already been terminated."

"That's harsh, Harmony. Do you want to go down this road? We can stop sharing information in retaliation."

"What do I have to lose? You're already limiting what you give me access to. I've hired a PI firm to get to the bottom of everything. They're willing to do what it takes to earn the bonus I've offered."

"You think some bottom-of-the-barrel PI can find evidence we can't? I've seen your bank account. That's all you can afford unless you spend the company's money."

"A little old man found Eli's phone. What else have all of you missed? My two holding companies? You've misjudged me. Again."

She didn't answer. The silence settled on the stairs like a Florida rain. But I wasn't in a hurry.

"When are you moving out?" she asked eventually.

"For Eli's sake and because Jake asked me to, I'll stay. That doesn't change our relationship. Not friends. Not enemies. Acquaintances, at most."

"I was looking forward to having a friend I could share my adventures with." Vanessa plucked a dead leaf off the geranium and tossed it to the ground.

Me too. But I wouldn't tell her that. "Putnam can decide who he wants in the office when the locksmith opens the safe. There's no reason for you to be there."

"What can we do to fix this?"

We? There was nothing 'we' could do. I channeled Chief Sorenson's calm demeanor when he scolded his officers. "Nothing. You took advantage of my moments of weakness and pushed me too far. I won't allow that to happen again.

"Here's the new plan. If I go anywhere, I'll text you before I leave. Give you the chance to follow me. Unless your boss decides it's a waste of your time. I've already provided all the information I can."

I stood and brushed off my slacks. "Ready?"

"Right behind you," she answered.

Chapter 28

"You summoned?" Lando asked, flopping into the guest chair in my office.

"I've got it set up for you and Scotty to visit Eli." I avoided his eyes by flipping through the stack of paperwork Darla had dumped on my desk earlier. "But I want to go with you the first time."

"That's fine, but what's the deal with the lady with the Feds?"

"Vanessa? She and I had a contest of nerves and I won." Or lost, depending upon my mood. "She'll be out of my hair from now on."

"Too bad." Lando grinned. "I was considering asking her for a date."

"I won't stop you."

"Nope. Whatever she did to hurt you puts her out of the running."

I wouldn't try to change his mind. "Can I depend on you to back me up when the locksmith shows up?"

He leaned forward. "What do you expect to find?"

"Expect? Boring paperwork. Petty cash. Hope for? Top Secret documents to get Putnam off my case."

"Count me in."

"If you're free this afternoon, I'll be trying to catch Eli when he's not in therapy to unlock his phone." I'd already told Lando and Scotty the story of how it was found. "Make sure Putnam doesn't copy the contents when he looks through it. Disable the WiFi and Bluetooth and any other way he could send the information to his systems."

"Spy vs. counterspy? Consider it done. The network gurus already changed the passwords to the areas Vanessa may have accessed."

"Close the door," I said, as a memory struck me.

He cocked his head and reached to give the door a shove. I waited to hear the click of the catch.

"Is there a back door into the Orlando Police Department's database?"

His eyes widened and his mouth open and closed. Several times. "You're treading in dangerous territory."

"Yeah." I pushed my chair away from my desk. "I'm not happy about it, but my choices are limited. I need to know everything the agencies aren't telling me, and I don't have access to their data."

"Think about this logically. Would the cops keep your info in their crimes history? More likely, there's a fat folder sitting in a drawer of Horace's desk."

"Which I can't touch."

"True. It's not like you can saunter into his office and search. He's probably in a cubicle with no privacy."

He was right. It wasn't like Oak Grove, where every detective had an office. Where I could waltz in and everyone on the force would talk to me.

"Besides," Lando continued with a slow smile. "I already checked and found nothing."

He was one step ahead of me. "When?"

"This morning. Don't worry, I concealed my tracks. Part of our contract is checking their system to ensure the database doesn't get corrupted. I did it a day early. And did an extra-thorough job to verify there'd been no outside intrusion attempts."

He had it covered. "Do you have a friend on the force?"

"Nope. They don't use local techs. They outsource everything."

That left it to the PI firm. They still needed to prove they were worth the money I was paying.

The locksmith knew what he was doing. At least, it looked that way. I wasn't technically needed in Darla's office while the middle-aged man drilled a hole in the front of the safe near the dial, but I wanted to watch. Lando was even more enthralled by the process than me. Putnam kept one eye on things while working on his phone, but there was no sign of Vanessa. Suited me fine.

The locksmith seemed unperturbed as he turned off the drill and wiped metal shavings from the front panel. "Now comes the fun part," he said as he pulled a snake light from his black tool bag.

A variety of other tools followed, ones I couldn't name. He adjusted his light and resumed work, keeping up a running commentary of what he was doing. He rocked back on his heels and smiled. "Done!" Then he turned the handle and the door opened a crack.

He stood, stretched, gathered up his tools and put them away. "I'll leave you folks to it."

Darla walked him out of the office. Neither Putnam nor Lando moved. It took me a few seconds to realize they were waiting for me.

"My turn?" I sat on the floor, wondering what I would find. Proof Eli was a secret agent for the government? Pictures of his mistress? Stacks of cash and rolls of coins?

I swung the door open the rest of the way. Nothing exploded. All I saw was a neat stack of envelopes and a few loose papers. Then I looked closer and spotted the small envelope tucked between the stack and the safe wall. I started with it.

"Petty cash," I announced, displaying the bundle of ones, tens, and twenties. "Nothing exciting."

I moved on to the paperwork. On the top lay copies of the documents giving me legal authority for the company. And the POAs for his personal life. I hadn't had to pull rank on Tillie and Rob, and hoped I wouldn't need to, but my copies were in my purse. Then came copyrights, trademarks, and patents. Behind everything else, I spotted floppy disks, CDs, DVDs, and flash drives, labeled with the code they stored.

I eyed the remaining stack of envelopes. "Where should I start?" I asked, trying to relieve the building tension.

"Everything we've seen suggests Eli keeps things in chronological order," Darla said. "So, start at the top."

I followed her suggestion and undid the metal prongs on the first envelope. It held a solitary piece of paper, filled with what I recognized as code. But I didn't understand it, so I passed it to Lando.

He studied the sheet. "It's not part of our active programs." Then he grinned. "That's how he did it. Bloody genius."

"What?" Putnam and I asked simultaneously.

"I told you I couldn't break into his GPS app? He updated the base code. These are the changes. And damn, they're good."

Would Eli ever code again? I shoved aside the knot of fear in my heart and picked up the next envelope. Its thickness gave me a glimmer of hope. But a glimpse at the top sheet chased it away, because it contained the working notes of his discussions with Claire on the needs of fire departments.

Putnam pulled up a chair to monitor my progress. Lando sat beside me, peering over my shoulder. Darla returned her attention to the bottomless stack of paperwork on her desk.

By the time I reached for the last envelope, an hour had passed, with no luck. Well, for Putnam. The contents of several of the envelopes enthralled Lando. To his dismay, I didn't let him copy them.

But this one was different. Instead of the standard

manila, it was a padded white envelope. Did that signify something?

I held it up. "Any bets?"

Darla spoke first. "I've seen him take that one out several times. He carries it to his office and I never get to see what's in it."

"Some super-secret code?" Lando suggested.

"Hopefully, my documents," Putnam said.

The envelope didn't have metal clasps, so I merely lifted the flap. The papers inside were stiffer and thicker than standard copy paper. I slipped the stack out and caught my breath.

The top sheet was a picture of me at the Oak Grove Library, taken from the second floor. I was surrounded by books, with a notepad to my right, and my laptop in front of me. Moisture pooled in the corners of my eyes. He valued this shot so highly he stored it in a safe. Did he still see me that way?

Putnam cleared his throat, and I flipped to the next sheet. Another picture of me, this one in my apartment, reading. Then, the two of us in the park. Picture after picture, most of me, but a few of us together.

I wanted to linger over the memories, but not in present company. "Another dead end," I said, running a finger across Eli's lips in one picture before placing them back in the envelope.

"When do you want to head to the hospital, Miss Duprie?" Putnam asked, reaching over and touching my shoulder. "To get access to the phone?"

Too many things were happening at once. All I wanted was to be alone. "Give me half an hour, okay?" I needed time to collect myself.

He nodded. "I'll update the others." He stood and pushed the chair to the corner where it belonged. As he reached the office door, he stopped, turned, shook his head and grinned. "A 180? On the interstate? I wish I'd seen it."

I stared at his retreating back. It seemed so out of character.

Lando distracted me. He stretched and put his hand on the safe. "Are you sure I can't spend some quality time with those envelopes? For a few minutes?"

Darla shooed him away. "The locksmith will return this afternoon," she said, "We won't have to worry about anyone getting into it overnight."

I clutched the envelope of pictures to my chest. So many, most I hadn't even known Eli had taken. "Darla, can you make copies of these?"

She hesitated. "That's an invasion of privacy."

"They're for Eli. His mom brought in a photo album to spur his memory, but he wasn't interested. He might react differently to these."

"It's worth a try." She looked doubtful, but when I held out the envelope, she took it.

I didn't want to spring too many people on Eli at once, so Putnam, Vanessa, and Lando stayed in the family waiting area while I checked if he was awake. The obstacle course to Eli's room featured a new roadblock. A maintenance man, working on repainting a section of the wall, created an additional hazard.

His coveralls didn't match what the others wore, but I guessed he was an outside contractor. I couldn't get close enough to read his nametag.

What bothered me the most was how he avoided looking at me. Not a friendly smile, a nod of acknowledgment, not even an annoyed glare. He bent down and stirred his paint as I went by. I wondered if there was anyone in the hospital to report him to.

Eli had the TV on but wasn't watching it. He stared out the window, but his eyes held the faraway look of someone seeing inward, not outward. Was he trying to place fragments of memories? Wishing he was outside, soaking in the sunshine?

"Hey, Sweetie," I said from the doorway.

He turned and his face lit up. "Buttercup! Is it that late?"

"No, I'm early. I brought someone to see you if you're up for company."

He nodded. "As long as it isn't another doctor. I'm tired of being poked."

"Nope. Stay here and I'll be right back."

That was a dumb thing to say. They hadn't even tried to get him to stand yet.

I didn't have to navigate around the painter, He'd moved down the hallway. But at the opposite end Lando, against my request, paced, instead of staying with Putnam and Vanessa. I waved, and he jogged my way, leaping over the tape barrier. Show off.

I led the way into Eli's room. "I'm back. And I brought a friend. Do you remember Lando?" And held my breath as I watched a variety of emotions flash across Eli's face. Puzzlement. Sadness. Thoughtfulness. A glimmer of recognition. An enormous smile erased the others. "Lando. Yes. We work together, right?"

"You got it in one." Lando offered a fist bump.

Eli hesitated, but responded with the correct motion.

Instead of following it up with his normal arcane ritual of hand signals and high fives, Lando resorted to giving Eli a simple hug.

"It's good to see you, boss man," Lando said. "You had us worried."

Shoot. I should have told Lando not to use that nickname. Would Eli catch it?

Lando covered his slip by rushing to change the topic. "We need a favor. The cops want to check your phone for clues, but it's locked. Can you unlock it? I'll make sure they don't get into any private folders or messages. You've trusted me to take care of your phone before."

"I wondered what happened to it."

"A fisherman found it near the crash location. It still works, although the screen is cracked. When the cops are done with it, I'll get the glass replaced."

"I don't remember the password."

"All we need is your finger. Harmony, will you do the honor?"

Eli's phone was in my purse, protectively wrapped in a hand towel. I didn't want the glass fragments to fall out. As I removed the cloth, interest sparked in Eli's eyes. It was almost a look of longing.

I handed him the phone. "Careful, Sweetie, the glass has sharp edges."

He winked at me. "Yes, mother. This isn't the first time I've broken a phone."

I exchanged a glance with Lando. "Oh? Tell me about the other times." I kept my voice light, nothing more than curious.

"It happened once in West Virginia," he said, "When Jake's car broke down and I got stuck in a dinky little motel in the middle of nowhere."

"You were missing for a week," I added to his story. "And spent your time working on a security app for your non-existent phone."

"Did I ever finish that development?"

Lando shook his head. "Not that you showed me."

"Huh. Hey, what was I doing driving Jake's car instead of mine?"

"You were bringing it to him after he was released from prison."

"Jake's done time? That doesn't match the man who's been sneaking in real food. Why was he in prison?"

"You should ask him when you see him. Tell me about another time you broke your phone," I said.

"Nope." He grimaced. "That one's classified. Too bad, because it would make you laugh." His smile returned. "But I remember. I was in the Rangers. I was a Ranger. Why didn't you tell me?"

A piece of my heart cracked like the glass in his phone. We'd had this discussion before. "The doctors want you to recover the memories on your own."

"That makes sense. Is that why my mother brought me the photo album?"

"Yes. And why I brought you these." I held out the envelope of pictures. "You can look at them after you unlock your phone."

One side of his mouth quirked. "Now that I have it, I hate to give it up."

"The sooner you unlock it, the sooner the cops get done with it, and the sooner I can get it fixed," Lando said. "Then you can surf the internet in your free time. Better than watching TV."

"I should be like Buttercup and give up watching television." Eli blinked. "Is that right?"

"If you don't count the weather or an occasional documentary, it's the truth." I put the envelope on the bed where he could get to it when he was ready.

"More and more is coming back. Trouble is, I can't tell what's a memory and what's a dream. Like, I dreamed there was a run-down house in the middle of nowhere. I barged in and you were tied up and I rescued you. Crazy, right?"

"Except that happened."

Eli's mouth opened and closed, but no sound came out.

"The guys responsible are still in prison." Most of them, anyway. Only the one in charge, Sallis, had been released. And I wouldn't share that worry with Eli. Or Lando.

"Look, you two can reminisce all day," Lando interrupted. "But there's an impatient cop waiting. How about unlocking it and giving it to me?"

"Is he always this bossy?" Eli grumbled as he

placed his pointer finger on the phone, the trembling nearly gone. The display lit up. So did Eli's eyes.

Before I could stop him, he ran his finger over the screen. He yanked it back and stuck it in his mouth. "Damn, that hurt." The phone dropped to his chest and Lando snatched it.

"We warned you," he said. "Now, keep each other entertained and I'll be right back."

"What's so important about the phone?" Eli asked once Lando disappeared out the door.

I tried to sound lighthearted. "Oh, the usual. Potential evidence, company secrets, state secrets, and hopefully, no recordings of our calls to each other." Some of them were not safe for public listening.

"State secrets? Does Florida have secrets? Even their ability to screw up elections isn't a secret."

"Not Florida. The United States. You have a super-duper security clearance." Or had. I wondered if they would pull it because of his memory loss. "Obviously, you don't talk about it. But the guy examining your phone has all the right credentials. I've checked."

"I should talk to him." He threw back his covers and swung his legs over the side of the bed.

I planted myself in front of him to either stop him or catch him if he fell. "Are you allowed to get up?"

"No one has told me I can't."

As far as I knew, no one had said he could, either. "I'll ask Putnam to come here."

"Putnam?"

"Special Agent Rodney Putnam of the Defense Counter Intelligence and Security Agency. He's in charge of making sure everything is protected until you're back in action."

"He sounds like an interesting guy."

"If you behave, I'll bring him to you." I pushed Eli against his backrest and helped get his legs back on the bed. "Wait for me."

"Do I have a choice?"

There wasn't a good answer, so I didn't reply before making my way through the obstacle course. The workman had changed his location and was closer to Eli's room. He ignored me again. My suspicions grew.

Was he listening in on our conversation?

Chapter 29

"We can't make it work," Lando said. "The phone's screen isn't responding because of the cracks."

I'd figured as much when I walked into the family waiting room, and Putnam and Vanessa weren't huddled around him.

"Eli will be upset if he doesn't get his phone tomorrow," I said. "He's counting on it."

"I got into his security setup and created a password." Lando grimaced. "That's all I did. But once the glass is replaced, I'll be able to access the information without getting Eli involved."

He grinned. "And yes, with great power comes great responsibility. I'll use my power for good, I promise."

I trusted Lando—mostly. "Are you okay with the plan?" I asked Putnam and Vanessa.

Putnam shrugged. "We'll make it work. When do you want to meet tomorrow?"

I needed to check my schedule. "How about we text you when the phone is ready?'

They nodded and stood.

"Before you leave," I said, facing Putnam, "Eli would like to meet you."

"It would be easier to station a guard outside Mr. Hennessey's room," Putnam said as he navigated around a mop and bucket.

"Hospital security made the call. They wanted to discourage the curious. Vanessa agreed." And I'd gone along with it, not having the energy to fight them. "Is there a reason to change the setup?"

"No," he replied in a voice just above a whisper. "None of our sources have picked up any information to indicate a threat."

We exchanged a hard stare, and he nodded. The menace was there, and we both knew it. Who was responsible for it was the answer we needed.

With a slight bow and a wave of his hand, Putnam indicated I should go first.

"I'm back, Eli," I announced as I swept into the room. "Did you miss me?"

The pictures I'd brought lay scattered across the bed. He swiped his eyes. "Why don't I remember these? I mean, some of them are familiar, but not all." He picked up the print of the two of us in his office. "Where was this taken?"

Now wasn't the time. "Here's Special Agent Putnam."

Putnam picked up on his cue and strode into the room, his hand extended. "My pleasure to meet you, Mr. Hennessey."

They shook, and I wondered if Eli would ever get his firm grip back. I got a kick out of watching him establish his dominance over his competitors. Still, he got straight to the point.

"What is your role in this mess, Agent? Harmony hasn't been exactly straightforward."

"She has good instincts and your best interests at heart."

That felt like high praise coming from Putnam. I turned and looked out the window to hide my blush.

"She still gets herself into trouble. Are you keeping her safe?" Eli asked.

Putnam chuckled, and I glared at him.

"We're keeping an eye on her."

"Good. So, tell me, what is she hiding from me?"

Putnam looked at me for guidance. I stuck my hands in my pockets and shook my head, having none to give him.

"Our records indicate you were in possession of privileged government documents at the time of your accident." Putnam chose his words with care. "My job is to locate and secure them. Miss Duprie has been most helpful, but we haven't found them. Where would you have put them?"

One of those random synapses in Eli's brain fired, and he sat upright. "Will you leave for a few minutes, Buttercup?"

"The agency has granted Miss Duprie temporary security clearance if you want her to stay," Putnam said.

"Breaking the rules again?" Eli winked and a tired smile lightened his face. "They were for the Department of Defense, right, Agent? I can't say why I have them unless they're tied to my time in the Rangers. Which I'm remembering pieces of. I came close to dying a couple of times but nothing like this."

He was rambling, but I didn't want to stop his train of thought.

"The one time in Africa was bad. Assigned to stop the fighting between two warlords, we got caught in the middle of a battle. It didn't go well. We lost three guys."

His eyes shuttered. Holding back tears or lost in the memory? I wanted to hug him but was afraid of how he'd react.

Putnam clasped his hands behind his back and waited. It appeared he'd done this before.

Beads of sweat dotted Eli's forehead. "It's there. Somewhere. What happened. It's on the other side of a wall and I can't climb over it. Like the night I was shot. The wall is too high."

"I've got your six," Putnam said. "Relax. We can try again later."

Whatever that meant, it worked. Eli's shoulders slumped. "I come so close and then it slips away."

"It'll take time. You're already ahead of my buddy who suffered a brain injury while in action. Took Jim months to get to where you are. Now he's a father to two of the cutest little girls I've ever seen. And I don't like kids."

Eli couldn't leave well enough alone. "What do the documents deal with?"

"A security leak in a recent SEAL mission. You were analyzing communications."

"That would require digital data."

I caught my breath. Even if it wasn't his official job, this was the first time Eli mentioned anything work-related.

"Yes. You received both digital and paper."

Why hadn't Putnam mentioned that when we searched Eli's house? Not that it would have made a difference. We hadn't found the papers. The two would have been together.

Eli closed his eyes again, and I studied his face, waiting for a lightbulb moment. From the corner of my eye, I caught the door opening a crack. No knock, like a nurse or any staff member would do. Not wanting to break Eli's concentration, I reached up and fiddled with my bun to catch Putnam's attention. It worked. I jerked my head towards the door and cupped my ear. A rotten version of charades.

Putnam read my unspoken message. He slipped his hand under his suit coat to where he kept his gun. Without a sound, he glided backwards and reached for the door handle.

Five thousand elephants raged through the hallway. No, it was a ladder tipping over, a bucket clattering, and two men yelling. One of them was Jake.

Putnam yanked open the door. I was right behind him. Jake stood in the middle of the hall, one bucket in his hand, another rolling away. He pointed towards the end of the hall. "He went that way."

As a man turned the corner and disappeared, Putnam took off, running after him. I stayed to guard Eli. And help Jake extract himself from the security tape wrapped around his feet.

"One guess. That was Putnam?" he asked.

"Special Agent Putnam. He's touchy about that. What are you doing here?"

He picked up a brown paper bag. "I couldn't make it this morning, so I'm bringing Eli's bacon. I try to pick a time to avoid Aunt Tillie and Rob but didn't expect to find you here."

"Tillie had an appointment. Lando and Salters are here, too. Someone found Eli's phone, and he needed to unlock it."

"I can hear you," Eli called. "Bring the bacon!"

Jake laughed. "Spoiled, much?"

While the two of them bonded over bacon, I texted the PI agency. They also supplied bodyguards. Not for me, for Eli. I was throwing money around like I had it. Which I did. If there was ever a time to spend it, it was now.

We crowded into Eli's room. Me, Lando, Vanessa, and Putnam. I wanted Eli to be part of the discussion. Jake had slipped away as soon as Vanessa and Putnam showed up.

Vanessa and Putnam discussed potential security plans while I sipped on a cup of coffee, courtesy of Lando. Putnam hadn't caught the intruder. Too much of a head start. Lando tried to interject his ideas into the conversation but was ignored. I watched the show, ready to jump in when the moment was right.

My phone vibrated, and I checked the message. The first bodyguard of the day was at the nurses' desk, waiting for permission to take his post outside Eli's room. Money had talked to make it happen so swiftly.

I focused my attention on Eli. He was struggling to follow the discussion and to stay awake. His eyes fluttered closed and open for about the tenth time, and I'd had enough.

"Out. Everyone. Now," I stage-whispered. "Let the man sleep. We can continue this in the cafeteria. Or at the office."

"We can't leave Eli alone," Lando objected.

"I've got it covered. He'll have twenty-four-hour security. It's been cleared with the hospital administration. Now, everyone out." I shooshed them out but hung behind, closing the door to give Eli and me a moment of privacy.

"Have a good nap, Sweetie. I'll be back later."

He blinked. "What are you up too?"

"I'm taking charge. Should have done it a week ago." I rearranged his pillow and straightened his covers, then leaned in to kiss him. "I'll be back later, I promise." I waited for his eyes to close before leaving,

❉ ❉ ❉

"New rules." I nibbled on the sandwich Darla had ordered. "Everything comes to me. I want the reports from all the agencies. Special Agent Putnam, make sure I have the clearances I need. I have a reputation to uphold."

"What reputation would that be?" Vanessa tore her sandwich in half but didn't take a bite. "The one that says you're a drug dealer? Or a show-off risky driver?"

Low blows, but I wouldn't let her get under my skin. "The one where I put together the pieces of the puzzle law enforcement misses. Where I find patterns and trends that everyone else overlooks. Vanessa, I want the analysis of the similarities of the fires to other incidents. Can you get me access to the database? I assume you have one."

"I'll talk to my boss."

I smirked. "Make sure word gets up the chain of command to whoever is calling the shots."

Then I turned to Putnam. "Special Agent Putnam, tell me what you're looking for. Not now, when we're in private. And get me the background checks the agency has completed. In fact, forget completed. Give me everything you've got."

My eyes drifted to Lando and Darla. "As far as I'm concerned, you two are cleared. Scotty, too."

Putnam pushed away from the table and shook his head. "No."

"Am I cleared or not?" I asked.

"Doesn't matter. You aren't getting those reports. It's against regulations."

"So is attempted murder. And snooping on us in Eli's hospital room. And setting houses on fire. What's one more thing to add to the list? While we're at it, Lando, I want electronic access to Marty's spreadsheets. In fact, I want access to his computer. And anything he stores on the network. No one else needs to know about it. Can you do that?"

"Who's Marty?" Vanessa asked.

"The accountant. He gives me paper reports, which I despise. Old-school, I guess. Or maybe it's deliberate."

Lando grinned. "Can I do that? Of course. Give me five minutes with your laptop and you'll have the keys to his kingdom."

"Darla, I'll lean on you to keep me organized. When I dive into these reports, I'll ignore everything else. Your role is to interrupt me when there's work to do."

"Like Eli when he's programming?"

"Exactly."

"What makes you think we'll go along with this fiasco, Miss Duprie?" Putnam asked.

"Because you need to close this security breach and I'm your best bet. You're as tired of me as I am of you. Unless you're stringing me along to make yourselves look good. Or bad, for some convoluted reason. Because you want to protect Eli and get to the bottom of everything. Not as much as I do, but you'll grab every opportunity to solve this case. And that means using every resource available. Including me."

"You're quite confident in your abilities, aren't you? Perhaps over-confident? If you're that good, why aren't you working for law enforcement? Or a big corporation?"

"You haven't seen her in action," Lando said. "She's good. Real good."

"Because I've turned down three offers, Special Agent Putnam. Something your records and interviews will never find." I chuckled to myself at the way his eyes narrowed. "I don't want to be boxed in by rules and regulations."

"I think we should give her a chance, Putnam." Vanessa cocked her head and rolled her shoulders. "She's a bundle of surprises. Bad for my self-esteem, but that's my problem."

"One set of top-secret paperwork has gone missing." Putnam's lips formed a tight line. "I'm not willing to risk anything else going astray."

I was strangely proud of him for standing up to the pressure, even if it made my research harder.

"What I will do," he continued, "is to allow you, Miss Duprie, to review their contents in my presence. You'll never be in possession of them."

He got full points for finding a way to bend the rules. "I can make that work." Two burdens off my shoulders in one swoop. I no longer had to research the employees and didn't have to worry about protecting the reports. I was counting on the PI agency to get me the full FHP report. It was my first test to verify their effectiveness.

Chapter 30

After trying to use my phone with no luck, Eli fell asleep early. So, I got back to the house while a hint of light still colored the sky. I pulled into the garage. Vanessa parked in the driveway behind me, her way of making sure I wouldn't take off in the middle of the night, forgetting how often I walked away while she slept.

As I unlocked the front door, the ever-present silver pickup drove by, going wherever it went each night. Only this time, the driver tooted its horn. Amazed, I stared at the vanishing taillights.

"Have you tracked down who that is?" I asked Vanessa. "It should be easy to get the plate."

"We did. It comes back as registered to a local nonprofit for vets. Part of their fleet. Without a warrant, they won't reveal who's driving a specific vehicle at any specific time. They haven't done anything wrong, so we can't request the records."

Another dead end. At least, they no longer felt like a threat. That's what I told myself as I bent to pick up the manila envelope tucked in between the screen door and the front door. Right where the PI agency had said I'd find it. We'd agreed to do everything electronically, but the copy of the FHP's report was too blurry to transfer to a digital format and remain readable.

I headed to my room to change and fire up my laptop. As much as I longed to read a book, there was work to do. I'd begin by reading the report and see what I hadn't been told. And what they missed. If Eli had thrown his phone out the window, what else might be hiding in the bushes and weeds at the crash site? I shot off an email to the agency, suggesting a search.

As I arranged my pillow to use as a backrest, a piece of paper fluttered to the floor. I picked it up before it settled.

A rough sketch of an angel decorated one side. I didn't need anything else to realize that Jake had been here.

It was his style. The note and the audacity to break into a house occupied by an agent of the law. Never mind the security guys upstairs. It was Jake's way of thumbing his nose at Vanessa and the ATF. And letting me know he'd be around if I needed him.

I placed the slip of paper between the pages of one of my books—The Wolf and the Witch. I couldn't imagine Vanessa ever reading it.

Knowing Eli was guarded and I was gathering the forces needed to find who was behind the attacks let me sleep a little easier that night. Like a queen rallying her allies to protect her king.

❊ ❊ ❊

Lando tapped on my office door. The conference call with Gavin Fairwood was wrapping up, so I waved him in.

He laid Eli's phone on my desk. A glance confirmed he'd gotten the broken glass replaced. He turned to leave, but I caught his eye and pointed to a chair. He got the hint and sat.

It was only moments until the call finished, and I focused my attention on Lando. "From the look on your face," I said, "You and Putnam had no luck."

"None," he said with a frown. "Although I did show him a few places to check he didn't know about."

A thought that had been nagging me for days broke to the surface. "Next, we tackle his laptop."

Lando held up his hands, shoulder height. "Nope. It's so locked down; I won't touch it. Hell, I'm not sure the damn thing won't self-destruct if I try to get in and fail too many times."

Which made it the obvious place to search for leads. But after seeing Eli struggle with my phone, I wasn't confident he could log into his laptop.

"Did you make the password something easy?" I asked as I picked up Eli's phone and ran my hand across the now-smooth surface.

"Why? You think he'll forget it?"

That was one reason. "I'm more worried about him being unable to punch the right numbers. His fine motor control is shaky."

"Hmm. Let me have it."

I handed him the phone and watched as he fiddled with it.

"This goes against everything I preach," he said. "But I'm making the password one-two-one-two. He should be able to handle that. Can I tag along when you take it to him?"

"What are you working on?"

One corner of his mouth lifted. "It depends upon your definition of working. I'm assigned to a nasty coding issue for the Oak Grove Fire Department project. But mostly I'm staring at the screen. I can't concentrate."

"And Scotty?"

"The revisions for the Smithfield setup. Supervising more than anything else. I think he knows the fix but wants the new guy to figure it out. Why? What do you have up your sleeve?"

"I heard a rumor you need to go pick up your van today. Eli's in therapy until eleven, and I have another call scheduled then. How about you two combine errands and take Eli's phone to him? I'll clear you with the PI agency and you can take as much time as you want."

Lando's grin spread across his face. "Have I told you you're my second-favorite boss?"

"Yeah, yeah, flattery will get you nowhere. Before you go, have you figured out how to give me access to Marty's computer?"

"Doing it is easy. But getting him out of the office long enough to make it happen is hard. If I rope our systems guys into the project, it will only take a few minutes."

"Do you trust them not to tell anyone?"

"Yep, they're good."

"Then do it." The sooner the better.

The call at eleven was boring with a capital B. While I pretended to listen to what the salesperson promised they could provide, I checked out the backgrounds of Stan and Raoul, our systems guys. Lando might trust them, but that didn't mean I had to.

The only reason I stuck with the call was because Eli had it on his calendar. I didn't know why he was interested in a small business loan unless he'd been thinking about expanding the company. If so, it would have to wait.

By the time the call ended, Stan and Raoul had joined the ranks of the cleared, and it was time for lunch.

I hadn't grabbed anything out of the freezer this morning, so I wandered down to the breakroom to see what the vending machines offered.

Several others stared at the machines. Chances didn't look good.

"There are two choices," Fiona said. "Hot dogs or stale ham sandwiches."

Neither was acceptable. "Somebody check where the nearest food truck is," I suggested.

Four phones were whipped out of pockets at once, in a race to find the information.

Jeremy, one of the help desk experts, found it first. "There's a mini food-truck rally over at the church on Eighth until two. Tacos, sausages, and burgers. Who's in? We can walk."

As we trooped out the front door, I noted Marty pulling into the parking lot. Maybe he'd taken an early lunch. I considered asking him to join us, but he stayed in his car, making it easy to exclude him.

I wasn't the only one who noticed. "You know what's weird?" Jeremy asked.

"What?"

"Every time one of those cops come to see you, he leaves."

I was slow on the uptake. "Who leaves?"

"Marty. Not right away, but five minutes later."

Alarms rang in my head, but I played it cool. "I've never paid attention. Does he leave often? On regular days?"

Paula answered. "He used to. When Eli was here. We figured he was running errands for Eli."

I'd never heard Eli mention anything like that. But we'd almost reached the church and the food trucks, so I let it drop.

In the security feed, I watched Lando's van pull in, closely followed by Scotty's car. Five minutes later, they tumbled into my office. It surprised me it took that long.

They tried to look serious but failed. Smiles broke through their frowns.

"It went well, I assume?" I asked.

They dropped into the nearest chairs.

"He remembered me right away!" Scotty crowed.

"Didn't even need a hint."

"Because he'd already seen me and figured it out because we were together," Lando said.

"Sure, sure. Whatever it takes to make yourself feel better. Jealous, much?"

"Argue after work." I tried to sound boss-like to hide my laughter. "I have a project for you two."

"What?" Scotty asked.

"I need a list of Marty's comings and goings during work hours. Include any time he entered the building outside of office hours. Go back two weeks before Eli's disappearance. Also, a list of each time any of my law enforcement contacts were here. How soon can you get that for me?"

They eyed each other. Lando held up two fingers. Scotty countered with four.

"What kind of bonus do we get?" Lando asked, always the mercenary.

"None. Eli spoils you two. Not me. Either you do it, or you don't."

"Three days." Scotty lowered a finger.

Lando raised one. "Three days."

I'd seen them in action enough to recognize the bullshit. "I'll give you two days. Better yet, tomorrow by five. It'll cut into your gaming time tonight, but you'll do it for Eli. Am I right?"

"Thursday morning," Scotty negotiated.

"Agreed. And don't share this with anyone."

"It'll be like doing a special project for Eli. Even without the bonus." Lando rubbed his hands together. "Everyone is so used to us working on special projects they won't even ask about it."

Good. I didn't want it to become part of the office gossip.

The end-of-the-day report from the agency, on an extensive report of the area where Eli had wrecked, didn't reveal anything new. Other than a couple of crusty old watches, plenty of beer cans, scrap metal and assorted garbage, they'd found nothing. I'd been hoping they'd find Eli's wallet and gun. No one had attempted to use his cards or pawned his gun yet, which eliminated robbery as a motive. And led me right back to revenge.

I needed to get Eli to remember more about the night. Tonight was not the time. Between therapy, Lando and Scotty's visit, and his frustration at not being able to work his phone, Eli wasn't in the best of moods.

The phone itself was fine. The problem was his fine motor control. He couldn't swipe or type correctly. We tried speech-to-text and while it helped, it wasn't a total fix.

I didn't know how to help. When he rolled over and asked me to dim the lights, I did. I sat in the darkened room with him until his breathing steadied and he was asleep.

❃ ❃ ❃

Vanessa tossed a flash drive on my desk. She closed the office door and silenced the sounds of keyboards clacking. "There you go. Everything we've dug up about the fires. And thanks to a push from up the chain, my boss caved. It includes the database listing historical incidents matching the methodology. Someone has their eye on you, Harmony."

Or Eli, and I was the path to him. "How much of this is classified?" I picked up the drive and rubbed it, like trying to get a genie to appear.

"None of it. So, you don't have to worry about some scary boogeyman coming after you to steal it." Without an invitation, she sank into a chair. At the same time, I watched the security feed as Marty slipped out the back door. I shot a quick text to Lando and Scotty.

"Well?" she asked.

"Well, what?"

"Do your magic. I want to see what you come up with."

"It doesn't work like that. First, I have to develop a structure for the information and determine what data is relevant and what isn't." And ask my experts to check out the contents of the drive to make sure it contained no spyware that would install on my laptop. I didn't suspect Vanessa of doing anything like that, but someone else in her agency might. "I'll get started this afternoon if I have the time."

"You haven't forgiven me."

"Are you surprised?"

"It's part of my life."

I understood. "But it doesn't have to be part of mine."

"You're not as innocent as you pretend."

"I'm also not as tough as I act."

"I can see that." Vanessa stood. "For what it's worth, I'm sorry."

Saying she was sorry was fine, but I'd figured out Vanessa's job would always be first in her life. She had something to prove. To her boss, to the world, to herself. I didn't feel the slightest bit of guilt when I dropped the flash drive on Scotty's desk and explained the situation.

"Can you find a link between the fires the ATF can't?" he asked.

"Probably not. But I might get lucky. It's past time for me to catch a break."

"I kept an eye on Marty when he left. All he did was go sit in his car and make a phone call."

Suspicious enough. I'd wait for the results from the review of the security video.

The drive was as clean as fresh snow, according to Scotty. But he was Florida born and bred, and what did he know about snow? I counted to three before sticking Vanessa's device into the proper spot and waiting for the explosion or dancing monkeys to spread across my screen. Nothing. Just the standard box acknowledging the new addition to my laptop. I didn't have time to start my analysis but was curious to see what information they'd given me.

A quick peek revealed my work wouldn't be easy. The way they arranged the data wasn't the way my mind worked. I'd be starting from scratch.

I couldn't resist browsing through the list of known arsonists. No names that I recognized. Thank heavens. I checked my calendar. It listed nothing for another forty-five minutes. I should go talk to the other employees. Or I could give into temptation.

Chapter 31

Darla knocked on my office door. "Your meeting is in three minutes, Harmony."

Drat. I was just getting warmed up. But I couldn't miss the on-line meeting with the trio of Maine police chiefs. Lando, who was working on the development for the joint effort, joined me in my office as I brought up the link on the big screen.

Lando's side of the project was all but complete, and Kris and Elena were finalizing the contract. I was nothing but the face of the company and the connection to Eli. I wondered if he'd be able to sign the final paperwork. He'd put so much into the initial design.

With no new issues to iron out, we ended the call ahead of schedule. I longed to get back to Vanessa's data, but needed to make a personal appearance in the main room and see how things were going. That's what Eli would have done. And would do again.

I passed by Fiona's darkened office on the way. It was early for her to have left for the day, but maybe she was out taking care of a public relations event. I hoped she was enjoying her new role. Darla hadn't mentioned any issues, and I took that as a good sign.

The email from Sarah held several surprises. She and Freddie were engaged. No date had been set for the wedding, although they were discussing a simple courthouse ceremony. She wished I'd be able to come home for it.

Home. The tears that fell on my desk were a mixture of happiness and sadness. Why hadn't she called? I'd hoped they would take the big step, but I should have been there to celebrate with them. At least I'd won the bet with Janine about when the engagement would happen. Too bad I wasn't in Oak Grove to collect.

The second part of the email was as unexpected. I'd forgotten I'd asked Sarah to research the possibility of buying the house, and forgotten to tell her to forget about it. The owner was willing to sell, but at a price well above what I was willing to pay. Did I want to negotiate a deal?"

As I picked up my phone to call and congratulate her, Scotty and Lando barged into my office without knocking. They didn't look as if they brought good news.

My mind jumped to a worst-case scenario. "Is something wrong with Eli?"

"No! Where did that come from?" Scotty asked.

"The looks on your faces. Like you lost your jobs, and the bank repossessed your vehicles."

Lando's frown deepened. "We were comparing results from the security footage. We aren't done but thought you should see the preliminary results."

I checked the time. It was quitting time, except for the evening support staff. I needed to find a way for them to work from home. There weren't many customers on the West Coast and calls trickled down to next to nothing this late. There didn't seem to be a good reason for the support team to stay in the office.

"Harmony?" Lando clicked his fingers in front of my face.

"Sorry. I got distracted."

"Yeah, I know the look. Write it down so you don't forget whatever brilliant idea you had."

I scribbled on the notepad. "What is Marty up to?"

"It's not Marty," Scotty said. "It's Fiona." Another flash drive dropped on my desk. "Take a peek."

I couldn't read their faces, so I plugged in the drive and opened the only file it contained. Despite my instructions, they'd started a preliminary analysis. Not only on Marty, but on several employees. But I'd forgive them based on what they'd found.

Fiona, after being given her new assignment, was spending lots of time out of the office. Not away from the office, just not in it.

"Is she taking a laptop outside to work?" I asked. I scrolled through the list of her comings and goings. Five minutes here, ten minutes there, but not official breaks. Twice a full half-hour. "Did this happen before she switched jobs?"

"Yes, but not as much. And she isn't taking a laptop. She hasn't been issued one yet. She's not even touching her phone. At least, not while she's in camera range."

"Is she a smoker?"

Scotty rubbed his neck. "Not that I've noticed. We don't socialize much."

Scotty was friendly, if reserved, with almost everyone. "She's gone for the day, right?"

"Yeah, why?"

"Why don't you like her?"

He and Lando exchanged a glance.

"It's like this," Scotty said, "When she started working here, she seemed nice enough. She did her job, chatted with everyone, figured out the ropes. Pretty soon I noticed her flirting with me. A lot. I was flattered, then I got talking about it with Lando and she was flirting with him, too. Okay, whatever, there's no rule that says she can't, and she wasn't trying to hide it."

"Then we figured it out," Lando interrupted. "It happened more when we were talking to Eli. She'd find an excuse to join in the conversation. She was using us to get to him."

"Which didn't work." Scotty grinned. "Once we noticed, we started freezing her out. And Eli never gave her any more attention than anyone else. Because he was totally in love with you, even if he didn't realize it back then."

I couldn't blame her for trying to catch Eli's eye. Unless there was more to it. "What if she tried to seduce Eli to get information to use against him?"

"That's quite the stretch," Scotty said.

"Not as much as you think. A while ago, Eli was

getting consistently underbid for jobs. He never told me the details, but it seemed as if someone saw his figures and leaked them to the competition. I suspected an inside job, like the attack."

Lando stood and planted his hands on the desk, leaning over so we were eye-to-eye. "Crap. Why didn't you tell us this before?"

"Because I have no proof. It's pure speculation."

"How about your law enforcement buddies?"

I quirked one side of my mouth. "Put it this way. None of them are my friends. Why do you think I cut Vanessa's network access? They've semi-promised to give me data when I ask for it, but they're still hiding things I should know. That's why I hired a firm to fill in the gaps and provide Eli's bodyguard. I can't do everything at once."

"The big scary guy outside Eli's room? I didn't think he looked like a hospital employee."

"Yep."

"Where's Marty fit into this?" Scotty asked.

"I don't know. I need time to review the accounting files."

"I'd offer to help," Lando said. "But I'm no good with that stuff."

"What you're doing with the security tapes is a big help. But Scotty, I have another job for you. I want you to track Fiona tomorrow. Follow her when she leaves, see where she goes, what she does. Is she meeting someone? Buying drugs? What is she up too? Do you think you can do that without her figuring it out?"

"I can help," Lando suggested.

"You stand out too much. Your blue hair is a giveaway. In this heat, you can't even wear a hoodie to hide it."

He put his hand over his heart. "For Eli, I'll dye it brown. Or black."

"We aren't at that point yet. That's what the PIs are for. If that changes, I'll come to you."

"Promise?"

"Promise. For now, I need your hacking skills more than anything else. You can keep your blue."

"Then we'll get back to work. There's a deadline to meet."

Thanks to a traffic jam caused by a minor accident, I had time for a nice conversation with Sarah on the way to the hospital. We talked about the proposal and potential dates for the wedding. She wanted to keep trying to get the price down on the house, and I agreed. That was after making a side trip and purchasing a pack of tablets and pens for Eli. The report from the agency had mentioned he'd been asking for them, and all the hospital staff gave him were tiny scratch pads. I liked having a second set of ears to tell me what Tillie forgot.

The bodyguard nodded as I strolled by. I didn't recognize him, but that was part of the agency's method. Switch up people often to keep them fresh. In the room, the lights were dimmed and the bed empty. My heart sank, then did a little dance as I spotted the figure looking out the window. In a wheelchair, but out of bed. Even from the back of his head, I recognized him.

"Hey, Sweetie, look at you."

"I never realized how different things look when you're in a chair instead of stuck in a bed. It's like seeing the world a whole new way." He tried to turn the chair around, but the wheels didn't want to move in the right direction. I hesitated, wanting to help, but not wanting to hurt his pride.

He gave up, and I took two steps to be closer. "Do you need a hand?"

"I did it earlier." He gave the wheel another weak shove, but it didn't respond.

"You're tired. Consider me your chauffeur. Where do you want me to take you?"

"Home."

I turned the chair so he faced me.

"Do you remember your home?"

"It's confusing." He stared out the window again. "I get flashes of my room when I was a kid. I'm even starting to remember my mother. Then there's a yellow house. It's mine, but it's just a place to stay. Then there's a little place in an old house. And every time it comes to mind, so do you. So, I'm guessing it's your apartment."

He didn't mention his house in Oak Grove, so I didn't either. "Did you tell your mother that you remembered her?"

"No, because I had her fooled, and I didn't want her to know I was lying before."

I chuckled. "You sound like a sneaky little kid."

He grinned. "I feel like that sometimes. How old am I, anyway?"

"You don't remember your birthday?"

"It's in the fall. October. But the nurses keep asking and I don't want to get it wrong."

I locked him in by putting a hand on each of the arms of the chair, positioning myself between his legs, and leaning forward. "And you thought you would trick me into telling you the exact day, so you could lie and tell them you remembered it on your own."

In the next moment, faster than I knew he could move, I found myself pulled against his chest.

"My legs may not work right, but my arms do." He tugged me closer, and I squirmed to get comfortable. Which made me aware that another part of him worked as well. Now wasn't the time to deal with it.

"You're trying to distract me," I said.

In answer, he blew a breath over the top of my head while moving a hand up my back. The awkward position didn't allow for kissing, but I moved my left hand to stroke his cheek. He rubbed my neck, and I relaxed at the touch. Then he slid his hand under the chain I wore. The one with his dog tags. The tags jiggled as the chain rotated, but they didn't go with it.

I grabbed his hand. "You aren't very good at being sneaky. Besides, your birthday isn't listed. The army doesn't do that."

He sighed and kissed the top of my head. "I've lost my touch. But it was worth a try."

"You almost got away with it." I maneuvered out of his grasp and stood. I needed to distract him. "Hey, guess what I brought you?"

"Not another stuffed animal, I hope." Eli fake-shivered. "My mother tried flowers and balloons, but the hospital doesn't allow them. Now, she keeps bringing stuffed animals. I don't think she realizes that the nurses take them to the kids' unit after a few days."

I'd wondered where the revolving supply of toys came from. "No, nothing like that. How about paper and pens?"

His eyes lit. "Like full-size and everything?"

I handed him the bag. "It isn't your birthday, and it's not Christmas, but enjoy."

He tipped the bag over and a three-pack of tablets and a twelve-pack of pens tumbled into his lap. I'd bought fat pens with rubber grips, figuring they'd be easier for him to hold. And the variety of colors would help if he wanted to track changes or mark sections. I'd learned something about his style in our time together.

He fumbled with the package, trying to break into the plastic cover. I plucked it from his hands. "Let me. These things are terrible to open."

I made a show of separating the clear front from the cardboard backing. "What color do you want first?"

"Red."

Odd choice, but if that was what he wanted, that's what he'd get. After handing a red pen to him, I tore the plastic wrap off the bundle of tablets and gave him one.

With no table handy, he laid the paper in his lap. He clicked the pen and wrote.

I craned my neck to see what words of wisdom would flow from his pen. At first, it was scribbles. Lines and circles and pointless dots.

He flipped a page and started fresh. Circles within circles. Boxes within boxes. Shaky, and lines crossed where they weren't meant to, but he didn't seem to care. If there was a meaning to his drawing, I didn't understand it. Or was he relearning how to control the pen? He turned to a fresh sheet of paper.

He seemed content, and that warmed my soul, but I was bored. I amused myself by gathering up the garbage and looking for a trash can. When I came back, I caught him ripping a page from the tablet and folding it in half. Badly, like a five-year-old would do, but he'd done it.

He waved it in the air. "This is for you. I can't come to you, so you have to come to me."

What game was he playing? Only one way to find out. I walked behind him and snatched the paper before he could turn.

"No fair!" he protested.

It only took a moment to unfold it. And turn me into a puddle.

The picture was simple. A misshapen heart with the words 'I love you' in block letters. The lines wavered and pointed in every direction. It didn't matter. The thought did.

I wrapped my arms around him from behind and kissed his neck. "Thank you. I love you, too."

The pen clattered to the floor as he reached up and clasped my arms.

A knock interrupted the moment. "Time to get

you in bed, Eli," a voice said. I recognized it as one of the nurses. "And no whining. We've already given you a half-hour more than what the physical therapist suggested."

Eli succumbed to sleep early, so I tackled more research when I got back to the house. With Vanessa in her room, it was the perfect time to rip into Marty's spreadsheets. I wished for a big screen to ease the strain on my eyes, but I'd have to make do with what I had.

Around midnight, I sneaked into the kitchen and made half a pot of coffee. I didn't plan on an all-nighter, but I needed one more hour to complete my analysis.

At two, I shut down my laptop. No matter how I manipulated the data, I found no flaws. His accounts were as clean as any I'd ever seen. But my gut wasn't convinced of his innocence. He was hiding something. I just hadn't uncovered it.

Chapter 32

"Ready for the hurricane?" Lando asked as he strolled into my office.

I put down my third cup of coffee and stared at him. "Hurricane?"

"Nothing to worry about. It'll slide up the coast and all we'll see is rain."

"Do I need to stock up on groceries in case the electricity goes out or something?"

"And how would you cook without electricity? Newbie." Lando laughed. "If it looks as if it's going to get bad, you can come stay with me. I'll protect you since Eli can't. But the most I expect is the hotels filling up with people leaving the coast and heavy traffic."

He was the expert.

"I actually came in here to give you this." He handed me a flash drive. "It's the report you requested."

"Find anything interesting?"

Lando used his foot to shut the door. "Gut reaction?

Marty's spying on you and reporting your movements to someone. He not only leaves when law enforcement is here, he's taking off when you're on conference calls. But not all the time. See if you can figure out a pattern. I couldn't."

Why hadn't Putnam given me a report on the employees yet? I needed to move Marty to the top of the list. "And Fiona?"

"At a quick glance, I wasn't able to correlate your activities and the times she leaves the building. Maybe she's slacking off." He rubbed his chin. "That's where Scotty is. Following her."

"I hope she's out feeding the homeless or something. I hate firing people."

"You can't do that until you know she doesn't have anything to do with the attack on Eli."

True. If she didn't suspect we were tracking her, she might slip and reveal needed information.

"Have you checked out Marty's files yet?" Lando asked.

"Last night. I'm not an accountant, but I didn't spot anything fishy."

"Don't the bad guys in the movies always keep a second set of books?"

I snorted. "That's so overdone it's ridiculous."

"But you'll let me wander around Marty's computer and check, right?"

I had to try everything. "Don't get caught."

He chuckled. "You know me better than that."

I reminded myself that I was the boss. I didn't need anyone's permission to allow Lando to search Marty's computer. But if Marty was innocent, I didn't want to lose him. He'd worked for Eli for a long time.

❊ ❊ ❊

I put on a bright face as I entered Eli's room. He sat in the small beam of sunlight by the window, but based on the pile of crumbled paper on the floor, he wasn't looking outside. As I stood there, another sheet joined them.

"Are you having trouble?" I asked.

"I can't remember." He tossed the tablet onto the small table beside him, a recent addition to the room. "I've got this perfect code in my head, but it goes away when I try to put it on paper."

He was trying. I picked up the tablet and stared at the assortment of letters, numbers and symbols. I recognized it as code, but that was the extent of my knowledge. "I can't help. You'll need to ask Lando and Scotty."

He frowned. "We work together."

"We do. But I'm a researcher, not a developer. I used to be a librarian."

His eyes glazed, the look of someone lost in their thoughts. "The company has a crazy name. Shift. That can't be right. It has nothing to do with cars. Tell me, Buttercup. What company do we work for?"

"You're close. Try again."

He focused his stare on me, as if searching my face for a clue. "Tech. Technology. What does shift have to do with that?"

"You're getting hot."

"Like the kids' game? Let me try again. Tech. Technology. Feels close. I still can't figure out what shift has to do with anything. Shift. Shifting. Shifts. Or I could get crazy like one of those movies. Shifter."

Beads of sweat broke out on his forehead. "Shift. No, shifter feels right, but that's nuts. Technology shift. Technology shifter. What would a computer geek look like as a wolf?"

Was he sinking into a nightmare? I didn't want to break into his thought process. He was so close.

"Technology. Technologies. Shift. Shift Tech. Shifter Tech. Shifting Technologies."

His breathing slowed. "Shifter Technologies. That would be a cool company to own."

Now I held my breath.

He grabbed my hand. "That's it. Shifter Technologies. Like in changing technology. And I own the company, right? Tell me I'm not making this up."

Happy tears welled in my eyes. "You're not making this up. You are the founder and owner of Shifter Technologies, Incorporated, a firm that specializes in software for police departments nationwide."

Eli grasped the arms of the chair and tried to stand. A gentle push from me had him right back in his seat.

"Where do you think you're going?"

"I have to get out of here and check how things are going. Is everyone being paid? Who's taking care of the business?"

I crouched, so I didn't loom over him and we were equals. "Me. You gave me emergency access a few months ago. That's where I am all day."

"And why you're all dressed up."

"If I'm representing you, I need to look the part."

"Is everything going okay?"

"You hired good people, Eli." Except for one or two. "They've got things covered."

"But none of them care enough to visit."

I put my hands on his knees. "Are you whining? Really? The hospital has limited the number of visitors you're allowed. I'm pushing the rules, getting Lando and Scotty in here. If everyone came, they'd be in the way and you'd never get any rest."

Was that a faint smile?

"I have the right to complain." He put his hands on top of mine.

"You do. But don't get used to it."

He leaned forward. So did I. Our lips met in the middle. A soft touch. Enough to convey our love.

"Is that why the cops haven't questioned me about the accident?" he asked after we pulled apart.

Where had that idea come from? "That's different. With your memory being unreliable, Richon decided to wait."

"Who?"

"Sergeant Alex Richon of the FHP. He's in charge of investigating the incident."

He shook his head. "Are you collecting cops again? Call him. Not tonight. Tomorrow. He and I need to talk."

Lando took one of Eli's button-up shirts to the hospital for the interview. I couldn't go to support him, but, as a precaution, Maria would stay in the room.

When he returned, Lando reported in. He slouched in his favorite chair and sipped on a soda. "I didn't realize how much weight Eli's lost until I helped him put on his shirt," he said.

I had. I pushed aside the paperwork in front of me to pay attention to Lando.

"He's going to need a new wardrobe," Lando continued. "But you know what was cool?"

"What?" I asked to prove I was listening.

"It was the change in attitude. Like he stopped being helpless and was ready to take charge. Like the old Eli was back."

I'd been seeing hints of it, but one of the cracks in my heart healed having Lando agree. "Hospital staff doesn't know what they're in for." I smiled at the thought. "He's going to demand things instead of playing nice."

Lando chuckled. "You're the only person who can handle him when he gets cranky."

That sounded like a compliment. "I'm sure they've dealt with it before. All they have to do is distract him with the coding books I've given him."

"He had one on the table by his bed. There were pieces of paper sticking out from between the pages."

I made a mental note to take him more tablets. And bookmarks.

"Anyway, Richon said he'd get a copy of the report to you through the proper channels. I tried to eavesdrop, but he chased me away."

"That means I'll get it in never and a day."

"That's what the PI agency guy said, too. He bet they'd get you a copy before Richon did. I didn't ask him how."

Another dead end. For the moment. "Has Scotty had any luck following Fiona?"

Lando grimaced. "Either she's on to him, or she's dealing with something personal. She wanders down to the bus stop every time, makes a call, and comes back. Nothing suspicious there."

"And Marty?"

"If he's hiding something, I can't find it. But I'm not done digging yet. There are lots of places you can hide files. If you know what you're doing, you can give it a system file extension and it becomes almost invisible."

I added asking the PI agency to research both Fiona and Marty to my to-do-list. I preferred to keep it in-house, but we weren't getting anywhere. Like everything else in the investigation. Putnam had emailed a few heavily redacted reports, which wasn't our agreement, but was better than nothing. They hadn't included either Marty or Fiona.

The daily email from the agency arrived early, marked as urgent. I didn't want any interruptions, so I shut my office door before clicking on the message. Had they got Putnam's report?

The attachment was a series of pictures. Blurry, out-of-focus, grainy, taken by a cheap security camera. Each shot featured the dark outlines of a vehicle by the gas pumps. I recognized it as well as I would recognize Dolores. Eli's car.

If I scrolled through the pictures fast enough, it reminded me of one of those old-fashioned flip books with cartoon characters. That didn't do me any good. I needed to study each image for clues.

The last set of pictures was different. A red car, the plate unreadable. A blurry face made almost inhuman by the pixelated features, No one I knew.

I watched again and again as the man and Eli talked. The man leaned over by a tire on Eli's car when Eli had his back turned. I thought I spotted a flash of metal in his hand. A knife?

The contact number for my lead investigator with the agency was programmed into my phone. He didn't answer, but I left a detailed message with what I'd seen. If the agency was as good as their reputation, they'd be able to get into the police impound lot and check.

On the way to the hospital, the pictures played in a continuous loop in my mind. It was the best lead we had. What was I missing? Eli clearly had his wallet because in the video I could see him take out a credit card to pay for the gas. But the poor quality didn't allow me to determine if he'd worn his gun.

My heart was lighter as I walked up the stairs to Eli's room. I didn't have answers yet, but at least I had clues.

Eli sat near the window, but he wasn't staring outside. The coding book lay open in his lap and one hand rested on a tablet of paper. The other held a pen he was using to tap the arm of the chair. Or was it a tremble he couldn't control?

I watched from the doorway until he looked up. "Hi."

"There you are. I was worried you weren't coming."

"Am I that late? Blame Orlando traffic."

"Yeah, I remember." His eyes lit up. "I actually remember. I kind of miss it. I can't wait to drive again."

"How did therapy go?" My report said he'd yelled at the therapist. I wondered if he'd confess.

He studied the tips of his slippers. "I'm not a very patient patient."

I couldn't help myself and giggled.

"Their equipment is old and worn out. I can afford better than that."

I waited until the realization hit him.

"Wait. I can, can't I? Buy better stuff?"

"Yes, you can. Maybe we can make a donation to the hospital later."

"How much would it take to buy my way out of here? Who do I need to talk to?"

I put my hand on his shoulder. "Slow down. You can't buy your way out. But no worries, I'm researching local facilities to find one I approve of for long-term care. I've eliminated all but two."

His eyes narrowed. "You're sticking me in an old folks' home?"

Exactly what I didn't want. "I've asked if you could be released to your home and go to a therapy center every day, but the doctor said not yet. He wants you in a medical facility for the time being."

Besides, it wouldn't be safe until we'd tracked down who was responsible for his assault. "The places I'm considering specialize in rehabilitation after accidents or surgery. I'll tour them before I pick one."

"Take me with you. I can help decide."

He should be part of the decision. I knew how to make it happen. "Do you remember how to make video calls?"

Eli rolled his head. "Where's my phone?"

I glanced around the room. "On the table by your bed."

"Will you bring it to me?"

In an automatic reaction, I started to. Then changed my mind. "Do it yourself. You're in that chair instead of in bed for a reason."

"You're mean," he grumbled, but not-so-gracefully jerked his chair around and got it aimed in the right direction. A few turns of the wheels and he reached his goal. I let him struggle with turning on the phone and unlocking it. His hands shook, but he reached the opening screen. "Now what?"

"It's easy. I'll call and all you have to do is accept." Once we connected, I went out to the hall to reduce the echo. "What I can do," I said, swiveling the phone from side to side, "is show you each facility this way."

"That'll work. Come back, now. I miss you."

I laughed. "You're laying it on awful thick," I said before ending the call. When I reentered the room, he had a huge grin on his face.

"I have an idea. You can call me from work, and I can see what's going on."

It was an interesting idea, but I could foresee

several flaws. Lack of security. Him butting in when he wasn't needed. The calls interfering with his therapy. Still, the more his mind was put to work, the faster his recovery. I hoped. "Let's focus on getting you settled into your new place and take it from there."

My phone rang. A quick glance revealed it was him calling.

"Just checking," Eli said. "Wanted to make sure I had the hang of it."

I'd created a monster. "Right. It only took you one try. What else can you do with the phone?"

"Nothing." He set it on the table. "I tried the other day."

"Have you tried since then?"

"You're pushier than my therapist," Eli muttered.

If I wasn't, he'd walk all over me. Not now, but once he was stronger. "Stop whining. It doesn't suit you."

He jerked his head. "Come here."

"Say please."

"Come here, please."

What was he up to?

He held out his hand, and I walked over and held it.

He tugged, and I ended up in his lap. I wiggled to get more comfortable, and he wrapped his arms around me. "I appreciate everything you're doing for me. But sometimes I need to vent."

"And I'm the only safe person for you to vent to."

"Yeah." He rubbed his cheek against the top of my head.

"Okay, I'll let you complain once in a while. But when I tell you enough is enough, stop. Deal?"

"Deal. Can we seal it with a kiss?'

It wasn't until I was driving back to the house that I realized how easily he'd distracted me. He never tried anything else on his phone.

Chapter 33

The tours went well. Scratch that, one did. The other not so much. It took me seconds to choose. I was afraid Eli would disagree because the therapist at the other one spent too much time flirting with him and not enough time explaining their program.

But the deciding factor was the other patients. My choice had a majority of younger patients that I thought Eli would be more comfortable with. The equipment looked newer to my untrained eye, and the facility felt cleaner.

We didn't have time to discuss it before Eli's therapy session. Which was okay, because I didn't want him pressured into making a decision. My refusal to sign on the dotted line disappointed the patient representatives—salespeople—at both facilities.

Vanessa was waiting for me on a bench outside of the second care home. I was immediately on guard. Why wasn't she relaxing in the air conditioning of her car?

"Have you heard from Hennessey? Jake?" she asked as she stood.

The question hit me as hard as the humidity. "No. But Eli didn't mention anything about him not bringing bacon this morning, so I assume he made his daily visit. Why?"

She thrust her phone at me. "Read this."

I squinted in the bright Florida sun to scan the small print. A police report from last night. A jewelry theft. "And?" I asked.

"Come on, it's not the first time Hennessey has been a suspect in a similar crime."

"And he's never been arrested for one. Even the FBI couldn't gather enough evidence to get a warrant. The cops are at it again. Picking a suspect and trying to prove it instead of the other way around."

"You think he's innocent?"

"Innocent? Never. Is he responsible for this theft? No. Here's a different theory. Stephen Sallis is doing this to get back at me. Or doing his darnedest to pin it on Jake. It wouldn't be the first time someone has tried and failed. Either that or it's a double whammy. Me and Jake in one shot."

"Where is Hennessey?"

"I don't know." I shrugged. "Off doing whatever he does to get himself trusted by folks who don't play well with cops. He'll show up when he's ready. Better question is, where is Sallis? Is law enforcement tracking him? They should monitor his phone calls. He could sit at home and give orders to the few friends he has left."

"Sallis hates you that much?"

"Hate isn't the right word. Me, a simple librarian, made him look bad. His reputation vanished, destroyed by the cops in a humble little nowhere town. He'll never live that down."

Vanessa bit her bottom lip. "So, revenge is his motive. There's a lot of that in the air. Are you sure he isn't involved in the attack on Eli?"

The idea hit me as hard as if she'd punched me. Was I responsible for Eli's injuries and the mess we were in? I collapsed on the bench. Vanessa hovered over me while I waited for my brain to switch off my emotions and turn on my logic.

"What's the timeline? When did Sallis apply for release? And when did he walk out of prison? Does he have associates here?"

"Good questions. Let us handle getting the answers. The internet won't have what you're looking for."

No, it wouldn't. Neither would any of the law enforcement databases I had access to. Or did. I wondered if Chief Sorenson had removed my privileges.

My mind switched to Jake. If he was in danger, it was time to call him in and off the streets. But just because I asked, didn't mean he would do it. He set his own rules.

"This changes everything," I said, twiddling Eli's dog tags. "And alters nothing. It's all speculation."

Vanessa sat beside me. "It's like you reminded me. We can't afford to decide who's guilty and set out to prove it. We have to dig for clues that point us to the guilty party."

She patted my knee. "It changes one thing. I'll be sticking to you like glue. If you think I was annoying before, you ain't seen nothing yet."

I couldn't come up with a smart-aleck response. My mind was going in too many directions at once.

❇ ❇ ❇

The contracts with both care centers were long and complicated. I didn't have my normal powers of concentration to study them. My first thought was to fax them to Dan because I always depended on him, but why? Not when I had a lawyer down the hall.

"What am I looking for?" Kris asked, ruffling through the paperwork.

"What kind of gotcha's can get hidden? Extra fees? No guarantee on the amount and kinds of therapy? An upcharge for better meals? Both places have good reviews, but they can fake those."

"I'll handle it." Kris moved the contracts to the middle of her desk. "What's the deadline?"

"Monday morning. Neither has an opening until Tuesday."

"Are you including Eli in the discussion?"

"He was on video calls with me during both tours." Except for the time he'd fallen asleep. "I'm going to ask his opinion tonight. Unless he calls sooner."

"He remembered how to use his phone? That's good news."

"I tried to convince myself of that when he called at four this morning, and I didn't have the heart to ignore him. He hasn't figured out how to get into his contacts yet, so the rest of you are safe." I smirked. "For now."

❋ ❋ ❋

The agency bodyguard stopped me in the hall. That was against every protocol the agency and I had established. Red flag number one.

"I'm Derek," he said, extending his hand. "We need to talk before you visit your friend. Can we go somewhere more private?" He eyed a couple leaving a room.

Red flag number two. We'd be leaving Eli alone. I ignored his hand. "May I see your agency ID?"

His eyebrows lifted. "Sure."

I tracked his movements as he reached into his pants pocket. A small gun would fit in it. But he drew out a leather case and retrieved a business card. He handed it to me.

I studied it. It looked authentic when I compared it to the one I'd received ages ago. "Alright, Derek, let's talk. But here, so we can both make sure no one goes into Eli's room that shouldn't."

"Your choice. You might want to sit while we chat."

He severely underestimated me. Unless Eli was dead, I was fine. And the hospital would have delivered the news, not a random employee of a private eye agency.

"Spit it out." I leaned against the wall, trying to look self-assured. Calm and in-charge.

"There's an unverified rumor that Stephen Sallis is in town."

If he expected me to faint, he was mistaken. I'd faced Sallis down once before. And won. And I'd do it again if I had to.

"We've checked through a partner in New York. He isn't at his home there," he added. Every time the agency slipped up and made me want to fire them, they redeemed themselves.

"Any idea of timelines?"

"We're working on it. In the meantime, we recommend you have a bodyguard, too."

"I have one. The ATF has it covered. I'll be fine."

"You need to be more vigilant. You come up and leave the same way every day. The back stairs aren't the most secure area of the hospital."

He was right. I knew better. "Thanks for the reminder. I can't do much about switching my schedule, but I can find different ways to get here. That'll change next week when we move Eli."

"Who were you talking to?" Eli asked when I walked into his room.

"A staff member." I didn't mention whose staff. We hadn't told him about his bodyguards. "We were planning for next week."

"Did you pick a place?"

"Nope. Wanted your opinion first. You saw most of what I saw. What do you think?"

"The aides were cuter at the first one. That's what Jake said."

I hadn't realized Jake was there. "That sounds like Jake."

"But the second one has a swimming pool."

"With a lift that can lower people into the water if they can't manage stairs. That impressed me, too."

"Can I swim?"

The question caught me off-guard, and I almost answered. I switched words at the last moment. "Can you?"

He licked his lips. His eyes narrowed. "Everyone who grows up in Florida learns how to swim. Good thing, because swimming in uniform during Ranger training wasn't fun."

His eyes glazed. I waited, almost fearful of what might come next.

"The water's in front of me. All I have to do is dive in. But I couldn't move, no matter how much everyone yelled at me."

I waited more.

His voice cracked. "I was a Ranger?" he asked.

Why did he keep losing and finding that particular memory? "Yes. You were a Ranger."

"But that's why the government asked me to review the records of the SEAL mission."

"I don't pretend to know what the higher-ups in government think, but it makes sense."

"Has Special Agent Putnam found what he was looking for?"

"Not yet. Do you remember where you hid the papers?"

Eli bounced his toes on the footrest of the wheelchair. Not like he was nervous, but as if he needed to burn energy. That was a new but good sign, in my eyes.

"It has something to do with the accident," he said. "I had them with me, but I'm not sure why. Something to do with keeping you safe, but I can see you're okay."

There was so much he didn't know, and I wasn't ready to tell him.

"The police didn't find any documents in your car."

"That's okay." His eyebrows furrowed. "I should be worried about it, but I'm not. Why?" His breathing quickened.

I put my hand on his knee. "Take your time, Sweetie. If you can't remember, it's okay."

"It's gone." He shook his head. "There's no way I'd take top secret documents with me anywhere. It must have been a bad dream. Like wanting to get out of the car and go swimming. The water was so close, and I needed to finish the training course. The one place has a swimming pool, right? I think I'd like that."

I got whiplash from the sudden change in topics. "That one's my favorite, too. Their equipment looked better taken care of. I have Kris looking over their contracts so there aren't any surprises."

"Kris?"

"The company lawyer."

"Is he any good?"

"She. And yes, she's good. You hired her, after all."

He blew out a hard breath. "I don't remember her."

"Maybe if you saw a picture? I don't have one but can get one. Or I can call from the office next week and you can see her over the phone."

His eyes brightened. "You can take me through the entire office. Help me remember where I work."

Had the knowledge that he owned the company escaped him again? "We can start slow. Start with Kris and Darla, and not until Monday."

"What is today? I lose track."

"Friday." I didn't remind him of the whiteboard near the sink with the day, date, and hospital staff names. "We won't bother them over the weekend."

"I can call you, right?"

He sounded whiny and worn out. "Yes. But not when your parents are here. And I'll be coming to see you."

He wrapped his hands around mine and captured my gaze with his. "I count the moments until you come back, each and every day."

That was a line Jake would use. "Have you been reading a romance novel?"

He tugged to draw me closer. "You're my anchor. The constant that I always remember when everything else escapes me. I worry that you'll tire of taking care of me. Or that something will happen, and I'll lose you. The only time the feeling goes away is when you're here."

One crack in my heart healed while another one formed. "Don't worry, Eli. I have people protecting me and keeping me safe. I'll always come back to you."

"But you hate bodyguards."

He remembered that, of all things?

"True. We've worked around it."

"We?"

"You've met Vanessa. She's become my shadow."

"I don't trust her. She's keeping secrets."

"And she doesn't trust me." I smirked. "But she's good at her job, so we declared a truce."

"I guess that's as much as I can hope for." He tugged me closer, and then there was no need for words.

❋ ❋ ❋

With the night's conversations weighing on my mind, I waited for Vanessa to wake up before going for my morning walk. Still, I couldn't shake the prickle at the back of my neck that told me we were being followed. Either that, or my imagination was working overtime.

I slowed, pulled out my phone, and pretended to take a picture of a garden of daisies. What I was actually doing was using the camera feature to look over my shoulder. I spotted nothing out of place.

"You're feeling it too?" Vanessa slid her hand into the pocket of her hoodie. The one that held her weapon.

"I'm not seeing anything."

She knelt and tied a loose shoelace, an excellent cover for some swift surveillance. "Do you want to cut your walk short?"

"And let them know we know? How about we figure out a way to make them reveal themselves?"

"I like it." She stood and stretched, swiveling from her waist up, working whatever muscles those were. The process gave her a better view of our surroundings. "What do you have in mind?"

"Continue to the end of the block, cross to the other side, and come back this way. If someone is watching us, they'll have to duck and hide. That should make them stand out." The only other people out this early were folks hoping to get their yard work done before it got any hotter.

"Good call." Vanessa grinned, the smile of a shark. "Let's do it."

Despite her outward confidence, Vanessa unsnapped the cover of her holster. I followed her lead and checked that Betsy was reachable in my pocket.

In almost military precision, we swiveled after we'd crossed the street. We spotted the anomaly at the same time.

"Beige car," I said. "Beat up and rusty."

"It's perfect for the neighborhood," Vanessa added.

"A little too perfect, if you think about it. Have you ever seen it around?"

"Nope. And did you notice it's parked facing the wrong direction?"

"Like they spotted us and pulled over as quickly as they could?"

She nodded. "Right. And they didn't bring guns into play. Interesting. So, what's their motive?"

An intense headache struck me. "They want to

grab me and take me to 'meet' with Sallis?"

"Or someone's checking to see if you'd lead them to Putnam's papers?"

I came to an abrupt stop. Vanessa backtracked to stand beside me. "I never asked for this. All I ever wanted was to be a librarian in a little town where nothing happens."

"Instead, you're here, running a multimillion-dollar business. Quite the difference. But you missed your true calling. Now, walk."

I didn't ask what she meant. I'd heard it from cops before. That I should be one of them. "Is that a good idea?"

"I want a look at their faces. A picture would be better. A license plate would be icing on the cake."

I made a series of quick calculations. Which yards had fences, what houses were unoccupied, the dogs that were friendly or snapped at everything. It might work. "Follow me."

We ducked behind the rickety wooden fence in the side yard of a retired couple. They had a habit of sleeping in, and the house provided us with additional cover. From there we merged into the property of a family who were on an end-of-summer trip up North. We squeezed by the trash cans in the next yard and ended up in the side street four houses down from the beige car. Behind them.

"Are we close enough to get a picture of the license?" I asked.

"Yep. Then I'll stroll up the sidewalk on the driver's side. You sneak up street-side and we'll see what magic we can make."

The plan was dangerous and had a serious flaw. "I need to be on the driver's side, if we assume it's me he's interested in." From this angle, it appeared the person was working solo. "He has to think I'm alone so he can make a move. With you on the passenger side, he'll be busy tracking me in the mirror and won't see you."

"If this doesn't work, I am so out of a job." Vanessa chewed her bottom lip. "But I can't waste the opportunity." She slid her revolver from the holster and nestled it in her hand. "Stay far enough away from the car that he can't grab you. On the count of three. Three!"

It was a turtle's pace to the finish line. I wished I could whistle as I sauntered down the sidewalk, avoiding the cracks. Vanessa kept a few steps ahead of me, staying in his blind spot.

I faltered as I reached the car's rear bumper. What if it was an elaborate trap? One step forward and I slipped my hand into my pocket, reaching for Betsy's metallic comfort. Two steps forward and I reviewed likely self-defense scenarios. Three steps and I wondered if the man in the car was awake. I hadn't seen him as much as rub his nose. Four steps.

The door flung open, almost hitting me. I side-stepped to avoid the collision and turned to face my assailant. The sun glinted off metal in his right hand as he climbed out of the car. He pointed the gun at my chest. "Get in the back. Now."

He hadn't done his homework. He was in the perfect spot for a side kick to the knee. Simple but effective. He staggered, half-falling into the seat.

I slammed the door, catching his hand in the frame. The gun clattered to the pavement, and I kicked it away.

Vanessa yanked the passenger side door open. "ATF. Don't try anything."

Chapter 34

By the time the North Crystal cops hauled away my attacker, a small crowd had gathered. They seemed disappointed that there'd been no gunplay, and no one got beat up. The cops got nothing out of the scrawny balding man, not even a name. He didn't have ID, and the car was stolen. I shouldn't have expected anything different.

"They'll transfer him to the Orlando facility," Vanessa said. "Better security. I'm sure Detective Horace will cooperate in making the arrangements. I'll request to be part of the questioning."

The interrogation, she meant. I bet she was good at it. "I'd like to observe."

"Which is more important? Watching the same questions being asked over and over and getting no answers or spending time with Hennessey? Because it'll be late by the time the suspect gets booked and transferred."

When she put it that way. "Eli."

"Thought so. Now, head home and lock the doors

until I get back. I want to hang out with the prisoner. You don't recognize him, by any chance?"

She knew everyone in Orlando I did. "No."

"Didn't think so. Anyway, wait for me. We need to talk. You never mentioned your martial arts training."

"Because I'm don't have any."

"Uh-huh. Not what I saw." She grinned. "We'll talk later."

With the adrenalin rush worn off, the short block home seemed like a mile-long hike. A cop car trailed me the whole way. But I had a reputation to uphold, and I didn't collapse until I reached the comfort of my bed.

I didn't sleep; just rested long enough for the shakes to subside. From the sound of things, the guys from upstairs had taken a sudden interest in yard work. One out front and one in the back, even though the landscaping company hired by the landlord had mowed earlier in the week. I wondered how much Vanessa had told them.

After starting a load of clothes, I tackled cleaning the kitchen, desperately seeking a sense of normality. I rearranged the spices and threw out expired boxes of pasta mixes. I wiped down every shelf in the cupboard and rearranged the dishes to make more room. I even tossed the cereal boxes that were almost empty.

Still, nothing felt normal, because it wasn't over. If Sallis had sent one attacker, he'd send another.

And if this first one wasn't sent by Sallis, it meant the person responsible still lurked in the shadows.

I was getting rid of expired salad dressing—and making a list so I could replace them—when my phone rang. I glanced at the screen before answering.

"Hey, Tillie," I said, putting on my best nothing is wrong in the world voice.

She sniffed. "We need you. Eli needs you. They threw me and Rob out of his room."

I raced to the bedroom to put on my shoes. "What happened?"

"All the machines. At once. We couldn't do anything," she sobbed.

"Let me talk," Rob said. I grabbed my purse and listened to fumbling sounds as Tillie gave him the phone.

"We don't know what happened," he said. "We were talking about which nursing home he should go to. He kept insisting you had it covered and told us about the tours. Then he turned white and stopped talking. The monitors beeped a few times, then the beeps turned into a steady sound. Staff rushed in and forced us to leave."

I locked the door behind me. "I'll be there as soon as I can. He's in good hands. Go find somewhere where you can wait for news."

"We're in the family waiting room."

"I'll meet you there." If Eli had a stroke or heart attack or something even worse, it would be a long day. "I'm going to hang up now so I can drive. Bye."

As I backed out of the driveway, I rolled down the window to yell at the guy out front. "I'm headed to the hospital. Eli's having a major issue."

He didn't try to stop me, but by the time I paused at the intersection, both of them were getting in one of their cars to follow.

Dolores' magic was in full force and the traffic gods were with me. I only hit one red light the entire trip. The parking valet's eyes bugged out as I handed him my keys and grabbed my receipt. I didn't have time to find a parking spot in the crowded lot.

The elevator had just discharged a load of passengers as I rushed through the lobby and only a few people waited to get on. They were all going to higher floors, so mine was the first stop.

"Any word?" I asked, dashing into the family waiting room. Tillie and Rob, hands folded, sat on hard chairs, staring at blank air.

"They took him for tests," Tillie sniffed.

I dug for my package of tissues in my purse and handed them to her. "Did anyone say what kind?"

"No." Rob said. The skin around his knuckles whitened as he clenched his fists.

I wondered where Eli's bodyguard was, and if he'd overheard anything. "Do you want something to drink?"

They both shook their heads. I'd get them coffee, anyway, after I located the guard.

But he knew nothing more than Tillie and Rob. The assistant at the front desk also claimed ignorance. I sat beside Tillie, bouncing my foot and using my second cup of coffee as a hand warmer.

What was taking so long? Shouldn't we have received an update?

My phone pinged, and my heart stopped. But it was only Vanessa. *"Meet me in the cafeteria."* That sounded ominous.

With the memory of the morning's encounter still fresh, I took a different route downstairs. She sat at her normal table where she could keep an eye on every entrance. She waved as I walked in, like I'd have any trouble finding her.

"How's Eli?" she asked as I joined her.

"We haven't been told anything. And it's been a couple of hours. That means it's serious."

"They say no news is good news."

It didn't feel like it.

I stared out the window, and she swirled her coffee while continuing to watch the doors. Her head never moved, but her eyes continually shifted from left to right, right to left.

"Why are you here?" I asked when the silence got to be too much. "You didn't come just to see how Eli was doing."

"I came in case you needed a friend. I know you don't think of me that way, but it's not like you've had the time to make any since you've been here. So, pretend I'm one and I'm here to support you."

"I figured you'd be at the cop shop giving the suspect a hard time."

The corner of her mouth twitched. "Mr. X has invoked his right to a lawyer at questioning.

Unfortunately, the public defender's office is overworked and understaffed. He'll enjoy the rest of the weekend in the tender care of the Orlando PD."

"That doesn't help."

"Think of it as psychological warfare. Mr. X has effectively vanished into the system. Whoever hired him can't track him down. That gives us a little breathing room."

I needed every bit of my breath when the doctor showed up in the family waiting room.

"Mr. Hennessey's family?" she asked.

Rob stood. "That's us." The sweep of his hand included me.

Vanessa stood, too. "I'll leave while you talk."

I wished she could stay, but Rob and Tillie would be more comfortable if she wasn't there. She wouldn't go far. She was in full guard dog mode.

The doctor looked as if she'd just graduated medical school. Or was that because I was getting older? I'd aged years since I arrived in Florida. She clasped her hands behind her back as if preparing to lecture.

"Mr. Hennessey experienced an arterial blood clot," she said. "Under the worst of situations, they can lead to heart attacks or strokes. Luckily, he was here.

"The clot wasn't near his heart, and we had time to treat it without surgery. If the staff hadn't responded as quickly as they did, it may have been a different story.

"We located the clot and dissolved it with medication before it did any damage."

She seemed quite pleased with herself. I wouldn't argue with her assessment.

"What caused it?" Rob asked.

"He has no known risk factors, so the best I can say is, it is likely a side effect of his injuries. We'll monitor him for a few extra days. This will delay his move to a rehab facility."

"The paperwork hasn't been signed, so I should be able to negotiate a change in date," I said.

She nodded. "Mr. Hennessey should return to his room soon, but I expect he'll want to sleep. He's on pain medications that will make him drowsy. He's had a rough day."

"Can we see him?" Tillie asked.

"Of course. Keep the visit short and stress-free." The doctor looked directly at me. "I assume you're the one he calls Buttercup?"

I blushed. His name for me had been our secret. "Yes. Why?"

"May I have a moment of your time? Alone?"

Like I'd turn her down. "Of course." I turned to Rob and Tillie and shrugged. I didn't want them to think I was keeping secrets from them. Although I was.

The doctor—her name tag read Fleuers—didn't mince words. "When Mr. Hennessey was under sedation, he asked for you numerous times. He mumbled about giving you secret papers. Which seemed odd."

Not as odd as she thought. "Did he mention where they were?"

Her eyes widened. "Sorry, no. He mentioned scratching his back in the spot you know about. What that has to do with it, I can't guess."

Neither could I. "Did he say anything else? No matter how crazy."

"He joked about going swimming. And needing to buy an exercise bike to add to his collection of equipment."

What collection? "It'll be awhile before I have to worry about that."

"His therapists can help you. I didn't read all their notes, sorry."

"You had more important things to do. Like save his life. Thank you."

She smiled. "That's what we're here for. Now, I have other patients to see." She held out her hand. We shook, and she hurried away.

"What was that all about?" Rob asked from behind me.

I turned to face him, wondering how much he'd overheard. "Eli was throwing my name around under the influence of the drugs they put him on and said a few things the doctor thought I should hear."

His eyes narrowed. "I heard something about paperwork. Have you lost company property?"

I held my breath and counted to ten. Twice. There were too many harsh words crowding in my mouth and I didn't want to say any of them.

"Are you talking about the papers Eli had with him the night of the accident?" Tillie asked.

"What?" I'd been so focused on Rob I hadn't noticed her join us.

"Didn't I tell you? In the bag of clothes I took home to wash was a stack of papers. They're wrinkled and bloody, and I didn't want to touch them. I considered throwing them away but figured I'd let Eli decide."

I fought to contain my excitement. "After Eli gets settled back in his room, can I come to your place and check them out?"

"Oh, yes, please. Stay for supper, too. I've been worried you're upset with us because you haven't come to visit."

"I'll make up for it. Promise. Dinner sounds nice, but not tonight." I sighed dramatically. "I left a load of clothes in the washer."

It wasn't a total lie. But if things turned out the way I expected, I'd be spending my evening with Putnam.

It didn't work out that way. It took longer than I'd guessed for them to bring Eli back. Then he was awake enough that he wanted to chat with all three of us. Each time we thought he'd dozed off, he'd start talking again. I had the impression he was recalling 'new' old memories but didn't want to ask him directly. Especially because of the happiness in Tillie's eyes each time he called her 'Mom' like he meant it.

Once he fell asleep for real, and we got to Rob and Tillie's house, she wanted to show me her latest project. She'd taken up making backpacks to donate to local schools, using leftover upholstery material from local shops. Another organization filled them with needed school supplies.

"I saw the cutest little girl wearing one the other day," she told me. "I wished I could've stopped and taken her picture, but that wouldn't have been right."

"They're nice. I wish I had one when I was a kid. I'm impressed."

Her cheeks turned a deep red. "Thank you. I give each one a different design to make them special. Would you like to see the pictures?"

I spent the next half hour scrolling through the photos on her phone. Which meant she started to cook supper, and I was stuck. I kept Vanessa informed of every delay by text. Each extra minute increased the risk. I spotted Vanessa driving by the house several times as she patrolled the neighborhood.

When Tillie suggested dessert, I turned her down, claiming I hadn't figured out a new exercise routine. Only then was I able to steer the conversation back to the papers she'd found,

"Are you going back to the hospital to see Eli tonight?" I asked. I hoped the answer would be no.

"I wish we could," Tillie said. "There was something different about him this afternoon. He seemed more like the old Eli, if you know what I mean."

"I felt the same way but didn't want to say anything, in case it was a side-effect of the medications. I don't want to be disappointed when they wear off."

"Make sure you give Harmony those papers you found," Rob said, doing my job for me. "Eli might remember them."

"They're in the closet in Eli's old room. I'll get them," Tillie said.

I held my face as unmovable as a stone, not wanting to reveal my emotions. Hope. Curiosity. Excitement. Fear. Anticipation.

She came back carrying a manila envelope. "I didn't want the blood to rub off onto his things." Her hands shook as she handed the envelope to me. "Not that anything was worth saving. They cut his shirt off, his pants are ripped, and his shoes ruined. But I can't force myself to throw them away."

I opened my arms to share a hug.

I pulled into a parking spot at a gas station a mile down the road. Vanessa snagged the next space. She jumped out of her car and rapped on the passenger side window. I unlocked the door so she could get in.

"Well?" she asked.

"I haven't looked yet."

"Putnam is on his way."

"Should we wait for him?" My hand shook as I reached behind the seat to retrieve the envelope.

"And make him come all this way if it's a collection of bad poetry?" Vanessa grinned.

The outdoor lights flickered on. If I didn't get to the hospital soon, I'd miss my chance to see Eli. I lifted the envelope's flap. Ever so slowly, I pulled out the document.

The evident blood stains—Eli's blood—chilled my entire body. But the print was still readable. The first page looked like every image of a top-secret document I'd found in my research. I hardened my nerves and flipped to the next page.

The blacked-out blocks of words put me further on edge. This was the information I didn't need to read. "I think this is it, Vanessa," I whispered as I passed the papers to her.

She flipped through the pages. "Checking to make sure the rest aren't blank, and Hennessey wasn't playing a joke on someone." She gave them back and pulled out her phone. "I'll update Putnam."

She sent off a quick text. We waited. And waited. Her phone buzzed, and I jumped. Just a little. I was too tired and too stressed not to react.

"He wants to meet at my office."

"I've never been there."

"A miscalculation on my part. I'll lead the way, but why don't you set the GPS on your phone as a backup?"

"You think I can't keep up with you?" I laughed.

She cracked a smile. "We'll test that one of these days. On a course. Not in public and not on an interstate and definitely not tonight."

She recited the address and I plugged it into my mapping app. "Ready," I said.

"I'll take the envelope." She held out her hand.

Warning bells clambered in my head. Once these documents left my possession, there'd be no need to keep me in the loop. "No. I'm responsible for them. Putnam has cleared me for the job, not you."

"I'm trained. You're not." Her hand remained hanging in midair. "If someone is watching us, I'd prefer to be the target."

Just because it was logical didn't mean I was comfortable with it. "If someone follows you, it's better if I keep the papers." I slipped them from the envelope and tucked them under my seat. Then, I made a big show of giving her the envelope. "You're the decoy."

As she returned to her own car, using the envelope to scratch her back, a piece of the puzzle slid into place. The reason the paperwork made it to the hospital was because Eli had them tucked into his shirt. Next to his spine. Where they rubbed against that one spot that he loved me to scratch. But why?

Chapter 35

For someone who prided herself on her driving abilities, Vanessa had a lot to learn. The white line on the right wasn't meant to drive on, and she needed to stay in the middle of the lane. In fact, she crossed the center line a time or two, now that I was paying attention.

Despite the heavy Saturday night party traffic and Vanessa's driving, we made it safely to the office building where the ATF was located. She parked under the brightest light illuminating the lot. I pulled in next to her but left Dolores running.

Vanessa turned off her car and got out but didn't approach me. Instead, she leaned over her front tire, examining it, reminding me of the video of Eli at the gas station. I wished I had a sweater to wrap around me as I shivered.

I rolled down my window. "Something wrong?"

"I thought I had a flat," she said, hands on her hips. "The steering felt off."

That explained her poor driving. "Maybe you threw a wheel weight."

"I'll get it checked out. There should be a tire shop open tomorrow somewhere."

Stores in Orlando stayed open a lot longer and more days than in Oak Grove. "How long until Putnam gets here? And what's the plan, when he does?"

"I've contacted Detective Horace, and he's arranging for patrols in the area. As soon as they show up, we'll head inside. Putnam is twenty-five minutes away, depending on traffic and the weather."

The first patrol car showed up in under five minutes. We entered the building under the officer's watchful eye. Putnam made it in twenty. Enough time for a pot of coffee to finish brewing.

To avoid the temptation of scanning through the top-secret paperwork while Vanessa ran downstairs to fetch Putnam, I studied her collection of magazines and books related to the science behind fires. If she understood them, she was far smarter than I'd given her credit for.

In the almost silent office, it wasn't hard to track Vanessa and Putnam's movements. First it was the sound of the elevator, followed by the front door opening and closing. The rhythmic drumming of their steps on the tile floor. Vanessa's indistinct murmur as she filled Putnam in on details of the day's events.

I was anything but relaxed when Vanessa held open the office door for Putnam. The stiffness of his posture revealed his anxiousness. This moment had been a long time coming.

"I hear you have something for me, Miss Duprie," he said, his voice a monotone.

Where was the excitement? I picked up the stapled papers from Vanessa's desk. I'd play it his way. Unblinking, I held it out. "It's a start, but I don't know where the flash drive is."

He gave me one of those manly chin-jerks and accepted the stack. I studied his eyes as he scanned the front page. He flipped through the papers, his expression never changing. "Did you read these, Miss Duprie?" he asked when he got to the end.

"No. I glanced through the first few and figured they were what you needed, so I didn't go any further."

He looked over at Vanessa and then back at me. "These were found on Hennessey in the hospital?"

"That's what I was told."

His lips narrowed.

"What?" I asked.

"They're forged. A good job, admittedly, but fake. Worthless."

"Eli almost died for garbage?" I asked.

"Well done garbage," Putnam answered, "I wonder if Hennessey created it. From what I understand, he's fully capable of the task. But why?"

"When he first regained consciousness, he kept worrying about me being safe. What if someone threatened to hurt me if he didn't give him the paperwork you're looking for?"

"You're thinking of Stephen Sallis?" Vanessa asked.

"Do you have any confirmation on his location?"

"I'm in touch with Horace, and Orlando PD hasn't been able to confirm anything. They're tracking down a few rumors, but their informants can't come up with any definitive leads."

"The PI agency is in the same boat."

"The ATF has feelers out nationwide, but nothing's coming to the surface. He's hiding deep," Vanessa said.

There was one source I hadn't heard from: Jake. He was the ace up my sleeve. I didn't need to put him into play. Yet.

"We're assuming Sallis knew Hennessey had access to top-secret documents. As much as I'd like to pin this on him, I can't make it work in my head," I said. "How would he have gotten the information?"

"People like him have connections everywhere," Putnam said.

"Which leads me back to my original thought. Someone at the company is responsible for the attack on Eli. It seems too far-fetched for him to be under fire from two different enemies at the same time."

A gust of wind rattled the window.

"You've got a point," Putnam said.

"And that's why I need those background checks. What's happening with them?"

Putnam grinned. "I was waiting for the last few, but I figured I'd bring along what I have." He tossed a flash drive onto Vanessa's desk.

"My kingdom for my laptop," I said, reaching for it. I hadn't thought about grabbing mine in the rush to get to the hospital.

"Do you think you'll find your answers there?" Vanessa asked.

I gave her a non-committal shrug. "I haven't found them anywhere else."

"I'd like to review these reports with you," Putnam said. "The three of us can collaborate."

"I'll snag a spare laptop," Vanessa said. "Be right back."

I sipped my coffee and listened to the wind howl as we waited. It didn't sound any worse than the winter storms that hit Oak Grove at least once a year.

"Who do you suspect?" Vanessa asked when she returned.

"There's two at the top of my list. Marty, the accountant, and Fiona. They both exhibit suspicious behaviors. Marty leaves the office whenever one of you drops by."

"And Fiona? She seems nice enough," Vanessa said, logging into the laptop.

"Her behavior has changed since her promotion. She leaves the office a lot and as far as we can see, she's stepping away to make phone calls. Maybe she's dealing with personal issues, but why does she have to leave?"

"As a receptionist, she'd have potential access to all kinds of information," Putnam pointed out.

I nodded.

"You could have fired them," Vanessa said.

"I remind myself regularly that they are Eli's employees, not mine. I won't fire anyone without proof of their misdeeds."

"Well, let's get started. You want to give me that

flash drive, Harmony?" Vanessa grinned and pointed out, "It won't do us any good if you crush it."

I opened my hand and stared at the imprint in my palm. I didn't realize I'd been clutching the drive that tightly.

Putnam and I leaned over Vanessa's shoulders to stare at the small screen. "How are the files labeled?" she asked as she wiggled the drive into the slot on her third try.

"Random number, last four letters of the last name, first three of the first name," Putnam answered. "It's my personal system."

Easy enough if you knew who you were looking for, difficult if you were guessing.

"Where do you want to start?" Vanessa poised her fingers over the keyboard.

Marty had been my original suspect, so he seemed a good place to begin. "S T O N M A R," I spelled out.

"He's number 842," Putnam said. He didn't consult a list, and I marveled at his memory.

I slowed my breathing as Vanessa scrolled to the right file. It was the moment of truth.

She peered at the screen and double-clicked. The screen filled with words in a font almost too small to read. She enlarged the size, and I adjusted my glasses as I leaned closer and started at the top.

Cold, hard facts greeted me. Names and dates of employment. People he worked with. Classes he took. Degrees and certifications. Nothing struck me as odd.

"Scroll down, please," I asked.

"Ready?" Vanessa asked Putnam.

He nodded. She brought a fresh page to the screen. It showed summaries of interviews with various people who knew Marty. The names were blacked out, but they were entitled to their privacy. Most of them talked about what a good guy he was. One mentioned they didn't talk much because he didn't like to party.

"How can anyone be this perfect?" I asked no one in particular. "Does he have any wants or warrants or even parking tickets?"

"Those are the next page." Putnam's mouth quirked.

Vanessa brought up those records. "Oh, look, he received a warning for a brake light being out. He got it fixed the next day, and the ticket was voided. Is that bad enough for you?"

It was a gentle teasing. I wouldn't object. "What else is there?"

Vanessa moved on to a screen filled with relatives' names. "His youngest son was an Army Ranger. Growing up, I wanted to be a Navy SEAL. Broke my heart when I found out they didn't allow women to join."

"Do you have access to military records?" I asked, straightening to look at Putnam. Well, as much as I could, considering he was several inches taller.

"Yes. What do you want to know?"

"Did Marty's son and Eli serve together?"

His eyebrows rose. "Interesting concept. It will take a while to check and I can't access that information unless I'm in the office."

Fair enough. But it would explain why Eli hired Marty.

A few more pages of small print and nothing of interest. I stretched. "I need more coffee."

The lights flickered as another gust of wind rattled the window. Putnam checked his phone. "Right on time. That's one of the first bands of the storm."

I'd forgotten about the hurricane. "Are we safe?"

Vanessa and Putnam exchanged a glance. "No worries, newbie," Vanessa said. "They've downgraded this system so many times it's nothing but a major thunderstorm. Horace said the chief has pulled most of the extra patrols off the streets and sent the officers home."

Rain rattled against the window, and the lights flickered again.

"We should wrap this up," Putnam said. "I don't want to be on the road when the worst of the storm hits."

I wasn't ready to give up. "We haven't checked Fiona's information yet."

"I've got a safe at the house." Vanessa winked at me. "We can keep the flash drive locked up when Harmony isn't using it."

Putnam rubbed the stubble on his chin. "With the pressure we're getting for inter-agency cooperation? I could live with that. As long as you accept the responsibility, Special Agent Salters."

A warm wind blasted us as we stepped outside. It held the threat of change and I shivered. "You won't drive back to Tampa tonight, will you, Special Agent Putnam?"

"No. On the way over, I arranged to stay with a friend."

That was good. He and I stood guard while Vanessa tucked the flash drive into a secret compartment in her car. I didn't peek to see where it was.

"Ready to go," she said.

"I want to stop and say goodnight to Eli on the way back to the house." I waved to Putnam as he got into his car.

"Isn't it after visiting hours?" she asked.

"There's a way to sneak in." I'd gotten the lowdown from Jake a few days earlier. "A set of stairs in the back hallway by the cafeteria. The staff at the nurses' desk will never see me."

"Okay, but just for a few minutes. It's been a long day."

Putnam beeped his horn. He was waiting for us to leave. Vanessa nodded.

"You lead the way," she said. "I'll be right behind you."

Dolores wasn't happy. She didn't like the wind and rain and didn't appreciate that I forced her to drive straight into them. When we turned into the now-familiar street leading to the hospital, she perked up and purred her approval when I parked next to a panel truck that blocked much of the storm.

It also put us nearer to an entrance close to the cafeteria. Once Vanessa pulled in next to me, I headed towards it at a half-run, not waiting for her to follow. I didn't want to spend an extra moment in the rain.

Inside, I shook like a wet dog, and waited for her. She was only a few steps behind.

"Nasty weather," she said. "Sure made it hard to maintain my lane." She pushed some wet hair away from her face. "Even worse than before."

"Are you going to go find a nice unmarried security guy to hang out with?" I asked, copying her movement.

"After I walk you upstairs. Not taking any chances after everything that's happened today."

That was fair. I wanted to run up the stairs to get to Eli faster, but took my time so she could keep up. At the top, she locked eyes with the bodyguard. They exchanged nods. Then she headed for the elevators to go wherever she disappeared to, waiting for my call.

Eli's room was dark, and I stood in the doorway, allowing my eyes to adjust.

"You're here." Eli's voice came from his bed. "I thought you'd forgotten me."

"Not a chance."

"I was worried you got stranded in the storm somewhere."

"Nope. I was stuck at your parents' house. Your mom made her famous spaghetti for supper."

"With canned sauce and overcooked noodles?"

"Exactly." I pulled up a chair. I didn't want to sit on the bed and drip on him. "You remember."

"I've been remembering a lot of things today. It's like the problem I had earlier shook something loose in my brain." He patted the bed. "Come, lay beside me. I want to hold you."

I plotted the best way to accomplish that. They had added a new monitor which meant more wires to avoid. If we kept a blanket between us, I wouldn't get him wet. "If you roll onto your right side, we can make this work."

It wasn't as easy as they make it sound in books. At least I didn't have to worry about his bruises. They were almost healed. I couldn't get as close as I wanted because of the electrodes glued to his chest.

But we got into a spooning position where his left arm draped over me. Not quite like old times, but it would do. He blew out a breath on the back of my neck.

"What did you and my folks talk about?"

He was fishing for something. I could tell by the edge in his voice. But what? "Your mom showed me the backpacks she's making."

"It makes her feel useful, and she has fun doing it."

"You remember?"

"Yes. More and more keeps flooding in. Sometimes I can't figure out if they are true memories or my imagination."

"What do the doctors say?"

He chuckled. "You're the first person I've told. I figured they'd want to run a bunch of tests when what I want is to sort things out."

That was understandable. "I'm honored. I wish I could turn over and kiss you."

He kissed the back of my head. "This will have to do for now."

A flash of lightening and the deep rumble of thunder intruded into the moment. "If this is a tropical storm, I'd hate to see what a hurricane is like," I complained.

"This is nothing. One of these days I'll tell you about the time we…no, I won't. The mission was top secret."

"I have clearance. Even if it is temporary."

Eli laughed. "Putnam—excuse me, Special Agent Putnam—wouldn't be happy."

"It takes a lot to satisfy him, I suspect."

"Was he happy when he found the document he's been looking for?"

I stiffened. "He hasn't found it. All we discovered was the fake you had with you the night you were attacked. Although he complimented you on the excellent forgery."

"I could have done a better job with more time. But I should be telling him this."

And Richon. And Vanessa. "Do you want me to call him?"

"Later. I need to discuss something with you first."

That sounded serious. In fact, it scared me. "You're not breaking up with me for one of the cute nurses, are you?"

"No. But I've been remembering things about you and Jake. About you being together. And it hurts."

It was tough, but I flipped over, so we were face to face. "Jake and I were over long before you and I ever met. But I'm grateful to him because he's the reason you and I are together." I reached to stroke his face, but he caught my hand.

"Jake still loves you. He's here because you asked him to come."

"Jake is in love with the fantasy of how he thinks he could change me. I'm not that person, and I didn't ask him to come." Eli didn't fight me when I laid my hand on his chest, over his heart. "Jake came because of you. He's out there doing whatever he does for you. You're his brother. Not legally, but that's how he sees you."

"You're sure you don't love him?"

"You asked me that once a long time ago. My answer hasn't changed. No, I don't love Jake. You're the one I love."

"Tell me again. Of all the things I remember, that's the most important."

I wiggled to get close enough that our noses touched. "I love you, Matthew Elijah Hennessey."

He tugged me closer. We were chest-to-chest, mouth-to-mouth, lips almost touching. And the alarms on his heart monitor beeped erratically.

I pulled away. A nurse rushed in, eyed the situation, smiled, but shook her head.

"You're supposed to be resting, Mr. Hennessey. The last thing your heart needs is extra stress."

I started to roll away, but Eli caught my arm. "Give us a minute," he said. "We'll be good. I promise."

The nurse sighed. "Don't make me regret this." With a wink, she left.

"I can't wait until I can hold you in my arms all night," he whispered in my ear. "There's something I have to ask you. I'm worried about the answer."

I waited, studying his eyes, hiding my impatience and anxiety.

"You won't leave, will you, when Putnam gets his papers? And you'll stay even when I can start running the company again?'

I crafted my answer. "I'm going to have to go back to Oak Grove and take care of things there sometime. But I don't plan on leaving soon."

"That gives me time to convince you to stay here forever."

It took me a minute to process that. "What are you asking, Eli?"

A knock on the door interrupted the moment. I expected to see the nurse, but it was Vanessa. "Go away."

"Sorry, but I need to talk to you, Harmony."

She wouldn't leave me alone until she got whatever it was off her chest.

"I'll be right back," I told Eli. I gave him a swift kiss and crawled out of the bed. Something about Vanessa's all-too-casual stance put me on high alert.

She waited for me down the hall near an empty room. "We've got to go. Horace had an informant tell him Sallis is hunting for you. We need to get you to a safe house, pronto."

"What about Eli?"

"The agency has extra people on the way. Now, don't argue and move it."

The world slowed down. "I didn't say goodnight."

She shoved me, and I staggered a few steps. "My purse," I objected.

"Sam," she called. "Grab her purse."

How did she know the bodyguard's name?

He jerked his chin and stepped out of view for a few seconds. He reappeared with my purse in his hands and tossed it to me. I caught it cleanly, thankful I'd left Betsy under the driver's seat.

"Where are we going?" I asked as Vanessa hustled me down the stairs.

"First stop is the police station to meet up with Horace. He's making arrangements to move us elsewhere. We'll take my car."

"No. Your car isn't reliable. How do we know it wasn't tampered with? Like Eli's was?"

She stopped in her tracks. Her face paled. A string of curse words equal to the best I'd ever heard poured from her mouth. "We'll take your car, then." She started back down the stairs. "But I'll drive."

It was my turn to stop. "No one drives Dolores but me." And Eli, but that would be a long time away.

"We don't have time to argue. I'm not happy about it, but you drive," Vanessa acceded.

I stopped again at the bottom of the stairs to send Jake a quick message. He needed to protect himself.

Vanessa put her hand on her service revolver. "Move it before I make you."

I stuck out my tongue and hit send. Not the most mature thing. I justified it as a reaction to the stress.

Chapter 36

As Vanessa and I walked toward the parking lot, a hospital security guard joined us. From the corner of my eye, I saw several more emerging from other doors. I felt like a prisoner being escorted to my jail cell as he and Vanessa flanked me on the way to Dolores. The rain had stopped, and the wind calmed down to a heavy breeze, making the weather almost pleasant. Even enjoyable, under other circumstances.

The security guard shone his flashlight in and under Dolores before allowing me to unlock her. In a last-ditch attempt to get me to give her the keys, Vanessa held out her hand. I clutched them tighter and shook my head. She grinned and headed for the passenger's side.

While she settled in, I dug Betsy out from under my seat and stashed her in the console.

"You need a real gun," Vanessa said.

That was the last thing I wanted to worry about. "She fits me."

Her phone pinged as she clicked her seatbelt.

"Horace," she said. "He's wondering where we are."

I patted Dolores' dash and started her engine. "On the way."

I couldn't read the traffic flow, and it made me nervous. Too many drivers who didn't signal their turns and drove too slowly. Or too fast for the slick streets. As a result, I couldn't track the headlights behind me.

Vanessa was twitchy, too. I sensed it from the obsessive way she kept checking the side-view mirror and leaning forward to glare into the vehicle beside us.

"There's a side street we can take a few blocks ahead," she said. Another car made a swift lane change, forcing me to step on the brakes. "It'll get us out of this traffic."

"Which is what someone wants to happen," I suggested.

She frowned. "Or they're looking to cause an accident. A diversionary tactic to grab you."

We were both paranoid. "How many of these drivers are innocent tourists and how many are part of the maneuver?" I asked. There were too many cars, and the darkness made it impossible to track any one vehicle.

"The side street is just ahead," Vanessa said.

I made a last-minute decision. If nothing else, we'd find out who was following us. Dolores' tires squealed as I swung hard to the right.

"We've got one." Vanessa turned around to watch. "No, two. And now three."

I didn't like the odds. "Hang on." I mashed the gas pedal. Dolores roared in delight as I jerked the steering wheel left and slid across the intersection.

The first car in the procession didn't make the turn. One down. But in the mirror, I spotted another set of headlights join the chain.

I knew nothing about this part of Orlando. I had to trust my instincts. A second left should take me back to the main street. A possible play.

I drifted to the left lane as if preparing to turn that direction. Instead, I went straight, blowing through the intersection in the merest gap in traffic. Vanessa sucked in her breath. Everyone behind us was forced to stop.

"How far to the cop shop?" I asked, checking my mirrors. And again.

"Another ten minutes."

Too long. Especially with the car behind us speeding to catch up. With all the streetlights, I couldn't pull into a driveway, turn off the headlights and disappear. I had to play this one out.

"If you go right, you'll be in an alley behind a mall," Vanessa said, studying her phone.

"Done." If I made it to the main parking lot, I'd have room to maneuver. At this time of night, about the only thing open was the movie theater, if the mall had one.

The speed bumps didn't slow me down. I flew over them and Dolores didn't complain. Vanessa mumbled a string of choice words.

Except for a few scattered vehicles, the parking lot was empty. That made my life easier. Only one car followed us. That should have been reassuring but wasn't. Where had the other cars gone?

My answer came in the glare of headlights approaching from the opposite direction, I hadn't factored in the probability of a second back entrance. And my followers being familiar with it.

"Shit. They have us sandwiched," I whispered.

Vanessa heard me. "They want to play chicken."

"What's the line? The only way to win is not to play?" I flipped off Dolores' headlights. The overhead lights provided enough illumination that I didn't need them. I slowed to a snail's pace.

"What's your plan?" Vanessa's voice crawled with tension.

"Don't know yet. Feel them out and see what their intentions are."

"We're sitting ducks."

"If it helps, the car doors have an extra layer of metal in them. The body shop added it after the last time I was shot at."

"That's marginally better."

"Have you contacted Horace and relayed the situation?" I asked.

"He's on his way."

We didn't have time to wait. We'd reached an impasse. I revved Dolores' engine. Who would make the first move?

Me. I stepped on the gas and aimed Dolores directly at the car facing us. Both the one in front and the one behind us matched my actions. If I didn't time things perfectly, we'd end up with total destruction.

My maneuvering room shrunk too fast. I swerved

from side to side to confuse them. Plus, they were being blinded, just for a moment, by each other's headlights.

The distance halved. I made my last move. But my timing was off. And I hadn't planned on the light pole being in my path as I yanked Dolores to the left. I especially hadn't counted on the gunshots.

The rear driver's side slammed into the pole. Glass exploded and rained on me. I swatted at the sudden sting in my left arm.

"Get us out of here," Vanessa hissed. She rolled down her window and fired off two shots.

I wiped the blood on my hand onto my jeans, grabbed Betsy and threw open my door. "We're not going anywhere." I had the sinking sensation someone was about to die. And it might be me.

I ducked behind my door to take cover. The overhead lights revealed the carnage left in my wake. The two vehicles smashed together, horns blaring and headlights faltering. That part of my plan had worked.

The strobe-light effect of the flickering lights outlined four people. They ran towards us. I fired one shot and ducked behind the door without waiting to see if I hit anyone. Vanessa let loose another. I listened for screams, but none came. I wished for more ammo. And the cavalry.

If this had been a movie, the villains would shout grandiose explanations of their prowess. But this wasn't a movie. Not a single word was screeched at the sky. Or at us.

I peeked around the edge of the door to survey the scene. Four people stood there, spread apart. Damn. Both Vanessa and I had missed. The one at the left end raised his gun, and I ducked back into my precarious shelter. The bullet slammed into Dolores, rocking the door on its hinges, but the extra metal plate did its job.

The odds weren't in our favor. I wasn't good enough to take them out one by one. I caught Vanessa's eye and raised four fingers. She shook her head and raised six.

Fuck. We didn't stand a chance.

"Any ideas?" I asked quietly.

"Pray. Pray hard."

That wouldn't fix anything. "What does your training tell you to do?"

"Call for backup. And run away, if you can." She glanced my direction. "You're bleeding."

"I got hit by flying glass."

She opened her mouth to say something and then closed it firmly.

I listened for sirens. They were still too far away to bring comfort. "It's me they're after." I swallowed to clear the lump in my throat. "If you see an opening to leave, take it."

"I'm your bodyguard, remember? I'm not going anywhere. But thanks for the offer."

A bullet whizzed by. I cringed. Another crashed into the windshield. Glass pellets sprinkled onto the seats and floorboard.

"Show yourself, bitch." The unforgettable voice of Stephen Sallis attacked my ears.

How stupid did he think I was? "Fat chance. Besides, you know what I look like."

"Your face is seared into my brain. Plotting for this moment kept me going in prison."

"And yet you are dying, anyway."

"The cancer? You'd be surprised what you can buy. That includes a false medical diagnosis."

"I told you to let me do the talking," one of the other men said.

"It doesn't matter. She's dead, one way or the other, as soon as we get done using her as bait," Sallis answered.

Bait? For who? They didn't expect Eli to show up, did they?

"I haven't decided which order to kill you in," Sallis yelled. "Maybe your little friend first to prove I'm serious. You'll be next. Fitting punishment for Hennessey."

He had to be talking about Jake. "You're barking up the wrong tree," I hollered. "The necklace Jake gave me was a replica. He never had the one you wanted."

Sallis snorted. "Good story. Do you believe it?"

"Yes." Well, most of the time. Some of the time.

I wanted to keep him talking. I was using his voice to figure out where he stood. If I had a chance to take a shot, I'd aim at him.

"Calm down, Harmony," Vanessa whispered. "Hold it together."

Oh, I was calm. I'd shoved every bit of my emotions deep inside. I was running on pure logic.

"Do we have enough ammo to take them out?" I asked.

"If we're lucky."

I felt my good luck had run out. "We'll have to do as much damage as possible. Sallis is mine. The old man."

"I figured that out. Prison didn't do him any favors. One shot and then back under cover. Keep them from trying to get closer."

"You go high. I'm going low." Nobody ever expected a shot to come from ground level. The angle shooting from under the car door was rough, but I was confident I could do it.

"On my count of three," Vanessa whispered. "One. Two."

I lied. When Vanessa hit three, I fired off two shots. One center mass at Sallis. The second aimed at the only female in the group. She hadn't said a single word, but enough light reached her face to make it recognizable.

Fiona.

I didn't hesitate as I squeezed off that second round. I shoved it on its way with every ounce of pain that Eli had suffered, every bit of rage I carried. I prayed for it to hit. And hit hard.

Then I pushed the limits and took a third shot. The man standing behind Fiona looked like the guy Eli had talked to at the gas station that night. A lifetime ago.

I expected the hail of bullets that followed. I crouched behind Dolores' door and waited for the end.

Then the world turned upside down.

The roar of engines. Lights of every color. The never-ending crack of gunshots. Men in camo everywhere.

Several ran by me. Oddly, one reminded me of Derek, the bodyguard from the agency. Another was built like Jake, but now I was imagining things.

I lost track of how many silver trucks circled us. They cut between Dolores and our attackers, spraying bullets everywhere. Well, not everywhere. None were aimed at Vanessa or me. I couldn't tell if any hit Sallis and his people either. They—whoever they were—were intent on keeping Sallis pinned.

"Friends of yours?" I yelled. I leaned against Dolores and wiped more blood from my left arm. The glass shard must have cut deep.

Vanessa shook her head.

Sirens interrupted my weariness. Like magic, all the trucks disappeared except for two. They maintained positions between us and Sallis until the police arrived.

I knew the drill. I clicked on the safety and put Betsy on the driver's seat. I didn't have the energy to stand, so I stayed where I was on the ground.

More sirens heralded the arrival of additional cops and the first ambulances. I wondered how many of Sallis' people needed one. Vanessa appeared to be unscathed, and I only had minor cuts. Except for the one that refused to stop bleeding. And hurt like hell now that I had time to pay attention to it.

I closed my eyes to shut out the bright lights and relax. Just for a moment.

"It's about time you opened your eyes."

I didn't want to. Open my eyes, that was. As long as I pretended to be asleep, I wouldn't have to face reality. But Vanessa—it was her voice—wouldn't allow me to fake it for long.

The steady beeping of machines, the sharp, antiseptic odor and the low murmur of voices talking nearby told me where I was. "Why am I in the hospital? Was the glass in my arm that deep?"

"Glass?" Vanessa snorted. "You were shot."

"No. Huh. Are you sure?"

"Your upper left arm. Open your eyes and look."

I blinked my eyes to wash away the sand that filled them. Then I tried to lift my arm to see what she was talking about. The pain made me want to scream, and I gave up. "I'll take your word. How bad is it?"

"You'll live," she said cheerfully, and I wanted to slap her. With my right hand. "It's a flesh wound. No major damage done. You needed stitches and lost a lot of blood, but I've seen worse. It'll be a couple of weeks until you can use it normally. Then we'll compare scars."

She'd never mentioned being shot. "Did anyone else get hurt?"

She nodded and stared at the wall. "Sallis is dead."

I didn't feel bad about it. "Did I kill him?"

"He was shot several times. Until the autopsy is

finished and forensics have completed their tests, no one will know which bullet was responsible. But there was one point of entry in his shoulder. That sounds like your style." She grinned.

"Except I aimed for center mass. I should be sad that he died. I'm not. Does that make me a bad person?"

One side of her mouth quirked. "That man had every intention of killing you. You did what you had to for yourself and for Hennessey."

Both of them. I kept that thought to myself. "Was that it?"

"All of Sallis' people were shot. Minor wounds, but enough to make sure they wouldn't be able to get away."

"Does that include Fiona?"

"You figured that out, huh? Yeah, she got shot twice. Once in the arm, once in a leg. She's in surgery to remove the bullets. We haven't determined whose jurisdiction will take precedence in questioning her. I'm out, though, because of my personal ties to the case."

"I'm sorry. I hope I didn't get you in trouble with your boss."

"He hasn't had time to decide if he's mad at me. I'm good for now." She stood. "Let me go get a nurse. They want to move you to a room for observation for the rest of the night. Oh, but first, here. I'm supposed to give you this." She reached in her pocket and pulled out a folded-up piece of paper. It reminded me of those paper footballs we played with as kids. "One of the guys in camo gave it to me."

With my right hand, I took it. "Who were they?"

"Same bunch that have been following you. They're a group of retired Army Rangers. They get together informally and make sure everyone's doing okay. The guy I talked to said Hennessey wasn't active with them but did them favors regularly."

"Like hiring Marty?"

"That would be my guess. So, with Hennessey in trouble, they made sure you were safe."

Or that I wasn't taking advantage of him. I'd reserve my judgment because they showed up when I needed them.

I counted to ten after Vanessa left, to make sure she wouldn't be back right away, before fumbling to open the paper. I only had partial use of my left hand, making it harder than expected. There was no doubt in my mind who it was from.

Without my glasses—where were my glasses?—I was nearly blind. I blinked and brought the sheet closer, but I still couldn't read it. I scowled. Was my brain that addled by the drugs they'd given me? Then I realized it was upside down.

With it turned the right way, I could almost make out the crudely drawn picture of a necklace, the one currently displayed in the Museum of Fine Jewelry. The one Jake gave me so long ago.

So, he had been at the scene of the shootout. At least I knew he was safe. As safe as Jake could be. Or let himself be.

Chapter 37

I'd hoped to see Eli before they stashed me in a room for the rest of the night, but it turned out I'd been taken to a different hospital. My phone was nowhere to be found, so I couldn't call or send him a message. After seeing me tucked into bed, Vanessa disappeared, so I couldn't ask her.

Now that I was fully awake, a nurse gave me something for the pain. And another pill to put me to sleep. As I closed my eyes, I realized I didn't have any idea what had happened to Dolores. Which jolted me wide-awake again.

But I was alone, with no one to ask. And nothing to keep me from falling asleep. So, I did.

"Those aren't my clothes," I said as Vanessa draped a bag over the chair in my room.

"Maybe you don't need your contacts after all," she said. "I brought them since your glasses broke."

I needed them, alright. I hadn't brought any of my spare pairs. After I got out of the hospital, I'd have to find one of those glasses-in-an-hour places.

"Anyway," she continued. "While I was looking for your contacts, I realized you own nothing in the way of Florida clothes. So, I bought you a sundress. It'll work with your sling better than any of your suits."

Yes, I was going to have to wear a sling for a few weeks. It would interfere with typing, but I'd adjust. The floral pattern on the dress was pretty, if not my normal style. I popped in my contacts to see it better.

"You didn't have to do that," I objected out of a sudden sense of insecurity, and not wanting to be beholden to her.

"Yes, I did. Your clothes from yesterday are ruined."

I studied the dress. "I'm not sure I can put it on."

"I thought about that. It buttons up the front. You'll be able to get your arm through the sleeve hole easy-peasy and if you have trouble with the buttons, I can help. Until we figure out who shot who, I'm on administrative leave and will have all the time in the world to make myself useful. Or get in your way, depending upon your point of view. You'll need a driver for a few days."

Which returned me to an earlier worry. "How soon can I get Dolores back?"

Vanessa took the dress out of the bag and pretended to smooth out a wrinkle. "The crime lab isn't done processing her yet."

"And?"

"And she's going to need major work. If she can be repaired. Between the broken glass, bullet holes and various body dings, she took a lot of damage."

Which insurance probably wouldn't cover. But Dolores was my friend, and I'd pay whatever it took to fix her.

"What other bad news is there?"

"The media is all over this. There are bunches of videos on social sites. We're letting Orlando PD take the lead to keep it as low-key as possible. Neither of us has been identified, but Dolores is a dead giveaway. It won't take long until our names come to the surface."

"And me without a PR rep," I said drily.

Vanessa chuckled.

"Looks like I have an opening on my staff," I continued. "Do you know anyone looking for a job? Preferably someone with no ties to a criminal organization."

Her chuckle turned into a laugh. I fought to hold a straight face.

"The last thing we need is for an influencer to call us the heroes they didn't deserve. Or Harley and Poison Ivy. Worse yet, Thelma and Louise."

"Without the dying part, hopefully," she added between laughs.

I couldn't help myself. I joined in. It was one thing I could do without my arm hurting.

❊ ❊ ❊

The black car following us shouldn't have made me twitchy, but it did. Even though I knew it was an agency car driven by another ATF agent. Vanessa's car was at a mechanic for a thorough diagnostic, and her boss insisted she use a government vehicle for the time being. The powers that be—there was a rumor that someone in the governor's office was involved—had ordered the precautions in case any of Sallis's cronies wanted revenge. My gut said the danger was over, but I'd thought that before, so I'd play along with the professionals.

A silver pickup beeped its horn as it passed, going the opposite direction. "Is one of your fellow agents in that Ranger group?" I asked.

"It's possible." She flipped on the turn signal to enter the hospital—Eli's hospital—parking lot.

We took the elevator up to Eli's floor. The short walk to the lobby wore me out. It was quiet, but Sunday's usually were.

As we turned the corner to head towards Eli's room, I noticed the agency bodyguard wasn't at their post. I'd wondered if I'd ever catch one of them on a bathroom break. I bumped into Vanessa on purpose. "You don't suppose the agency withdrew their person without me telling them to, do you?"

She stopped and grabbed my arm. My good one, thankfully. She shoved me against the wall and touched her fingers to her lips. I got the message. Stay put and be quiet.

She crept up to the door and tilted her head to peak into the room. Then, without a glance back at me, she disappeared inside.

All the warning bells rang in my head. Instinctively, I reached for Betsy. She wasn't in my purse, of course. Until the police completed their investigation, she'd remain in their evidence locker.

What did I have to use as a weapon? Even my shoes were lightweight and flat-soled. Not a sharp edge to be found.

But I had a mirror buried in my purse, under the paperback with a half-naked man on the cover, and a packet of tissues. I inched closer to the door and positioned the mirror to see inside without being seen.

The reflection was blurry and the point of view wrong. All I could make out was Eli's empty bed. No help there.

I adjusted the angle and got floor. All floor. I tried again. And nearly dropped the mirror. Vanessa and a man I assumed to be the agency guard leaned with their faces against the far wall, hands high over their heads and feet spread apart. But why?

With a little fine-tuning, I saw more. And wished I hadn't. Eli sat in his wheelchair. But the cracks in my heart reopened because of the man standing behind him, holding a gun to Eli's head.

I pushed myself tight against the wall. I should run and find security. But the only way I foresaw this ending involved a lot of innocent people getting hurt.

There were three trained professionals in the room. Well, two and a half if I accounted for Eli not being able to walk. Maybe two, if Eli's memories had slipped away again. If I created a disturbance, surely one of them could seize the opportunity I provided. I didn't have the strength to do much more.

I gathered my weapons. The paperback book.

The mirror. My purse. If I rushed into the room, there'd be additional items to grab. This wasn't a precision operation.

But I wanted to start with a message.

I fought to pull off the chain around my neck with one hand. If I threw the dog tags to the right spot, Eli would see them and know I was there. Small enough comfort, but a ray of hope.

The bedframe was my initial target. I didn't wait for the clang of metal against metal to tell me if my aim had been good. The paperback, thrown in Eli's general direction, followed the dog tags. Next, the mirror and my purse.

By then, I was halfway into the room. I grabbed the closest stuffed animal and hurled it at the attacker's head. Instinctively, he raised his right hand—his gun hand—to fend it off. He knocked it away, and it hit the floor and started singing 'It's a Small World.'

Everyone moved at once. I lunged in Eli's direction. From the corner of my eye, I saw Vanessa and the guard swivel. Eli grabbed the man's shirt, pulling him forward and knocking him off balance. The gun clattered to the floor. The man reached for the wheelchair to balance himself, but Eli twirled one wheel to steer it away.

I got to him first. My momentum took him to the floor, and I landed on top of him. Ignoring the pain in my arm, I pounded him with my fists. Both of them. No fancy moves, just plain old pummeling whatever target I could connect with. At least until Vanessa pulled me away. And still the ditty played on.

❀ ❀ ❀

"I thought you took all of Sallis's people into custody last night," I complained to Detective Horace while a nurse checked my stitches.

"Based on the count reported by Special Agent Salters, we thought we did. It appears she missed one in the confusion."

Her number had been closer than mine.

They'd broken us up into separate rooms for our initial interviews. Detective Horace had drawn the short straw and got stuck with me.

"But it explains why the others were reluctant to identify themselves," he continued. "None of them carried an ID."

"Like our 'friend' from the tan car yesterday morning. Who is this new guy, anyway? I'll feel better putting a name to the face."

"Niles Jonas. He has a long rap sheet of minor crimes, including arson. A patrolman recognized him."

"What does he have to do with Sallis? What did Fiona have to do with any of them?"

The nurse interrupted. "Your stitches are fine. The bleeding was minimal, but the next time you might not be so lucky." She glared at me. "Use the sling."

I started to object. I had been using it. But I had the distinct impression that she'd heard every excuse in the book, so I kept my mouth closed.

She finished re-wrapping my upper arm and turned to frown at Horace. "Keep her out of trouble,

Timothy. I don't want to see her back in my ER. Don't disappoint me."

"Yes, ma'am," he said quietly, but there was an amused glint in his eye.

"You know her?" I asked after she swept out of the cubicle.

"We're members of the same church. I fear I often don't live up to her expectations."

I grinned. "Or they're set too high. Back to Niles. What are his connections to Sallis?"

"What you should ask is his relationship to Miss Varela."

"Fiona?" I held out my hand and Horace helped me off the examining table.

He nodded. "He made and received numerous calls to her and from her. We retrieved that info from his phone."

That explained what she was doing when we tracked her leaving the office during work hours. "I still can't make all the pieces fit. Why would Sallis be interested in the documents Putnam is looking for?" As far as I knew, Eli hadn't revealed their location yet.

"One of the suspects will talk," Horace reassured me. "And we'll get your answer."

They didn't allow me to see Eli until the officers finished getting his statement. It seemed to take an unnecessarily long time, but I supposed he was as busy extracting information from them as they were from him. It gave me time to prepare for the onslaught of questions I was sure he'd throw at me.

Detective Horace kept me company in the cafeteria while we waited. Rather, he made sure no one disturbed me as I nursed a glass of iced tea and tried not to mess with the gauze wrapping my arm.

Once they allowed me to go upstairs, Horace continued in his watchdog role. The bodyguard outside Eli's room was different, and I wondered if the first guard was all right. Horace threw his arm in front of me to stop me from going further. The guard and Horace glared at each other, sizing each other up. After a synchronized chin jerk, Horace lowered his arm and let me enter Eli's room.

Eli faced the window but wasn't looking outside. He held his phone and tapped furiously at the keyboard.

"Hey, Sweetie," I said.

"I remember," he said without glancing up.

"What?" From behind him, I put my hands on his shoulders and bent over to kiss the top of his head.

"All of it. How to code. How to create a program. All of it."

"Now you can start ignoring me when you go into coding comas," I teased.

He put his phone down, "Never again. You'll always come first."

I walked around his chair and stood in front of him. "It's part of you. I won't ask you to change."

He patted his thigh. "Come here. I need to hold you."

It was an offer I wouldn't refuse. I wanted his arms wrapped around me, to feel loved. I laid my head on his shoulder and he hugged me, being careful to avoid my bandages.

We sat in silence. He ran his fingers through my hair, which had fallen out of its bun long ago. In return, I lightly ran my fingers up and down his forearm.

His chest heaved, and I realized he was crying. I sat up and wiped his eyes. "Do you want to talk about it?"

"They told me everything. About last night." He gulped for air and control. "I wasn't there to protect you. And that was my gun he had. If he hurt you, it would have been my fault, and I'd never be able to live with myself."

"But you were there. In the form of the retired Rangers, sure, but they stood in for you just like you've been there for them. That counts.

"And think about it. You're the one responsible for Jonas being captured. Even in this chair with your own gun pointed at your head, you figured out how to throw him off-balance and save all of us."

"The minute my dog tags came flying through the door, I knew you were here. And when you followed them, I thought I was in a dream. Or a nightmare. But never tell my mother you used her latest stuffed animal as a weapon."

"I hope that song haunts him for the rest of his life."

"You should ask your cop friend to have it piped into his cell on a continuous loop."

I grinned. "Tempting. But wouldn't that fall under cruel and unusual punishment?"

"He'd deserve every minute."

I laid my head back on Eli's shoulder. "We work well together."

He tightened his arms around me and kissed the top of my head. "We do everything well together."

There was a long silence, and I used it to enjoy being with him. We'd had precious little of that.

But the moment couldn't last forever. "I have an investment opportunity for you," Eli said. "There's this little software business I know of. The owner is tired of running it and wants to get back to basics. He's hoping for a partner to help manage the business side. Word on the street is that you have the right experience to step into the role."

Was he talking about what I thought he was talking about? Okay, I'd play along. "How much of an investment am I looking at?"

"It's negotiable, but fifty-fifty is the standard arrangement."

"I think the current owner should ask for fifty-one percent just so he keeps majority control. What would my duties be?"

"Same sort of things you're already doing. Payroll, reviewing contracts, paying invoices. Although I hear there's a sudden opening in public relations if you're interested."

"And the perks?"

"Better than average salary. A share in the profits. Free housing. A private swimming pool. Good neighborhood. A comfortable bed. I can't guarantee how much sleep you'll get in that bed."

"So, I'd have to move here if I took the offer?"

"That would be a big plus. But the owner will discuss alternative arrangements."

"What's the catch?"

His chest rose and fell. Rose and fell.

"It's a two-part proposal," he said after a too-long pause, "that's the first part. The second part is harder. When I said partners, I meant it."

He tightened his hug so I couldn't get out of his grasp. Not that I wanted to. Besides, I'd been rendered motionless by his words.

"I can't do the whole get down on one knee thing. I don't even have a ring. But I can't wait that long to ask you. Will you marry me, Buttercup? Please?"

I tried to think logically, to plot out the details. Would we take turns between living in Orlando and Oak Grove? Did it matter? How would we split up the responsibilities of running the company without getting in each other's way? But logic was on hold. My brain and my heart were too busy screaming to tell him yes!

"Harmony?" Eli asked tentatively.

"I won't lie to you. I've thought about it and didn't see how we'd make it work. I still don't know. But…"

"But?" he sounded dejected.

"I love you, Eli. I can't imagine not spending the rest of my life with you. The marriage vows say for better or worse, and I think we've been through the worst. Yes, I will marry you." Logic be damned.

Epilogue

We didn't tell anyone about the business and personal plans, deciding to wait until Eli healed and returned to the office. That way, no one would accuse me of taking advantage of him.

Lando and Scotty, working with the tech at the care home, fixed up Eli's room at the rehab facility with a setup to give him direct access to my office. He could participate in meetings and conference calls. Depending upon his therapy schedule, of course.

So, he got to take part when Detective Horace gave me the final update on the case. "It's complicated." Horace's melodious voice filled my office. "Without Special Agent Putnam's background information, it would have taken us longer to pull the pieces together."

"The check I did when I hired Fiona didn't turn up anything," Eli objected.

Horace and I exchanged small smiles. "On paper, she was clean. No wants, no warrants, not even a traffic ticket or juvenile history. Her only known association with Jonas was having her car serviced at the garage where he worked. The same one you used, Mr. Hennessey."

"I thought he looked familiar that night." Eli rubbed his chin. "I asked him if we'd met, but he claimed he was from out of town and the plates weren't local, so I didn't think twice about it."

"The car was stolen," I said.

Eli grimaced. "Of course. So how do I fit into any of this?"

"We're getting there," Horace said. "Varela and Jonas were in a relationship the entire time. We suspect being hired by you was a deliberate move, but she won't admit to it."

"If she was already working with Jonas, it explains why she tried to get your attention. She figured she would seduce you and use that to wrangle information out of you," I explained.

"She tried to seduce me?" Eli's eyes widened.

I laughed. "That must have frustrated the heck out of her, that you didn't even notice. Lando and Scotty had your back and put an end to it."

Horace nodded. "As your receptionist, she had access to your schedule, your mail, and it's possible she listened into calls that passed through the front desk instead of going directly to your phone."

"And she fed that information to Jonas. But who is he and what does he have against me?" Eli asked.

"We figured that out thanks to Miss Duprie. She gave us a list of competitors that went out of business after your company got started. Jonas is a cousin of Jules Fellows."

"Crap." Eli's lips tightened. "Fellows Electronics."

"Yes. We can't prove that Fellows had any involvement, but it provides motive."

"How does this tie into Sallis?" I asked.

"We received an anonymous tip that Sallis hired Jonas to help him get revenge on the two of you. Mostly you, Miss Duprie."

I wondered if Jake had anything to do with the tip.

"Using information retrieved from Jonas' computer, Special Agent Salters connected him to a dark web forum frequented by scum who share knowledge on fire-setting techniques. As a result, she's developed new leads on several open cases which has led to two arrests. She's still working on finding the person who set fire to your house in Oak Grove, Mr. Hennessey."

No wonder she'd been looking so smug lately. I hadn't given her nearly enough credit for her crime-busting abilities.

"We also tracked money coming from Sallis' holdings to Jonas' bank account starting several years ago."

Holy premeditation. "That makes it a charge at the federal level, right?" I asked.

"Possibly. I don't get to make that decision. But perhaps you can tell me how your cousin fits into this, Mr. Hennessey."

Jake? He was back in Cleveland, according to the one text I'd received. The reports of a jewelry shop getting burgled the night of the shootout had nothing to do with him.

"Jake?" Eli asked. "Sallis had a misplaced grudge against him."

"But it seems like a stretch to think Sallis would attack Eli to lure me here, to use me as bait to get Jake to come here. It would have been easier to attack each of us individually," I said.

Horace shrugged. "I agree, Miss Duprie. And Putnam's paperwork was nothing but a means to throw you off-kilter, Mr. Hennessey. It was of no use to either Sallis or Jonas."

The document was back where it belonged. Eli had revealed its location to Putnam—inside a safe in one of the air-conditioning vents in his house. I'd always wondered why it didn't blow as cold as the others. Eli had completed his analysis the night of the attack. So much for his story about catching up on coding techniques.

"But we'll never be sure," Horace continued. "Sallis is in no shape to tell us. By the way, you didn't kill him, Miss Duprie. Your bullet struck him in the leg."

I'd tried. And I didn't feel guilty about it.

"A clean heart shot killed him. The ballistics don't match any of the weapons belonging to yourself or any of the authorities."

"Did one of the Rangers shoot him?"

"We can't determine that. The weapon was recovered at the scene. No prints, no serial number."

"Jonas shot him and dumped the gun?" I asked. Or had Jake executed the ultimate revenge?

Horace nodded gravely. "We've considered the idea. A move to take over what was left of Sallis's organization. Of course, it would have made more sense to use Mr. Hennessey's weapon."

"Criminals don't always think logically," I muttered.

"That's what keeps me employed, Miss Duprie."

"I'm going to miss you," Vanessa said as she shoved another suitcase into her car. "We make a good team, even if you drive me up the wall."

She was headed to Georgia for an advanced training course. After that, she was taking a couple of weeks off to visit her parents.

"At least you don't need to worry about breaking down on the way. The best mechanics in Orlando have gone over your car with a fine-tooth comb," I said.

"Luckily, the sabotage was minor stuff." Like loosened lug nuts and slow leaks in her tires. "Are you going to be okay here by yourself? With the guys upstairs moving to a place closer to work, so they don't have to fight the traffic every day, I'm worried."

A familiar gray van rumbled by and tooted its horn. I waved, recognizing it as one from the PI agency.

"Alone?" I laughed. "I have so many people planning to drop by and check on me I won't have time to breathe."

Not that I'd be staying at the house for long, even though I was buying it. As soon as I signed the closing paperwork, contractors would get to work on the first floor and start restoring it to a reflection of its original glory. I'd move into Eli's in the meantime. But Vanessa didn't know any of that.

When she was gone, I headed to the garage where Harry waited for me. Yes, Harry. A two-year-old white BMW 5 series. A car that Eli could get in and out of without too much trouble.

Dolores had been pronounced dead by the local body shop that specialized in high-end vehicle repair. It wasn't the bullet holes, or the broken glass, or the shot-up engine that did her in; it was the bent frame. The expert explained that even after straightening it, he wouldn't guarantee she'd ever handle the way she used to.

I donated her to a local tech school that taught automotive repair. She'd live on, even if she never hit the road again. That was after I cleaned out all my belongings, and sat in her for a good hour, crying softly, remembering stories about our time together and saying goodbye. She'd saved my life, and I owed her.

Harry and I were still getting to know each other. Today was the day for Eli to size him up. He'd been nagging the rehab staff to allow him to go on a field trip, and they'd caved. For the first time since the attack, Eli was coming to the office.

He was waiting at the front door when I pulled up, sitting in one of those collapsible wheelchairs, his two canes leaning against the wall. The canes let him walk farther than a few steps on his own, more or less.

With the help of the therapist, he got into the front seat. I wrangled the wheelchair into the trunk. At the office, there'd be plenty of people to assist him in getting out.

We took the long way. Heck, I took an entirely different route than normal to allow Eli to enjoy the ride. But he was eager to get to the office, so I cut the tour short.

'His' parking spot out front remained empty, as usual, and I pulled into it. Before I got around to the passenger's side to open the door for him, Lando and Scotty boiled out of the building, whooping and hollering. I hadn't told them about the visit, but Lando had the habit of monitoring the security cameras.

Between the two of them, they got Eli out of the car. I could have done it myself, but it was too much fun watching them get in each other's way in their eagerness to help. Once he was standing, I took his canes out of the back seat and held them out.

He shook his head. "I'm going to do this on my own."

It wasn't a long path to the door, but farther than he normally walked. And there was nothing for him to grab onto if he lost his balance. Like a mother hen, I hovered a few steps behind, more as moral support than anything else. This was Eli's moment.

The world held its breath as he took a break halfway up the sidewalk. He wobbled and Lando reached for him, but I shook my head and he backed off. Eli gathered himself and continued.

He almost made it inside before he stopped again. I realized there was one step in his way. He hadn't tackled stairs yet.

I read his body language and stood beside him. "You can lean on me, Eli."

"We'll do this together, eh, Buttercup?" he asked and winked at me. Our secret.

I matched my pace to his. He applied only a little pressure to my good shoulder as he raised one foot and set it back down, then the other, and made it up the step with no problem.

Applause erupted when he walked through the door that Lando held open.

"Take me home, Buttercup," Eli said from the doorway of my office.

I put down the contract I was reviewing. "Are you alright?"

"Worn out, that's all. It's been like an extended therapy session."

I grabbed my purse. "Any place you want to stop on the way back to the center?"

He grinned, a tired but happy grin. "Who said anything about that? Home. Take me home. I want to sit on my own couch, lay on my bed, and hold you. No interruptions, no one else around, just you and me. It's been too long."

"Home it is." I dug into my purse and pulled out the keys and my phone. With a wink, I turned it off. Our private language. No one would be able to disturb us.

His smile broadened, and he repeated the motion with his own phone. "Out the back door?"

Lando would know. And Darla. Neither would rat us out. I wrapped my arm around Eli's waist. Subtle support. He didn't resist.

"You know," I said as we slowly made our way towards Harry, with Eli using both canes, "We're going to get yelled at."

We stopped at the corner of the building on the one spot not covered by the security cameras, so Eli could lean against the wall and take a break. We took advantage of the privacy to share a kiss. A long, deep, soul-touching kiss that left me longing for more.

"I've analyzed the risk and the rewards." Eli licked his lips. "The risk is worth the reward. I'll make it worth your while. After that kiss, I could almost run to the car."

"Don't push it." We resumed our slow walk. "You've got to save your strength. You made me a promise."

"I remember. And it's one I intend to keep for the rest of our lives."

That's when it happened. The remaining cracks in my heart snapped shut. I put my hand on top of his. "Let's go home, Eli."

The End

Dear Reader,

We've reached the end of the Harmony Duprie Mysteries. As much as I love her, it's time I give Harmony and Eli a chance to rest and recuperate, and to figure out how the change in their relationship is going to work.

Could Harmony return in the future? They say never to say never.

This doesn't mean I'm going to stop writing. I've got a new heroine in the works. Watch for Annie (C.T.) McGregor and her story.

Thanks for reading!

P.J. MacLayne

Other Books in the
Harmony Duprie Mysteries Series

THE MARQUESA'S NECKLACE

Harmony Duprie enjoyed her life in the quiet little town of Oak Grove—until her arrest for drug trafficking. Now she has to figure out who is behind the sinister incidents plaguing her, and why.

HER LADYSHIP'S RING

Harmony Duprie is back, and so is trouble in Oak Grove.

Her ex-boyfriend Jake is out of prison and a suspect in a murder. Can Harmony clear Jake's name and solve the mystery of her own heart?

THE BARON'S CUFFLINKS

What starts as Girl's Night Out ends in murder, and Harmony Duprie is a suspect.

She's innocent, of course, but with no alibi, the sheriff's department won't remove her from the list of suspects. But caution isn't Harmony's middle name and she plunges head first into danger to defend her honor.

THE CONTESSA'S BROOCH

A firebug is stalking Oak Grove and internet researcher Harmony Duprie is on the case. It starts as a simple data analysis project for Police Chief Sorenson, but things get personal when the house she renovated is targeted.

The arsonist is in it for the glory, posting videos of his exploits on social media. Can Eli, Lando and Scotty, Harmony's favorite computer hackers, help her track down the pyromaniac before someone gets hurt? Or, worse yet, killed?

THE SAMURAI'S INRO

Harmony Duprie has it made. Or so she thinks.
New job.
New routine.
A quiet life in the quiet little town of Oak Grove.
Oh, and Eli.

But trouble has a long memory and it's playing a deadly game.

Books in
The Free Wolves Series
by P.J. MacLayne

WOLVES' PAWN
Book 1

Dot McKenzie is a lone wolf-shifter on the run. Can she survive when she becomes a pawn in a pack leader's deadly game?

WOLVES' KNIGHT
Book 2

Tasha Roeper knows what it means to protect your own. Torn between tradition and a changing world, will Tasha risk everything to save a friend—including her own life—when old enemies arise?

WOLVES' GAMBIT
Book 3

Free Wolf Lori Grenville has made it her life's mission to help unhappy shifters escape from overbearing alphas and dangerous situations. She hasn't failed in a mission yet. This one may be the exception.

P.J. MacLayne
can be reached at

NEWSLETTER
eepurl.com/cL73Cz

WEBSITE
PJMacLayne.com

FACEBOOK
facebook.com/pjmaclayne

TWITTER
twitter.com/pjmaclayne

BOOKBUB
bookbub.com/profile/p-j-maclayne

www.ingramcontent.com/pod-product-compliance
Lightning Source LLC
Chambersburg PA
CBHW051528100726
47898CB00005B/1612